"No, you won...   to the color of the sea on a stormy day, but the grin that cracked his face was still devilish. "It's little enough punishment for the way you've tormented me, and you know it. Besides, who'd believe *you* would set up a squawk over a kiss or two?"

She turned her head aside, her lashes fanning down over a glitter of moisture. "If I'm so wicked, why do you want to anyway?"

Zach cupped her chin and turned her face back to his. "Angel, haven't you ever heard of loving your enemy?"

This time his mouth settled over hers gently, like a benediction of healing and atonement. She murmured, but Zach allowed no protest, kissing her with such intensity that she quaked and sighed. She was sweetness and spice and utter beguilement, soft and giving and intoxicating.

In that moment of discovery and desire, Zach knew that he had to have Beth Ann Linder, come hell or high water . . .

If You've Enjoyed This Book
Be Sure to Read These Other
AVON ROMANTIC TREASURES

FASCINATION *by Stella Cameron*
FORTUNE'S FLAME *by Judith E. French*
MASTER OF MOONSPELL *by Deborah Camp*
SHADOW DANCE *by Anne Stuart*
VIRGIN STAR *by Jennifer Horsman*

Coming Soon

LORD OF FIRE *by Emma Merritt*

Angel Eyes

Suzannah Davis

An Avon Romantic Treasure

AVON BOOKS ◆ NEW YORK

ANGEL EYES is an original publication of Avon Books. This work has never before appeared in book form. This work is a novel. Any similarity to actual persons or events is purely coincidental.

AVON BOOKS
A division of
The Hearst Corporation
1350 Avenue of the Americas
New York, New York 10019

First Avon Books Printing: December 1993

For Diane, Kathey, Marian, Peggy, Penny, and Sandra
for keeping me centered

For Barbara Dawson Smith
for keeping the faith

And for Cody and Devon

Chapter 1

Arizona Territory, 1871

It looked promising. Very promising indeed.

Zach reined his tired buckskin to a halt in a grove of cottonwoods on the banks of the Gila River. Ahead in the purple Arizona night, golden lantern light gleamed in the windows of a spacious stone and adobe hacienda.

Traveler's Rest Way Station. Just like Tom said. Welcoming. Prosperous. Ripe for the plucking.

Built into a hill overlooking the best fording place on the river, the stagecoach inn sported wide porches and broad front steps. The ground dipped away on one side, making space under that end of the porch for kitchen and storerooms. Lingering scents of woodsmoke and fresh-baked bread drifted on the cooling breeze. Corrals and outbuildings lay in the shadows to the rear.

Though amber bars of light spilled into the packed-dirt yard, nothing stirred. All was serene, comfortable, complacent.

Zach rubbed his palm over his stubbled jaw, anticipation bubbling in his veins. Since leaving Prescott days ago, he'd eaten enough trail dust to choke a buffalo, but it wasn't just the promise of a drink and a meal that made him grin. No, it was the same optimism he experienced every time he felt called to a new mission. Some might even declare it was a heavenly gift, this vocation of his that made him incapable of resisting a unique challenge, a fresh opportunity.

Zach's crooked smile grew even broader. In this case, the opportunity might just turn out to be a golden one.

Knowing the importance of first impressions, Zach slapped the grit from his new frock coat and straightened his unfamiliar collar. Then, setting his wide-brimmed hat at its most dashing—yet still respectable—angle, he kicked his mount into a canter.

No one challenged him when he entered the yard. No stable hand rushed to take his horse. No welcoming host came to the porch to greet the latest arrival. Grumbling a little under his breath about the early hours country folk kept on a Saturday night, Zach realized he'd have to tend to his own livery duties, so he rode around back to the corral.

As he dismounted, he grimaced at his own stiffness. While he preferred to earn his bread with his wits and his charm, his lean, hard-muscled limbs proved he knew how to work when the occasion demanded it. But no matter how much physical activity a man was accustomed to, having to leave a place in a hurry took a toll in sore thigh muscles and saddle blisters.

Ignoring the inquiring nickers of horses within the corral, Zach opened the gate and walked his mount inside to unsaddle the weary animal. Just as he reached for the cinch buckle, a large gray lop-eared mule trotted out of the herd, heading straight for the open gate.

Since one did not impress one's prospective host by letting his stock loose at the first opportunity, Zach gave a sharp whistle and waved his arms. "Get back, you!"

The mule stumbled to a clumsy stop, then took exception to Zach's command with an ear-piercing bray.

"I said, back!" Zach threw up his arms again, and the mule retreated a pace, braying fit to bust a gut.

Scowling, Zach reached again for the cinch, swiftly stripped off the bedroll and saddlebags, and then swung the saddle itself up on the fence rail. When you grew up around a livery stable, you got to know livestock. And Zach hated mules. Especially mean-eyed ones that made enough noise to wake the dead.

He slid the bridle out of his buckskin's mouth, then sent it to join the herd with a slap on the rump. Each of Zach's moves was accompanied by the mule's amazing cacophony of noise. Behind the protesting animal, the other horses stamped and snorted restlessly, disturbed by their companion's tantrum.

"Jee-sus H. Christ! Will you shut the hell up!" Exasperated, Zach swung the bridle at the mule's grizzled muzzle.

The animal shied, squealing his fury. With a slash of sharp hooves and a savage snap of equine fangs, the gray monster charged—straight at Zach!

Beth Ann Linder sat up in the tin bathtub too fast, jolted out of a doze by Old Henry's harsh brays. Tides of soapy bathwater swirled around her breasts and kneecaps, and sloshed onto the snug kitchen's rough stone floor.

"Sweet sassafras, what now?" She scowled, resenting this intrusion in her Saturday night ablutions.

For once, she had Traveler's Rest to herself. There were no stage passengers to see to, Paw had gone the five miles into Destiny for his deacons' meeting, and Buck, that worthless cowpoke, was snoozing his supper off somewhere. This private time was her sole indulgence, the only way she had to armor herself against her inevitable Sunday humiliation at the Gospel Assembly Chapel.

Strumpet! the memories whispered. *Who does she think she is?*

Images burned behind Beth Ann's eyes. The condemning glances, the turned-up noses, the cold looks and intentional snubs of people she'd once counted as friends.

Her lip curled. At least she always showed them they couldn't beat her down. Why, the seductive looks and imaginary kisses she'd thrown Mayor Ike Cunningham during last week's sermon had nearly sent that bald-headed hypocrite into an apoplectic fit. And most of the menfolk hadn't heard a word of the lesson, not when she'd pretended to be too warm and removed her jacket, lingering over every button in a flat-out tease that had every male in church squirming by the time it was over. It made having to stand up before the congregation while they tried to pray her into true contrition almost worth it.

Almost.

Absently Beth Ann rubbed the fading shadow of a bruise on her upper arm, put there by her paw's brutal grip as he forced her to stand up every Sunday and take it. *For her own good.* She grimaced. Yes, sir, Wolf Linder sure knew how to make a sinner repent.

Hussy ... a bad'un through and through ... whore!

With a wince, she pushed the hurtful whispers away, cocking her head to one side to concentrate on the raucous echoes outside. Since she had no love for the cantankerous animal, she shrugged and sank back down into the cooling bathwater. A single lantern illuminated the tidy kitchen with its heavy oak table and well-stocked cupboards, the neat pile of clean clothing on a straight chair, the high, narrow windows with homespun curtains pulled tight against the starlit sky.

"I hope the Apaches roast and eat that loco mule," she muttered, reaching for her precious sliver of rose-scented soap. "Serves him right for gobbling my marigolds."

With a sigh, Beth Ann admitted to herself that the past week of cooking and cleaning for the folks traveling the old Butterfield stage route to California had worn her to a frazzle. The prime location of Traveler's Rest and a reputation for the best food within a hundred miles of the Superstition Mountains kept trade brisk and Paw grinning like a weasel in a henhouse over the clank of coins in the till. Why, he'd been so tickled with this week's take, he'd hardly complained about the ghostly pain in the leg Doc Sayers had amputated last year because of a festering snakebite.

Beth Ann, on the other hand, was glad things had eased up a little. And she certainly wasn't about to abandon the only earthly pleasure she had left to see about a bad-tempered mule with a bellyache! But the braying continued unabated, disturbing her well-earned respite.

"Shut up, damn you!" she shouted in the direction of the back door. "What the hell's the matter with . . . Oh, my God!" Struck by a horrible realization, Beth Ann shot to her feet, spraying water and perfumed suds like a miniature geyser. "Apaches! Nellie!"

Indians hadn't raided for horses in over a year, but no one thought the roving bands had lost their taste for fresh horsemeat for good. And Nellie, the sorrel mare Beth Ann's mother had given her for a tenth birthday gift before running off with the traveling dentist, was due to foal any day.

In a panic, Beth Ann pulled her white cotton wrapper on over her wet skin and grabbed the Winchester rifle from its place beside the chimney. Bathwater streaming down her legs, she threw open the door and dashed out of the kitchen.

Mindless of the rough ground and her bare feet, Beth Ann sped silently through the dark tangle of cottonwood striplings behind the house toward the corrals. The damp wrapper clung to her legs, impeding her steps, and the night-cooled April air raised gooseflesh on her skin.

She'd never understood why her paw had let her keep Nellie after the shame of Eleanor Linder's desertion had driven them out of Wickenburg. When he'd struck a modest paydirt in the Superstitions, they'd settled down at Traveler's Rest, but Wolf sure hated anything to do with her maw. Beth Ann guessed he was just too much of a skinflint to give up a fine piece of horseflesh like Nellie, whose foals had made their string one of the best in the territory.

But this foal of Nellie's was more than special. For a desperate woman, it was a last chance.

For months now, Beth Ann had been counting on the money from the foal's sale to leave the little town of Destiny, her paw, and her Sunday penance behind for good. She was sick to death of lectures and prayers and ministers who preached forgiveness but never actually forgave anyone. Twenty-two wasn't too old to start a new life, not if she could go someplace where no one knew or cared what she'd done two years ago with Tom Chapman.

As she neared the corral, Beth Ann's nerves jangled at Old Henry's strident bellow. A disturbed drumbeat of hooves vibrated on the sage-scented breeze as the herd of horses inside the corral cantered this way and that, churning up clouds of blinding, choking dust. Grimly determined, she set her jaw and gripped the rifle tighter.

It would be a cold day in hell before she'd let a damn marauding Apache rob her of her one chance of deliverance!

Zach cursed and dived out of the mule's path, yelping as a hoof glanced off his foot. He hit the ground hard. Mad as the devil now, he ignored the pain and rolled upright, intent on foiling the animal's attempt to escape. It would be a cold day in hell before he'd let a damned jackass outsmart him!

Waving his hat and whooping loudly, Zach limped for the gate and latched it hurriedly as the braying mule came after him again.

"Hold it right there, you varmints!"

The shrill warning, followed by the sharp report of a rifle, froze Zach in his tracks. Pandemonium erupted. The herd panicked and bolted, charging in circles, banging against the fence, raising dust and confusion. Even the mule forgot about the gate and joined in the stampede.

"Holy hell!" Frenzied animals rounded the corner of the corral straight at Zach, and he made a desperate vault for the fence. Handicapped by his sore foot, he clung to the railing as the herd swept past, craning his neck to find the source of the shot.

In the midst of the billowing dust clouds inside the corral, a wraith materialized, a dark-haired figure in a long, flowing white robe. Thunderstruck, Zach gaped and squinted through the dust and darkness as the feminine apparition floated toward him. He received an instantaneous impression of a sweetly curved form beneath the diaphanous gown, angelic features, and fiery eyes. Wildly he wondered if he'd really seen the flutter of white wings, and then realized that the vision—whoever or whatever she was—stood in the path of the crazed herd!

"Look out—"

Zach's warning congealed in this throat as the angel lifted a rifle to her shoulder and aimed it right at his heart!

Nearly blinded by dust, Beth Ann strained to see through the murky darkness. A flicker of movement drew her attention to a human shape skulking near the fence. Heart pounding, she pumped another cartridge into the rifle's chamber. "Stop, or I'll blow you into next week!"

Above the thunder of panicked hooves and shrill whinnies came a hoarse cry of surprise, and the figure ducked out of sight. Beth Ann drew a sigh of both relief and elation. She'd routed the interloper! The next instant she was on the ground, the wind knocked out of her by a collision with a shaggy gray beast, her ears ringing with Henry's harsh brays and the ear-shattering explosion of the rifle.

The herd shied again and dashed toward the opposite corner of the corral, huddling winded and heaving in a nervous group. Shaken, Beth Ann wheezed for breath while levering herself to her hands and knees.

"Miss Beth Ann! Great balls of fire! Are you all right?" A gnarled old cowhand scaled the fence, his voice trembling querulously. "What's going on out here?"

"Buck." Gasping, Beth Ann shook her head to clear it. "Indians. After Nellie."

Buck hastened to help her to her feet, his tone aggrieved. "Good God almighty, Miss Beth Ann! You shoulda hollered for me!"

Beth Ann let that go. Sometimes she felt aeons older and wiser than the wizened cowpoke, and a sight more competent. Even her paw agreed Buck was generally about as useless as a bucket of hot spit, but Wolf kept Buck on as an extra watchdog, so he could go into town without fear of his daughter's wicked escapades.

"Never mind, Buck. I—" She froze. A shadowy form lay on the hoof-churned ground beside the fence. "Oh, my God!"

"By gum! You hit the bugger!" Buck crowed.

Stricken, Beth Ann stared at the motionless body. She'd only meant to scare the intruder away! Damn that Henry! "See if . . ." She had to swallow hard. "See who it is, Buck."

The old cowboy hobbled on his permanently bowed legs to inspect the casualty. " 'Tain't no Injun," he called over his shoulder.

"Horse thief," Beth Ann mumbled, staggering after Buck. The smell of burnt gunpowder filled her with sick dread. When she reached the fence, Buck snapped a sulfur match on one horny thumbnail and raised the flame high.

A clean-shaven white man lay sprawled on his back, bleeding profusely from a hole high on his shoulder. In the orange flare of the match, the ever-increasing pool on his frock coat and pristine white shirt looked black as pitch. There was something odd about his shirt collar . . .

Beth Ann drew in a sharp breath of horror. The match flame reached Buck's fingertips, and he dropped it with an oath that echoed in the darkness.

"Holy jumpin' Jehosephat, Miss Beth Ann! You done kilt a goldanged preacher!"

"Don't argue with me, you old coot!"

Every muscle in Beth Ann's body ached with strain from manhandling the preacher's limp and surprisingly heavy form up the hill and into Traveler's Rest's best guest bed. She threw the wild, drying mass of her black curls over her shoulders and glared icily at Buck. "Go fetch Doc Sayers like I said!"

The wiry cowpoke's weathered mahogany features twitched, and he tugged at his grizzled mustache uncertainly. "But your paw told me not to leave you alone—"

"Hell's bells!" Beth Ann grabbed up sewing scissors from her mending basket and began to cut the unconscious man's clothes away.

Crimson soaked his shirt, but she was just as concerned by the already-swelling welt in the shape of half a horseshoe on the side of his dusty face. He must have caught a blow from a flying hoof after he'd fallen. Her stomach knotted at how close he'd come to being trampled into mincemeat. But his troubles were far from over. She hissed at Buck.

"He isn't dead yet, but he will be if I don't get this bleeding stopped! Ride for the doc, or they're going to blame you as well as me if he dies!"

That convinced Buck. He set down the lantern he held in such a rush that mad shadows danced across the quilted coverlet and glittered in the age-spotted mirrors of Beth Ann's prized walnut armoire. "Yes'm. I hear you, Miss Beth Ann."

"And hurry!"

She didn't bother to watch him leave, her hands and mind busy on the tasks ahead if she was going to keep this ignorant, Bible-toting jackass alive until the doc arrived.

What had a preacher been doing skulking around their prize horseflesh in the first place? Sweet sassafras! Considering her aversion to clergymen, no one was ever going to believe she'd shot him by accident! Her lips twisted in disgust. Well, public censure was nothing new to her. Besides, she wouldn't let even a polecat bleed to death.

Muttering imprecations, she peeled off the remnants of the shirt and coat and sucked in a ragged breath at the sight of the ugly bullet wound oozing blood. For all that it was a clean shot through the fleshy part of his left shoulder and, praise be, seemed to have missed both bone and lung, she knew that the exit wound was probably worse. If she waited for Buck to locate Doc Sayers, some other minister of the Word would soon be reading a funeral service over this preacher. *Then* what would people say about her?

Beth Ann stripped her best cotton slips off the bed pillows, made a pressure pad for both sides of the wound, then raced down the inside staircase to the kitchen for water, clean linen, and supplies. Within moments, she was again bending over the injured man.

He was tall and, for a cleric, surprisingly well muscled in a lanky way. His brown hair might have held a touch of red beneath the coating of buff dust, but it was the scarlet already seeping through the makeshift bandages that commanded her attention. She'd had to help when the doc amputated Paw's leg. Surely this was nothing compared to that! Steeling herself, she got to work.

By the time she cut the final knot of her stitches, tied the bandages tight, and gently eased her mercifully unconscious victim into a comfortable position on the clean sheets, she was limp and light-headed. Gulping rapidly, she fought the threatening blackness. She'd stopped the bleeding; the rest was up to the preacher. She wasn't such a pussy willow that she'd faint now that it was all over!

Drawing a steadying breath, Beth Ann really examined the man stretched out in the bed for the first time. He wasn't old, not even thirty, she reckoned, but more than that, she couldn't say because of the streaks of dirt obscuring his features. Another damfool itinerant missionary, she guessed, come out from the East to convert the heathen. And this one obviously didn't have a teaspoonful of common sense, sneaking into a strange place in the middle of the night. She regretted her role in his injury, but she knew very well that she'd be the one to pay the price of his folly.

Her shapely mouth clamped in a resentful line, she reached for the basin and cloth, then carefully sat down on the edge of the bed to sponge his battered face. The metallic odor of blood had abated, only a faint reminder mingling with the fragrance of male musk, sweaty leather, and horses in a tangy mixture of manly scents. She gave a brief, longing thought for her own interrupted bath, then got to work.

With the first touch of the cool cloth, the man flinched, rousing slightly. His sandy-colored eyebrows were incongruously lighter than the whiskey brown curls springing over his ears and forehead, and they drew together in a puckered frown of pain. Ignoring his faint groan, Beth Ann grimly mopped the dirt away, taking special care around the swelling on his bruised cheekbone. His jaw was strong and square, his cheeks long, his nose slightly crooked. Under his tan, he was so pale she could make out a light dusting of rusty freckles. In repose his features were tolerable enough to be called handsome, she supposed, but his carved mouth hung downward in a manner she thought indicative of a particularly petulant and spoiled personality.

"Jee-sus," he muttered, the word a croak.

"Be quiet," she ordered unsympathetically. "Time enough for prayers later, Reverend."

With impersonal thoroughness, she washed his thick neck and swept the cloth over his tanned chest above and below the white bandage. A sprinkling of freckles winked through the crisp brown hair that whorled around his nipples and down his flat middle before disappearing were a stripe of lighter skin started at his waistband. Although he was muscular and hard, he wasn't as bulky or as heavily furred down his brisket as Tom.

At that unbidden thought, a sharp, unexpected sensual pang swept through Beth Ann from breasts to belly, heating her middle in a way she hadn't experienced since that last time with Tom. She leapt off the bed as if lightning were sizzling along the sheets, ruthlessly tamping down those wicked feelings.

It's all your fault, she thought, glowering at the stranger with pure venom in her gray eyes.

For two years she'd kept herself well in hand, ignoring longings and needs that clamored for attention. But now in a split second, all the repressed pleasures came rushing back in a molten torrent of memory. Stolen kisses, daring caresses, whispered words of love and passion. Beth Ann moaned helplessly. She didn't want to remember the delicious tingles that melted a woman's innards when the right man touched her skin.

But Tom Chapman hadn't been the right man, had he? a voice inside her head sneered. What else would you expect from a man who'd ended up in the territorial prison for robbery? The sweet-talking bastard had only wanted one thing from Beth Ann—and humiliatingly enough, it hadn't even been her virtue.

With a strangled sound, she flung the washcloth into the basin and moved toward the door, unable to stand another moment with the stranger who unwittingly evoked such dangerous and provocative remembrances. She'd done all she was morally bound to do until Doc Sayers arrived.

The preacher groaned again, his long legs shifting uncomfortably. Beth Ann halted in the doorway, chewing her lip in guilty indecision. Reluctantly she edged toward the foot of the bed, then reached to tug off the preacher's worn and scuffed boots. He lurched reflexively when the second one came off. When she peeled off his socks, she noticed the painful red outline of a hoof etched on the side of one instep—evidently another injury picked up during that mad stampede inside the corral.

Beth Ann was almost glad. Her lips pursed in an irritable pucker. Damn him, anyway! Coming around Traveler's Rest and causing all this trouble and extra work. She drew the sheet up to the preacher's chest, her mind already busy with thoughts of the beef broth and custards a convalescent would need. She'd have to ask Ama, the Pima Indian squaw who helped in the kitchen, to bring more eggs . . .

The man pushed fretfully at the sheet, a low vibration of pain rumbling deep in his throat.

"Oh no, you don't!" Bending over him, Beth Ann caught his hand to still its restless course.

His fingers turned and grabbed hers with startling strength, holding her when she would have pulled away in surprise. Sandy lashes fluttered once, twice, as if their owner strained with the fiercest effort to lift them. Finally he succeeded, and Beth Ann drew a tiny startled breath at the brilliant blue-green of his eyes, a flash of turquoise, unfocused but potent.

"Who . . . ?" His whisper was almost inaudible.

Beth Ann knew his question. *Who shot me?* In a sudden flare of nerves, she chose to misunderstand him. "I'm Miss Linder. You're at Traveler's Rest. You're safe."

"Safe?" He pressed her fingers to his chest. The light thatch of hair felt crisp against her fingertips, his skin warm and velvety. "Good."

Startled at the immense satisfaction in that gravelly whisper, she met his gaze again, and somehow became entangled in its intensity, her palm frozen over his heart. His hand slid across her wrist, then up her arm. Her lips parted to protest the familiarity, but no sound emerged, only a rush of indrawn breath as he reached inside the gaping neckline of her wrapper and touched her naked breast.

Immobilized with shock, with the white-hot surge of sensation that coursed through her like lightning and lodged, throbbing, between her legs, Beth Ann tried to breathe—and couldn't. His fingers were work-roughened, the raspy feel of them against the sensitized satin of her skin more pleasurable than anything she'd ever imagined. Gently he explored the heavy underside of her bosom,

and her blood ignited, fire streaming through her
veins, burning her lungs, melting her core.

She couldn't move; she couldn't think. All she
could do was *feel*. The stroking touch changed, became harder, possessive. His thumb caressed the
crest of her dusky rose nipple, and it instantly
tightened and puckered into a hard pearl of
arousal, pouting against his fingers, demanding
his attention. Expertly he squeezed it, rolling it las-
civiously between thumb and forefinger. Beth Ann
arched her throat and groaned wildly at the exquisite sensation.

It was that sound, the unrecognizable moan of
some mad, wild thing, that brought her to her
senses. With a strangled cry, she slapped his hand
away, her knees quaking so badly, they could
barely support her.

"You ... you lecherous cur!" She struggled for
air, trying to form words sufficiently scathing.
"How dare you! How ..."

She couldn't finish. Scarlet, dazed at the wanton
response of her own traitorous body, she choked
on her mortification. How dare this ... this *man of
God* behave in such a reprehensible fashion! Well,
she certainly knew his true colors now. Even in a
semiconscious state, the man was a rutting, lustful
beast! She didn't know whether she was more furious at him for taking liberties, or herself for allowing it for even one stunned moment!

Almost hysterically Beth Ann assured herself it
was only shock at such a blatant outrage, not a liking for what his skillful touch had done to her,
that had kept her still. She pushed those wanton
sounds of pleasure out of her memory and struggled to regain her composure. He was watching
her from beneath his sandy lashes like a sleepy

predator, his lips curled into a drowsy half smile that infuriated her beyond caution.

"Keep your hands to yourself, damn you!" she hissed. "You don't know who you're dealing with!"

"I know." He was groggy, his words slurred by pain and shock, but his smile was so full of boyish charm, his face was transfigured into something beyond mere good looks. "My angel. *Mine.*"

Beth Ann's cheeks burned. She was anything but an angel, as Wolf Linder would gladly tell anyone who'd care to listen! Before she could voice the vitriolic reply such an asinine assessment deserved, however, the stranger slipped into unconsciousness again.

Still angry, but startled and alarmed by his abrupt lapse, she bent over him, touching his face, feeling for his heartbeat, appraising the shallowness of his breathing. He'd better not die on her, not before she had the chance to tell him just what she thought of him!

"Woman, have you no shame?"

Beth Ann jumped guiltily at her father's bellow. Wolf Linder filled the doorway, as big as a bear, his silver-streaked black beard bristling with indignation. His shirt collar was tightly buttoned beneath his corpulent neck, and his waistcoat bulged like a sausage casing. A gold watch chain swung across the expanse of conservative brocade.

"What is the meaning of this outrage?" Wolf's bass voice rumbled as loud as Jehovah's. Eyes like black buttons shone from his weather-beaten face, inquisitive, sharp, missing nothing.

He crossed the well-swept plank floor toward his daughter, the peg he wore below the knee in place of his right foot *ka-thump*ing in rhythmic counterpoint to his cane. Dr. Samuel Sayers, a small cricket of a man with scraggly side-whiskers, appeared from behind Wolf and scurried toward the patient.

Beth Ann felt herself shrinking. "It . . . it was an accident, Paw."

"The hand of the Dark One is surely upon you, woman!" Wolf thundered. "To shoot the anointed of the Lord is bad enough, but to find you here with hair streaming, indecently clad, reeking of scent like a whore—it is too much for a God-fearing man to bear!"

Beth Ann glanced down at herself, then flushed furiously. In the heat of the emergency, she'd forgotten she wore nothing beneath her thin wrapper—at least until the preacher had reminded her in such an unnerving fashion! Though the garment was mostly dry now, it still clung to her body in embarrassing places, and streaks of the preacher's blood blotted the fabric. Her feet were bare and dirty, and she had no doubt that her hair looked as wild as a banshee's.

"I—I'm sorry, Paw." She backed away instinctively. "But he was bleeding, and—"

"Get thee gone, you Jezebel!" Wolf shouted, thumping his cane with menacing emphasis. "And hope your meddling hasn't made Doc's job an impossible one!"

"Indeed not, Mr. Linder, sir," the smaller man interjected with a jittery smile. "I couldn't have asked for better work. Why, just look at these stitches. God willing, this young man should do just fine. We'll get him out of these britches so he can be more comfortable—"

"See, Paw?" Beth Ann demanded, lifting her chin and shaking back her hair with renewed spirit. "I did all right . . ."

"Comport thyself, child of Eve," Wolf snapped.

"You bring ignominy down upon my house at every turn. Better that I should have strangled you in your swaddling clothes than lived to see you dishonor my name yet again! Heaven knows what kind of explanations I'll be forced to make to keep the sheriff from hauling you away for this outrage against both man and God!"

Beth Ann's mouth dropped open. "It was an accident! Henry bumped me. Buck can tell you—"

"Silence!" Wolf roared. "By Jove, you're going to learn a lesson one way or the other! You'll let me deal with this as I see fit, or I'll let the law have you. We'll see just how high and mighty you feel then."

Beth Ann had learned long ago that in time of trial she was never to count on her father for support, much less justice. The refusal to hear her side, the willingness to believe the worst, the deafness to others' compliments—none of that was new. She kept the hurt in a special place where no one could see, and now she pulled the shell in tight around herself and tilted her chin again in well-practiced insolence.

"Go ahead, Paw. Do your damnedest. Frankly, a nice quiet cell with nothing to do sounds like heaven to me." She shrugged. "Who knows? Maybe in a year or two you might actually learn to fix something edible for the paying customers."

The thought of doing without Beth Ann's expert culinary services made Wolf's scowl even blacker.

"You foulmouthed strumpet! Get out of my sight! I'll deal with your transgressions later."

Beth Ann flinched imperceptibly, but her tone was purposefully rude. "Sure you will, Paw. God knows, I'd hate to deprive you of your favorite sport!"

Turning on her heel, she left her father spluttering. She sought the sanctuary of her room, knowing in her heart that things were far from over.

Double-damned preacher! It's starting again, and it's all his fault!

He hurt like the devil all over.

No, Zach thought muzzily, there were parts of him—a very few, admittedly, but some—that only felt as though he'd been beaten up. He was sure the rest of him had been trampled by a thousand-head herd of the orneriest, walleyed, snot-slinging longhorns this side of the Rio Grande. Twice.

The only bright spot in the haze of pain was the dark-haired angel with the pouty mouth who materialized periodically. There was something familiar about her, but no sooner did she appear, and he would almost grasp the thing that eluded him, than she'd vanish again, replaced by the wrinkled nut brown countenance and grizzled mustache of a face Zach decided must belong to Old Nick himself. If he could just convince the angel to stay awhile, he might even consider returning to the land of the living someday. But for now, the gray clouds on which he floated were as soft and silvery as her angel eyes, and it was just too much trouble.

When Zach climbed out of the cloud bank again, it was to a sound like thunder. The rumbling gradually became words, took on sense and meaning.

". . . wake him up!"

"Doc said he'll rouse when he's ready, Paw."

The husky weariness of the second voice—a feminine one—caught Zach's interest, and drew him upward through mists that dissolved and reformed into a face. It was his angel, but so changed—her rich ebony hair drawn back in an

unforgiving knot, her cheeks pale, her lips compressed tightly. And her eyes, those wide gray
orbs that haunted his dreams—God, he'd never
seen or hoped to witness again such unhappiness.
And suddenly his heart hurt even more than his
body.

"See?" the man's voice accused. "There he
comes now. Never underestimate the Lord on His
own day."

"I would never presume so much, Paw."

"No, you only harden your heart to the message." The deep voice reverberated with righteous
indignation. "Standin' there like a stone in church
while the good folk pray for your salvation. You
ain't worth such a blessing, but I'll be boiled before I let you end up like your maw!"

Zach's head rested on a fluffy pillow, and he
turned slightly toward the source of that outburst.
A robustly built older man stood beside the
roughhewn poster bed on which Zach lay. The late
afternoon sunlight poured through the window
behind him, washing the flat adobe plaster walls
with golden warmth and making the brass handle
of the man's cane gleam. Bushy-bearded, in
Sunday-best shirt and string tie, Wolf Linder was
an easy man to recognize from his description.
And that meant . . .

Zach tried to sit up. It was definitely a mistake.

"Whoa there, Reverend! Be still before you start
bleeding again." Wolf pushed Zach down. "You
ain't a-goin' nowhere."

Since he had gone instantly queasy and light-
headed from the fierce, stabbing pain in his shoulder, Zach had to agree. In a hoarse rasp, he said,
"A drink, for God's sake."

"Get him something, daughter," Wolf ordered.

The woman hastily slipped her arm under

Zach's neck and brought a tin cup to his mouth. Cool liquid slipped past his lips and he drank gratefully, then choked. Lemonade!

"Don't try to take too much," she advised in a voice as soft as crushed velvet, then eased his head down again.

Thankfully the throbbing began to relent, but in its place came a sudden wave of dizziness at her nearness. She was dressed in stiff black gabardine, trussed up like a Christmas turkey. Everything from the high neck of the gown to her severe hairstyle aimed for modesty and plainness, but it was a sham, a thin disguise that only showcased the purity of her profile and elegant bones. The tiny tintype photograph in his saddlebag had not prepared him for skin as translucent as porcelain, straight, well-marked brows, and a sultry mouth the color of ripe peaches. Her smoky eyes were veiled now, so that he might have dreamed the misery he'd glimpsed there before, and her gaze was cool and unreadable except for one unmistakable element—hostility directed squarely at him.

Instantaneous wariness chased away the vestiges of fog in Zach's head. A rapid assessment of his physical status reassured him that all his parts seemed to be in reasonable order, except for a bruised face, an eye that was nearly swollen shut, and the hot poker sizzling through his shoulder. But the bed was soft, it appeared he'd been well cared for, and there was no one holding a gun on him. So why was she looking at him as though she'd like to draw and quarter him at the first available opportunity?

He frowned, attempting to reconstruct the incident that had brought him to this bed. He'd ridden in late ... His thoughts circled the confused gaps in his recollections.

Wolf noticed his bewilderment. "I'm Wolf Linder, proprietor of Traveler's Rest. This here's my daughter, Beth Ann. And you are . . . ?"

"Zach . . . ah, Reverend Zachariah Temple." The raspy whisper that was his own voice surprised him. "Beg your pardon, Mr. Linder. I had no idea I'd have to make your acquaintance like this."

Wolf's black eyes narrowed. "Heard of me, have you?"

"Your generosity is well known among travelers like me."

"I like to offer hospitality to all the Lord's hand-servants, Reverend Temple." The burly landlord's prideful puffing dissolved into an expression of extreme chagrin. "But, uh, I'm afraid you've had something of a mishap."

Beth Ann gave a delicate snort. "Didn't anyone ever warn you about sneaking around like a horse thief? You nearly got your ass shot off!"

"Beth Ann!" Wolf jerked her arm. "I won't have that kind of talk in front of the reverend. Forgive her, son, she's a willful hellion, though I try to teach her better."

Eyes narrowed, Zach studied the woman, seeing in his mind's eye the face in his dreams superimposed over the face of—a dusty angel with a rifle!

Son of a bitch! He'd been shot by this woman! Zach felt as though he'd been walloped between the eyes with a gun stock. If this ever got out, he'd never hear the end of it. The more Zach thought, the madder he got.

"Mishap, huh?" he grunted, his good eye burning with blue-green ire. "It was you who did this to me, wasn't it, Miss Linder? Are you crazy, or simply a man-hater?"

"I thought you were an Apache trying to steal my mare," she said defensively. "The mule wal-

loped me, and ... and the rifle went off by accident, and ..." An angry flush rose up her slender
neck and stained her cheeks bright pink. "And
anyway, only an idiot greenhorn would take a
chance like you did! You were lucky to get off so
lightly!"

"Lucky?" Zach spoke carefully through his teeth
because the whole side of his face ached. "You've
got a mighty strange notion of good fortune,
lady!"

"We could be planting you six feet under today," she pointed out stiffly.

"Thank the Lord for small mercies." Zach raised
his eyes to heaven and took a deep breath to regain control. He didn't intend to foul things up
any worse than they already were by losing his religion in front of these two.

The part of Wolf's face not covered by his beard
was beet red with embarrassment. "Hope you'll
pardon her, Reverend. Women ain't worth shucks,
generally, and this one's been a thorn in my side
since the day she was born."

Beth Ann shrugged out of her father's grasp,
her mouth a sullen line of resentment. "I was looking out for *your* property, Paw! What if it had been
Apaches raiding our stock? Even a newcomer
should have better sense than to sneak around a
stranger's place in Indian country!"

"That's enough, woman!" Wolf gave his daughter a hard, quelling look, then turned back to Zach.
"I don't want you to worry about a thing, Reverend. Buck's taking good care of your buckskin,
and he fetched in your saddlebags and gear, too."

Zach followed Wolf's pointing finger. His
leather bags, still buckled tight, lay draped over a
plain wooden chair with a cowhide seat. Breathing
a silent sigh of relief, he nodded his thanks.

Wolf beamed, and his tone took on a sly heart-iness. "So, Reverend, where you headed?"

"I hear Tucson is a lawless town in need of sal-vation." Despite the fact that he lay flat on his back wearing nothing but the bottoms of his long johns, Zach's small, pained smile was a coura-geous and charming portrait of valiance in the face of adversity. "But it seems my work will have to wait."

"Now, don't you fret, Reverend," Wolf inter-jected hastily. "I personally guarantee that you'll receive every care and comfort here until you make a full recovery. Beth Ann will see to it."

His daughter's lush mouth turned down at the corners. "I've got to get supper started, Paw. Buck's been helping out, so he can play nursemaid from now on."

"You'll serve the man kindly, and make proper atonement as a sin offering, or I'll take it out of your hide!" Wolf shoved Beth Ann to the side of the bed. "Look to that bandage like Doc said."

Beth Ann's delicate jaw clenched. "I know what to do, Paw."

"Then shut up your yapping and do it!" Wolf smiled encouragement at Zach. "You rest easy, Reverend Temple. We're going to take good care of you."

Zach felt a little glow of satisfaction ignite, but carefully banked it down. It wasn't hard, for fa-tigue was dragging at him, but he strove to make his tone sufficiently grateful. "Your kindness has not been exaggerated, sir. I hope someday I can re-pay your benevolence."

"Well, we're a small congregation, without a permanent pastor yet. And since there are some who could stand a proper chastisement from a real minister—" Wolf speared his daughter with a dark look "—maybe you can preach for us when you're recovered. You get some rest, and we'll talk later. See to him, gal."

Wolf thumped out of the room, being very careful to open the door to the veranda wide for propriety's sake. Zach's energy left with Wolf, and he watched Beth Ann from an ever-increasing distance. She stood rigid for a long moment, and he sensed the fine quivering of an inner struggle beneath her outward composure. Finally she leaned over and gingerly lifted one edge of Zach's bandage.

The sweetness of roses engulfed him. Even in his weakened condition, the feminine scent evoked a basic masculine response, a reflexive tightening of his loins that almost made him groan aloud. What was it about this woman that called to everything male in him? She was a hellion, and an unpredictable and dangerous one, at that. Even his palms tingled, almost as if he knew what it felt like to touch her, to stroke breasts whose womanly fullness no expanse of black gabardine could ever truly disguise. Zach closed his eyes to shut out the sight of her looming over him and battled with his lustful thoughts. When she tugged at the bandage, he sucked in a pained breath, biting his tongue to stop the words that leaped to his lips.

"I'll be done in a moment. It doesn't look too bad." Even though her tone was grudging, her touch was gentle. She worked quickly, rapidly replacing the dressings, then straightened. "If we can keep the fever down, I reckon you'll do."

Zach opened cautious eyes, then tucked his stubbled chin to his chest and peered at his shoulder as best he could. "A tidy job. What doctor do I have to thank for the stitching?"

In a show of efficiency, Beth Ann straightened the sheet and pulled a colorfully striped woven blanket from the foot of the bed to cover him. "I did it. There wasn't time for anyone else."

He imagined her delicate hands working over him, the cool head and sheer guts it had taken to patch up a bloody stranger—even one she was responsible for plugging!—and he blew out a shaky breath.

"I guess I ought to thank you for that, at least, Miss Linder." He favored her with a rather snide smile. "On the other hand, don't you think you owe *me* an apology?"

She stiffened as if he'd goosed her through her corset, her eyes sparking silver fire. "I'm certainly sorry . . . that you're so blamed stupid!"

Zach held on to his temper by the slimmest of threads. "The Lord works in mysterious ways. Perhaps this is a test of my vocation."

Bracing her hands on her slim hips, she glared at him, her mouth twisting with contempt. "Oh, so you're another one of those self-righteous hypocrites come to 'redeem' the scarlet woman, are you? Well, think again, preacher!"

He frowned. "Hold it. Scarlet woman? Who, you?"

Beth Ann's chin hardened. "Around here, that's what they call a woman if she runs off trusting a man to marry her and he doesn't."

Zach blinked. He hadn't expected this. "Oh."

She gave a brief, bitter laugh. "Yeah, Tom was all for marriage as long as he thought I'd end up with Traveler's Rest and Paw's played-out claims. But when Paw caught up with us on the trail, swearing he'd disown me first, Tom lit out of there like a cat with his tail on fire." She heaved an exasperated sigh. "So I haven't got much of a reputation in these parts. In fact, there are some who'd be flat scandalized to know I'd laid a finger on your sanctified flesh!"

"I'm not complaining," Zach drawled.

Something in his tone raised her hackles, and she spit at him like an enraged tigress. "I don't have much use for men in general, and preachers in particular, so save it!"

His head reeled at her vehemence. "I don't understand you."

"I'm just giving you fair warning." Belligerence tinged her words with acid. "Preacher or not, you lay a hand on me again and you'll draw back a nub."

Honest bewilderment clouded his expression. "Again? When did I ever . . . ?"

Zach broke off, for his palms were tingling again and something niggled at his brain, a fleeting impression from a dream, velvety skin and the lush heaviness of feminine flesh beneath his fingertips. One look at Beth Ann's incensed expression convinced him of the reality of his erotic fantasy, leaving him both thrilled and dismayed. "Oh, Lord."

She looked down her nose at him in icy hauteur. "Mighty interesting behavior for a preacher, I'd say."

Flustered, Zach struggled up on one elbow. "Look, I was out of my head. You can't hold something like that against me. Besides, the Lord says we should forgive those who do us wrong."

Beth Ann's breath hissed between her teeth. "Don't you preach to me about forgiveness! Paw's made me get up in church every Sunday for two years and confess my sins, but no amount of humiliation is ever going to be enough to satisfy this town."

"I'm not so hard to please." He gave her a crooked smile guaranteed to melt any feminine heart. "What do you say we let bygones be bygones? Wipe the slate clean and start over, so to speak?"

Suspicion lurked in her silvery eyes, and her mouth was petulant. "The only thing I'm interested in is getting you well enough to leave my house!"

Zach wasn't used to having his overtures rebuffed so firmly. Irritation and the throbbing of his head and shoulder made him lash out. "Not very charitable of you, now is it, Miss Linder? What are you so scared of? That I might in my delirium mistake you for Delilah again? Or that if I did, you'd enjoy it too much?"

At that thrust, she went pale, then crimson. "You ... you mangy, despicable hound! You dare—"

His taunting laughter broke into her tirade. "My, my, for a fallen woman, you play the offended virgin quite impressively. I wonder what other roles you know."

Beth Ann gulped, too outraged to speak coherently.

"By the way," he said smoothly, "I'm still waiting for that apology."

"When hell freezes over!" she managed.

Gingerly lying back against his pillow, Zach *tsk*ed between his even teeth, his good eye glinting with turquoise malice. "Well, even without your apology, sister, I do most heartily forgive you. It's apparent you need all of that most merciful and precious commodity you can get."

She glared at him, but when she opened her mouth to speak, all that came out was a strangled "Oh!" Infuriated, she stamped toward the door.

He called her back. "Miss Linder?"

"Now what?" she barked, facing him again with her fists fastened to her hips, prickly as a porcupine with a sunburn.

Zach made his expression innocent. "Would it be within the bounds of your Christian charity to direct me to the nearest privy before my bladder explodes?"

Beth Ann choked, and her face flamed. "Don't you dare get up! You'll bust open those stitches, and I don't want you around here any longer than absolutely necessary."

The strain was beginning to show on Zach's face. "Then you'd better come up with another suggestion before I piddle on your clean sheets."

"There's ah—a convenience under the bed." She backed toward the door. "I'll get Buck to help you."

"Just hand me the damn thing before we're both embarrassed!"

"I—oh, hell's bells!" Crimson-cheeked, she dove under the bed, slapped the flower-strewn china pot onto the mattress, eased him onto his side, and hightailed it out of there.

"Thank you, Miss Linder," Zach called, both laughter and relief accompanying the sound of liquid tinkling against china.

Beth Ann paused on the threshold, her backbone rigid with outrage. "Save your gratitude, Reverend. I'm only sorry my aim wasn't better!"

She disappeared with a disdainful flick of her skirts. Zach grinned ruefully. Waking up with a bullet hole in his shoulder might not be the most salubrious beginning he'd ever made, but he'd discovered one very interesting fact.

Beth Ann Linder was no more an angel than he was a preacher.

His initial assessment was right on the money. Things were very promising indeed.

Chapter 2

There was one thing about prison, Zach thought. You met a better class of scum.

Perched with his saddlebags open on the bed beside him, he carefully unwrapped his last clean shirt from around a flat leather wallet and removed the creased and sweat-stained tintype print of Miss Beth Ann Linder. It was the kind of picture a traveling photographer would take, a stiff, posed portrait of a pretty lady decked out in all her frills and ruffles and gewgaws so the old folks or her beau would have a likeness to cherish.

Only she'd given this one to her lover. Even in the pale dawn light, it was easy to see it didn't do her justice.

"Tom, you son of a bitch," Zach muttered. "I always knew you were a goddamned liar."

It was a good thing Tom Chapman was still in Yuma in the territorial prison, Zach decided. Otherwise, he'd probably be whaling the tar out of one Zach Madison for lifting this little trophy of Tom's most notorious feminine conquest. Tom liked to show off the picture like it was a scalp or something, endlessly retelling the tale of successful seduction. Of course, in jail there wasn't much you could do after the day's labor but jaw, and Zach had been as guilty as the next man of listening.

At the time, Zach had been working out a six-month sentence for hoaxing a crooked barkeeper out of his nest egg. The fellow had deserved it, after all, but how could Zach have known the barkeeper's brother-in-law was the sheriff? Not that he couldn't handle his first spell in jail, but there were nights in that stifling, stinking hellhole when Tom's voice weaving fantasies in the darkness was the only relief that counted.

Zach turned the little photograph toward the growing light, studying the face that had been the focus of countless convicts' fancies. It was damned hard to reconcile the flat image with the prickly, razor-tongued termagant he'd met yesterday, much less the hot-blooded honey of Tom's accounts.

Tom had loved to talk about his sweet Beth Ann, so trusting, so loving, so desperate to get away from that fat-assed, Bible-thumping paw of hers that she'd believe anything, even a snake-tongued desperado's lies of love and devotion.

"Hell, boys," Tom had said, laughing in that ugly way of his, "it was easy as shooting fish in a barrel and twice as much fun!"

Recalling every succulent detail, Tom's gravelly basso enthralled his listeners until their flesh strained against their britches and they groaned with the carnal images dancing behind their eyes.

Tom told of the first time he'd stolen Beth Ann's hair ribbon and seen that rich, curling mass of black hair falling down about her shoulders. The wine and spice of her mouth when he'd taught her how to really kiss, no maidenly pursing of lips, but a real tongue-sucking exchange of tonsil juice. How timid and blushing and curious she'd been the first time he'd gotten his hand inside her blouse. Her nipples rosy and sweet as candy; her skin like honey and cream, "all over, boys, *all over.*" And her hips, lifting to meet a man's power—sweet Jesus! So tight and hot, her legs long and strong, her need so fierce, she sucked a man dry and left him crying, it was so good . . .

"Pure heaven, boys," Tom always ended when the murmurs and groans up and down the cellblock became too restless. "My own little piece of heaven."

Zach passed his hand over his burning eyes and licked his dry lips. He wasn't immune even now, despite his having made the lady's acquaintance by way of a bullet that shattered all his illusions.

The rest of the story of Wolf Linder and Traveler's Rest had come in bits and pieces during those long evenings of torture, a secondary thing to everyone but Zach. He spent just as many nights with his manhood making a tent out of his blanket as the rest of them, but somewhere in all that sensual stewing, a germ of an idea was born, so half-formed at first, he hadn't really known why he'd made certain the last thing he did before leaving jail was swipe that little tintype picture.

Now, six months after his release, he'd had another unfortunate disagreement with the law and needed to lie low awhile. Sooner or later the authorities would find themselves too busy with a new killer of Tom Chapman's ilk to worry about Zach Madison's escapades. After all, he upheld his own code of honor, of sorts. What was a little fraud or a crooked soap game or even impersonating a peace officer in the grand scheme of western law and order? He never broke a law when he could get what he needed with a little guile. Not that he wouldn't bend the rules when he found something unfair or senseless, but he never hurt anyone or took advantage of those less astute in the matters of survival than himself. In fact, he always chose a mark for one of his schemes with particular care, likening himself to that old fellow Robin Hood who took from the rich and wicked to give to the poor.

Hell, Zach thought, he was only using the gifts the Lord had given him, a silver tongue and innate charm that taught him early he could catch more flies with honey than vinegar. Yes, sir, he'd made his way into card games, front parlors, and even his share of female beds with nothing more than his winning smile. Even though lately he sometimes felt a nagging dissatisfaction way down deep at the way he let Lady Luck blow him from town to town, drifting was what he knew, freedom what he craved, and living by his wits his strong suit. He couldn't abide being trapped—not by a place, a job, a woman—and there was no way in hell he was going back to jail again—*ever.*

So what better place to wait things out off the beaten path than Traveler's Rest, where Zach might pursue the challenge Tom Chapman had been unable to meet—getting his hands on Wolf Linder's gold mine? Yes, sir, glittering, fabulous gold, straight out of the rich heart of the Superstition Mountains. Zach had worked a claim or two before and new enough about minerals and mining to make a sure thing pay off. With spoils like that, a man might buy into a San Francisco gambling palace and make some real money.

Frowning in concentration, his sore shoulder making his movements awkward, Zach carefully wrapped the incriminating tintype in a clean bandanna and stuffed it down in the bottom of his saddlebags where no one could find it. The stakes of the game this time were too high for blunders.

Tom said everyone knew old Wolf had mines hidden up in the Superstitions. The old codger would disappear for weeks, then come back with his grub sack full of nuggets and deposit it right in the Destiny Savings Bank. Lots of men had tried to trail Wolf to find the location of his glory hole, but the old buzzard was clever, and always managed to lead his followers on a wild-goose chase before losing them.

"Amateurs," Zach murmured in disdain.

Including Tom. Imagine, shackling yourself to a wife to latch on to a fortune! There were so many easier ways to run a swindle. Of course, it might not be such a hardship with a gal as pretty as Beth Ann Linder, especially if she was as hot and insatiable as Tom boasted. Too bad it hadn't worked. Clever Wolf, making marriage between Tom and Beth Ann a worthless proposition. It was all it took to drive Tom off.

That failure, buried under all Tom's bragging, was the item that caught Zach's imagination. In his experience, self-righteous hypocrites made easy marks. Despite Tom's amateurish attempt, Wolf Linder, with his complacent faith in himself and his God, was still ripe for the picking. And Zach Madison, alias the Reverend Zachariah Temple, was just the one who could do it.

Zach riffled through his saddlebags for his razor and laid out his clean shirt. After having spent an uncomfortable night trying to find a position to ease his throbbing shoulder, he was ready to get on with the business at hand. And since circumstances had robbed him of a good first impression, it might behoove him to do something positive about the second.

Holding his left arm close to his rib cage, Zach tugged up the waistband of his sagging long johns and eased to his feet. He yelped when he tried to put his weight on his injured foot and grabbed the bedpost as the stone floor seemed to dip and tilt like a ship's deck. Damn! He was more muzzy-headed than he realized, and his mouth was so dry, he could have spit cotton.

Zach limped to the washstand, a twig-and-rope affair with a plain china wash set, and drank tepid water directly from the pitcher's lip. Pouring the rest into the bowl, he balanced the pitcher on the edge of the stand, then splashed his face and neck, one-handed, relishing the chill against his overwarm skin before reaching for his shaving soap.

It was a decidedly awkward business, working up a lather with one good hand, especially when his vision kept growing brighter, then dimmer, in a most annoying fashion. Frowning, Zach scrubbed the suds into his stubble, then reached for the straight razor. With the first swipe, he nearly took off the tip of his nose.

Cursing under his breath, he made an O of his mouth and promptly nicked his upper lip. He'd never noticed how much a man needed two hands to get this masculine chore done properly. Scowling his ill temper, he slung suds off the edge of the blade in the direction of the bowl. His knuckles grazed the pitcher, which perversely leaped off the washstand and smashed itself on the flagstones with a sickening crash.

"Shit."

Zach regarded the shards around his bare feet with disgust and dismay. Miss Beth Ann would have his hide now.

No sooner had the thought formed than the door swept open and the lady in question charged in with a covered tray, firing questions like a Gatling gun.

"What happened? Are you all right? What—no, don't move!"

"No, ma'am," he said meekly. After all, what could he do, balanced half-naked on one foot amidst the pottery shards, one arm strapped by pain to his side, the other raised up like some dad-blamed fandango dancer! Under the layer of suds, his cheeks burned.

Surrounded by the fragrant aromas of hot coffee and fresh bread, Beth Ann hastily set the tray on a nearby table. She dropped down on her haunches and began tossing the fragments into the cupped lap of her pink striped apron.

"Bullheaded, arrogant . . . *man!* What in the world are you thinking? You shouldn't be up! Look at this mess. It's a wonder you haven't cut your toes off!"

Kneeling at his feet, she caught his ankle between her thumb and forefinger and moved his foot into a clear spot. The astonishing contact sent a tremor up Zach's leg.

"Move over," she ordered, exasperation coloring every word. "Honestly, men have no more sense than children!"

Suds dripping from his chin onto his bare chest, Zach watched in mute amazement as she rapidly cleared the floor. Her hair was bundled back from her face in a thick braid that ended in the middle of the back of her starched white shirtwaist, and a fascinating inch of lace-trimmed petticoat peeked from under the bunched-up hem of her sprigged black calico skirt. Her morning-fresh appearance contrasted to his sweat-stained dishevelment made him feel at a disadvantage, a sensation that suited him not at all.

"There. You can put your foot down now." Rising, Beth Ann untied the sash of her apron and wrapped the remnants of the pitcher into the makeshift bag. "Whatever were you—" She broke off, frowning at him in accusation. "You're fever-ish!"

His denial was automatic. "You're loco, lady!"

Reaching up, she brushed his curls back from his forehead and laid her cool palm against his brow. "Just as I thought. Are you trying to kill yourself just to spite me? Get back in bed this instant!"

Why did all women think they were your mother when you were ailing? Zach asked himself irritably. At least, scolding and petting you at the same time was something he would have expected his own mother to do, if he'd ever had one. Since he couldn't remember having parents, he'd had to imagine that kind of thing when he was a hungry, snot-nosed kid with sticky fingers and a talent for blarney. In his boyhood, Zach had only had old Boone, the owner of the Red Garter Saloon and Livery Stable in Calliope, Texas, who'd set him to working for his keep when he was only knee-high to a grasshopper. Later, Miss Hortense Small had come along, a prune-mouthed, do-gooder spinster who'd been responsible for the little bit of proper schooling and religion Zach had ever gotten.

Zach smiled at the recollection. "Miss Tensy" had bullied him into sitting through Sunday after Sunday of boring sermons, but it was well worth it when she filled him up afterward with the best dinner he'd get all week—fried chicken and fluffy potatoes, smothered green beans and squash, and real, honest-to-God coconut cake every time because, even though he was a rambunctious scamp, she knew he liked it best. It wasn't a half-bad trade, giving the lonely old maid some company in return for her cooking. Hell, he'd even gotten one of his biggest belly laughs when she'd dragged him to the tent revival meeting and he'd

seen everyone whooping it up, "amens" and "hal-
lelujahs" flying all over the place!

But if there ever had been a time when he'd
dreamed of a family of his own, he'd quickly
learned to appreciate the freedoms of growing up
half-wild. When he left Calliope, he'd never once
looked back. Drifting beat the settled life all to hell
and gone, especially when there was always the
excitement of a new game in the next town down
the trail. Zach had to admit, though, there was a
certain comfort in a woman's concerned touch . . .

Whoa there, partner! Zach jerked himself out of a
fool's paradise and pulled back from the enticing
pleasure of Beth Ann's fingers on his parched skin.
He wasn't so chuckleheaded that he'd let this
woman slip under his guard this way. He fixed
her with an overbright glare.

"Isn't a man entitled to any privacy around
here, Miss Linder? I'd be obliged if you'd let me
finish my shave in peace."

"I think not, Reverend Temple." Her voice vine-
gary, she deftly plucked the razor from his grasp.
"You've lost enough blood without adding to the
account with fresh lacerations."

"Now, just a damn minute! Blast it, there are
certain rituals a woman has no business poking
her nose into, and this is one of them. And I'm not
going anywhere until I've had a shave!"

"Don't be a stubborn mule! You'll only end up
scalping yourself." She dragged the cowhide-
bottomed chair in front of the mirrored armoire
and indicated it with the razor. "Have a seat. If
you insist on being such a baby, I'll do it for you."

"Let a bossy woman like you come at me with
a razor?" Zach looked from her expectant face to
the shining steel and back again in alarm, then
shook his head. "Honey, I've already taken one

licking from you. I'm not crazy enough to risk it again!"

She flushed to her roots with guilty embarrassment, then said stiffly, "Your breakfast will be stone-cold if you insist on shaving one-handed. And you really do have a hectic color. The sooner you're quiet and resting again with a dose of my sage tea inside you, the better." When he still hesitated, she plunged on. "I'm experienced. I kept Paw's beard trimmed up when he got hurt last year."

He gave her a considering look. "I'll admit I'm not as steady on my pins as I'd like this morning . . ."

"So I see." She gave a disdainful sniff, glancing at the apron full of fragments.

"And this soap is beginning to itch . . ."

"Well, at last you're seeing reason!"

"Hold it a minute." A devilish turquoise light gleamed under his lashes. "I might consider your offer. *If* I get that apology you still owe me."

She spluttered indignantly. "I will not!"

He shrugged his uninjured shoulder. "Too bad. Never know what kind of relapse a man in my condition might suffer. Now, return my razor, please. Or is thievery also on your list of sins?"

"You vile—" Their gazes clashed and she broke off, seething, her hands making white-knuckled fists at her sides. She was the first to look away. Finally she ground out, "I apologize. I was unreasonable before. I hope you'll forgive me."

"Now, that's more like it." His voice was husky with suppressed laughter. "Apology accepted."

She flashed him a hot look. "Then plant your butt in that chair, preacher, and let's get this over with!"

Grinning, Zach complied. "My, such language from a lady!"

Beth Ann tugged a sheet from the bed and swept it around Zach's bare shoulders, muttering. "I never said I was a lady. But you're the sorriest excuse for a gentleman I've seen in a coon's age!"

With a jolt, Zach realized she was right. If he expected the Linders to accept him with the respect due a minister, he'd have to remember to play the part. Not the easiest thing in the world since this beautiful shrew had a knack for bringing out the worst in him. He had to stifle his inclination to rile her while he found a way to sweeten her up a bit. She might eventually divulge information about her father's mines, or at least where he kept his cache of nuggets. While if he'd had his druthers, he'd have forgone a bullet wound, having a genuine excuse to remain right where he wanted was going to make things a lot easier—as long as he didn't make some kind of jackass mistake and reveal himself!

"I'm afraid I'm taking my irritability out of you, Miss Linder," he murmured. "I beg your pardon."

Surprised, she looked up from the washbasin, where she'd been lathering her hands, then said gruffly, "That's all right. Are you ready?"

Settling back, Zach nodded. She transferred the suds on her hands to Zach's cheeks with circular strokes until he wanted to purr like a contented pussycat. The fresh scent of soap was overlaid with a subtle hint of her rosy fragrance, and it teased his nostrils and the back of his throat in a peculiar fashion.

"I should have brought some hot water," she said. "I'll go get some—"

Prolong what was fast becoming pure torture?

Zach swallowed convulsively. "No, don't go to the trouble. Where I come from, I'm used to cold."

"Oh?" A small pleat appeared between her dark brows as she concentrated on stroking the white suds evenly across his lean cheeks. "Where's that?"

Zach nearly blurted "prison," but caught himself. "Oh, here and there. The Lord's work has taken me into rough country more than once."

"I see." Chewing her lush lower lip, Beth Ann studied him with some trepidation, then raised the razor and went to work on his whiskers with grim determination.

Trying to keep his mind off the luxurious way her fingers felt against his face, Zach searched around for a safe topic. "You've a fine place here. In fact, I've rarely enjoyed the luxury of an inn as comfortable as this."

That was certainly true. Most way stations expected their paying customers to flop down with one another on a dirt floor for the night, along with any assorted livestock that might be in residence, from the ubiquitous bedbugs to the occasional pig. Plastered adobe walls and polished wooden floors, fresh linens and china washing facilities, were accommodations fit for the emperor of Mexico, or at least his ambassador.

"Traveler's Rest is our home, Reverend." Beth Ann tilted Zach's chin upward and scraped away the red-brown stubble sprouting underneath. "I'd like to believe each guest receives every courtesy."

Zach's faintly mocking glance collided with hers, and she blushed but did not make further comment, resolutely concentrating on her task. Zach pursued the conversation in the idle fashion that he hoped did not show his true interest.

"Your father's, er—unfortunate disability must burden you with heavy responsibilities."

"Oh, Paw." She was offhand. "He can still do just about whatever he pleases. Except go off prospecting, of course. That's how he came to lose the leg, you know."

"No, I didn't."

"Uh-huh." She tugged his earlobe out of the way, carefully outlining his jawbone with the blade. "Snakebite. I told him he was too old to venture out all alone, but my father's a stubborn man. Still thinks he's going to find the mother lode after all this time."

"You don't think so?"

She snorted. "As much time as he's spent in those mountains, he'd have found it if it was there. Haven't you ever heard that a miner is a liar with a hole in the ground? Not to say Paw hasn't done all right over the years. We bought Traveler's Rest with what he earned running placers early on, but it's no kind of life for a man his age."

Zach considered. Was she lying? Or had her father kept her in the dark about his mines? Or worse, was it the truth? Hellfire! How was he going to know if he was wasting his time here or not?

"I understand prospecting gets in your blood for life. Surely he misses it?" he said.

"I suppose. But he's lucky to be alive, leg or not. Nowadays he and Mr. Barlings at the bank spend a lot of time on church and civic projects for the betterment of Destiny. That's safer than risking your neck looking for gold, I say."

"Very sensible."

Zach only wished his reaction to Beth Ann's nearness were as sensible. Unfortunately, she was having a peculiar effect on him as he admired the thickness and length of her dark lashes and the satiny texture of her perfect, golden complexion. Her feminine aura was overwhelming in his present weakened condition, for his thoughts kept turning to how that skin would feel if he tested it with his lips . . .

Looking beyond Beth Ann in an attempt to regain control of his wayward thoughts, Zach caught a rather vertiginous view of himself reflected in the armoire's spotted mirror. His eye was developing a rainbow of colorful bruises—yellow, purple, green. It was a dizzying sensation to feel Beth Ann's gentle touch while simultaneously watching her from another angle.

In the mirror's reflection he could see her skillful hands at work as well as the outline of her rounded bottom through her skirts. She'd almost uncovered all of his face, and he realized with something of a shock that the countenance that gazed back at him from that mirror had a satyr's lecherous blue-green eyes. It would be nothing for that lascivious beast to lift his hands and cup her hips, pull her into the throbbing vee of his legs, and bury his nose in the valley between her soft breasts. Then he could place tender love bites on the underside of those sweet mounds until she moaned with pleasure . . .

But he couldn't. He was the Reverend Mr. Temple, Zach reminded himself fiercely, and above such outrageous actions—not to mention mere thoughts! The only certain way to foul up his plans would be to give Miss Linder reason to wonder about him. Right now he was the saint, and she was the sinner, and he'd better damn sure keep it that way if he expected anything to come of this scheme!

She took a towel and, bending closer, carefully

wiped the residue of the suds from his cheeks. It was too much. Zach covered the backs of her hands with his, holding her palms and the towel against his face. The swiftness of his movement made Beth Ann gasp softly. She pulled away, and the towel fell into his sheet-covered lap, but he didn't release her. His gaze locked with hers, and despite his earlier reasoning, Zach knew he had no choice but to find out if she was really as soft as his vague remembrances told him she was.

"R-Reverend?" Her gray eyes widened in alarm.

With surprising strength, he tugged her closer, mocking her. "Miss Linder."

"Let me go." She sounded strangled.

"Not nervous of me, are you?"

She jerked her hands, but he held firm. "Varmint!"

"No, just a man with an unsatisfied curiosity."

Tilting her chin, she glared at him. "I've got no answers for you!"

With a laugh, Zach slipped his good arm around her waist, dragging her against his side. Since he was still seated, his mouth was on a level with the upper swell of her bosom. If he bent his head just a bit . . .

"Maybe I just want to know the questions," he said thickly.

"Oh, is that how it is?" Suddenly she seemed to understand, and her voice became a purr, her silver eyes sultry. "You're no different from all the other bull calves around here, are you?"

He smiled. "Why don't we see?"

Grabbing the curls at his nape, she pulled his head back. Only a whisper separated her mouth from his. "You'd like that, would you?"

His eyes glinted. "More importantly, darlin', I guarantee *you* would."

"Muy macho hombre, eh?"

"There's one way to find out," he rumbled, smoothing the curve of her hip suggestively.

With a malicious laugh, she whirled out of his grasp. "No, thanks, preacher. I don't take on charity cases or cripples. I believe I'll wait for a real man!"

Nonplussed, Zach blinked. "Cuss it! I'm no—"

A thunderous knock shook the door, and it flew inward. A tall figure in a long duster and broad-brimmed sombrero stood poised on the doorsill. "Hell in a bucket, Beth Ann! Lemme see that feller you plugged!"

"Jean!" With a cry of pure delight and a smile as radiant as sunshine, Beth Ann launched herself at the intruder and was gathered up in a huge bear hug.

Stunned, Zach watched with his mouth open. That smile had transformed Beth Ann's lovely features, producing an indentation in her cheek that was more intriguing than a mere dimple. More than that, however, it revealed a liveliness and vivacity and intelligence, and he understood then that all of Tom Chapman's boasting had not been in vain. Happy and excited, laughing and flirtatious, Beth Ann Linder was a force not many men could resist.

Not himself. Not the man in the doorway.

Zach's stomach sank with disappointment and an unsuspected twinge of pure jealousy. But why wouldn't she have found herself another man in the two years since Tom left her high and dry? What was so damn surprising about that?

"When did you get back? Why didn't you tell me you were coming?" Beth Ann was almost giddy with happiness.

"Hell, them bullocks came downhill so fast this

trip, I nearly met myself coming!" The tall figure turned toward Zach. "Damn, Beth Ann. He's still alive. Didn't I teach you to shoot better'n that?"

"Next time I'll take more care," Beth Ann returned, slanting Zach a meaningful look.

"Well, I guess I'm tickled you ain't actually kilt nobody." Sweeping the large hat off a thatch of mouse-colored hair, Jean stepped forward and stuck a huge, callused hand in Zach's face. "Put her there, son. How the hell are you, anyway?"

"Uh." As Zach's hand was soundly wrung, the truth finally dawned on him. This mountain of a man—was a woman!

"You've rendered the reverend speechless," Beth Ann commented. "At last. But let me introduce you. Reverend Zach Temple, meet Whiskey Jean, the best bullwhacker this side of the Pecos!"

"How do, er—ma'am?" Zach answered in a voice rocky with shock.

"Just fine, son! Say, you look a mite peaked."

Beth Ann nodded. "I knew he was rushing things! You really don't look at all well, preacher."

"I think I'll lie down now." Dragging the sheet with him, Zach stood and lurched toward the bed.

"That's the ticket, son! Get some rest." Whiskey Jean clapped Beth Ann on the shoulder. "Say, I've been dreamin' of sourdough biscuits for the last forty miles!"

"Sure thing." Catching Jean's arm, Beth Ann moved toward the door.

The bullwhacker threw a shrewd look over one brawny shoulder. "Take care of yourself, son."

Zach stared after them, then began to laugh softly. He must be a *lot* feverish to be so damn glad Beth Ann's "real man" had turned out to be a female!

* * *

"More coffee, Paw?" Beth Ann asked a bit later.

Wolf left off arguing with Sam Pritchard, the stage driver, about whether or not the railroads would see fit to build lines across lower Arizona long enough to let Beth Ann fill his cup from the huge graniteware pot. Without thanking her, he took a sip and continued to make his point, loud enough so that Mr. Pritchard, his guard, Pat Tucker, and the four other male passengers gobbling up Beth Ann's pan-fried ham, eggs, hot buttered biscuits, and saguaro fruit conserve couldn't fail to be impressed with his grasp of the subject.

Beth Ann caught the gleam of Whiskey Jean's smile from the other end of the long trestle table and returned that amusement with a wry wink. Wolf never bothered to include her in the table conversation. After all, a female who'd wear men's britches was an affront to nature. In fact, everything about the woman raised Wolf's hackles. Everything, that was, except her cash money.

Never mind that Whiskey Jean was the best freight man in the region, tough and reliable, a loudmouth giantess who handled her teams better than most men, who drank, spit, and cursed with the best of them, and who always got her supplies to the mining camps on time. A frowsy-haired and genial amazon, her lined face generally encrusted with enough road dirt to plant potatoes, "whiffy" with the smell of mules and sweat, Whiskey Jean had enjoyed the cooking at Traveler's Rest for years, befriending Wolf Linder's lonesome, motherless daughter in the process.

She was the one who'd had a frank talk with a frightened girl about the mysteries of a woman's body and what measures you could take if a man tried to get too personal with you. Unfortunately, when Tom Chapman had come sparking Beth

Ann, Whiskey Jean had been absent on one of her long hauls. Otherwise, Beth Ann believed now, the old woman's savvy could have saved her a lot of grief. She was just about the only person, man or woman, who hadn't condemned Beth Ann for a jade and a harlot after Tom deserted her and Wolf had brought her home in disgrace. And Beth Ann loved her.

"I'll have some more of that jamoka, too, iffen you don't mind, Beth Ann," Pat Tucker said from the other side of the table.

Beth Ann stiffened with dislike. Greasy and disagreeable, the beefy stage guard fancied himself a ladies' man and considered Beth Ann fair game. After all, if she'd spread her thighs for the likes of Tom Chapman, it was only a matter of time before her resistance to Pat's heavy-handed wooing collapsed. Beth Ann shuddered every time he undressed her with his eyes, and she did her best to ignore his crude innuendos. Unfortunately, her coolness just seemed to make him more determined, and she'd had a bellyful of fending off his unwelcome attentions.

Reluctantly, her features stiff, she carried the hot pot to his place. Using the corner of her apron to steady the bottom, she poured the scalding, black-as-sin brew into his tin mug.

"Yer lookin' mighty fetching this morning," Pat said, leaning on his elbow to screen their conversation from the men at the end of the table. He smirked at her through his scraggly beard and waggled his eyebrows suggestively. "How's about you and me steppin' out for a breath of fresh air?"

Beth Ann's teeth clicked together in distaste. "I'd just as soon set up housekeeping with a pack of tarantulas."

"You're a hardhearted woman, Bethy Ann."

Pat's oily voice took on a wheedling tone. "C'mon, honey, let me show you what a real man can do for you—"

Bold as brass, he pinched her bottom through her skirt, a sure enough goose right in the tender area at the top of her thigh. In the next second, Pat was on his feet with a lap full of hot coffee, squalling like a scalded cat.

"Yeow! Goddammit!" Hopping and stamping, he blistered the air with curses. "What the hell did you do that for?"

"Enough!" Wolf roared. "I won't have blasphemy in this house, Mr. Tucker."

"But she . . . she . . ." Pat spluttered, plucking at his denims.

"You're the clumsiest female I ever saw," Wolf scolded his daughter. "Clean up that mess!"

"Right away, Paw." Hiding a smile, Beth Ann set Pat's tin cup upright again and mopped at the steaming liquid with a spare napkin.

"Hey, Pat!" Whiskey Jean cackled. "You best change them drawers, son. Everybody'll think you done made wee-wee in your britches."

The passengers sitting around the table snickered. Pritchard gave Pat a sharp nod. With a venomous look in Beth Ann's direction, the stage guard stamped out of the room.

"Hey, Wolf!" Whiskey Jean called. "Pass me some more of them sourdoughs, will you? All this hilarity's done worked up my appetite again."

Distracted, Wolf shoved the platter of biscuits down the table.

"Much obliged, Wolf." Whiskey Jean always called Wolf Linder by his first name just to annoy him. She stuffed double handfuls of the fluffy biscuits into the kangaroo pockets of her ancient duster and twinkled at Beth Ann. "I'd love to stay and jaw with you, Wolf, but daylight's burning. You got change fer a dollar?"

All these interruptions to his pontificating made Wolf's whiskers quiver in annoyance. He jerked his chin at Beth Ann, more than anxious to rid himself of Whiskey Jean's company. "See to it."

"Yes, Paw." Beth Ann dropped her sopping rag onto the table and led the way out of the dining room to the front parlor, a public room where visitors could relax and visit on the chairs and benches. The front door stood open to let in the cool early morning breeze. A large rolltop desk served as the Traveler's Rest business office.

"Cain't say when I've had such a belly laugh," Jean chuckled, patting the belt buckle holding up her voluminous, dusty trousers. "But I reckon you made an enemy of Pat, honey."

Beth Ann snorted her disdain. "I'm not afraid of that ass."

She quickly added one breakfast to the tally in Wolf's big green book, the one he kept in his own shorthand code to keep prying eyes out of his business, then sorted out Whiskey Jean's change from a tin box in the middle drawer. "And if Pat Tucker lays so much as a finger on me again, he's going to wish his only problem is scalded privates!"

"Figurin' on taking a plug out of him like you done that preacher feller?"

Beth Ann wilted, then gave Whiskey Jean a wry look. "It's pretty fair sport, but shooting a man turns out to cause just too damn much trouble."

The friends looked at each other a moment, then broke out laughing. After the last couple of days, the simple release felt wonderful to Beth Ann.

The preacher was trouble, pure and simple, and Paw's making her wait on him wasn't helping matters. Why, it had been all she could do to ignore his state of undress this morning, but only a blind woman could have missed the impressive width of Zach Temple's bare chest. She'd been amazed at the way a pair of worn long johns could reveal the handsome muscularity of a man's lean buttocks and thighs, too.

Sobering, Beth Ann stifled an inward groan. And why had she offered to finish shaving him? She'd never endured anything so nerve-racking in her life! It was a wonder she hadn't sliced him to ribbons! Of course, she'd done her utmost not to show how touching his skin affected her pulse, but his smile had been so boyishly mischievous and yet so knowing that her breath had quickened involuntarily and her legs had quivered like dry leaves in a winter storm.

Perhaps there really was something wanton in her nature like Paw said, Beth Ann thought morosely. Maybe that was why Zach had touched her as he had. Perhaps all men just had some sort of sixth sense when it came to knowing which women would have trouble controlling their animal urges. The preacher was arrogant and infuriating and so damned attractive, she had a sinking feeling he could be more of a temptation than Tom Chapman ever was. But she'd be damned if she'd let anything like that happen again! She had the willpower, and if Zach Temple tried anything else, well . . . next time she'd shoot him where it would *really* hurt!

Beth Ann glanced at Whiskey Jean, who was wiping away the last of her chortles with a not-so-clean bandanna. "How'd you hear about what happened, anyway?"

The bullwhacker grinned. "You know what a

big mouth that pip-squeak Sayers has. It's all the talk in Destiny."

"Damn." Beth Ann chewed her lip. "I didn't mean to shoot the preacher, honest. I thought he was an Apache wantin' to steal Nellie."

Whiskey Jean shrugged. "Well, you know how folks like to take a thing the wrong way around here."

"Yes, I know." Beth Ann's mouth drooped, and her gray eyes were wide and forlorn as a lost child's.

"Your paw been ridin' you hard?" Whiskey Jean asked sympathetically.

"No worse than usual."

There was little Whiskey Jean could say to that, so she changed the subject, digging into one of many pockets to retrieve a small package wrapped in brown paper. "Nearly forgot. Thought you might could use this."

"Oh, Jean, thank you!" Beth Ann smiled and sniffed the sweetness of her favorite rose soap through the wrapping. Paw frowned on such frivolities, and since he kept her on such a short leash—almost a prisoner, she guessed, though she would have avoided town anyway—she rarely got to shop for such small feminine necessities. But Jean never forgot.

Beth Ann kissed the older woman's cheek. "You spoil me."

"Seems to me somebody ought to," Jean muttered, whacking her battered sugar-loaf sombrero against her knee, her weathered cheeks bright with pleasure at Beth Ann's affectionate response. She cleared her throat and said gruffly, "Gotta git outa here, gal. Buck'll have them bullocks of mine watered up real good by now, and them miners up on Tapamoc Ridge'll be hollering they ain't got no ter-baccy if I don't get there by tonight."

Beth Ann walked with Whiskey Jean onto the porch to make her farewells, but they both drew up short as a shiny black buggy carrying a trio of female passengers pulled up before Traveler's Rest.

"Uh-oh." Whiskey Jean whistled softly through her teeth.

"What on earth?" Beth Ann wondered.

"Looks like trouble." The older woman jammed her sombrero on her wispy hair and shot Beth Ann an apologetic look. "Sorry to run out on you, gal, but I'd rather face a herd of sidewinders than a delegation of virtuous women any day. See you next time. And watch your back."

Jean clopped down the steps to where Buck waited, his hat politely doffed as he held her team. She didn't give the females climbing out of the buggy so much as a glance. One look at the stiff-laced, poker-backed matrons, and Beth Ann wished she could skedaddle, too.

Dressed in proper, unrelieved black from bonnets to boots, they were the spiritual models and leaders of Destiny's feminine society. Beth Ann recognized Mamie Cunningham, a horse-faced woman whose ambitions had been fulfilled with the election of her livery-stable-owner husband to the position of Destiny's mayor, and Anita Kellogg, the spinster schoolmistress. The third was younger by at least a generation, a pretty blonde with a nervous expression. Beth Ann gasped in recognition and wary pleasure.

Kitty! She and Kitty Gallen had been bosom school chums before Kitty had married Douglas Hardy, the storekeeper, and Beth Ann's duties at Traveler's Rest had taken up all her time. That was before Tom had come along, of course. No one from town came calling on her anymore. They were afraid she might taint them with her scarlet behavior.

Beth Ann's heart tripped over in sudden trepidation, but she hid it beneath a cool smile. "Long way from home, aren't you, ladies?"

"The harlot's on the doorstep to stop us, Mamie," the schoolmistress said in a shocked tone. "It is beyond all Christian decency!"

The trio paused at the base of the porch steps. Mrs. Cunningham's squinty blue eyes blazed, and Beth Ann could have sworn she heard the rousing strains of "Onward Christian Soldiers" in the distance.

"Out of our way, you murderous Jezebel!" The feathers on Mrs. Cunningham's bonnet quivered with a zealot's determination.

Beth Ann had expected nothing less, yet still she stiffened, pricked to her sensitive and wounded core, but damned if she'd sacrifice what was left of her pride by showing it. They saw what they wanted to see, anyway. Really, she hated to disappoint them.

Animosity gleaming in her eyes, Beth Ann hiked up her skirts, planted the heel of her shoe on the porch rail, and made an elaborate production of checking her garter and stocking, right there in broad daylight! To her immense satisfaction, the action provoked three shocked gasps. She smiled, and her voice was a husky, suggestive contralto.

"I think you'd better state your business first, Mrs. Cunningham."

Red-faced, Mamie Cunningham practically choked on her tonsils, then took a deep breath and announced, "We've come to deliver poor Reverend

Temple from this iniquitous den of sin and degradation! Even if we must storm the very gates of
hell itself, we will not be turned aside!"

Beth Ann's lip curled, and she actually laughed.
"So who's stopping you?"

Chapter 3

"Shameless hussy!"

Beth Ann laughed again at Mrs. Cunningham's indignant splutter, then sauntered down the veranda to Zach's door. Throwing it open, she leaned against the casing, hip cocked provocatively and chest thrust out, gesturing in careless invitation.

"There he is. Have at him."

The three women exchanged distrustful glances, then Mrs. Cunningham lifted her hems and stomped up the steps to the porch with her entourage in tow. Wolf Linder met them at the front door.

"Well! Good morrow to you, Miz Cunningham." Wolf's eyes were flat with puzzled suspicion. "What brings you ladies to Traveler's Rest?"

"Out of our way, Mr. Linder!" Mamie Cunningham swept him aside with a vicious thrust of a chubby forearm.

The schoolmistress's thin mouth puckered like a prune as she followed. "Highly improper, Wolf Linder! How you could countenance such a situation is beyond comprehension!"

"Wha—what?" Wolf scowled in confusion.

"There is some—ah, concern about the reverend's welfare," Kitty murmured in a hesitant voice.

"Don't beat around the bush, Katherine Hardy!" Mrs. Cunningham snapped. "It's intolerable! An

58

affront to all that's holy! A man of God under the same roof as this piece of tawdry baggage—it's indecent!"

Wolf's bulbous features froze. "I'll thank you to mind your business, Mamie Cunningham. I can control my daughter."

"Yes, we all see how well you've managed that so far!" Mrs. Cunningham's voice was shrill with sarcasm. "The community is in an uproar. Have you any idea the damage this could do to Destiny's reputation? I don't understand why the sheriff hasn't hauled this girl off to stand trial for attempted murder!"

Beth Ann stiffened, unnerved by that threat and uncertain of her paw's reaction. He wasn't accustomed to having any woman question him, and his black and silver beard quivered with indignation.

"Sheriff Nichols knows the shooting was accidental," Wolf said. "Besides, I need Beth Ann here to look after me and keep Traveler's Rest running. Would you take away a poor cripple's livelihood and leave me to starve?"

Beth Ann fumed at that predictably selfish response, forcibly reminded that everything revolved around Wolf Linder's own dignity and benefit, nothing for his maligned daughter—ever. Wolf continued in a stentorian tone that grated on her raw nerves and rawer emotions.

"It's a fair penance for her to nurse the fellow. It'll teach her proper humility—"

"There is nothing *proper* about this at all, Mr. Linder!" Mrs. Cunningham interrupted. "Now, stand aside!"

The plump matron marched into the preacher's room, holding herself as far away from Beth Ann as possible to avoid contamination. The other two women followed, Miss Kellogg with her thin, pointed nose in the air, Kitty Hardy without meeting Beth Ann's eyes. Scowling, Wolf stumped in behind them.

Roused from sleep by the arrival of this unexpected delegation of visitors, Zach lifted his tousled head, then painfully levered himself into a half-sitting position against the pillows. The colorful blanket puddled modestly at his waist, but his bare chest with its heroic swath of white bandage was fully exposed. Heavy lidded, sleep-flushed, he had the beguiling innocence of a small boy in need of mothering and the slumberous sensuality of a sybarite rising from a three-day bacchanal. He was clearly not the middle-aged evangelist Mamie Cunningham was expecting.

"Oh, my," she breathed, wide-eyed. "Reverend Temple?"

Zach blinked, then his mouth crooked in a slow, intimate, just-for-you smile guaranteed to raise any female's temperature. "Yes, ma'am?"

"I had no idea . . ." Mamie's pudgy hand fluttered at her bosom in girlish bashfulness. Her companions were equally floored—Miss Kellogg looking like a frog catching flies with her mouth hanging open, and Kitty gazing anywhere but at the preacher's bare chest while wave after wave of increasingly hot color stained her cheeks.

"Dear sir, how do you fare?" Mamie asked anxiously.

"Tolerable, ma'am." Zach sighed deeply, and his three visitors automatically drew closer with a sympathetic chorus of sighs of their own. "But ours is not to question the trials the Lord sends us. Unlike Job, I will not chastise my God, amen and amen."

"Amen!" Wolf rumbled piously.

Zach gave another brave smile. "I thank you for your concern, Mrs. . . . ?"

"Mamie." Her face went bright pink. "Er, Mamie Cunningham. And this is Miss Kellogg and Mrs. Hardy. Here, let me adjust those for you." Simpering, she plumped the feather pillows into shape and settled them comfortably behind his shoulders.

"You must be parched, Reverend." Not to be outdone, Miss Kellogg snatched up a half-full water glass from the bedside table, her plain features twitching like an excited prairie dog's. "Would you care for a drink?"

"You're kindness itself, ma'am." Zach accepted the glass, and as he sipped, his turquoise gaze fell with masculine approval on Kitty Hardy. She grew an even deeper shade of crimson.

Amused, he lifted the tumbler again to hide a smile, his eyes twinkling as he met Beth Ann's sour glance over the rim of the glass. Mrs. Cunningham followed the direction of his gaze and instantly stiffened at the sight of Beth Ann lounging indolently against the door facing.

"This is intolerable." Giving the man on the bed another quick, appreciative once-over, Mrs. Cunningham nodded emphatically. "We must take the reverend into town immediately. It's the only thing."

Beth Ann threw her head back, exposing her throat, and her laugh was a rich gurgle of amusement meant to be both insulting and provocative. "They're afraid I'll try to corrupt the preacher, Paw!"

Wolf looked ready to explode. "Not under my roof, by God!"

Running a suggestive finger around her neckline, she feigned a pout. "But how can a proven sinner like me resist him, when he's pretty enough to tempt even these saintly ladies?"

Mamie spluttered indignantly. "Why, we never—that's the most preposterous, offensive thing I ever heard!"

"But, Mamie, you're quite right!" Beth Ann was serious and guileless as a wide-eyed kitten. "I had considered keeping Zach here as my very own fancy man, but he's kind of skinny, and as it turns out, I can't abide a man with freckles on his ... well, with freckles."

Her brazen confession evoked another round of horrified gasps. Wolf roared in angry mortification. "Beth Ann!"

She shrugged. "I'm not the only one who appreciates the way a man fills out his trousers, but I *am* the only female here honest enough to admit it."

"You uncivilized strumpet!" Mamie shouted, outraged. "How dare you compare yourself to us!"

"Mrs. Cunningham, ma'am," Zach began, only to be drowned out as Miss Kellogg added her two cents worth to Mamie's tirade.

"No God-fearing Christian should be forced to endure this hussy's scandalous conduct for even a moment!" The schoolteacher plucked the now empty glass from Zach's surprised grasp and positioned herself protectively at his side like a knight facing down a fire-breathing dragon. "We must remove the reverend from this unholy house this instant!"

In the folds of her skirts, Beth Ann's fists clenched, and her eyes narrowed in pure loathing. Interfering, self-righteous, meddling biddies! Preening and cooing over the preacher while they tried and convicted her without so much as a hearing! And as for Kitty—well, that hurt so much, she couldn't even think about it right then. She was caught in a red haze of rage, and nothing mattered but thwarting these interfering sows any way she could.

"By all means, take the preacher!" Beth Ann urged. "He's more trouble than a calf with the slobbers anyway."

"Indeed we will!"

Against the white pillows, Zach's flushed face took on an expression of mild alarm. "Ma'am, that won't be necessary—"

Beth Ann inspected her nails, her tone indifferent. "Just don't blame me if he dies on you."

As if released from a spell, Kitty spoke. "Dies! Oh, no!"

"Doc said it might kill him to move him too soon, didn't he, Paw?" Yawning her unconcern, Beth Ann stretched luxuriously, letting the movement accentuate the voluptuous lift of her bosom. "And that was before the preacher got a fever, too. See how flushed he is?"

Miss Kellogg was startled by this news; her pinched mouth shrank another two sizes. "Ah, perhaps we shouldn't act in haste."

"No, no! He's a nuisance to wait on," Beth Ann said. "Just make sure when you carry him out that he doesn't bleed all over my clean floors."

"Oh, my!" Kitty pressed a plump white hand against her rosebud mouth in dismay.

"Ladies, please." Zach's deep voice sounded like a frog's croak. A frog in dire extremity, at that.

Miss Kellogg caught his hand and patted it reassuringly. "We know how distressing a man of your sensibilities must find your present situation, sir. But now . . . well, we must consider the reverend's health above all, mustn't we, Mamie?"

Mrs. Cunningham gnawed her lip in frustration.

"It's unclear which course would be most advisable."

"Look, I'll just get Buck to hitch up the wagon, shall I?" Beth Ann offered brightly. "Why, ten to one, my little sweetheart here won't lose enough blood to kill him before you get him back to Destiny. Leastwise, he can have a proper burial in town."

"Ohh," Kitty moaned, chewing her thumbnail. "We can't do this, Mamie! What if—"

"Hush up!" Mrs. Cunningham ordered. "What's right is right, no matter what the cost, so—"

"Ma'am!" Grimacing in pain at the force of his own shout, Zach reclaimed his hand from Miss Kellogg's possession. "I'm right grateful for your concern, but I can't go."

With a furtive glance at Beth Ann, Miss Kellogg bent closer to whisper. "The impropriety . . . Reverend, you don't understand."

Although his voice now sounded as weak as watered milk, his determination was readily apparent in the firmness of his chin. "The Lord brought me down this trail for a reason. He went among the Philistines and tax collectors to preach repentance to sinners. Can I do less? Should I not serve as the instrument of redemption for the one in this house who needs it most?"

He looked pointedly across the room at Beth Ann, who cringed in angry humiliation.

"Of course," Mamie Cunningham said, awestruck by the revelation. "A mission. A holy crusade."

"You do understand." Zach slumped back against the pillow, exhausted. "Bless you, ma'am. Bless you all."

"We daren't interfere with the Lord's work, then." Mrs. Cunningham transferred her gimlet gaze to Beth Ann. "The reverend stays. For the time being. And God speed his holy work!"

Dismayed, Beth Ann realized what her temper had done to her. Instead of getting rid of the preacher, her little show for the ladies had convinced the turquoise-eyed devil that he had been sent to Traveler's Rest specifically to rescue her from eternal damnation! Good Lord, he might even prolong his visit indefinitely to pursue that aspiration! Down deep, a secret part of her was terrified by the prospect of continued contact with Zach Temple's not inconsiderable physical attraction. Choking on her chagrin, her fury directed not only at the trio by the bedside but at her own foolish behavior, Beth Ann pushed away from the door with a glare that could blister paint.

"You're addled if you think I'll listen to anything that braying jackass has to say!"

"Woman, keep a civil tongue in your head!" Wolf shouted. "These good women know what's best."

"Like hell! They're drooling all over the preacher because not a one of them has ever had a real man in her bed!" Ignoring a chorus of indignant cries, Beth Ann raked the group with a scornful glare, then pointed contemptuously at Zach. "Well, I guarantee this mealymouthed milksop has nothing to fear from me—because I have!"

With that final sally, she stormed out. Crossing the yard toward the lower paddock, she was too angry even to acknowledge Mr. Pritchard's farewell call as he and his passengers loaded up to leave. Muttering fervent curses and kicking the dusty soil into little puffs, she let herself through the gap in the rustic stick fence and gave a low whistle. A sorrel mare swollen with imminent delivery trotted out of the herd.

"N-Nellie." The word came out almost a sob.

Suddenly it was all too much. Holding on to the mare's mane, Beth Ann laid her cheek against the horse's neck and let the tears fall in a salty torrent of frustration, rage, hurt, and despair. Nellie stood patiently under the onslaught, giving what comfort she could as her mistress soaked her hide and clung to her neck as if her life depended on it.

When the moment of weakness had passed, Beth Ann raised her head again, clucking softly and praising the tolerant animal. Nellie never condemned her. Nellie's love was always unconditional. What would it be like to have that kind of love from another human being? Beth Ann couldn't begin to imagine it. As long as she could remember, the place where love should have been in her heart was as empty as the desert stretching out between Traveler's Rest and the distant mountains. For a time Tom Chapman had pretended to fill it, and that had been a lie.

Beth Ann worked her fingers through the knots and snarls in Nellie's ivory-colored mane. She wasn't sure now if she had been in love with Tom or merely in love with the idea of love and desperate to escape the drudgery and sterility of life with no affection. Her hands moved over Nellie's protruding abdomen.

Soon.

Soon she'd have the means to leave it all behind, and this time she wouldn't depend on anyone but herself. With the stake from the foal's sale, she could find a new life. She could go to California and find a job at one of those fancy city hotels, someplace with a real chef who could teach her all about haute cuisine and European cookery that she'd only read about in her cookbooks. She would never again be forced to endure the slurs and condemnation of all around her. What a blessed relief that would be!

In the meantime, she'd get by somehow, just as she always had. And she wouldn't put up with a preacher set on "redeeming" her, either! Beth Ann's sultry mouth firmed with determination.

So the Reverend Temple thought he'd been called to reform Destiny's fallen woman, did he? He'd soon find out differently. Her temper had gotten the best of her today, but she knew of a few things that might change his mind about hanging around. She smiled and rubbed Nellie's velvety muzzle playfully, her optimism returning.

Yes, sir, by the time she'd finished with Reverend Zach Temple, he'd be more than willing to leave Traveler's Rest for greener pastures. No, he'd be *begging* to go. And that thought made Beth Ann laugh out loud.

It wasn't the round of mustard plasters or the blistered skin they left behind that tipped Zach off.

It wasn't even having his bedroom fumigated with a noxious bitterweed smoke to clear out the fleas she was certain had invaded the premises, or going buck naked for a day and a night while his clothes were treated with lye soap and boiling water so that they came back in virtual shreds. He didn't even wise up when Beth Ann insisted he take a "healing potation" that tasted like cow dung and hot chili peppers. She stood over him while his eyes ran and his gullet blazed until he'd downed the whole blamed thing!

No, it was three days after the visit of the ladies' delegation, when he woke up to the realization that he was slowly being starved to death, that Zach knew Miss Beth Ann Linder was capable of holding a grudge.

He'd had to do some quick thinking to prevent those busybodies from carting him off to Destiny, but who'd have guessed Beth Ann would be so sensitive? Jeez, you'd think he'd tried to baptize her in her shimmy or something. He had no intentions of following through with any plans to "redeem" her anyway. Far from it. In fact, there were times when he caught a hint of her rosy fragrance or noticed the feminine lift and sway of her full breasts that he was sure it might be a hell of a lot more fun to experiment with a short fall from grace.

In the meantime, she was making him pay. Maybe a convalescent diet of weak teas and baby pabulum had been a wise choice the first day or two, but those pots of sage tea she'd poured down him had done the trick on his fever, and ever since it had broken, he'd been ravenous. He was treading a fine line, it was true. Although he felt better and stronger by the day, he couldn't afford to mend too quickly or Wolf Linder might question why he didn't hurry on to his mythical assignment in Tucson. But if he pretended to be any weaker than he was, he'd continue to get nothing but boiled rice and potato water!

As Zach gingerly tugged his shirt on over his sore shoulder, his belly grumbled with hunger. The sun was a glowing orange ball on the western horizon, and all evening the smells of frying meat and baking bread wafting up from the kitchen had tormented him. He was damned if he was going to wait around to see what invalid's portions appeared on tonight's supper tray. No, he reckoned he was due to make a public appearance, and the first thing he was going to do was march himself into the kitchen and demand nourishment!

Zach buttoned up the shirt and ran fingers

through his curly hair. With a grimace at the armoire's mirror, he headed out the door. At least he wasn't limping any longer, and the bruises on his cheek had almost disappeared. Except for the sling holding his left arm, he was just about back to normal.

It was definitely time to open up a conversation with Wolf Linder about the dangers of worldly wealth, and how a gold mine was a millstone that could drag a God-fearing man straight to hell. What was that about the rich man passing through the needle's gate? Or was that the camel's eye? Damn, he'd have to look that up. No matter. Maybe the old coot could be persuaded to tithe.

Zach followed his nose across the ramada and down the outside stairs to the basement-level kitchen. He found Beth Ann stirring a caldron on top of the black cast-iron stove beside the massive fireplace. Neat as ever, she wore a modest calico dress topped by a crisp bib apron. Her cheeks were flushed a becoming pink from the stove's warmth, and damp ringlets that had slipped from her thick braid curled beguilingly about her temples.

She hummed a tune under her breath, moving about her well-ordered domain with easy familiarity while a very short, extremely round Indian squaw in a voluminous sack dress swept the spotless floor. A collection of well-thumbed cookbooks sat in a place of pride on a wooden shelf above a locked spice cabinet. Dipping the wooden spoon, Beth Ann stirred the delicious-smelling concoction she was brewing, then reached into the crockery saltbox and carefully adjusted the seasoning.

Zach leaned against the door opening in the three-foot-thick adobe wall and sniffed appreciatively. "Mind if I have a bit of whatever that is?"

Beth Ann jumped and nearly dropped her spoon. "Dang it, preacher! Didn't that bullet in your shoulder teach you anything about sneaking up on folks?"

The corner of his mouth lifted briefly. "Hunger has driven me from my sickbed."

She had the grace to look shamefaced for an instant, then she tilted her chin and met his gaze with a challenging look. "Then you're in luck, for I've just prepared a very special dish just for you."

Zach didn't like the sound of that. What was she planning for him now? Turnip broth and oatmeal gruel? He gave her a dark look. "Miss Linder, I'm exceedingly weary of soup. In fact, I'd sure like to grease my chin with a two-pound steak."

"Oh, it's not soup," she assured him. Digging into the pot, she lifted a meaty joint dripping with succulent gravy. "A very nourishing ragout especially to aid in blood replacement and tissue growth. Quite tasty, too, I might add."

Zach's mouth watered. Pulling a chair up to the plain board table, he said, "Miss Linder, as long as it doesn't slither, I'll eat anything."

Her lips twitched, and her gray eyes gleamed as she laid out a crisp cotton square, eating utensils, then a substantial plate of the stew. Zach barely had the presence of mind to bend his head for a quick, if calculated, blessing before he picked up his fork and dug in.

It was sheer heaven, and he ate with a concentration that was a compliment to the cook. Beth Ann poured him a glass of milk and brought slices of sourdough bread, and a canning jar of "lick," the syrup that was the cowboy's favorite. Within minutes, she had to dish him up a second helping.

"Delicious, Miss Linder," he said around a

mouthful. "Quite an unusual flavor, too. What did you call it again?"

"Ah—ragout."

The squaw looked at Zach, her black eyes sparkling, and said something in her own language. Beth Ann answered in the same tongue, and the woman giggled, then scurried out the door.

"What's the matter with her?" Zach asked, sopping gravy with the last crust of bread.

"Ama is ... er, bashful around strangers, but she's good help in the kitchen." She busied herself washing a few dishes in the big speckled tin pan of soapy water, slanting him quick, furtive looks from beneath her sooty lashes. "I enjoy using native herbs to season my dishes. Sometimes Ama brings me special ... ingredients from the Pima village."

Finished, Zach pushed his chair back and patted his flat stomach, beaming with well-being. "That was wonderful. Thank you, Miss Linder."

"No need, Reverend." She came to the table and began to gather up his dishes, but she didn't meet his eyes, and her voice seemed rather smug. "Paw and I guarantee good service—of one kind or another."

Zach felt so much revived, he hated to return to that prison of a sickroom. "Is your father about? I've got some things I want to discuss with him."

"He's got guests, but since he prefers preachers over almost anything except maybe a sack of gold dust, I suspect he'd be delighted." Her mouth twisted suddenly, her expression turning as sour as clabber. "No doubt you two stinking polecats'll whoop it up together planning my 'redemption.' "

"Beth Ann." Zach caught her wrist, and she froze with her hands full of dirty dishes, her silver eyes wide and wary. His thumb traced circles across the delicate tendons on the inside of her wrist where the pulse jumped erratically. "The first thing we need to work on is that sharp tongue. Folks wouldn't take so much offense if you weren't so prickly all the time."

"Much you know about human nature, preacher," she scoffed, her lip curling in derision. "The folks around here have already made up their minds about me. If I were sweet as a honeycomb, it wouldn't make a bit of difference. So keep your fool advice to yourself!"

She wrenched her arm free and dumped the dishes into the tin pan with a bad-tempered crash.

"Doesn't take much to get your dander up, does it? All thorns and barbs like a cactus," Zach mused. He rose and stood beside her, watching her swish suds over the plates. "Works like a charm so no one can see how soft and scared you really are inside."

Beth Ann ruffled up like a sage hen in a rainstorm. "You must be studying to be a half-wit, preacher. I never heard anything so idiotic in all my life."

Zach knew when he'd touched a nerve. "You wish I'd go straight to perdition, don't you?"

"Yes!"

"So you could forget you put this hole in me."

Her cheeks blazed. "It was an accident. I apologized."

"So there's no reason to think you'd do anything . . . uncivilized to encourage me to think twice about convalescing at Traveler's Rest?"

"It's only Christian to hope you recover as quickly as possible, of course," she said in a stiff voice.

He nodded sagely. "I see. And mustard plasters

and hot-as-blazes potations are just part of your tender loving care?"

"Of—of course."

Zach nudged her chin up with his forefinger so he could look into her stormy eyes. "I just want you to know that I'm on to your little schemes, honey."

"Schemes?" Her expression was both alarmed and guilty, and her breathing accelerated revealingly.

"Trying to make me so miserable that I'll leave isn't going to work."

For an instant she looked as though she might blurt something out, but then reconsidered. Then, damned if she didn't look him straight in the eye and deny everything!

"I don't know what you mean."

"I mean it's time you got over this resentment you have against clergymen—me, especially— because I'm not going anywhere until I'm good and ready."

Beth Ann slapped his fingers away. "I might have known! You're just another freeloading preacher. But don't think you're going to loaf around here eating up all my vittles indefinitely!"

"I wouldn't make threats, Beth Ann," he taunted softly. "The Lord doesn't take something like that lightly—and neither do I."

"I'll worry about the Almighty by myself, thank you, but *you* don't frighten me!"

"Oh, no?" Smiling slowly, he leaned so close, their noses nearly bumped. "Then what exactly is it I do to you?"

Her eyes were as wide and startled as a fawn's, her breathing suddenly erratic. "Nothing," she managed, then, with more spirit, "except make me spitting mad!"

"There's something very intriguing under all that anger, honey." Zach's voice was a husky purr, a predator toying with small prey. "Something that makes your heart pound and your belly melt, something that makes us both wonder what it'd feel like if I touched you again."

Hot color flooded her cheeks, and her peachy lips parted in surprise and confusion and just enough guilt to make Zach's loins tighten in anticipation. No, she hadn't forgotten about that earlier dreamlike encounter any more than Zach had, lying there in that lonely sickbed these past days with only his fantasies for company. He groaned inwardly at the unconsciously provocative invitation of her lush mouth, damning the self-imposed restraints of his masquerade. If he could just have one taste . . .

From abovestairs came a bellowed demand for pie and coffee.

Beth Ann jumped, skittish as a jackrabbit rescued from a snake's hypnotic stare. With a fulminating glance at Zach, she scurried off to load a tray.

"I'm coming, Paw," she yelled up the stairwell. Then in a savage undertone to Zach, "You keep away from me!"

He watched her slicing pie with vicious stabs of the knife and took a cautious step back. When he could finally draw a steady breath again, it occurred to him that he'd just made a lucky escape from an impulse that could have landed him in serious trouble. Damn, but this woman intrigued him, pricking his curiosity with her blunt ways and feisty demeanor. Everything about her enticed him to probe deeper, to explore the softness he sensed beneath that starchy exterior, and to damn the consequences.

But he knew better than that. You never felt sorry for your mark. If you allowed yourself to feel the least bit sympathetic, you were likely to come out empty-handed in the end. He'd do well to remember that. So he'd best forget about any diversion Miss Beth Ann Linder presented and concentrate on her father, starting now.

"Put a cup for me on that tray and I'll help you carry things upstairs," he offered.

"I don't want your help!"

"You know," he said thoughtfully, "you put me in mind of old Nathaniel facing down that sore-pawed lion in his den."

She frowned, puzzled and faintly scornful. "That was Daniel."

Oops! Zach winced, and renewed his vow to study up on the Good Book before he peppered his speech with any more biblical references. The last thing he needed was this sharp-eyed gal discovering he didn't know Leviticus from liver spots!

"Of course. Isn't that what I said?" he replied, covering the slip with an easy smile. Picking up a set of forks, he went to wait at the bottom step. "At any rate, you've got my help, so make the best of it."

Her pretty lips clamped in a tight, forbidding line that would have made a lesser man quiver in his boots. "Oh, hell's bells! Suit yourself!"

In a manner that won Zach's admiration for her agility and her temper, she picked up the tray and flounced up the narrow stairs to the front parlor. Heavy wooden chairs and benches and a couple of brass spittoons made up the sparse furnishings, and the adobe walls were bare, but someone— Beth Ann, Zach expected—had set out pungent sprigs of early-blooming lavender heart's delight and white angel's-trumpets in fat earthenware jars, and starched gingham curtains decorated the deep window enclosures.

"Reverend Temple, good to see you up," Wolf boomed at their appearance. "Come in and meet some folks!"

Zach sat down in a comfortable armchair whose wooden bottom was slick from years of fanny-polishing. As Beth Ann served everyone coffee and pie, Wolf introduced him to Robert Barlings, the owner of the Destiny Savings Bank, and his grown son, Bobby. Zach chewed a mouthful of apples and took stock.

Robert Barlings looked the typical banker with his thinning, gray-streaked brown hair and tiny wire-rimmed reading glasses perched on his knobby nose. He was in his late fifties, and a pronounced paunch rounded out the burgundy brocade waistcoat he wore with his good wool suit. Prosperous and genial, he made easy conversation about the unusually mild weather and complimented Beth Ann's pie.

Bobby, on the other hand, took some figuring out. A slight, pleasant-looking young man in his early twenties, he was dressed in a starched chambray shirt, pressed trousers, and striped suspenders. His light brown hair was parted in the middle and combed to each side, but a wayward lock stood straight up from the cowlick on his crown. He sat awkwardly on a deacon's bench, his ankles rolled in, trying to juggle his plate and cup, looking baffled and uncomfortable until Beth Ann took pity on him and placed his cup beside him on the bench.

That's when Zach realized Bobby Barlings wasn't quite "right." His hazel eyes were vacant except when he stared adoringly at Beth Ann, and everything about him—actions, mannerisms, even the way he talked—seemed more like a small child than a full-grown man.

"It's heartening to see you on your feet so soon after your ... er, accident," the elder Barlings said to Zach.

"Miss Linder sees tenderly to my care in a most compassionate and Christian manner," Zach responded, hiding a smile when he saw Beth Ann's spine go rigid.

But Zach had no intention of revealing her campaign of subtle tortures to her father or anyone else. No, it would be a pleasure to pay her back by keeping her in suspense. And having something to hold over her head might prove useful down the line.

"I'm always glad to see a young man like you answering the Lord's call," Mr. Barlings said. "Where did you attend seminary, Reverend?"

Zach gulped. "Ah-Calliope College of Heavenly Light back in Texas."

The elder Barlings frowned, perplexed. "Can't say that I ever heard of it."

"Oh, it's a very popular training institute," Zach assured him solemnly. *For a brothel.* Indeed, the "instructors" upstairs at the Heavenly Light had given Zach quite an education! "It's esteemed by all its graduates."

"You studied the usual, I assume? Bible history, theology, divine literature ... ?"

"Certainly. Why, I can recite 'begats' with the best of them," Zach fibbed, hoping lightning wouldn't strike him dead where he sat. "Oh, yes, indeed, I know 'em all like the back of my hand. Nebuchadnezzar and Habakkuk, philodendron and ... and Tippecanoe and Tyler, too!"

Mr. Barlings's brow pleated in puzzlement, then

he suddenly laughed out loud and slapped his
knee. "Sir, you are a wit! Tippecanoe ... My, my,
quite humorous, indeed!"

Zach gave himself a mental kick in the seat for
making such a blunder. Feeling a mite too cocky
for his own good, he'd almost put his own tail in
the proverbial crack that time! He gave Mr.
Barlings a weak grin. "Well, they say laughter is
the best medicine, sir."

"Then your recovery is certainly assured."

"You can tell that to Mamie Cunningham the
next time you see her in town, Robert," Wolf said,
stretching out his peg leg. "She was good enough
to concern herself with the reverend's recuperation."

"Be glad to." Still chuckling, Barlings blotted his
lips delicately with his napkin, then reached into
his vest pocket and pulled out a leather cigar case.
He caught Beth Ann's eye. "Do you mind if I
smoke, Miss Linder?"

Busy with the coffee things, Beth Ann shook her
head. "Of course not, sir."

"Gentlemen?" Barlings offered the case around.
"Straight from Havana, hand-rolled especially to
my specifications."

Both Zach and Wolf declined. With a disapproving scowl, Wolf watched his friend take a cigar
from the case, remove the gilded paper band with
its distinctive eagle logo, bite the end off, and light
it. Barlings puffed heartily and gave a sigh of pure
pleasure.

"How you can pollute your lungs with that stogie
is beyond me, Robert," Wolf grumbled. "Now, a
good chaw is one thing, but this stinking—"

Surrounded by a cloud of aromatic blue smoke,
Barlings sat back and admired the glowing tip.
"Allow me to enjoy my only vice without having

to listen to another of your lectures, Wolf. At my age, there aren't so many pleasures left."

Wolf squirmed for a more comfortable position. "Well, at least you don't have a woman like Mamie Cunningham after you about it all the time." Wolf leaned toward Zach in a conspiratorial manner. "Mamie's a fine churchgoing lady, but when she's got a bee in her bonnet, she can sure make the menfolk jump. Especially her husband, Ike. He's so henpecked, he's sprouting tail feathers. What excuse did he give for not coming with you tonight, Robert?"

"Something about a quiltin' bee or some such nonsense."

Wolf snorted. "Bet Mamie's got him washing the dishes."

"They're having chocolate cake," Bobby said brightly.

"How's that, son?" Robert asked with an indulgent smile.

"Mrs. Hollis next door. She made a cake to take to the party. She let me lick the bowl." Bobby glanced down at the half-eaten piece of pie on his saucer, then back to Beth Ann with a worried look. "But I like your pie better, Miss Beth Ann."

"That's nice. Thank you, Bobby." She held the empty tray against her chest and backed toward the door. Bobby blushed furiously and scuffed his foot.

"Won't you visit with us awhile, Miss Linder?" Robert asked politely. "We bachelors don't get to enjoy feminine company very often. Scoot over, Bobby, and let her sit next to you."

The young man moved over on the bench, red-faced but as eager as a puppy for attention. Beth Ann glanced at her father, who nodded sharply. With some reluctance, she seated herself beside

Bobby while Robert smiled benignly at the pair. Zach blinked, wondering whether to believe what his instincts suspected. Did Barlings have aspirations in Beth Ann's direction for his imbecilic son? The idea made Zach's gut ache.

"Well, mayor or not," Wolf began again in a voice laden with disgust, "Ike wouldn't have been much help anyway. He ain't got a lick of experience when it comes to mining claims and such."

Zach's ears perked up. "I hear the country around here's fairly rich in precious ores."

"For the lucky few, Reverend Temple," Robert Barlings said. "But if Destiny is to grow and prosper as we all desire, then the town has to offer incentives to potential investors and settlers alike, and that means law enforcement, a proper assayer's office—not just the little laboratory setup I keep in my vault—and a railroad spur. The list is almost endless."

"That's a businessman for you!" Wolf grumped, shaking his head. "Nary a word about the thrill of finding color for the first time."

"I gather you've had your share of that kind of excitement, Mr. Linder," Zach remarked helpfully.

"Yes, sir, you can say I'm a self-made man."

"That relieves the Almighty of a heavy responsibility," Zach muttered into his coffee cup.

"Pardon?"

"I said the Almighty has blessed you with a full life."

"You could say that again and it wouldn't be a lie." Wolf reared back in his chair. "I recollect the time in the Superstitions I ran into that Mexican vaquero . . ."

Zach listened to Wolf's tales, asking skillful questions to keep the reminiscences flowing. You never could tell what information might come in useful at a later date. Although Wolf wasn't forth-coming about exact details—like the location of his own mines—Zach still got a sense of what the man had been capable of accomplishing in his prime, and learned that Wolf Linder not only had "diggings" but that he was champing at the bit to try his hand at them again.

At the same time, Zach was conscious that Beth Ann sat beside Bobby Barlings, trapped into a one-sided conversation as the young man breathlessly shared all he knew about the quilting party. How "everybody" was going, and the food the neighbor lady had prepared, and the patterns of the quilt tops the ladies would stitch together, Wedding Ring and Log Cabin and Lone Star.

Her hands were folded demurely in her lap, but with a talent for observation cultivated over his motley career, Zach couldn't miss her knuckles, which grew whiter by the minute, nor her expression, which grew more and more wistful. In that unguarded moment, her silver eyes were crystalline with naked yearning—over a goddamned *quilting* party, Zach thought in amazement. When her lower lip suddenly quivered, Zach felt as though he'd been punched in the gut.

With Wolf's voice droning in his ears, Zach really thought about what being ostracized by the entire town was like for Beth Ann Linder. No girlfriends to gossip with. No beaux to come calling of an evening. No friendly faces to pass the time of day with when she went to town—hell, she probably *never* went to town, if the treatment she'd received at the hands of the ladies' delegation was any indication! She was trapped out here at Traveler's Rest with no one but her ornery paw and a few stage passengers for company. For all her bristly ways, the poor girl was pure-down, soul-deep lonely.

Way down in a place that he didn't look at too often, Zach knew how that felt.

On impulse, he clutched his shoulder and groaned. It brought Wolf's storytelling to a screeching halt.

"Reverend? You all right?" he demanded.

Zach put on a martyred expression. "Just a twinge. Nothing to—" He broke off with another groan of feigned agony.

Robert Barlings looked at him with alarm in his flat brown eyes. "How bad is it? Should we send for Doc Sayers?"

"No, no." Zach shook his head and levered himself to his feet with a show of difficulty. "I've overdone it a bit, that's all. I'm sure a round of evening prayers and meditations will facilitate some relief. Perhaps if Miss Linder could help me back to my room . . . ?"

"You heard him, girl!" Wolf barked.

"Yes, Paw." Beth Ann rose, her eyes shuttered and suspicious.

Leaning heavily on her arm, Zach bid the others a pained good night, and together they hobbled from the room.

Darkness had fallen when they reached the veranda leading to Zach's room, and the sweetness of night-blooming cactus mingled with the river's moist scents. Insects chirruped, and from a distance a small animal's shrill scream was abruptly cut off by a predator.

"You sure took a sudden turn in there." Beth Ann's skeptical tone said more than her words.

"I'd had enough, and you looked like you needed rescuing." Grinning, Zach reluctantly released her arm. "Just think. If your little persuasions had worked on me, you'd still be sitting there with poor old Bobby babbling in your ear. Good thing I stuck around, huh?"

"I did not need *rescuing*," she stated in a frigid tone. "Bobby doesn't bother me."

"Well, his father's plans for you should."

"I'm sure I don't know what you mean."

Zach raised an eyebrow. "I hadn't taken you for a fool, Miss Linder. Has Bobby always been like that?"

She shook her head. "Oh, no. When we were in school, he was normal as anyone, until the big black stallion his father bought him kicked him in the head. They didn't think Bobby would live for a while, and when he finally woke up—well, you see how he is. Mr. Barlings is a widower, and Bobby is his only child. It just about killed Mr. Barlings when it happened."

Zach paused outside his room. "And the old man still hasn't learned his lesson. What Bobby wants, Bobby gets. And unless I miss my guess, Barlings has got his sights set on you."

She scowled. "That's ridiculous. Bobby's sweet and harmless."

"Don't be naive, honey." Laughing softly, Zach tugged her braid. "He may be a child intellectually, but he's got a man's body with a man's needs. Barlings is looking for a wife and caretaker for that son of his, and if you're not careful, you could be it."

"You have a talent for being truly offensive, Reverend!"

A frown puckered Zach's brow. "Maybe I'm not getting the full picture here. Maybe you want Bobby to court you?"

"Why should I?"

"Because his daddy's rich. And because Bobby

Barlings is about the only man in Destiny who'd marry another man's leavings."

Her slap caught Zach across his still sore temple and made his ears ring. With a growl, he grabbed her by the wrists before she could strike him again. "What the devil!"

"You're just like all the rest!" she hissed, her eyes like silver blades. "I wouldn't—I'm not—aghh!"

Inarticulate with rage, she bit his hand. With a yelp, he released her.

"Jesus! Are you crazy?"

"Yes! Moonstruck. Loco!" She glared at him, wild-eyed with rage. "I'll put a Pima hex on you! The coyotes will tear out your belly and carry you off to the underworld. You'd better stay away from me, if you know what's good for you! I'm warning you!"

He laughed at her. "I think I'm man enough to handle anything you can dish out, darlin'."

"Is that so?" She was goaded past caution; her vengeful laughter trilled to the stars, an eerie keening that raised the hairs on the back of Zach's neck. "We'll see."

Turning, she strode down the veranda and skipped down the broad wooden front steps. "Well, come on, Reverend! Or aren't you *man* enough?"

Baffled, Zach frowned, then followed her into the darkness. What was the hellion up to now? He caught up with her just as she reached the back corner of the barn and paused to light a lantern.

"Are you cockeyed?" he demanded irritably. "If you want party games, I think spin the bottle—" He broke off as she raised the lantern high. "Holy hell! What's *that*?"

Propped against the rear wall of the barn, a

scaly, ghoulish carcass was strung on a wooden skinning frame. The monstrosity was mostly the skin of whatever it had been, but it still had teeth and claws and scales.

"A little going-away gift from Ama and me." Triumph and malice tinged her voice.

"I told you, I'm not going anywhere," he said, frowning. "But what *is* it?"

"Chuckwalla. Tans out real nice. Makes good belts, hatbands, boots—and ragouts."

Zach gulped. "You mean ... I ate ... *that?*"

"Two helpings." Beth Ann tossed her head and taunted him. "What's the matter, preacher? You liked the taste of lizard well enough before."

Zach's stomach lurched. "You little ..."

"You're as green as that poor little chuckwalla's belly, preacher! And after all those sweet compliments about my cooking! I went to such special trouble to lace my ragout with snake eggs and toad livers, too!"

Zach stared incredulously. "You viper! You've poisoned me!"

She broke out laughing. "You aren't going to lose your dinner, are you, Zach? God, that's something a *real man* would never do!"

"No, I—" Zach's belly heaved again, and suddenly he wasn't so sure. Sweat broke out on his forehead. "I ought to wring your damn neck ..."

She backed away from him, her laughter still taunting. "I'm 'dishing' it out, preacher! So you'd better run, and fast, because I promise you, *that's only the beginning!*"

With a flip of her skirts, she turned and headed for the house.

"Wait a damn minute, you harpy!" He jumped after her and caught her elbow, demanding roughly, "Just tell me the truth—is it going to make me sick or not?"

"Why don't you stick your finger down your throat and find out?" she returned sweetly. Thrusting the lantern at him, this time she made good her escape.

Cussing a blue streak under his breath, Zach juggled the hot lantern back onto its hook, then kicked a dirt clod into smithereens.

Bitch! And to think that for a moment he'd even been feeling sorry for that little viper! Well, to hell with her! She wasn't his problem, and he'd be damned if he'd let that crazy woman drive him away from a chance at a real gold mine! The sly little cat deserved to be taught a lesson she wouldn't soon forget, and—hell, yes!—Zach Madison was man enough to do it!

A wave of queasiness reminded him that he had a more immediate problem. His mood murderous, he knew there was only one safe course of action. Grimly he stalked toward the bushes to follow Beth Ann's advice.

Chapter 4

She didn't trust him as far as she could pitch a stagecoach.

"Don't go to any trouble, Miss Linder," the preacher said, so bland that Beth Ann's spine tingled with apprehension. "I'll just have whatever your paw is having."

It was beyond anything! She thought for sure Zach would clear out after a night sweating out a dose of chuckwalla. Now here he sat at her breakfast table in his rather threadbare shirt and worn trousers with a "butter wouldn't melt in his mouth" look on his handsome face, shoveling in steak and eggs with complete aplomb and with apparently no intention of tattling on her to Paw.

Somehow Beth Ann couldn't believe even a preacher could turn the other cheek so blithely, and as she began to clear the table, she knew how that French queen had felt waiting for the guillotine's blade to fall.

"Glad to see you up and chipper this morning, Reverend." Wolf used a biscuit to swab the last speck of yellow yolk from his blue speckleware plate, then stuffed the wad into his mouth, scattering crumbs like snowflakes over his bushy beard and the string tie dangling down the front of his chambray shirt.

"A man would be ungrateful indeed if he did not flourish under all the tender and generous care

87

you and your daughter provide, sir," Zach replied smoothly.

Stacking dishes, Beth Ann gave a delicate, disdainful snort. "I should say so. You ate enough for three cowhands. Hope you stopped to bless it first."

"I'd have been afraid not to," Zach remarked obliquely, but Beth Ann took his meaning quite clearly and her cheeks flamed. Breakfast had been fried beefsteaks, not rattlesnake, for God's sake!

Zach took a sip from his coffee mug, his sandy lashes veiling his satisfied expression. "I know I shall miss Traveler's Rest when I leave."

Beth Ann's spirits perked up. So her attempts at coercion were working after all!

"Now, Reverend Temple," Wolf rumbled, "it's much too early to talk about that."

"Paw, the reverend has been delayed long enough," Beth Ann interjected hastily. "I'm sure he has pressing business in Tucson."

She wiped her damp palms on her apron and tried to ignore the stickiness that made her starched shirtwaist cling under her armpits. She was glad that she'd pinned her hair up in a topknot since the day's warmth was already penetrating the thick adobe walls.

"When I require your opinion, girl, I'll ask for it," Wolf snapped. "You chafe for the preacher's departure because his presence here is a brand that burns your sinner's hide."

Zach clucked in mild reproof. "I understand a parent's role can be trying, Mr. Linder, but remember, 'a soft word turneth away wrath.' "

"Hmmph," Wolf snorted. " 'Spare the rod, spoil the child,' I always say, and this hellion would try the patience of a saint."

Zach shook his head, all charity and forgiveness.

"Despite the unfortunate circumstances of our meeting, I've found your daughter sweet-tempered, hardworking, and contrite. One has only to look around to see the care she takes of you, sir, and the woman's touches that make this house a home as well as a successful station house."

Thunderstruck at this rather fanciful and unexpected championship, Beth Ann was too astounded to protest when Zach took her hand and squeezed it warmly.

Scowling, Wolf combed the crumbs from his beard with his sausagelike fingers and gave a grudging nod. "I'll admit this place wasn't much when we first came, but I never took to all them female notions of curtains and furbelows. Heathenish fripperies, and expensive for a poor miner, too."

"The improvements paid for themselves, Paw!" Beth Ann protested. She was uncomfortably aware of the warmth and texture of Zach's skin against her own, and the way his thumb on her knuckles made her shivery all the way to her earlobes. Ignoring his slight smile, she wiggled free, still making heated objections to her father's statement.

"I never asked for one cent of your prospecting profits after we got on our feet. I had to save up two years to buy my stove as it was. And as many times as you disappeared into the mountains and came home happy as a flea in a doghouse, you could have spared your own flesh and blood a couple of ounces of gold dust."

Wolf's eyes narrowed dangerously. "It ain't none of your never mind what I found, girl. That's betwixt me and the Lord."

Beth Ann looked disgusted. "If He's as stingy as

you, the pearly gates are made out of old corncobs and pine burrs."

"Frugality is a virtue." Zach folded his hands in pious contemplation and gazed at Wolf over the peak of his fingertips. "As long as the Lord receives His portion."

"I never short the Almighty," Wolf said stiffly.

"Then you'll be rewarded, brother," Zach replied. "Yea, 'the Lord loveth a cheerful giver.' Would that I could find someone as generous to aid in my mission among the godless cowpokes who spend their hard-earned cash drinking and fornicating in those hellholes on Congress Street. Every varmint who's been run out of California or passes through the Yuma Territorial Prison settles in Tucson. If ever there was a place in need of salvation, that's one of the worst."

Wolf scratched his chin. "A minister could find his vocation right here in Destiny. We need a pastor, you know."

Alarm raced down Beth Ann's spine. Reverend Temple a permanent fixture? Not if she could help it!

"No doubt the reverend would be bored with this town's little sins." Beth Ann tilted her chin belligerently. "He's after bigger fish. I'm the only one remotely interesting, and since you've already made my life a purgatory, Paw, there's no sense in a preacher wasting his time around here."

"Don't sass me, girl!" Wolf's jaw snapped shut in annoyance, and he looked to Zach in appeal. "Tell me what I'm going to do with her!"

"She's just spirited, Mr. Linder, like a high-strung filly." Zach's turquoise eyes glittered with challenge. "All she needs is a strong hand. With proper instruction, I'd say there was real hope for her."

Beth Ann spluttered and choked on pure gall. First false praise from the preacher, now unwanted advice! Well, if he intended to teach her humility by heaping coals of fire upon her head, he could think again. "I'm not a horse you can tame, preacher."

So don't you even try, her narrowed look said.

The brilliant light in his eyes made ample reply. *Count on it.*

For a long moment their gazes clashed in a war of wills. When Wolf shoved his chair back and stood up, Beth Ann was the first to look away.

"You see what I'm up against?" Wolf demanded. "Stubborn, sharp-tongued harpy, just like every one of Eve's daughters—it's enough to drive a plain man to hard liquor! There ain't no stage today, so I'm going to town. You're welcome to come, Reverend. In fact, I'd be right proud to show you around."

"I'm still a bit sore and unsteady on my feet, Mr. Linder," Zach demurred. "Perhaps after the stitches come out. Besides, if I could trouble Miss Beth Ann for a bucket of hot water, it's time I got rid of some of my dirt. 'Cleanliness is next to godliness,' you know."

"Sure enough, Reverend. You tend to him, Beth Ann, you hear?"

"I'll have Buck bring the water," she muttered, stacking dishes onto the tray again. "I've got to put the beans on for supper."

"Not beans again," Wolf groaned.

"We'll have fresh vegetables from Ama's people soon." The Pima were expert farmers, having used irrigation for thousands of years. Beth Ann shot a malicious glance in Zach's direction. "There'll be chuckwalla to go with the beans, though."

Wolf's bushy brows meandered up his broad

forehead, and he smacked his lips in anticipation. "Well, why didn't you say so? Ever had it, Reverend? That sweet-fleshed lizard's quite a delicacy among the Indians. Beats a tough old javelina hog any day."

The look of consternation on Zach's face was purely comical. Had he sweated it out all night long, Beth Ann wondered, or taken action to rid himself of the "poison"? He swallowed loudly, the vengeful light in his eyes and the sickly smile on his lips all the answer she needed.

"I don't think the reverend's *delicate* constitution should be asked to deal with anything so exotic, Paw," Beth Ann interjected with every evidence of solicitous care.

"Nonsense!" Wolf gave Zach a hearty slap on the back. "You'll love it. Believe me."

Here was the perfect opening to recount the trick she'd pulled, but Beth Ann knew instinctively Zach wouldn't take it. So he knew now she hadn't really tried to poison him—the effect was still the same. What man wanted to look a weak-stomached fool before another? Gathering the remainder of the dishes, she perched the loaded tray on her hip, unable to resist tweaking Zach's pride just once more.

"Don't worry, Paw. I'm so sure the reverend will like my chuckwalla, I'm going to make certain he gets *two* servings!"

Long after her paw had driven off in his buggy and after she'd sent Buck along with the hot water, she was still chuckling at the memory of the sick look that had crossed the preacher's face. Kneeling on the floor of her room, Beth Ann worked at the blanket loom Ama had taught her to use, swiftly passing the shuttle wrapped with colorfully dyed wool between the fine strands strung from the top of the wooden frame, combing the fibers down, then beginning the process again. Occasionally she traded one shuttle for another loaded with a different color as she worked the pattern, a simple one that Ama called "Eye of God."

It was rare that Beth Ann found a few moments alone to indulge in any leisure pastime, but no stage today meant she had a respite from her kitchen duties, and the rhythm of weaving was sometimes almost hypnotic, a way to move outside of herself to a place where things were better, easier. She'd woven more than her share of blankets in the past two years. It was harder to find the peace she sought today, however, and she knew it was because of Zach Temple.

Couldn't that stubborn preacher take a hint? She had just about exhausted her bag of practical jokes and dirty tricks, and she was really loath to come up with anything else. Besides, what more could she do to make it clear that he was no longer welcome at Traveler's Rest, short of taking the rifle again and shooting him dead this time? She didn't want their conflict to escalate into all-out war—she just wanted him to leave!

Sighing, Beth Ann set down her shuttle and rubbed the stiffness in her neck. The preacher was right about one thing. She tended to arch and spit like a mountain lion when provoked, but she mostly kept her true feelings bottled up so that she felt ready to explode like a keg of bad beer. Even the solitude of her room didn't soothe her, although the rope bed with its own striped blanket and the old knotty pine chifforobe looked no different than usual. The door beside her loom stood open to the steady glare of a cloudless midday, and the breeze flowed over her, cooling her temples before drifting past the lace-edged curtains at her window. The narrow blanket on her loom now would become a rug beside the bed—if she stayed long enough to finish it.

Beth Ann toyed with the edge of the loom, staring at the emerging design without seeing it. She'd miss Traveler's Rest itself, but not the contention, not the staring eyes, not the unrelenting unhappiness. Just as soon as Nellie foaled . . .

"Could you give me a hand with this?"

Beth Ann jumped. Zach stood bare-chested in her doorway, his shirt in one hand, the end of a bandage in the other. She'd almost forgotten what a truly magnificent chest he had, broad in the shoulder, tapered at the waist, with freckles that played hide-and-seek beneath that enticing bramble of crisp brown hair.

"Beth Ann." Zach stepped into the room, smelling of shaving soap and clean male skin, his brow puckered at her apparent stupefaction. "If you could?"

"Oh!" She scrambled to her feet, a flush traveling from her breasts to her hairline, embarrassed and wary. She took refuge in offended dignity. "It's not proper to enter a lady's chamber half-dressed, sir!"

That produced a grin. "Make you nervous, do I?"

"Of course not."

"Liar. Don't you know better than to bear false witness?" He took a step closer, his grin tilting another infuriating notch. "And you should be nervous, my dear, after what you've done."

Supremely conscious that he stood between her and the door, the breadth of his shoulders blocking her escape, the warmth of his skin radiating across the narrow space that separated them, she still refused to back down. "You deserved it!"

"And you intend to feed me lizard again for supper?" His tone was silky.

Biting her lip, she looked somewhere beyond his ear. "M-Maybe not."

"Ah. You're learning." Zach stepped even nearer, then pressed the bandage into her fist. "I'd be much obliged if you'd tie this up again. I can't quite seem to manage."

Her heart thumping wildly, Beth Ann chanced a glance up into the blue-green depths of his eyes. They were cool and, she thought, deceptively placid.

"Are you sure you trust me to do this?" she murmured warily.

"It's a little late to worry about your nursing skills now."

Peeking under the bandage, she nodded in satisfaction at the healthy, healing flesh, then deftly rewrapped his wounded shoulder. His breath stirred the tendrils of hair that had fallen free of her topknot. The tickling sensation made Beth Ann shiver, almost as if she had an ague. She neatly tucked and tied the ends of the bandage.

"There. All done," she said brightly, but since she was trapped by the wooden frame of the loom pressing at her back, she couldn't step away as her instincts insisted.

"Thanks." He held up his shirt. "How about some help with this? I'm still pretty sore."

Beth Ann gave him a suspicious look, then gingerly edged the shirt sleeve over his arm and injury, reaching behind him to pull the other side over his back. He was entirely too close, and for some inexplicable reason, she couldn't catch her breath.

"Having trouble?" His voice was mild, amused.

"You're crowding me, preacher!"

"That's the general idea—*hey, watch it!*"

Before she could react, he caught her with his good arm, crushing her against his chest while performing a peculiar, stomping dance.

"What's the matter with you?" Beth Ann pushed ineffectually against him. "Are you loco? Let me go, you—"

"Scorpion."

Beth Ann yelped and grabbed at Zach so hard, he grunted in pain. "What? Where is it? How—"

"I got it, honey." Zach ground his booted heel against the plank floor in a succinct and telling movement.

Relieved, Beth Ann wilted against him, shuddering. "I hate those things."

"Yup. I've seen men big as mountains lie down and squall like babes over a scorpion sting." He cradled her gently, smoothing his big hands over her back, pressing her closer so that her breasts flattened against the muscular wall of his chest, bared by the half-on, half-off shirt. His breath whispered in her ear. "It's all over now."

His loose-limbed strength enfolded her in a cocoon of warmth and safety, and for a fleeting instant Beth Ann reveled in the sensations of hard male muscle beneath her fingertips and the tantalizing musk of his skin. Then realization of the absolute impropriety of their embrace made her suddenly flustered, and she tried, rather unsuccessfully, to put at least an inch of daylight between them.

"Yes. Well, ah—thank you," she stammered. She strained away more forcefully, but they were pressed hip to hip. Embarrassed, she babbled, trying to regain her composure with mundane conversation, craning her neck to see his boots. "How big was it? I hope it doesn't have a mate. Let me see."

"Uh. Bound to be nasty. Sure you want to?"

"Better to know what I'm up against, I guess." Zach's mouth twitched. "Right."

He moved his boot. There was nothing under it. Beth Ann's head jerked up, and she glared at him.

"Why, you dirty, low-down—there wasn't any scorpion!"

"Sure there was. Must have gotten away." His expression was as innocent as a newborn's.

"Louse!" Spluttering indignantly, she tried to shake free of him, but Zach held her easily by the shoulders. The wooden pole of the loom frame pressed into her back. "You just wanted an excuse to grope at me," she accused. "Let me go, you varmint!"

He looked hurt. "Beth Ann, would I do such a thing? I'm a man of God, after all."

He was laughing at her, and it infuriated her. Her voice rose. "Filthy, carrion-eating coyote! Take your hands off me, you damned, double-dealing son of a—"

Zach swooped and covered her mouth with his, effectively damming the tide of invective so that the epithet went unfinished, lost in a gurgle of astonishment. Shocked to her core, Beth Ann opened her eyes wide at the electrifying impact. His lips were warm and pliant, impossibly appealing. Horrified at her own reaction, she wrenched her mouth free of his.

"Scoundrel!" she raged, straining away frantically. "You're a minister! How could you do that?"

"Preaching the gospel doesn't make a man dead below the waist." Zach's eyes had darkened to the color of the sea on a stormy day, but the grin that cracked his face was still devilish. "And if I can keep you from the sin of blasphemy, I'm bound to do it—any way I can."

Her gray eyes shot silver sparks of fury. "You sorry—" She broke off with a frightened gasp when she read the renewed intent in his expression. "Don't you dare do that again! I'll scream!"

"No, you won't. It's little enough punishment for the way you've tormented me, and you know it. Even Pharaoh didn't suffer as many plagues! Besides, have you never heard of the boy who cried wolf? Who'd believe *you* would set up a squawk over a kiss or two?"

The question pierced her in her most vulnerable spot. She stared back at him with stricken eyes and answered truthfully. "No one."

Zach flinched. Remorse and something else flickered across his face. He bent toward her again.

"Don't." She turned her head aside, her lashes fanning down over a glitter of moisture. "If I'm so wicked, why do you want to, anyway?"

"Angel." Zach cupped her chin, his fingers gentle on her peachy skin, and turned her face back up to his. His voice was husky. "Haven't you ever heard of loving your enemy? Besides, I don't think you're so bad."

This time his mouth settled over hers gently, like a benediction of healing and atonement. She murmured, but Zach allowed no protest, gathering her close again, kissing her with such intensity and power that she quaked and sighed. His tongue probed the seam of her lips, and she opened for him.

Jesus, how he wanted her!

Zach knew he was in big trouble, but he groaned and slanted his mouth the better to taste Beth Ann. She was sweetness and spice and utter beguilement, soft and giving and intoxicating. In that moment of discovery and desire, Zach knew that come hell or high water, he had to have Beth Ann Linder.

The trouble had begun the minute he'd seen her angel's face hovering over him. Now that he'd discovered the sweetness that lay beneath her fire, he'd never be satisfied until he possessed her fully. Hadn't all Tom's stories been leading him to this? And damned it he could separate the fantasy from the reality when what was real was the way she moved in his arms, fitting so perfectly, responding so generously, that he knew he'd find heaven in her bed for the time they had together.

Sure, it would complicate things some, but he could do a little circumspect wooing while he worked on her paw. After all, he'd seen the inside of a lot of bedrooms in his time. An overprotective watchdog of a father was no challenge to the likes of Zach Madison. The ladies just couldn't resist his beamish face, and the way Beth Ann kissed him back proved she was just as susceptible. With the evidence of his own need pulsing and hardening between his legs, Zach swept his tongue over the roof of her mouth, and she tensed and shivered with need.

How could a kiss make her want so badly?

Beth Ann was so lost in the sensual magic of Zach's mouth, she could barely think. Tom had never kissed her like this, as if there were nothing else in the universe but the two of them, as if she were the sweetest nectar of paradise, and he could never get enough of her. Her knees buckled, and she clung to Zach helplessly, tossed like a thistle blossom caught in a maelstrom.

When she thought she would surely perish for lack of breath, but knowing she would gladly die before she gave up so much as an instant of this pleasure, Zach finally raised his head. She lay against his chest, panting, slowly coming to the realization that his heart beneath her ear was pounding fully as hard as her own and that his fingers tangled in her hair shook ever so slightly.

"Well." Zach's voice held a wry, strained note. "That should teach us both a lesson."

Humiliation flooded through Beth Ann, burning away the mists in her brain so that she stood revealed in all her wantonness. Her response had been undeniable—to a *preacher!* Her weakness and shame lay naked for him to see and condemn. Bile scorched the back of her throat, and her chagrin knew no bounds. She pushed free of Zach, only to have him catch her wrists, holding her before him in all her mortification.

"Let go, you snake handler!" she hissed.

Zach blinked at her vehemence. Damn, this woman was contrary! How could she go from melting sugar to stinging nettle in the blink of an eye? He made his tone placating.

"Now, honey, I didn't mean to rile you."

"You did that on purpose just to get back at me." God, he was vicious! Beth Ann thought. He had known just what to do to destroy her pride. Tears burned behind her eyes, but she'd be damned if she'd cry in front of him.

"Not exactly," Zach drawled, irritation edging his husky voice, "though I wouldn't recommend your playing any more nasty tricks on me."

She wrenched free of his grasp, spitting defiance to cover her utter devastation. "You vile, hateful good-for-nothing! You won't get another chance to insult me in such a disgusting fashion!"

"Fine." Zach's angular jaw flexed. "Just remember I'm on to you, and if you try anything childish again, you'll pay the price."

"Don't you threaten me!"

"Would that be Christian?" he mocked. "As long as you behave yourself, I think we can be friends." His expression took on a sudden wolfish gleam. "Real close friends."

"You delude yourself." She was so infuriated, she nearly stamped her foot, but that remark about being childish held her off. She pointed an imperious finger at the door. "If you're quite through, get the hell out of my room!"

Zach was beginning to enjoy this. Though he had no doubt of the finish, the chase looked to be might entertaining. "Such language from a lady. Think I ought to discipline you again for swearing?"

"Get out!" She nearly shrieked the words.

"As you wish." He swaggered toward the door, his whiskey-streaked brown hair tousled where she'd run her fingers through it, looking very male and magnetic in his open shirt, and not at all preacherlike. He shot her a final glance, his blue-green eyes glittering.

"In a way, I hope you can't resist temptation, honey. I can't say when I've found a more enjoyable form of correction!"

A shuttle wrapped with scarlet yarn whizzed past his head. Laughing, Zach ducked. With a little screech of impotent rage, Beth Ann hurled another shuttle loaded with emerald thread. A clatter and a howl of pain erupted on the porch outside.

Horrified, Beth Ann dropped the other shuttles she'd grabbed for ammunition and hurried through the door. Zach was already squatting by the slight figure sprawled on the dusty boards.

"Buck!"

"Ow!" The wiry, wrinkled cowpoke swayed to a sitting position with Zach's help. He held on to his forehead where a small purple goose egg was already developing. "Christ Almighty, Miss Beth Ann. Why'd you have to go and wallop me like that for?"

Totally flustered, Beth Ann helped him to his feet, apologizing profusely. "Buck, I'm dreadfully sorry. It was an accident."

"This kind of thing is sure gettin' to be a habit with you," Buck groused.

Beth Ann's cheeks flamed. Now that Zach could see that the old man wasn't seriously hurt, he began to chuckle. Beth Ann shot him an icy glance, then turned back to the ranch hand.

"Here, Buck, let me get you a cold compress. I—"

"Hell, it ain't nuthin' much. I'll be all right." Buck waved her away, looking around for his battered, greasy hat. "I only came to tell you Nellie's down."

"What? She's going to foal now? But mares almost never deliver in broad daylight!"

Buck shrugged his bent shoulders. "Well, it ain't stopping Nellie this time."

Delight and relief and anticipation replaced Beth Ann's earlier anger and chagrin. Good old Nellie! Her timing couldn't be any better. So what if Beth Ann couldn't convince this detestable preacher to go? She'd soon have the means to leave Traveler's Rest herself! Losing her head with the reverend had only made her escape more imperative than ever. The memory of what his kiss had done to her made her shiver, but she told herself it was revulsion, not desire, that was the cause. Heck, once she'd gone, Zach Temple could take up permanent residence with Paw for all she cared.

"Do you think she's very far along?" Beth Ann asked Buck.

"Dunno. But I reckon you best get down there if you don't want to miss the excitement."

"I sure don't! Thanks, Buck."

Spirits restored, Beth Ann cast Zach a triumphant look, then picked up her skirts and hurried across the sun-beaten yard to welcome her salvation into the world. To her vast annoyance, Zach fell into step beside her, and Buck brought up the rear of the little procession.

"Mind if I tag along?" Zach asked.

"Yes! You'll only disturb Nellie."

Mischief dancing in his eyes, Zach shrugged into the dangling sleeve of his shirt but didn't bother to button the placket. "But you might need some help."

Beth Ann's glance was contemptuous. "Not from you, preacher."

"You never can tell when an extra set of hands might be needed."

Beth Ann's lips compressed, but she made no answer as they threaded past the stippled shade of the cottonwoods and came to the paddock. A few moments later, however, the prophetic nature of Zach's easy words shocked her.

Something was very wrong with Nellie.

The sorrel mare lay on her side in the corner of the paddock in obvious distress, her heaving flanks glistening with placental waters. A few curious horses stood nearby, observing the labor of their companion like a pack of gossipy midwives.

"Why didn't you tell me she was like this, Buck?" Beth Ann demanded in alarm.

"Like what, Miss Beth Ann? Old Nellie's just doin' her work, same as always."

"Dang fool," Beth Ann muttered under her breath.

Even she could see that the mare's labor wasn't

progressing along normal lines. But Beth Ann had
no real notion of what to do, either. In the past
Nellie had always foaled with absolute ease. But
she had to do something—nothing must happen
to this foal! Beth Ann swallowed and made her
voice forceful.

"Turn those other horses out so she won't be
disturbed by how close they are."

"Yes'm."

"And bring a bucket of water and ... and the
lye soap and some iodine. And hop to it!"

"I'm moving as fast as I can." Waving his
scrawny arms to shoo the other horses, Buck hobbled off to comply.

Beth Ann tucked up her skirts and went to Nellie's head, crooning low to soothe the straining animal. "Easy, girl. I'll help you, I promise."

"Hold her head, Beth, honey," Zach said quietly.
"I'll take a look."

Beth Ann had all but forgotten the preacher.
Now she looked at him with alarm and suspicion
and appeal mingling in her expression. "Do you
know anything about horses?"

Zach squatted and lifted Nellie's tail out of the
way. "Enough. I grew up around livery stables. It
taught me real quick what I *didn't* want to do for
a living."

Beth Ann knelt and grabbed Nellie's halter, trying to settle the restive animal. Her gray eyes were
wide and skeptical as Zach busied himself at the
business end of the horse. "Can you tell what's
wrong?"

"She's working awfully hard. Must be a big
foal."

"Paw bred her to Bobby Barlings's stallion."

"Might take a while, then—no, I take that back.
Here's the bubble already."

Beth Ann craned her neck to see the leading edge of the placental sack. "That's a good sign, isn't it, Zach? I mean, Reverend?"

"Zach will do," he replied, preoccupied. "And yes, it's a good—"

He broke off with a string of curses that made Beth Ann's mouth drop open in shock. No preacher of her acquaintance even *knew* half of what came out of his mouth! But then no preacher she knew could or would have kissed her the way he had, either! But even more alarming than the vitriolic stream of swearing was the way Zach stripped out of his shirt and hollered at Buck to hurry with that water.

"What is it?" she demanded, fingers of panic tugging at her innards. "What's happened?"

"There's only one hoof showing." Zach shook his head in disgust and weary resignation. "Jeesus, I hate this. Damn!"

Beth Ann started up as Buck bustled forward with the bucket. Zach plunged his arms into the water and began to lather himself.

"Tell me!" she insisted. "That means one of the foal's legs is turned under, isn't it?"

"Or hooked behind its head."

Beth Ann swallowed hard. The foal couldn't move through the birth canal as nature had planned. If it was born in that position, it would probably be dead by the time it came out, and as for Nellie ... Beth Ann shuddered with fear for Nellie and for her own future. "We've got to do something!"

"You just hold her head!" Zach barked.

"But—"

Zach's mobile mouth twisted downward in a grimace of impatience. "Look, neither you nor Buck are strong enough to reach inside past the labor contractions and turn the foal, so it looks like I'm elected. Unless you have a better suggestion, Miss Linder?"

Biting her lower lip in distress, Beth Ann shook her head. "But you're hurt. Can you do it?"

Zach's jaw squared. "Only one way to find out."

Chapter 5

It was hot, hard, brutal work.

On his knees in the dusty paddock, Zach pushed his arm into the straining mare's birth canal, fighting against the powerful muscular contractions that sought to expel the infant from the mother's body. The space was tight and feverishly hot. The contractions squeezed Zach like a vise, but the foal was lodged, stuck like a cork that no amount of pressure could release.

"I feel . . . it," Zach panted, sweat dripping from his brow.

The contraction eased, allowing him to explore with his fingertips—a velvety nose, the curve of an ear, the bony elongation of the foal's leg tucked at an excruciating angle behind its narrow head. Zach groaned and laid his cheek against the mare's wet haunch at the discovery. Another contraction began, and his groan deepened.

"Zach!" Beth Ann's voice was shrill with panic. "Are you all right?"

"Jim-dandy." Grinding his teeth, Zach rode out the contraction. The instant it relented again, he began shoving the foal back, trying to find purchase and room to rearrange that captured leg. "If . . . I . . . can . . . just get the shank . . . over where it belongs . . ."

Another contraction forced him to stop. Then he tried again. And again. And again.

Over and over, straining against an animal that

107

outweighed him by hundreds of pounds until he thought his own heart was going to pop and the stitches under his bandage screamed for mercy.

What the devil am I doing here? he asked himself after an eternity of struggle.

Trying to ingratiate myself so thoroughly, Beth Ann won't be able to resist my overtures, was the not-so-lofty answer.

Zach moaned as another contraction compressed his arm painfully. His image of a grateful and dewy-eyed angel coming willingly into his arms might be a trifle premature, he realized. Especially since he was liable to be nothing but a smear of grease in the dirt when this ordeal was over!

Zach shook off the depressing vision, sheer stubbornness making him hang on. He'd opened his big mouth. The least he could do was make good on his brag. Sweat dripped into his burning eyes, made him blink and mouth silent obscenities. He was vaguely aware of Beth Ann ordering Buck to take the mare's head, then she was at Zach's side, wetting her apron and wiping it over his salty skin, offering the support of her weight against his back so he could get the leverage he needed. Zach knew neither he nor the mare could last much longer. Straining with all his might, he dredged up the last morsel of energy in his body and pulled.

"Almost . . . got it," he panted.

Half inch by millimeter by hairsbreadth, the foal's leg began to shift . . . then snapped down into position in a rush. With a shout, Zach fell backward against Beth Ann. "Here it comes!"

Two tiny black hooves appeared side by side, then withdrew. They came into view again, this time with the tip of a satiny nose behind them.

"Help her this time!" Zach ordered. When the hooves reappeared, he and Beth Ann knelt shoulder to shoulder, and each grabbed a tiny leg. "Gently," Zach urged. "Work with her—now!"

With a single great final heave, the mare expelled her burden. A wet, shiny bundle of bones and black hide flew into their laps with a gush of fluids.

"Peel the sack off its nose, quick!" Zach ordered, his breath rasping harshly.

Beth Ann joined her efforts with his, stripping the remnants of the amniotic sack from the foal's nostrils. The angular bag of bones quivered, jerked, then took its first breath.

"Look! He's all right!" Beth Ann was jubilant.

"Looks to me like *she's* a filly, Miss Beth Ann," Buck said at Nellie's head.

Beth Ann's laughter rang in joyous exultation. "A filly, then! And she's fine!"

She was so delighted that despite his exhaustion, Zach responded with a feeble squeeze to her shoulders. But when he tried to lever himself to his feet, the blue sky suddenly went dim, and the next thing he knew, he was sitting on his backside in the dirt again.

"Zach!" Beth Ann knelt beside him, her face worried. "What is it?"

"Just a little . . . dizzy," he mumbled, shaking his head as bells clanged in his ears. "I'm fine."

"No, you're not. You damned near killed yourself! Here, lean on me."

The wave of light-headedness was fast receding, but Zach wasn't about to miss an opportunity to play on her sympathy—or to get his hands on her again. Helping each other, they staggered to their feet, Zach leaning on Beth Ann more heavily than he'd intended, every morsel of energy wrung from his weary body. For several breathless seconds, both horses and humans rested in companionable silence. Then Nellie lifted her head and nickered an inquiry.

"Hold her, Buck," Zach instructed. "Don't want her getting up while the blood is still flowing through the baby's cord."

"What pretty things you are." Beth Ann praised both mother and child with a smile that transformed her own dirty face. Fatigued though he was, Zach thought he'd never seen anything quite so lovely, and the fire ignited again down low in his belly.

Beth Ann pointed. "Look, Zach, the cord broke."

Zach nodded with a grunt of satisfaction and reluctantly began to disentangle himself from Beth Ann's supporting arms. "Get me that iodine, Buck, and I'll tie it off and burn the end clean. We don't want this little filly getting the cord-ill after all this. And let the mama up now. She needs to get busy on her young'un."

Within minutes, Nellie was on her feet and doing just that, licking her offspring from hoof to forelock with maternal care. The little animal shivered and stared, then struggled up on her tiny hooves, swaying and staggering like a cowboy on a three-day bender. Like proud parents, the three humans enjoyed her antics while Nellie nickered and guided her offspring to a teat to nurse.

"That's a fine one, Miss Beth Ann," Buck said. "Look how deep her chest is, and those straight legs. She'll be a runner for sure!"

"She's beautiful, isn't she?" Beth Ann breathed, blotting her damp forehead with her sleeve.

"A champion, if I'm any judge." Moving stiffly, Zach splashed water from the bucket over his arms and chest, then reached for his discarded shirt, grimacing as he slapped the dust out of it.

Beth Ann watched his strained motions with concern. Water droplets glistened in his chest hairs, and his shoulders drooped with exhaustion. "You've hurt yourself again."

"I'll mend."

Beth Ann was filled with a welter of conflicting emotions. She couldn't forget the excitement she'd experienced at Zach's touch, nor the humiliation when she'd realized he'd kissed her to extort his own brand of punishment. But how could she be angry at a man who'd just struggled so hard to save her most valuable assets? Who had, albeit unknowingly, rescued her chance for a new life? But to acknowledge her gratitude meant she might be forced to reassess her view of Zach Temple—the preacher who saved her precious Nellie couldn't be all bad, could he? Beth Ann couldn't resolve so many opposing elements in so little time, so she ignored her inner turmoil by concentrating on outward necessities.

"Come along, Reverend. You need to wash, and that bandage will have to be changed again. Buck—"

"Take care of the preacher, Miss Beth Ann," the grizzled cowboy interrupted. "I can tend to things here."

Now that it was over, Zach had to admit that he felt as though he'd been pulled through the proverbial knothole backwards, so he didn't offer any objection as Beth Ann herded him back toward the inn. Minutes later, he was seated in a kitchen chair, allowing her whatever liberties she chose to take. Unfortunately for his baser instincts, she was completely in her hausfrau mode, bustling about washing, bandaging, even bringing him one of her paw's old shirts since all of his were the worse for wear. While he tucked the outsize garment into his britches, she fetched him a glass of buttermilk and a slab of cold cornbread and honey as a late lunch.

Zach looked at her quizzically. "Does this mean you're feeling a bit more charitably toward me again?"

She had been preoccupied with the little domestic chores—pouring out his wash water, changing her apron, checking on the beans simmering on the back of the stove—but now her expression clouded, changed.

"You'll never know what that foal means to me." Though her tone was slightly ironic, her luminous silver gaze had never been more serious. "Thank you for everything."

Zach wiped his milky mustache on the napkin she'd laid out for him. It was a simple nicety that touched him as much as her little speech did, a starched napkin for a man she had little reason to either trust or respect, but set out as the decent thing to do. He was beginning to suspect that there were greater depths of decency in Beth Ann than most people wanted to give her credit for. And that intrigued him.

Hell, if he was honest with himself, he'd admit she'd fascinated him from the moment he'd seen that tintype picture. Now that he had tasted her fire, nothing would stop him from having her. Winning her gratitude had sent the first brick in the wall of her defenses crashing to the ground. With a little patience and a subtle and continuing assault, she'd come around. Yes, sir, sooner or later, Jericho would fall and she would be his.

Zach gave Beth Ann a lazy grin. "The Lord's miracle of birth is really something to see up close, isn't it? Even for a poor servant like me. Are you willing to admit I'm not such a villain now?"

"I'll admit you're the first preacher I ever saw who knew anything about work," she said, flushing furiously. To cover her discomfiture, she pushed the tendrils of dark hair back from her brow and asked a question of her own. "Where'd you learn to cuss like that?"

Nonplussed, Zach looked at her blankly, then his long cheeks suffused with his own hot color. Damn, if she wasn't sharper than a tack! He would have to watch himself closely to keep this charade from disintegrating altogether.

"Oh. Er, well, I wasn't always a clergyman, you know." He grinned again, sheepish. "I'll have to do a powerful lot of penance to make up for that, won't I?"

Grabbing up a dishrag, Beth Ann began to dry a stack of clean dishes with more enthusiasm than they deserved. "You've done me such a favor, surely the Lord will overlook that as a minor infraction."

"And what about you? Are you going to hold that moment of weakness this morning against me forever?"

The spoon she was drying bounced on the stone floor with a metallic clatter that matched her suddenly brittle tone. "I'm sure that it would be best if we didn't mention that again, Reverend."

He heaved an aggravated sigh. Rising to his feet, he went to her side, leaning his elbow on the dry sink where she worked so that he could see her face better. "There, you're doing it again."

"What?" The glance she cast him from beneath her dark lashes was both startled and wary.

"Calling me 'Reverend' in that chilly little voice as if I was something that had crawled out from under a rock. Why can't you pretend I'm just another cowpoke and call me Zach like you did before?"

A peachy tide washed her cheekbones, and she stiffened. "It wouldn't be fitting. You really should go to bed and rest now. You overdid it, and I don't want you to relapse—"

"In a minute." Zach made an impatient gesture, then caught her hand, forcing her to cease her nervous wiping of silverware and turn toward him. "You're prejudiced against my breed, Beth Ann, but I'm not your enemy."

She bristled up like a porcupine. "I'm not so sure of that!"

He laughed and rubbed his thumb over her knuckles in a way that made her stomach go weightless.

"Why? Because I kissed you? I'll admit it seemed a great way to teach you a lesson or two at first. Just because I wear my collar backwards doesn't mean I can always control my temper. But now that I've had a sample, kissing you has wonderful appeal."

Beth Ann snatched her hand away, her hackles rising. "Just because everyone calls me loose, that doesn't mean I'll let you!"

Zach gave her a disgusted look. "You know, if you weren't so all-fired touchy, you might find out that I'm trying to apologize!"

"Oh." Her eyes narrowed suspiciously. "Why?"

"Because if we can quit sniping at each other long enough, we might discover we can be friends."

She looked uncomfortable. "Why should you want that?"

His grin was wry. "You never look in a mirror, do you?"

"That doesn't mean anything." Her words were bleak with past disappointments.

"No, the fact that I find you lovely is only a start," he agreed seriously. "But the more I learn about Beth Ann Linder, the more I think there are qualities in her that have been overlooked. You know, if we could call a truce, I sure would like the chance to discover them."

Despite herself, the cold shell Beth Ann had cultivated as a defense and a pretense thawed just a little. But before even a glimmer of hope could emerge, she realized the futility of such foolhardiness and shook her head.

"What's the point? You'll be going sooner or later, and I—well, never mind that." She broke off, unwilling to reveal her own plans. "Anyway, it's not worth it."

Zach controlled his exasperation with an effort. He had to find a way to get past Beth Ann's defensive bastion if he was ever going to get close enough to woo her. If sweet talk didn't work, there was one thing a feisty woman couldn't resist—direct challenge.

"Too yellow to take the risk, huh?" he goaded gently.

"I'm not afraid of you!"

"No, just of finding out all preachers—or men—aren't ogres and demons. You're right about me not being around much longer. Wouldn't you rather make peace than war for the duration?"

"Well . . ."

The way her white teeth worried her peach-colored lip gave Zach a hungry feeling right down in the pit of his stomach.

"Come on, honey," he cajoled, "I'm tired of fighting, aren't you?"

More than he could know, Beth Ann thought.

Besides, she couldn't abide the idea that Zach Temple would brand her a coward! She gave an inner shrug. What difference would it make in the end, anyway? No doubt the remainder of the preacher's recuperation would pass more quickly if they weren't constantly carping at each other. And now that Nellie's foal was safely here, she had, as Paw loved to say, "other fish to fry."

Eyeing him carefully, she held out her hand. "All right. Pax, then."

Zach clasped her fingers gravely. "My dear Miss Linder, I promise you won't regret this."

But from the way her skin tingled at his touch, Beth Ann feared that she already did.

Over the next few days, Beth Ann had reason to regret her hastily accepted challenge more than a little. It wasn't that Zach reneged on their agreement. Oh, no, far from it. He was the essence of all that was gentlemanly and cordial. That was the problem. Without the pressure of constant squabbling to keep her guard up, Beth Ann found herself dwelling on the preacher's superior physical and spiritual attributes far more than was safe for her peace of mind.

He *had* overdone it helping Nellie's foal into the world, to the extent that he spent another two days in bed grappling with a sore shoulder and the return of a low-grade fever, much to Wolf's disappointment when the preacher couldn't attend Sunday services with them. Despite his discomfort, Zach remained invariably cheerful and easy to please, so charming, in fact, that he actually made Beth Ann laugh with his jests when she brought in his supper tray that Sunday evening, easing her from the testy black mood that being made a spectacle during her weekly "penance" at church always produced.

By the next evening, Zach was recovered enough to play a poor game of chess with Wolf out on the veranda, laughing good-naturedly at his own ineptitude and letting Wolf lecture him endlessly on the finer points. In fact, he and the older man were becoming quite cozy, Wolf especially glad for an audience for his reminiscences and countless opinions. Beth Ann thought it was downright charitable of Zach to listen to all the boring talk of lost mines and hazardous adventures in the mountains, not to mention Wolf's endless dissertations on the latest milling techniques to separate various minerals and the efficacious benefits of the new oxidizing and chloridizing furnaces for amalgamating copper and silver. Zach actually pretended a rapt interest, questioning Wolf at length about every conceivable aspect of the subject.

No, indeed, Zach Temple certainly didn't act like any preacher Beth Ann had ever encountered. He didn't condemn her or avail himself of every opportunity to lecture her on her sins; he didn't offer to go down on his knees with her to pray for her immortal soul or bombast her with promises of eternal retribution, as had the clergymen whom Paw had summoned in the past to counsel with his wicked offspring. Those stern individuals were more interested in using her as an example than in hearing her side, so she'd reacted with defiance that had only brought her more trouble.

Maybe Zach understood that. All Beth Ann knew was that she was grateful for his restraint. And she couldn't help being flattered by the admiration in his eyes when he looked at her. "Lovely," he'd called her, as if she were no different from any other respectable young lady of his acquaintance. And for a moment, she'd almost believed it.

It was most unsettling.

Perhaps that was why her skin seemed ultrasensitive and every sense heightened, so that she knew without looking when Zach entered a room. Perhaps it was her overactive imagination, but he seemed to be everywhere she was, borrowing a book, looking into her cook pots, passing her with an innocent brush of their bodies, always so close that she could feel his breath on her neck. Once she'd met him on the kitchen staircase, and she'd been so overwhelmed by his nearness and the clean male scent of him, her heart had nearly pounded free of her chest before they'd negotiated that narrow space safely.

It wasn't just that he was a handsome man or that she knew what he looked like under his shirt, either. No, it was as if Zach Temple radiated some sort of special energy that affected her nervous system in peculiar ways, so that she found herself at the most inopportune moments thinking about what it would be like if he kissed her again.

It was dangerous. It was delightful. It wasn't to be borne!

Finding her recalcitrant thoughts wandering into forbidden territory yet again, Beth Ann tossed the potato she'd been holding as if it were the Holy Grail itself into the waiting pot, muttering self-admonitions under her breath. From her seat beside the sunny kitchen doorway, Ama regarded her mistress impassively, then went back to plucking the brace of prairie hens meant for supper. Gathering up the potato peelings in the lap of her apron, Beth Ann stepped past the Indian squaw and tossed the scraps into the yard for the birds.

How on earth, she wondered irritably, was she

going to get a solitary thing done around this place when her mind wouldn't obey her simplest instructions? This daydreaming had to stop! How humiliating if the preacher guessed she had more than a passing interest in the shape of his mouth. Beth Ann stifled a groan. Sweet sassafras! She had more reason than ever to hope he left Traveler's Rest soon, before she totally disgraced herself!

Every thought fled from Beth Ann's head at the sight of the bare-chested man crossing the yard from the vicinity of the corrals. She knew that Paw was stretched out on the horsehair sofa in the parlor, snoring up a storm in his customary midday siesta, but she'd thought that Zach was resting in his room as well.

Shirt in hand, he sauntered toward the house in that loose-hipped gait of his, his back glistening with sweat under the intense Arizona sun, his rusty brown curls clinging damply to this brow. As he walked, Zach rotated his shoulder to test its mobility, grimacing slightly. The white swath of his bandage was a stark contrast against his tanned skin and the crisp brown curls that feathered around his flat male nipples, then arrowed down to his navel.

Stunned by his blatant virility, Beth Ann fought for breath. Whatever his vocation, Zach Temple was definitely all man, and one who had no need of a sickroom any longer. The knowledge was strangely dispiriting.

Zach caught sight of her in the doorway, and his cheek creased into a grin. "Howdy, ma'am."

Beth Ann closed her mouth with a snap, chagrined at being caught gawking. She put on her best schoolmarm expression to cover her discomfiture. "I might have known you'd be up to some kind of dad-blamed foolishness! Where have you been?"

"Just trying to work some of the soreness out. Took a look at that new filly of yours. Did you know Buck is calling her 'Bullfrog' because she jumps so much?"

"That's ridiculous."

"Well, what are you naming her?"

"I'm not." No, that would be for her new owner to do when the time came, she thought with a pang, then confessed softly, "If I were going to call her anything, it would be 'Hope.' "

Zach lifted one sandy eyebrow. "Curious name for a horse. Anyway, then I walked down by the river. There's a sort of pool . . ."

"Yes, of course. We've been bathing there for ages." She eyed his sweaty chest critically. "But you're hardly well. You could have done yourself some more damage. You should have told someone—"

"Don't fret. I'm fine." He shifted uncomfortably and tugged at the bandage. "All except for these damn—er, excuse me—these stitches. I think they need to come out. Will you do it?"

Beth Ann froze. Voluntarily touch those broad shoulders again? Feel the latent strength of hard muscle and sinew within that brawny arm? Relish the sensation of satiny skin and silky chest curls beneath her fingers? Her middle liquified in a sensual shudder at the thought, but alarm bells clanged in her head.

"Ah, I'm sure it would be best if Dr. Sayers saw to that, Reverend," she said, backing away.

"I trust you more than any old sawbones." Zach gave her an imploring smile. "Come on, honey, these things are about to itch me to death! Have a little mercy. You aren't afraid, are you?"

That snapped her head around. "Of course not!"

"Well?"

She sniffed. "If you have no more regard for your own skin than to take a chance on an amateur, then so be it."

Beth Ann said something swiftly to Ama, who vacated her chair and ambled inside the kitchen, returning momentarily with a sewing basket and a corked brown-glass bottle. The squaw showed Zach a brief, snaggled grin, then picked up her cleaned birds and disappeared inside again, giggling.

"Have a seat." Beth Ann dragged the chair across the hard-packed dirt into the sunlight. With a dubious look at the departing kitchen maid, Zach sat.

Biting her lip, Beth Ann gingerly cut the bandage free with her scissors. She breathed a small sigh of relief at the sight of the healthy knitted flesh, then uncorked the bottle. "Hold still. This might sting."

Zach grunted when she daubed the pungent liquid over the protruding stitches on both sides of his shoulder. When she set the bottle back down in her basket, he lifted one sardonic eyebrow. "Whiskey, Miss Linder?"

"For medicinal purposes only, Reverend Temple."

"Like snakebite, huh?"

"Exactly."

"From the amount left in that bottle, some old snake around here must be getting mighty tired," he teased.

"I have no time for jocularity, sir. Shall we get on with it?"

"By all means."

"Fine!"

Though her voice was tart and businesslike, Beth Ann was shaking inside from both an overload of her senses and the fear that somehow she wouldn't be adequate for the task. But this is what she'd been working toward, wasn't it? Removing the stitches would be the signal of Zach's complete recovery, and he'd have no further excuse to tarry at Traveler's Rest. Why did that give her no joy? It wasn't that she'd miss the preacher, was it?

Refusing to pursue that course of thought and beginning to perspire now herself, Beth Ann carefully clipped the knotted ends of all the stitches one by one. Then, positioning herself at Zach's back, she took a pair of tweezers and swiftly jerked the first thread free.

"Yeow!" Zach shot to his feet. "Hellfire and—"

"Reverend! You're cursing again."

"Ummph!" The alcohol seared the small flesh wound left by the removal of the stitch, and strangled sounds of distress continued to rumble from behind Zach's clamped jaw.

"Sit down," she said, pushing at his shoulder. "Don't be such a baby."

His eyes squeezed shut, and he panted between bared teeth. "Jee-sus. That burns like a bitch!"

Beth Ann's cheeks were on fire, too, and embarrassment made her belligerent. "Look, do you want me to do this or not?"

His face screwed in a tight knot, Zach eased back down in the chair with all the enthusiasm of a condemned man facing the gallows. He snatched the whiskey bottle from the basket and took a long pull. Still holding the bottle, he coughed once, braced his arms on his knees, and nodded. "All right. Do it."

Beth Ann blinked, taken aback. "Are you sure—"

"Just get it the hell over with!" he roared.

"Don't you shout at me!" Beth Ann snapped, rattled, angry, and affronted.

Gritting her teeth, she plucked out the stitches on his back in rapid-fire succession. Zach jerked at each extraction, and the cords in his thick neck stood out in strain. When she came around to work on the front of his shoulder, she could see the beads of perspiration pearling Zach's brow, but he said nothing, merely took periodic swigs from the brown bottle.

"Done," Beth Ann said at last in vast relief.

"Douse it with what's left of this," Zach ordered tightly, offering her the bottle.

Beth Ann looked at the rows of bloody pin-pricks left in his flesh, and gulped. "Zach, please . . ."

"Don't want infection setting in after all the trouble you took, do we?"

She shook her head slowly, making the end of her braid wag against the middle of her back. She took the bottle, feeling weak-kneed and light-headed at the prospect of causing Zach more pain. But after all, she was the one who'd begun this. It was right that she finish it properly. Zach, how-ever, wasn't the only one in need of succor by this point.

Glancing around in the empty yard, Beth Ann swiftly lifted the bottle, placing her lips where Zach's had been, and took a generous sip of Dutch courage. She choked on the fiery liquor but forced herself to swallow, feeling the burn of the whiskey and what she imagined was a lingering taste of Zach himself all the way from the back of her tongue down to the pit of her stomach. It was strangely fortifying. Not allowing herself to think, she poured the remainder of the bottle over Zach's wounds.

"Ch-rist." Zach groaned deeply.

Beth Ann dropped the bottle and bent over him, one hand braced on the back of his chair, puffing out her cheeks and blowing her breath gently over the burning areas. She kept it up until some of the tension went out of him. But as she continued her ministrations, that tension became her own.

Fascinated, she watched her breath stir the fine curls of brown hair on his chest. The flat coin of his nipple puckered in reaction to the cooling draft, amazing her and making her breasts feel heavy, their tips tingling and contracting beneath her sedate shirtwaist. She wondered vaguely if Zach shared any of the myriad sensations curling through her like waves upon a distant beach.

He glanced at her out of the corner of his eye. "Whatever you're doing, that feels better."

"Didn't your mother ever do this?" she asked between puffs of air.

"Never knew my maw." Zach's voice was low, husky. "Or my paw, either."

Startled, Beth Ann looked up at his stony profile. She was so close, she could see the bristles of his afternoon stubble glinting in the sunlight. The not unpleasant tang of whiskey filled her nostrils. It seemed a moment for sharing. "My mother ran off when I was ten."

His words seem to come from far away. "At least you have some notion of where you came from. I was born in the back room of a saloon and grew up sleeping in the livery stable's loft. Luckily, old Boone appreciated an extra set of hands, even if it was attached to a mouth to feed."

Beth Ann had never thought herself fortunate until then, and a poignancy for Zach's lonely childhood filled her throat. Bending closer, she pressed her lips to the top curve of his muscular shoulder in a feather-soft kiss. She tasted salt and the unique essence of man, of Zach himself.

Zach stiffened, then turned his head to the side. When she raised her face again, their noses almost touched.

"What was that for?" he asked quietly.

"I'm sorry I hurt you." Her husky whisper meant so many things.

I'm sorry for shooting you. I'm sorry I'm so difficult. I'm sorry the whiskey burned. I'm sorry you had no family of your own. I'm sorry I won't have the time to know you.

"I'm sorry," she repeated softly. "So I kissed it better."

Zach's gaze fell to her mouth, and his glance was like a physical touch that drew her to him as a moth to a flame. Her lips felt full, throbbing, yearning, and her heart fluttered in her throat as helplessly as the foolish moth that saw only the glittering beauty of the fire and none of the danger. With a little sigh of surrender, Beth Ann crossed that infinite span—as close as the space between two heartbeats, as distant as the most remote galaxy—and touched her lips to Zach's.

How firm his lips were! How sweet, with the punch of whiskey to accent their flavor. Heady and exciting, that tentative brush of mouths, a tender melding more precious than a shower of gold dust and as ephemeral as the impulse from which it had arisen. And Zach let her savor him, making no move to claim the moment for himself, simply letting it happen, though in the end his lips clung to hers as she lifted her head.

Beth Ann knew she'd surprised him. She'd surprised herself with that freely given kiss. But then the realization of what she'd done hit her. Fear that he'd find her brazen, that he'd misjudge the innocent gesture and brand her a wanton temptress, made her tremble. Scalding color flooded her cheeks, and she tried to pull away.

Zach would have none of her withdrawal. He cupped her chin, holding her face steady while they examined each other's expressions for a timeless moment. Hers was confused and uncertain, his ... well, Beth Ann couldn't read it, she only knew that she couldn't have torn herself free of his mesmerizing turquoise gaze if her life depended on it.

And he must have seen that, for something ignited behind Zach's eyes, and he smiled crookedly, at once tender and triumphant with masculine satisfaction. Beth Ann shivered, suddenly fearful, and tried to move away, but he tugged her back with a murmured endearment. "Angel."

His mouth hovered over hers, and Beth Ann realized helplessly that she'd made a terrible mistake. But in that endless moment, as Zach touched her and excitement and anticipation trilled through her core, she didn't—couldn't—care.

From the kitchen at their backs, Ama's shrill chatter erupted in a spate of incomprehensible gibberish that broke the fragile spell. Startled, Beth Ann jerked away, hearing for the first time the identifying thump of her father's unwieldy steps, then his ill-tempered snarling.

"Cut out that jabber, woman! Who's doing all that howling?"

Beth Ann spun away from Zach just as Wolf barreled through the kitchen door. To hide her blazing cheeks, she kept her back turned and made a production of gathering up the old bandages and her sewing equipment. Shame and chagrin and a sensation that could only be frustration nearly choked her. Fortunately, Zach appeared to be having no such difficulties.

"Sorry if I disturbed you, sir." Zach leaned the straight chair back on two legs and gave Wolf an engaging grin. "Miss Beth Ann was good enough to take my stitches out, and I fear I disgraced myself horribly."

Wolf scowled at his daughter's back. "You daft, girl? You should have let the doc do it."

"It's done now," Beth Ann replied sullenly.

She continued to rummage in her sewing basket, looking for composure, amazed and more than a little annoyed. How could Zach be so glib and sound so normal when every nerve in her body screamed in embarrassment? He must be made of stone! Or had he been playing with her? Worse, laughing at her?

Mortification surged through her every vein. She'd kissed the preacher—of her own volition! What had she been thinking to do such a fool thing? The devil must indeed be tempting her! If Paw had seen—she shuddered at the thought.

"Did she hurt you, Reverend?" Wolf demanded. His anger focused on his favorite target. "Prideful hussy, thinkin' she knows everything—I ought to give her the back of my hand for that!"

"No need for violence, Mr. Linder." Zach rose from the chair, his eyes darkening so they looked almost emerald. Smiling tightly, he pounded his chest. "See? Good as new."

"Now, let's not be premature," Wolf said hastily. "Stitches or not, you've got to get your strength back, and I won't hear of your leaving Traveler's Rest until I'm satisfied of your complete recovery."

Zach drew on his shirt. "You're most kind, sir."

Wolf dismissed Zach's gratitude with a wave.

"I'd say getting shut of Beth Ann's embroidery is cause for a celebration. What say you and me take the buggy into town? I sure would like to show you around our little community. We might even get a peek at that old Mexican map Robert Barlings has been promising to show me." Wolf nudged Zach in the ribs and laughed. "Why, it might even tell us where to find the *Planchas de Plata*."

"Planks of silver?" Zach puzzled.

"Sure! You've heard of it, haven't you? Old Spanish mine lost somewhere around here a hundred years ago. Sheets of silver so pure, it'd make your head spin, lying right on the surface in gigantic 'planks.' " Wolf winked. "Course, if it had been that easy to find, someone would have done it long ago, Apaches or not. So, Zachariah, what do you say? You up to a little excursion?"

"I do feel amazingly well," Zach said thoughtfully, then added, "praise the Lord."

"Amen, brother. So you'll come?"

"I'd be glad to see a bit of the country. Will Miss Beth Ann be joining us?"

Beth Ann whirled around so fast, she nearly dropped her basket. Had the whiskey finally gotten to the preacher's brain? She was so mortified by her brazen display, she couldn't look him in the eye, much less keep him company all the way to town!

"No. No, thank you," she stuttered. "I've got so many things to do here—"

"But your daughter's been such a conscientious nurse, Mr. Linder," Zach protested. "Surely she deserves a day off?"

There was something about the mischievous gleam in Zach's eye that made Beth Ann very nervous. "I prefer to stay here."

"You'll do as you're told, girl!" Wolf ordered sternly. "You've been griping at me to pick up them supplies you want, so you might as well come and do it yourself. Anyway, it won't hurt to prove to the townsfolk—and especially Miz Cunningham—that the reverend is all right and there's no hard feelings betwixt us."

Beth Ann's stomach flip-flopped, then sank alarmingly. Until she could get control of herself, spending time with Zach was the last thing she needed! Moreover, she had no desire to parade herself through the streets of Destiny. "But, Paw—"

"If the preacher is charitable enough to want you along, that's exactly what he's going to get," Wolf Linder said in no uncertain terms. "So go fetch your bonnet, and be quick about it!"

Chapter 6

S he was as good as his.

As Zach helped Beth Ann out of the buggy in front of the Destiny Savings Bank, he felt her fingers tremble within his grasp and mentally congratulated himself. She gave him a wary flash of those soft silver eyes from under the brim of her slat bonnet, then lowered her lashes and stepped down into the street, retrieving her hand a mite too quickly for courtesy. Zach hid a grin. Yes, sir, unless he had sadly miscalculated, Miss Beth Ann Linder would soon be sharing his bed.

Damn if it hadn't worked just like always. Give a woman something to think about, then ease off, and the next thing, her curiosity or her pride landed her right in your lap. Zach chuckled to himself at what the upstanding citizens of Destiny might do if they could see the lusty, carnal thoughts lurking behind his respectable clerical collar. The things he planned to do with Beth Ann, the passion he was certain he could unleash now that he'd won her over, would send the likes of Mamie Cunningham into screaming fits. Zach knew the thought of it made him hard as hell.

On top of that, after dropping enough hints in Wolf's hairy ears, the old coot had finally picked up on the fact that the Reverend Temple, in return for a donation to his Tucson mission, might be willing to lend his services for a little prospecting expedition into the foothills of the Superstitions.

That Wolf missed the life and was desperate to go back—to check on his mines, Zach sincerely hoped and prayed—was a foregone fact. But the old man knew his disability made it next to impossible for him to go alone. Hence, a helper. A trustworthy person with a strong back who could keep a confidence. And who was more trustworthy than a man of God? Now Wolf was insinuating that he had a "proposition" for Zach. The old fire-breather probably even thought it was *his* idea! For Zach Madison, life was good, and nothing, not even his first view of this dusty, godforsaken little town, could spoil his ebullient mood.

"We'll just step in and say howdy to Robert," Wolf said, puffing as he levered himself carefully down from the buggy.

Zach would rather have spent time figuring out just where he and Beth Ann would do it. Her bedroom? His? Perhaps there was a soft pile of hay in the barn. He'd always enjoyed a romp since the day the stableman's oldest daughter had cornered him and shown him the difference between boys and girls. Instead, he nodded easily to Wolf and gestured for Beth Ann to follow her father up the boardwalk into the bank. As he headed after them, he gave Destiny a cursory glance.

It wasn't much of a town as towns went, just a single dust-covered street wide enough to turn a wagon and team between two rows of tan adobe buildings with overhanging shed porches and warped boardwalks. During the brief early summer rains the rutted thoroughfare would become a morass of mud. Here and there, a sad-looking yucca plant poked its pointed spines toward the sky, the stem of white, bell-like blossoms stained by a coat of red grit. In the stifling heat of midafternoon the only evidence of activity was one

other rig, a few bored horses tied to a hitching rail,
and a couple of Mexican peons drowsing under
their sombreros in the shade of an alley.

The more prosperous establishments announced their success behind wooden facades attached to the fronts of their adobe structures.
Zach noticed a few signs with highly embellished lettering: Lamb's Merchant Tailors;
Mullett & Hellar, Wagon-makers and Black-
smiths; Harry Campbell, Barbering; D. B. Hardy,
General Merchandise. There was one saloon, a
mortuary parlor, the sheriff's office and jail, and
a druggist. The Destiny Savings Bank was the
sole building in town built of brick. It was the
only thing that looked out of place to Zach.

Inside the bank, Robert Barlings left a private office and came around the walled tellers' cage
through a gate in the waist-high divider to greet
them. A large walk-in vault that would have been
the pride of any big-city bank stood open behind
an iron grille. Zach had an impression of highly
varnished oak and vast amounts of brass trim before the banker claimed his attention.

"Wolf. Reverend Temple. Miss Beth Ann." Hastily discarding a half-smoked cigar, Barlings shook
hands with the men and nodded to Beth Ann.
"Good to see you all. What brings you to town?"

"Just been showing the reverend here our
church," Wolf boomed, leaning on his cane.

"And what did you think of our edifice?" the
banker asked. The light reflecting off his spectacles
made his expression hard to read.

"The love and care for the Lord's work is truly
apparent in this town." *If you like crude adobe huts
with hard benches and no ventilation*, Zach thought.
He'd seen more welcoming rooms inside the Terri-

torial Prison. "You have a right to be proud of your accomplishments, sir."

During this exchange the other bank patrons, an older matron and two men, looked up from their business transactions. They noticed Beth Ann almost simultaneously. The woman gave an audible sniff and turned her back, then dragged the man who was obviously her husband around, too. The other man was a clerk of some sort with elastic bands on his sleeves. On his way out the door, he sent Wolf a swift look to make certain his attention was engaged, then gave Beth Ann a highly suggestive leer. She looked elsewhere and didn't seem to notice. Zach was certain she had and frowned to himself.

"You'll have to come out to Traveler's Rest soon, Robert," Wolf said. "Got a nice filly out of that black of yours. You ought to take a look at her."

"Thanks, perhaps Bobby and I will ride out there in a day or two." Barlings smiled at Beth Ann and patted his paunch. "Especially if you'll promise us another piece of that fine apple pie of yours, Miss Beth Ann."

"You're always very welcome, sir," she replied. Her voice was quiet, though a bit strained, and her cheeks were almost as pale as the crisp white shirtwaist she wore with a muted brown and gold plaid skirt.

The matron at the counter stuffed a wad of papers into her drawstring reticule and announced in a strident voice to no one in particular, "It's a fine how-do-you-do when decent folk can't conduct their business for all the trash on the streets. Come along, Harold. I need some air."

Harold dutifully trotted after his wife, who sailed out of the bank like a ship under full steam.

Beth Ann appeared engrossed in the brass trim of the waist-high room divider.

"Look here, Reverend," Wolf said, "I gotta talk me some business with the banker. I'd be obliged if you'd take Beth Ann to the general store."

Beth Ann looked up from her inspection of the woodwork with a flicker of alarm in her grey eyes. "I'd just as soon wait in the buggy until you're done, Paw."

"I got better things to do than jaw with Douglas Hardy over the price of baking powder and coffee, gal. You get them chores done so's I don't have to be bothered, y'hear?"

"I'll be glad to escort you, Miss Linder," Zach interjected with an engaging smile. "You can show me some of the town as well."

"Do what I tell you, gal." Wolf hobbled toward Barlings's office. "Me and Robert got some things to do."

Behind the brim of her bonnet, Beth Ann's expression showed her reluctance, then her mouth firmed in that customary mixture of courage and resignation that Zach admired, and she nodded. "Yes, Paw."

Zach held the door for her as they left the bank, offering his arm in a courtly manner.

"Better not, preacher," Beth Ann muttered, lifting her hems clear of the dust as she stepped into the street. "It's going to ruffle enough feathers, your being seen anywhere near my vicinity."

Zach paused just long enough to admire the turn of her shapely ankles encased in button-up shoes, then he caught up with her and slipped her hand through the crook of his arm. "Why don't you let me worry about that?"

She cast him a look that called him a fool, then

shrugged. "Suit yourself. But don't say I didn't warn you."

When she looked at him with that full lower lip in such an irresistible pout, Zach didn't care what anyone thought. Arm in arm, they crossed the street, then mounted the steps and entered Hardy's General Merchandise.

After the brilliant outdoors, the high-ceilinged mercantile was cool and dim, floating dust motes visible in the shafts of afternoon sunlight pouring in past the window displays of garden tools, leather goods, and sewing supplies. A few desultory shoppers wandered between tables laden with goods. Redolent with coffee and saddle soap and musty sacks of seeds, filled to capacity with every article a rancher or cowboy might need, the store seemed as magical as Aladdin's cave. Rows of glass jars filled with brightly colored candies sat on the long wooden counter at the rear of the store. The array of striped peppermints, multicolored sour balls, and black and red licorice whips was more fascinating than any jeweled treasures to a trio of wide-eyed children clutching their harried mother's skirt as she paid the young blond woman behind the counter.

"My idea of Christmas," Zach said, nodding at the row of jars.

"Theirs, too." Beth Ann smiled at the towheaded children and the candy, her gaze lingering on one particular item. Remembering her chores, she disengaged her arm and removed a penciled list from her pocket. "I need to look for a few things."

"Fine. I'll just poke around until you're done."

Zach watched Beth Ann wander off to inspect the stacks of tin washtubs and cast-iron griddles. She was all business until she reached the dry goods section, then her indifference deserted her and her fingertips lingered on the bolts of rainbow-colored fabric—calico, serge, jean, even a few silks and satins—with both appreciation and avarice. A tempting millinery confection of veiling and feathers and robin's-egg blue satin ribbons sat on a display stand. Zach saw Beth Ann hesitate, lift a hand to touch the delicate webbing, then draw back before she made contact, as if she weren't good enough even to covet such a ladylike creation.

Zach's jaw tightened. There hadn't been enough pretty things in Beth Ann's life, but he could change that. Once she was his, he'd see she had all the ribbons and feminine, silky things a woman like her should have. Whatever her heart desired. He smiled and headed toward the counter. Including him.

Beth Ann was still staring at the fetching little bonnet when he walked up to her a moment later. "Why don't you try it on?"

She jumped guiltily, and her cheeks flushed scarlet. "Don't be absurd."

"It's awfully pretty."

She heaved a tiny, regretful sigh and turned away. "Yes. Not for me, though."

Zach unwrapped a piece of paper and offered her a red licorice whip. She hesitated, slanted him a tiny smile of pure puzzlement, then accepted a strand. "It's my favorite. How did you know?"

He quirked an eyebrow at her. "Divine revelation?"

Beth Ann frowned at that bit of irreverence, then pursed her lips around the thin string of red candy, sucking gently at the sweet in a manner that made Zach's mouth go dry and the blood throb in his loins. He had visions of his tongue questing within her mouth, lapping up the flavor that was certain to linger there.

Then she bit off the string and broke the spell. Chewing happily, she smiled again at Zach, revealing the brief flash of dimple he found so delightful. "Thanks."

"Take it all." He pressed the paper bundle into her hand, curling her fingers around the package when she tried to protest. "No, take it. I bought it for you."

Beth Ann's cheeks flushed with pleasure and embarrassment and confusion. She bit her lip, and Zach thought he'd go insane. Jesus, he had to get her alone and soon, before he totally lost control of himself and jumped her like a randy youth.

"Well, thank you again," she said awkwardly. Taking a little breath that reassured Zach she wasn't totally unaffected by him either, she turned and pulled a bolt of fabric from a shelf. "I'm going to get this for a new dress for Ama. She wanted something bright. What do you think?"

Zach ran a finger over the red sprigged calico. "What woman wouldn't love it? I'll carry it to the counter."

"Don't strain your shoulder!"

Zach looked at Beth Ann from beneath his lashes and said in a drawl only she could hear, "Maybe I want you to kiss me better again."

"Oh!" Gulping, her face ablaze, Beth Ann gathered up the bolt herself and hurried toward the counter, with Zach's soft chuckles trilling along her overstretched nerves. She was supremely conscious that he followed her, so unnerved that she practically flung the bolt onto the counter. She came up short when she found herself face-to-face with an astounded and chagrined Kitty Hardy.

Beth Ann swallowed hard around the lump of

pain that materialized in the center of her chest.
"Hello, Kitty."

Kitty touched her blond curls nervously, then
self-consciously smoothed her starched apron.
"Er—could I help you, Miss Linder?"

Beth Ann winced. Kitty's schoolyard friendship
had evaporated, and with sufficient cause, Beth
Ann admitted, but it still hurt to be treated as a
stranger with a loathsome disease. It was especially galling, knowing that the preacher stood right
behind her. Beth Ann laid her list on the counter
beside the calico.

"I'd like twelve yards, please, and the rest of the
items here."

"Certainly." Kitty's blue eyes wouldn't meet
Beth Ann's gaze, but she measured off the yardage
and cut it with her scissors. Her plump hands faltered as she gathered up the material to fold, and
her regard flicked from Beth Ann's face to the man
behind her and back again.

Zach nodded in recognition, his expression
guarded. "Mrs. Hardy."

Kitty flashed him a strained smile, then turned
back to her former friend. "Uh, Beth Ann?"

Beth Ann's lips parted, and she regarded her
old chum with surprise and even a bit of hope.
"Yes?"

"About the other day . . ."

"Katherine!" Douglas Hardy, a tall, lanky man
with thin sandy hair and a bookkeeper's perpetual
stoop, appeared at his wife's side. He grabbed her
by the arm and propelled her from behind the
counter. "You're needed in the back."

"But, Douglas—" Kitty stumbled as he pushed
her toward the rear of the store.

Douglas Hardy spoke through clenched teeth.

"Go on, my dear. You've been on your feet too long. I'll help this . . . customer."

The way he said the word made Beth Ann feel tainted. Kitty cast Beth Ann a helpless look, then disappeared through a doorway in the back. Several other shoppers, including Harold and his matronly spouse, who'd exchanged banking for marketing, gravitated to within earshot of the curious commotion at the counter.

Beth Ann felt the sweat pop out on her temples. She hated being the center of attention, and the way Douglas had hustled Kitty out of the picture made it clear he feared his virtuous wife was in danger of being tempted into a life of depravity by Beth Ann's mere presence. All she wanted was to conclude her business and leave as quickly as possible. But to her surprise, Zach took that moment to step up and introduce himself to the proprietor.

"Mr. Hardy, I presume? I'm Reverend Temple."

Douglas Hardy inspected Zach while darting little glances at Beth Ann, confused as to the connection. However, he couldn't ignore the hand Zach extended. He took it, mumbling, "Please to meet you."

"Same here." Zach grinned. "I just wanted to thank your lovely wife for calling the other day at the Linders' place."

"Kitty . . . er, had pressing duties elsewhere," Hardy said stiffly. "I'll relay your message, though. I felt it was . . . appropriate that she accompany Mrs. Cunningham."

"Ah." Zach nodded. Though his manner was easy, almost jovial, his lids were hooded, his turquoise eyes narrowed like a stalking cat's. "Your idea, then? Well, I appreciate your interest. I'm quite sound again, as you see, and able to fend for myself."

The preacher's chitchat and the growing crowd unnerved Beth Ann. She began to feel suffocated with the need to flee. "Could I have the rest of these supplies, please?"

Douglas Hardy looked down his nose at her as if she were a cockroach who'd dared scamper through his sugar barrel. Snatching up her list, he filled the order for coffee, salt pork, flour, and nutmeg and tied the staples into a brown-paper bundle with a grim swiftness that revealed his eagerness to be rid of her. Beth Ann was just as eager to go. She produced the coins and bills Wolf had grudgingly provided from the till, then hurriedly began to fold the red calico—anything to help end this uncomfortable situation without losing face with an all-out retreat.

When Hardy at last pushed the bundle of groceries toward her, he had a hard look on his narrow face. "I'll ask you not to come in here again."

The other shoppers couldn't help but overhear his warning, and Beth Ann flushed, folding the calico with an irritated snap. "My money's as good as the next person's, Dougie."

His face darkened at her impertinence. "Your presence disrupts my customers. Send your father next time. And stay away from my wife. She doesn't want to see you."

Seething, Beth Ann asked too sweetly, "Then why doesn't she tell me that herself? Or did Kitty lose her voice as well as a mind of her own when she married a jackass?"

"Why, you—" Douglas Hardy spluttered in indignation.

"Give Kitty my love, will you, Dougie? And don't worry, I wouldn't come back to this filthy, low-class, vermin-infested hole in the wall for all the gold in California!"

With the paper bundle under one arm and the bundle of fabric under the other, Beth Ann turned and passed through the little crowd of onlookers like Moses parting the Red Sea, chin up and imperious. Harold's wife's shrill, outraged voice jangled the rafters.

"Lookit what that scarlet woman's done bought herself! That's right, you hussy! Wear that red dress so's decent folk'll know you for your true colors!"

Beth Ann froze in midstride, then turned and said in an icy voice, "Madam, if I had a nose as long and ugly as yours, I'd try to keep it out of other people's business."

"Well!" Snickers and snorts of laughter exploded from the other shoppers, and the woman puffed like a bullfrog. "Harold, did you hear that? Do something! Harold?"

Beth Ann stalked away, her arms full and her back ramrod-stiff, refusing to run in front of these gawkers. By God, she wouldn't give them the satisfaction!

"Let me help you with that." Zach was before her at the entrance, opening the door and reaching for her bundle.

She jerked away. "I can take care of myself!"

"So I see."

All the same, Zach followed her outside, pulling the door shut behind them without so much as a rattle of the glass. He took the heavy bundle of groceries from her despite her protests. Clutching the calico to her chest, her cheeks nearly as red as the fabric, Beth Ann angled her chin up another notch in disdain.

"So many *good, charitable* Christians here in Destiny, aren't there, Reverend?"

Zach frowned. "You can't let that bother you—"

"Miss Beth Ann, wait!" Bobby Barlings's glad shout interrupted Zach. The boy hurled himself down the boardwalk at them, looking for all the world like an exuberant puppy. His light brown hair flopping into his face, he skidded to a halt in front of Beth Ann, his changeable hazel eyes bright with bashful pleasure. "Papa told me you were in town."

"Hello, Bobby." Beth Ann smiled as best she could with the thump of hurt feelings and dashed hopes beating behind her eyes in the beginnings of a headache.

"You look pretty." Bobby scuffed his foot and grinned from behind the childish fringe of hair. "I'm glad you're here. Did you buy something? What ya doin' now? We've got new kittens at my house. I love baby things, don't you?"

Beth Ann couldn't help but smile a little. "Of course. My Nellie had a little filly the other day, the daughter of your big black, and she's beautiful."

"No foolin'? That makes her partly mine, doesn't it? Can I come see? Please?" Bobby looked at Beth Ann with appeal and naked adoration shining in his eyes. "You're the only girl I know who likes the same things I do."

Though in some ways Bobby was a balm to her wounded sensibilities, Beth Ann couldn't deal with the poor boy's overwhelming adulation at that moment. The painful and petty humiliations of this visit to town made it hard to keep her stoical facade intact. She needed a respite, an escape from everything and everyone—the preacher included—and she felt so raw than anything more than gently deflecting Bobby's attentions was beyond her. As a desperate diversion, she held out the small paper-wrapped package.

"Look, Bobby, licorice. Would you like this?"

His eyes got big. "Would I? Yeah!" Then he frowned. "Don't you want it anymore?"

Beth Ann looked away. "I've lost my taste for it."

"Well, gee. Thanks!" Bobby bit off a string and smacked appreciatively.

But the young man's childish gratitude couldn't erase the hostility of Destiny's "decent" townsfolk, nor the pain that clogged Beth Ann's throat along with the dust raised by a familiar train of bullocks crossing the street at the other end of town. Feeling trapped and suffocated, Beth Ann knew she'd had all she could take of Destiny for one day.

Impulsively she pushed the calico into Bobby's arms. "I've got to go. Will you help Reverend Temple carry my purchases to Paw's buggy?"

"Sure. I guess." Bobby looked disappointed and uncertain.

"Thank you. You're a dear." She touched the young man's cheek, restoring his doting expression.

Befuddled, his arms full of groceries, Zach scowled. "Wait a minute! Go where?"

"None of your business, preacher." She set off down the street.

"Now, see here! I told your paw I'd look after you."

Beth Ann glared at him over her shoulder. "So you're going to follow me into the privy?"

Zach's face went crimson. "Oh. Beg your pardon."

"I don't need anyone to look out for me, and

I'm not in the mood for company—especially yours. Just watch my packages and see that Bobby gets back to the bank. I'll find my own way home."

"Beth Ann, wait! What the hell—dammit!"

Ignoring the preacher's lapse into profanity, Beth Ann hurried down the street, then took a shortcut through an alley and began to run, her feet pounding on the hard-packed dirt until she came to the road leading toward Traveler's Rest.

Breathing hard, she twisted her mouth in a wry grimace. She took full responsibility for Zach losing his religion so regularly these days. It was downright depressing to realize one was so wicked and provoking that not even a man of God could keep to the straight and narrow with her around! And as for that kiss this morning . . . she couldn't even think about that! Lord, maybe she was Eve reincarnated. Today's experiences only confirmed what she'd known for a long time—she had to escape Destiny's narrow-mindedness, Paw's indifference, and her own wayward impulses before she became just what they expected, and she had to do it soon! At least she had one friend she could turn to.

"Whiskey Jean, wait up!" Grasping for breath, Beth Ann waved and hollered until the gnarled bullwhacker heard her above the bellowing of the oxen.

"Land's sake, child!" Beneath the broad brim of her battered sombrero, Jean's lined face showed her surprise. "What cloud did you drop out of?"

"Just seeing if you were heading my way." Still trying to catch her breath, Beth Ann grinned at the empty blue sky, shrugged, then fell into step beside the older woman as the tan abode buildings

of Destiny vanished behind them in the dust
clouds kicked up by the bullocks' hooves. The rutted track led through barren country dotted with
yucca, sagebrush, prickly pear, and little else,
while to the north, the rusty foothills and purple
peaks of the Superstition Mountains rolled into the
distance. "Mind if I walk along as far as Traveler's
Rest?"

"Course not." Jean cracked her whip over the
animal's backs. "Been to town, have you?"

"And seen all the 'respectability' I want to,"
Beth Ann agreed dryly.

"Yup." Jean dug in a voluminous pocket of her
long duster coat, pulled out a plug of tobacco, and
cut herself a "chaw" with a wicked-looking hunt-
ing knife she retrieved from another pocket. Tuck-
ing the wad of tobacco into the side of her cheek,
she regarded Beth Ann from under her puff of
frowsy, mouse-colored hair. "Civilization can be
downright wearing at times."

"You said it." Beth Ann's bonnet had fallen
down her back after her wild run, and she lifted
her heavy braid off her damp neck to catch a
breath of coolness. Skipping a little to keep up
with the taller woman's longer, distance-eating
strides, she blew out a shaky breath. "You've got
to help me get out of this town—out of this
country—before I do something desperate."

Whiskey Jean's expression remained placid. "Finally decided, have you?"

"Yes."

"Honey, I ain't got much, but whatever I have is
yours."

"Oh, Jean, thank you." Beth Ann's lower lip
trembled and tears prickled her lids at Jean's instant and unconditional response. "But you don't
have to do anything like that. I have a plan. I just

need to find a buyer for Nellie's filly without Paw's meddling around and spoiling things."

"If she's as fine as the rest of Nellie's foals, that won't be no problem."

"Oh, she is! I called her Hope, and she's the prettiest one ever. Robert Barlings's black stallion is her sire, you know. But I can't wait the five or six months it will take until she's weaned to sell her. Do you think there might be somebody willing to take the both of them?"

"You mean to sell Nellie, too?" That appalling thought did shock Whiskey Jean.

It hadn't been in Beth Ann's plans, but after today there was a new urgency within her. Somewhere over the horizon a storm was brewing, and she had to act quickly or she would be caught in the path of its destruction. As badly as she hated it, she knew she would sacrifice Nellie if necessary. Perhaps Eleanor Linder had foreseen her daughter's need with that long-ago gift. The thought gave Beth Ann a feeling of kinship with her mother that hadn't been there before. But there were other alternatives to selling Nellie that Beth Ann intended to explore first. She shook her head.

"I'm not going to leave Nellie at Traveler's Rest if I can help it, but no, I'd prefer to find a buyer for the filly who will board Nellie until the foal is weaned. By that time, I should be settled somewhere, and maybe I can send for her somehow."

"And where will you be?"

"California. San Francisco maybe. The hotels need cooks, and I've always wanted to learn fancy stuff from a real chef. I mean, I can do plain food just fine, but this is a chance to make a real career and find my independence—like you have. I guess it doesn't really matter where I end up, though."

"It might."

Marching beside the bull train, eyes straight ahead to the future, Beth Ann considered, then shook her head. "Not really. Just as long as it's somewhere I can forget about Tom and . . . and everybody in Destiny. Except you, of course."

"O'course." Whiskey Jean spit a stream of brown tobacco juice into the brush with such force, she flushed a sage hen. "I imagine there's a rancher or two along my route who might be interested in adding a blooded filly to their breeding stock and wouldn't mind the mama coming along for a while."

"That would be wonderful. I'll take whatever you think is a fair price."

"Don't worry, honey. Whiskey Jean is an old horse trader from way back." The older woman winked. "Shouldn't take long. I'll let you know as soon as I get something settled, all right?"

Relief left Beth Ann weak, and the thought of finally taking hold of her future made her knees shake. "F-Fine."

"You look plum tuckered out. Climb up on old Bullet there and ride a spell."

Taking Jean up on the offer, Beth Ann tucked up her skirts, then, using the harness for help, scrambled up on the lumbering animal's back to ride astride. She made an outlandish picture, her slim, stocking-clad calves showing all the way to the garters at her knees, hair falling out of her braid, singing the bawdy songs Whiskey Jean had taught her over the years until they reached Traveler's Rest.

"I gotta make a few more miles before sundown," the amazon said. "Tell Buck I said 'hey,' will you?"

"Sure will." Beth Ann gave Whiskey Jean a grateful hug. "Take care, and thanks."

"Anytime, gal. You start packing. I'll be in touch real soon."

Beth Ann waved her on her way, then headed for the house feeling better than she had in ages. Ama's giggly reaction to Beth Ann's dusty, sticky, disheveled state, however, convinced her that she'd be better off presenting a clean and tidy appearance before she had to face her paw's wrath for her rash desertion in town. Informing Ama, Beth Ann gathered up her rose soap, towels, and fresh clothes, then hurried down the embankment behind the house, through the cottonwood grove, and over a low, gravelly cliff to the secluded pool that was her special favorite.

The pool was nearly an oxbow of the river, but no more than thirty feet across and framed on all sides by concealing gravel cliffs and a curtain of willows. At times the water was waist-deep, sometimes no more than inches, but it always ran slow and clear so that you could see the multicolored pebbles dotting the sandy bottom. In her more adventurous younger days, Beth Ann had loved to swim naked here, relishing the freedom from the constrictions of clothing as well as the sense of wickedness and the sensual, hedonistic pleasure of water and sunshine on bare skin.

With a sigh for days past, she put that out of her mind, knowing that her mission at the pool today was to get cleaned up as quickly as possible. She undid her braid, stripped down to her shimmy and knee-length drawers, then waded out into the middle of the deliciously cool water and sat down to wash the grit out of her hair. Lathering herself thoroughly, she washed her body and underthings at the same time, paying scarce mind to the fact that the thin, wet cotton of her garments was all but translucent in the late afternoon sunshine. Then she floated on her back and thought about Zach Temple.

Now that she had made the decision to leave Traveler's Rest as soon as the filly was sold, she could be a bit more objective about her obsession with the preacher. It was simply that she led such an isolated life that she was so susceptible to his masculinity, she decided. Just because she found the shape of Zach Temple's jaw breathtaking, and the flex of muscles across his back so stunning they left her weak-kneed, didn't mean the preacher was any more able or willing to provide the things every woman dreamed of—home, husband, family—than Tom had been. All it meant was that she needed to expand her horizons and meet some amicable men whose prejudice against her checkered past wouldn't prevent them from finding out that she was basically a very nice person.

Yes, that was it. As soon as she put some distance between herself and the preacher, she'd get over this peculiar trembling in the stomach every time he looked at her. In fact, she was positive that within mere days she wouldn't even remember the incredible color of his eyes. It was a matter of perspective, after all, and as soon as the filly sold, Beth Ann would be able to afford some of that underrated commodity.

Beth Ann took a deep breath, sat up, and began to wring the water out of her hair. A slide of pebbles rattled somewhere close by, and she froze like a doe scenting danger. Though the pool was secluded, it was near enough to Traveler's Rest that they'd never been really worried about Apache raiders—but there was always a first time. Every muscle tense, Beth Ann felt around the rocky bottom until she found a fist-sized stone, then carefully eased herself toward shore.

The warm air on her water-cooled skin made her shiver. Every nerve ending tingled with alarm. Making no sudden movements, she picked her way toward the pile of clothes she'd left on a dry rock. Water streaming, she scooped her clothes up with one arm and continued up the embankment as though completely oblivious. Another rustle in the underbrush made her freeze again, and she felt eyes burning into her back. Pivoting slowly, she scanned the thicket.

A large, black-tailed jackrabbit stood on its haunches, calmly nibbling willow shoots and inspecting her with huge, solemn eyes. Beth Ann laughed, giddy with thankfulness and annoyed at her own jittery nerves. The sound startled the jackrabbit, who bounced once and disappeared into the undergrowth, and she laughed again.

Out of nowhere, hard hands grabbed Beth Ann from behind. Shrieking, she instinctively swung around and slammed the rock she clutched into her assailant's head. He howled and ducked, and the awkward movement sent them tumbling together down the sandy embankment, rolling over and over until they landed in a tangled heap at the river's edge. Beth Ann struggled frantically, the harsh breaths of two winded people rasping in her ears. Hands grasped her wrists and pushed her onto her back.

"Dammit, will you *quit!*"

"Zach!" She stared up into his angry face, his cheekbone marked with a streak of blood where the rock had grazed him. Beth Ann went limp with relief, then rigid with outrage. "You—you bastard! You scared me to death! What do you think you're doing?"

Turquoise eyes burning, Zach bared his teeth in a wolfish grin and deliberately cupped her breast. "What do you think?"

Chapter 7

Shock made Beth Ann's eyes shine like pools of molten silver, and she gasped aloud at Zach's words. He took full advantage of those parted lips, covering them with his mouth, probing the sweet recesses within with his tongue in a rapacious plundering that set his blood to singing. As good as he'd imagined it would be, this was better.

She was all but naked in his arms, her flesh cool and silky from the water, the buds of her puckered nipples showing dusky through her translucent shimmy. The crest of the breast he held poked against his palm in a manner so erotic, he went nearly mad with wanting. Groaning, he deepened the kiss even more, as if he had to devour her very being or die deprived of her sweetness. Running his large hand over the lush contours of breast, waist, and hip, he tortured himself with the lithe feel of her.

Beth Ann arched and shivered, pushing at his shoulders, and he insinuated his knee between her thighs, pinning her down on the sandy strand with his weight, going light-headed with the sensation of her pressed tightly against his tumescent manhood. Lifting his head at last, he trailed hot, openmouthed kisses across her jaw and down her neck, inhaling her scent and inciting himself to riot.

"Zach." She panted for breath. "What . . . ? Oh, please—"

"Anything, angel. Anything you want." He groaned into the fragrant hollow of her shoulder.

"I don't understand . . ." she wailed softly.

"Why did you run off like that?" He bit her collarbone just hard enough for her to feel the edge of his teeth, then laved the place with his tongue and felt her quake uncontrollably. "You were upset. Didn't you know I'd worry?"

"No. Yes. Why?"

"After this morning, you know why," he growled, pushing the swell of her breast upward, then lowering his head to flick the budded tip through the thin fabric with his tongue. She went wild, writhing and moaning, little choking sounds catching in her throat that drove Zach ever closer toward the brink of insanity.

"I didn't mean to hit you," she cried in a panicked voice. "You frightened me. I thought you were an Apache."

"Again? This confusion of yours continues to astound me." He turned his attention to her other breast. "Am I that much a savage?"

"Oh, God, stop! How can you be so cruel? I know you're just punishing me again," she accused tearfully.

Surprising the little hellion to teach her a lesson about caution might have been Zach's original intention, but the fact was, watching her play the mermaid from behind the willow fronds had driven him so nearly berserk that he'd all but forgotten why he'd followed her to this secluded pool. The way those thin garments clung to her womanly curves was more tantalizing than blatant nudity. The shadowy triangle between her legs, the rounded fullness of her buttocks, the fascinating tilt of her bosom—everything about her enticed him past all prudence.

Half-hypnotized with need, he'd known only that he had to hold her, and her startled reaction had surprised him as much as it had her. He should have known he'd pay a price for his audacity, but he'd never expected her to wallop the hell out of him with a goddammed rock! She surely deserved a beating, but did she honestly think that's what she was getting?

He threaded his fingers through the ebony silk of her hair, holding her face between his palms, his mouth hovering over hers. "Does this feel like punishment?" he demanded roughly.

"I don't know what you want from me!"

"Don't you?"

Her eyes grew round; the gray irises dilated. "No. You can't. You're a preacher."

He closed his eyes and groaned. "Don't remind me."

"But—"

"I'm no different than other men, whatever my ... calling, honey. I can be tempted." His hands tightened, and he feathered kisses over her dark lashes, the tip of her nose, the enticing arch of her upper lip. "Yea, beloved, you tempt me mightily."

She gulped, squirming on the damp sand, her fingers digging into his forearms in frantic strength. "Zach, this isn't ... We shouldn't ..."

"Sin? I'm not so sure what sin is anymore. All I know is that I want to touch you all over. I want to be inside you so deep I can feel your heart beat. I want you to wrap those lovely legs around me and let me feel you come. And then I want to bury myself in your softness until the universe shakes apart around us and time stops. That's how much you tempt me."

Beth Ann's breathing had faltered and stopped during this husky, carnal recitation, and now her breath leaked out in a shaky sigh that was part denial, part yearning.

"You want me, too, don't you, honey?" Zach whispered, his raspy breath hot in her hair, against her earlobe. "You feel it here."

He cupped her feminine mound through her thin drawers, and smiled to himself in triumph when she arched reflexively against his hand. Rubbing her intimately, he caught her high squeal of surprise within his mouth, sucking her tongue voraciously, coaching it past his lips, then twirling his own tongue around hers in an erotic joining that left them both frenzied with desire.

The fingers that had been pushing him away now tugged him closer. Zach sensed the tension within Beth Ann building to a passionate crescendo, and his stroking grew stronger, more rhythmic. His loins burned and throbbed, and he smiled against her lips and reached for his trouser buttons.

"All lies," she mumbled, breathless and melting. "It was all lies."

Alarm trickled through Zach's veins, freezing him. Was he found out? He asked a cautious question. "What is, honey?"

"The things I told myself." Dazed by passion, she gently caressed his grazed cheek in mute apology, then touched the rusty brown curls at his nape, and peppered tiny kisses along his jawbone. "That's why I had to get away. I ... I was tempted, too, but I thought it was because I've been alone so long. But it's not, Zach. You're the only one who makes me feel like this, so special, so wanted. You know who I am, and you still care."

Zach winced, and some of the muzzy haze of desire lifted from his mind.

The hell of it was, he did know her, and knew under all those prickles how truly vulnerable and soft she was. Hadn't he seen her valiance in the face of the town's censure today? Growing up nameless as he had, his own childhood had been fraught with similar incidents, and he knew how it felt. Hadn't he wanted to tell them all to go to the devil for her sake? Bedding Beth Ann Linder had seemed an imminently good idea when she meant nothing to him, but now that he knew her pluckiness and her courage firsthand, and had seen the hurt and loneliness she kept so close and revealed to so few, how could he use her simply to slake his own lust and then move on? She was like a cactus spine that had gotten under his skin and then worked its way straight into his heart.

Heart? Zach reined his tumbling thoughts to a screeching halt. *Whoa, partner! No woman gets to Zach Madison's heart.*

It was simply a matter of honor, Zach told himself. Beth Ann might not be a total innocent, but she was far from worldly-wise. His private code of conduct had never yet let him take unfair advantage of someone who simply had no chance of winning against his schemes.

Hell, Beth Ann had already lost—and she didn't even know it! What kind of snake's belly did that make him? Zach felt like a fool for suddenly developing a conscience at this late date, and his body was already screaming out in frustration at the very idea, but he knew he couldn't do it.

Not to Beth Ann.

Not to himself.

"Beth, honey," he croaked, reaching up to disentangle her hands from around his neck.

"Kiss me again, Zach," she murmured, soft and dreamy and pliant. "I like the way you do it."

Flame surged through his straining manhood at her innocent confession, and he ground his teeth around a groan of sheer pain. He had to get shut of this, and quick, or it would be too late for both of them!

"You ever been baptized, angel?" Slipping his arms under her knees and shoulders, he stood, lifting her high against his chest.

Her features soft with surrender, she blinked up at him, not understanding. "Uh-huh."

"Considering the state you're in, twice won't hurt." With a grunt, he heaved her into the pool.

She landed in a tremendous splash of flailing arms and legs, then came up spluttering and cursing, black hair streaming into her eyes. Humiliated, every vestige of passion dashed by the unexpected bath, she was a vindictive fury in transparent underthings.

"You low-down, conniving bastard! Puking, lizard-sucking coyote! Yellow-bellied buzzard!"

Standing on the riverbank with his hands on his hips, Zach threw back his head and laughed. "Watch your language, angel, or I'll have to dunk you again for good measure."

His laughter and his scorn infuriated her past endurance, and she shrieked and kicked water at him in a veritable torrent of aquatic and verbal abuse. "I'll make you pay, you dung-eating, hypocritical *preacher!*"

Zach sidestepped another wave and gave a pained grin. "Calm down. It was for your own good, honey."

"Me! I didn't start this! You're the one bustin' off his britches buttons! You invade my privacy and manhandle me, and you say it's *my* fault?" She screeched and searched the pool bottom for a projectile, then launched a good-sized rock in his direction. "Get out of my sight, damn you!"

The rock missed easily, but Zach's face tightened. "You'd better learn to control that temper. And next time, don't take off like a bat out of hell without weighing what can happen to an inconsiderate brat!"

With an inarticulate howl of rage, she reached for another rock, slipped, and sat down with a gigantic splash. Then she burst into furious tears. Zach took a step forward.

"Did you hurt yourself?"

Water lapping at her chest, she planted her elbows on her upraised knees and buried her face in her hands. "Why won't you let me alone?" she sobbed. "Go away. I hate you!"

Her words thrust through his chest with a peculiar sensation of pain, but he glowered at her ominously. "I trust you'll keep that thought in mind. It'll be safer for both of us."

She lifted her stormy face and glared at him through her tears. "Why don't you just *go?*"

Zach's jaw hardened. She didn't just mean leave the riverbank, and maybe she had a point. Gold or not, it looked as though he had worn out his welcome at Traveler's Rest.

"Maybe it is time, at that." He gave her a long look, then turned and began to climb the embankment. "Don't be too long, or I'll have to come looking for you again."

"Go to hell!"

Zach grimaced. "I'm doing my best."

He climbed through the stand of willows at the top of the cliff, walked a little way, then doubled back, squatting in the brush and listening to Beth Ann weep. The sound made him hurt inside. After what seemed a long while, when the light had gone purple with the settling dusk, she finally stopped crying. He heard her coming out of the water and gathering up her scattered clothing. Only when he was certain that she was safely headed back to Traveler's Rest did he move that way himself, his decision made.

Despite the swindling charges still hanging over his head from his visit to Prescott, he'd leave first thing in the morning. The only thing he had to do now was tell Wolf.

It wasn't that easy.

"Leaving?" Wolf said at the supper table that evening. "But, Reverend! What about my proposition? You could be a real help to me, if you would."

Zach cast a swift glance at Beth Ann sitting with her head bowed across the table, her tasty pan-fried veal dinner virtually untouched on her plate. She'd taken Wolf's loud chastisement with considerable calm when she'd returned from the river earlier, listening to him threaten to lock her in the windowless kitchen larder and bluster about courtesy and obedience without so much as a blink of her eye or a word of protest. Her subdued attitude had done much to conciliate Wolf's temper so that he was satisfied with a good tongue-lashing. But Zach knew it was their scuffle at the pool that had squashed Beth Ann's usually resilient disposition. For that, he was especially sorry.

On the other hand, greed was Zach's particular vice, so if Wolf was finally coming around, it wouldn't hurt to play out this hand, would it?

"Perhaps you'd better tell me just what you had in mind, Mr. Linder," Zach said, already thinking about pack mules and mining plats, and how he could convince Wolf he was trustworthy enough to learn the location of his glory holes.

"Well, it's like this, Reverend." Wolf leaned eagerly across the table, his long, bushy beard dripping into the gravy on his plate, a hectic light in his black button eyes. "I've got to make me a little trip."

"Oh." Zach nodded as if just understanding what that entailed. "You need an able-bodied man to assist you on your journey. Well, certainly. You've been so obliging here, like Ruth of old, I would be privileged to travel with you wherever—"

"No, no, no." Wolf waved his hands. "Me and Robert Barlings are going to Tucson to talk to some mining investors interested in developing the area around Destiny. I can handle an easy trip like that with no problem."

Zach scratched his head and gave Wolf a puzzled smile. "Well, then?"

"It's Beth Ann."

Her head popped up, and her expression was both wary and truculent. "What about me, Paw?"

Wolf ignored her. "You see, it's like this, Zachariah. I'll be gone four, maybe five days, and I don't rightly like to leave the girl here with only old Buck for protection, if you know what I mean."

Beth Ann drew a huffy breath. "I am perfectly capable of—"

"Shut your yap, gal!" Wolf gave Zach a toothy, ingratiating grin. "What I need is a chaperon to keep her in line. After that stunt of hers today, you can see why. So what do you say? I know it's an imposition, but will you stay on at Traveler's Rest, leastwise until I get back?"

Zach met Beth Ann's eyes across the table. One look at those glowing silver orbs told him she was still furious. Still fiery. Still utterly desirable.

He groaned inwardly. He'd made one noble sacrifice today already, dammit! How many more could he expect of himself? He certainly couldn't guarantee his forbearance if they were left here alone! All things considered, however, with Wolf out of the picture, maybe Zach could poke around in some of the older man's papers and get what he needed without having to toady up to the black-bearded buzzard anymore. Weighing options, Zach glanced at Beth Ann again and saw the defiant, angry challenge in her gaze. It was more than he could resist.

Wanting to grin, but knowing better, Zach turned to Wolf. "What I say, Mr. Linder, is you've got yourself a chaperon."

The next five days were the most intolerable Beth Ann ever endured in her life, five days in which she gleefully contemplated murder by poison, bludgeon, dagger, and garrote, reciting the merits of each method like a litany of prayers before bedtime each night. Although she took exception to the hard-line stance of some of His servants, if Beth Ann hadn't basically, deep-down believed in the existence of the Almighty and the possibility of eternal damnation, she would have cheerfully shot the Reverend Zach Temple's worthless hide so full of holes that he would have looked like a cabbage leaf after a hailstorm. God, she hated that man!

Beth Ann smacked the loaf of bread dough she was kneading on the kitchen table, then squeezed it with both hands as though it were Zach Temple's neck. The pale stuff oozed between her fingers in a most agreeable fashion. With malicious glee, she poked two eyes in the doughy mass, then smashed her fist right between them. The sensation was so satisfying, she did it again, punching and kneading furiously.

Plotting mayhem was some release to the roiling anger and humiliation that had consumed her over the past days, but it didn't do much for her bruised pride and battered self-esteem. That she'd succumbed so easily to Zach's lovemaking made her skin burn with shame. But his rejection was even worse. His playing on her needs just to prove her depravity was the most degrading experience of her life. Furthermore, it was beyond comprehension why a man who'd been as obviously aroused as Zach had been would deny himself the ultimate satisfaction—even if Beth Ann was grateful that he had. Maybe he loved manipulations and playing games. Maybe he was just plain mean—or crazy.

If only she never had to see Zach Temple's loathsome face again. This "chaperon" business of Paw's was the last straw! The only bright spot was that with Paw out of town, she'd been spared her Sunday ordeal, flatly refusing to attend church services in Destiny, and being faintly surprised that the preacher neither insisted nor attended himself, saying he preferred to meditate on God's majesty alone at sunrise. She thought in disgust that he was just taking his "watchdog" duties far too seriously.

Over the past days she'd avoided Zach by spending her time either in the kitchen, letting Ama and Buck serve the stage passengers, or in her room working at the loom. Since she wasn't sleeping much, she'd even finished the Eye of God blanket and begun another one. When she hadn't been able to avert a meeting, she'd been as frigid as an Arctic breeze. His dirty work done, Zach had exhibited no interest in conversation, either, for which she was profoundly grateful. So great was her chagrin, she couldn't have been held accountable for her actions if he'd uttered so much as a syllable of a sermon.

After dividing the bread dough, Beth Ann placed it in two loaf pans and set them in the warming oven to rise. She'd already baked four loaves in preparation of the midafternoon stage run, and a pot of venison stew simmered on the back of the stove to accompany the bread, smothered green beans, and a dried peach cobbler. She stepped to the kitchen door for a breath of coolness, frowning at the sound of bootheels pacing the porch planks over her head.

That damned preacher. He wasn't so pure and unstained himself, curse him. Hypocrite! She hoped he'd been wrestling with his demons those late nights when she'd heard him wandering the house. And she hoped the demons won.

A mental picture of Zach Temple roasting over Satan's coals for the sins of lust and cruelty made her smile. If she were a bit more sanguine about the situation, Beth Ann thought, she might even swallow her repugnance and anger long enough to offer the preacher more "temptation" in the form of her own person, just so she could have the pleasure of pushing him into perdition herself, then ruining him publicly. While she knew in her heart she was too cowardly to take any such cold-blooded action, she told herself she refrained from risking that kind of dangerous revenge because finally, thankfully, her deliverance was at hand.

Whiskey Jean had found a buyer for the filly.

Wiping her hands on her apron, Beth Ann slipped her fingers into her pocket, touching again for reassurance the folded letter that had come with the early morning stage. A rancher near Yuma was willing to take both Nellie and her foal for a fair price, and Beth Ann could ride with Jean the next trip she made in that direction. From there, she could take the stage to California. With some hard work and a little luck, she'd soon be learning culinary arts from a real chef, thus insuring her independence and her future. It was a giddy feeling, both frightening and wonderful, to know she was so close to a new life.

"Stage a-coming in, Miss Beth Ann." Buck shuffled around the corner of the kitchen with this announcement. "And unless my eyes are crossed, I think that's your paw's buggy right behind 'em."

Beth Ann puffed out a wry breath. She'd never anticipated a time when she'd welcome her father's return, but surely the preacher would leave Traveler's Rest now. Perhaps she'd have a few days of peace afterward to gather herself and prepare for an uncertain—if wished-for—future. But now she had not only Paw, but also a stage full of hungry passengers to see to.

The next few minutes were spent in a bustle of

confusion—stage passengers disembarking, the team being unhitched, Wolf bellowing for Buck, then stomping up the veranda to greet the preacher. Beth Ann scurried up and down the kitchen stairs with loaded trays and pots of food, then stayed so busy serving plates and pouring coffee that she could spare her paw no more than a cursory hello when he finally joined them.

"Behaved for you all right, did she?" Wolf asked Zach around a mouthful of venison stew.

"No problems at all." Perched on the window ledge, Zach watched Beth Ann blandly over the rim of a coffee cup.

She resented being discussed in such a fashion in front of strangers, not to mention Mr. Pritchard and a smirking Pat Tucker, but she held her peace. Mouth clamped tight in mulish silence, she dished up the peach cobbler and fresh heavy cream while Wolf gave everyone a lavish report of his trip to Tucson—the state of the roads, the miserable food, and the Indian raids being reported from up north.

Traveler's Rest had never suffered the bloodthirsty depredations of the roving Apache bands, but for the past year and a half, the hostiles had brought fear to many areas on Arizona with kidnappings, murder, and torture. Now Wolf reported that just ten days earlier, a group of citizens irate over the failure of the army to control the Indian assaults had taken the law into their own hands, massacring women and children at Camp Grant. Some weary settlers hailed the perpetrators as heroes, but the authorities were already demanding an investigation into this disgraceful episode that had set back the efforts of the federal Indian policy with a vengeance. And the Apaches, now more than ever, had cause to raise their war parties against their white enemy.

"So if you aim to head north, Pritchard," Wolf finished, "I recommend you take extra care to hang on to your scalp. Them savages will be looking to pay back every white man in the country now."

"That's why I have Pat along," Mr. Pritchard replied, tossing down his napkin. "You're a dead shot, ain't that right, Pat?"

"I usually hit what I'm aiming for," the greasy stage guard drawled, following Beth Ann with his eyes.

She stared back at him, refusing to let him see how uncomfortable his lecherous, oily glare made her. Finally Pat threw his napkin down, muttered something about visiting the privy, and left. Wolf's loud opinions eventually drove the passengers out to the veranda to smoke or talk among themselves while Pritchard checked the coach and made the rest of his preparations before departure.

Beth Ann began to clear the litter of dirty dishes. Wolf was describing yet again to Zach how he and Robert Barlings had impressed a group of important bankers and mine investors when she chanced to look up and caught a flash of a familiar sorrel mare through the front window. The stack of plates she held hit the table with a crash. Scowling, she hurried to peer through the glass pane, uneasiness making her overlook Zach's disturbing proximity. Buck, looking rather unhappy, bounced past the building atop his swayback gelding, hauling Nellie after him on a lead rope, the few foul frolicking behind.

"Where's Buck going with Nellie?" Beth Ann demanded. "And the filly! That lamebrain cowpoke!" Whipping off her apron, she lit for the door. "I'll have his worthless hide—"

"Leave him be, girl," Wolf rumbled, slurping the last of his cream and peaches. "I told him to take them into town."

Beth Ann stumbled to a halt on the threshold, her palms suddenly damp with apprehension. "You did *what*? Why?"

Unconcerned, Wolf wiped the back of his hairy hand across his mouth. "I sold the filly to Robert."

The earth dropped from beneath Beth Ann's feet, and she reeled back dizzily. "No! She's *mine*!"

"Bobby wanted her," Wolf said, as if that explained everything.

Beth Ann saw her careful plans disintegrating and her future vanishing before her stunned eyes. "You can't do this to me!"

Wolf shrugged. "The boy wanted the baby, and Robert made me such a good offer, I sold him the mama, too."

"Nooo!" With a frenzied cry, Beth Ann swept the pile of dirty dishes from the table. Food splattered and crockery shattered on the stone floor at Zach's feet. "Damn you, not Nellie, too!"

Wolf struggled up from his seat, his lap full of table scraps and assorted utensils, his face thunderous. "Cease this at once, you hellion!"

"Honey, take it easy. It's just a horse—" His expression alarmed, Zach caught Beth Ann's upper arm. She shook him off.

"You have no *right*!" Distraught, she took a step toward the door. "I have to stop Buck! Nellie was a gift from my *mother*—"

Wolf's hamlike palm lashed out in a stinging slap that knocked Beth Ann to the floor.

"Stop this at once. You're hysterical," he said coldly.

Zach made an inarticulate sound low in his throat and reached for her, but the venom in Beth Ann's silvery eyes froze him in his tracks. She looked up at the two men before her with equal loathing and contempt, condemning them as two of a kind with a single glance. Then, holding her cheek, she scrambled to her feet and rushed from the room.

"Hey! Come back here and clean up this mess!" Wolf bellowed after her.

Tears stinging her eyes, rage clogging her throat, her every hope stripped from her, Beth Ann sought the dubious sanctuary of her room, frenetic thoughts whirling in her paralyzed brain. What to do now? Should she go after Nellie? But why would Robert Barlings give her back the filly he'd bought and paid for? Distraught, she knew she couldn't stay here at Traveler's Rest another minute! She had to leave, but how? The obvious answer came like a flash of revelation.

She opened her dresser drawer, scooped up clothing, and stuffed it into a pillowcase. She added the little painted tin box that contained her life's treasures, the bits of cheap jewelry she'd collected and her few hoarded coins, tips for well-cooked meals that Wolf knew nothing about. It wasn't much, but it would have to do.

Checking outside to make certain no one was watching, she left her room, hurrying across the rear yard to the barn, where the fresh team stood hitched up in their harness ready to go. With Buck gone to deliver Nellie, it had taken a bit longer to change teams than usual, but in a matter of moments, Pritchard would pull the coach around front and load up his passengers again. Thank goodness she hadn't missed him. The clank of buckles and rustle of leather drew her inside the shadowy structure.

"Mr. Pritchard?" Beth Ann hurried into the central aisle, straining her eyes to see into the stalls lining both sides. The air was heavy with the smell of old manure and the dry hay stored in the loft. Golden bars of light poured through the cracks in the roof. A movement to the right caught her attention, and she breathed a sigh of relief as a man in a floppy hat came toward her.

"Mr. Pritchard, I've got to be on your stage today. I don't have much for the fare, but I'll do anything—"

"Now, that's right interesting, Bethy Ann," Pat Tucker drawled, stepping into a dusty beam of pale light. "Anything, you say?"

She caught her breath, unnerved by Pat's scraggly-bearded face and the lust—for vengeance—shining in his dark eyes. "Where's Mr. Pritchard?"

"You don't need him." Pat caught Beth Ann's wrist and swung her up hard against the barn wall, crowding her with the bulk of his rank-smelling body. "Talk to me sweet, and I'll be right accommodating."

"Let go of me, you swine!" she hissed.

"Come on now, sugar, you owe me, and you know it."

"I just need to ride the stage," she insisted, real fear creeping into her voice. "You'll be late. Mr. Pritchard will come looking—"

"What I want isn't going to take long, not with all the practice you've had." He grabbed her breast and rubbed his foul mouth across her cheek.

Panicking, Beth Ann knocked his hand away and tried to knee his groin. Growling like an ani-

mal, Pat squashed her with his weight against the
wall and ripped open her shirtwaist. Buttons flying everywhere, he brutally mashed his lips
against hers. Suffocated, repulsed, Beth Ann struggled wildly—and then suddenly he wasn't there
anymore.

To her amazement, it was Zach who snatched
Pat back by the collar. With an inarticulate growl,
the preacher smashed his fist into the startled ex-
pressman's face and sent him sprawling in the
hay-strewn dirt. Pat came up roaring, his nose
spurting blood. He hesitated when he saw who'd
so rudely interrupted his fun, then spat in the dirt.

"All right, preacher, let's see what you're made
of."

His first swing was wild, and Zach easily
sidestepped it, plowing a kidney blow into Pat's
side as he charged by. Pat recovered, and landed
a hard right jab to the side of Zach's face. Horrified, Beth Ann shrank against the wall while
they pummeled each other. She'd never imagined that Zach Temple, man of God, could look
so ruthless, so intent on death, and that frightened her even more that Pat's assault had. It
must have scared Pat, too.

Zach landed a blow that sent the bigger man
to his knees. Breathing hard, fists clenched and
poised, Zach hovered over the downed man, every aspect of his posture daring him to get up.

"You touch this lady again, and I'll kill you,"
Zach ground out. "You understand me, you son of
a bitch?"

Pat nodded. "Yeah."

"Then get the hell out of here."

Dragging himself up, Pat turned tail and ran.
Zach swung back to Beth Ann, and the look on his
face froze her against the wall. His eyes trailed

lower, and she looked down at herself in mute dismay, her blouse open, the creamy swell of her bosom rising and falling at the exposed top of her shimmy. Outside, harnesses rattled, and the familiar sounds of the coach pulling out of Traveler's Rest rent both the hot afternoon air and Beth Ann's future hopes.

Zach's voice was guttural. "Did he hurt you?"

Eyes closed, neck bowed, she shook her head.

Zach took an uncertain step toward the doorway. "I'll get your father."

"No." Her voice was infinitely weary. "He won't believe it. Or he'll say I asked for it. Everybody knows what kind of woman I am."

The strain in his face intensified, then he noticed the small bundled pillowcase lying in the dirt. "You were running away, weren't you? Over a horse, for God's sake! Are you crazy? Do you have any idea what can happen in this country to a woman alone?"

"It couldn't be worse than here." Her hand fluttered at her torn bodice, and her voice cracked. "I failed, anyway. That should make everyone happy."

Something gave way inside of Beth Ann then, and she slid soundlessly down the wall, crumpling with defeat, shaking uncontrollably. Zach kneeled down next to her, his hands hovering helplessly, as though he were afraid to touch her lest she shatter. Finally he hauled her into his arms, pressing her cheek into the curve of his shoulder, rocking her as though soothing a child.

"Bastards," he muttered. "We've all hurt you, haven't we?"

She couldn't answer. Nothing was left. Existing past this moment took more effort than she could muster, and she could only cling helplessly, hopelessly, to the rock that embraced and held her against his beating heart—Zach.

"Don't cry, angel," he whispered, though her eyes were still dry. "I'll take care of you."

And then she did begin to weep, because that sounded so beautiful, so perfect—and so utterly impossible.

Chapter 8

So much for his good intentions.

Zach had known better than to touch her again. Wasn't that why he'd kept his distance these past days? But a woman's tears got to him every time, and what else was a man expected to do in the face of female waterworks but hold on and hope for the best, even at the price of his own sanity?

The feel of Beth Ann shuddering in his arms tugged at his heart in ways too overwhelming to define. He was furious—at that bastard, Tucker, but also at Beth Ann for her headstrong foolishness . . . and what? Her attempt to leave *him?* Zach knew how irrational that sounded, but it was true all the same. But as she quivered against him, all he could really think of was how sweet she smelled and how much he wanted her, and how her tears were breaking his heart.

"Aw, come on, honey, don't," he begged, his own throat clogged with a suspicious thickness.

Looking around, he spied the open door into Buck's little lean-to room. Lifting Beth Ann from the hay-strewn floor, Zach carried her inside, kicking the door shut behind them. Still holding her, he sat down on the colorful striped blanket—some of Beth Ann's handiwork—that was neatly draped over the old cowpoke's narrow cot. Buck's extra clothes hung on pegs around the board walls, colored pictures from an old soap calendar were tacked in precise rows opposite the bed, and a cracked canning jar full of sage grass and wild-flowers sat in lonely splendor on an upended packing crate.

"You've got to stop, Beth," Zach urged in the helpless way of all menfolk faced with feminine tears. Stroking her dark hair back from her fore-head, he placed a soft kiss at her hairline. "You'll make yourself sick."

"Everyone would be better off if I died any-way," she said with an odd hiccuping sob.

"Don't say that!" He caught her chin in a hard grip and jerked her face up to his. His turquoise eyes held a fierce, burning light. "Don't even think it again!"

She blinked at his vehemence, but still the tears slid down her cheeks in silent defeat. "What dif-ference would it make to anyone?"

"Jesus, how can you ask such a dumb question? You're very special." Releasing her chin, he cocked a crooked grin at her. "Didn't I just take on Goli-ath to prove it?"

That provoked a watery smile in return.

"Yes, you made a very credible David." With a little sigh, she settled against his shoulder and pushed at the moisture trailing down her face with her fingertips. "I didn't know preachers were allowed in fistfights."

He toyed with the end of her braid. "Sure we are, on the side of right. The Bible's chock-full of all sorts or warriors. David and Joshua and such like."

Zach grinned to himself for pulling those names out of his hat. He'd vented his frustrations over the past days by studying the Bible for just such an occasion. To his wonder, he'd discovered some pretty interesting things between its covers—not just teachings, but poetry and songs and down-to-earth rules for getting along with folks. He'd also stumbled across some surprisingly racy stuff. Some of those old kings had led quite the life.

Beth Ann watched Zach, and now her hand timidly drifted up to examine the growing puffiness of his jaw where Pat's punches had landed. "Thank you for what you did. You're always getting hurt because of me."

"Believe me, I've had worse. I'm just glad I was here when you needed me." He cupped her hand against his cheek with his own, then turned it and dropped a kiss into her sensitive palm. He felt her instant tension, and a reciprocating chord vibrated deep within him. "What is it, angel?"

"Let me up," she said, suddenly breathless.

Zach frowned. "I'm not like that bastard Tucker. I won't hurt you."

"I know." And somehow she did. But the stunning failure of all her plans, even that pitiable attempt to run away, made her feel very raw and vulnerable, misdirected and so emotionally volatile, it was her own uncontrollable urges she feared. Blushing, she fell back on an old defense, one he had to acknowledge. "It's just not proper, that's all."

A warmth burned low in Zach's belly at the sight of the flush of desire spreading over her cheeks. She was as aware of him as he was of her. He grinned wickedly. "I always say homemade sin is the best kind."

She jackknifed to her feet. "Don't tease me!"

Zach pulled her back down, his arm supporting her neck, his other hand cupping her waist, and his smile turned rueful. "I don't mean to tease you, honey. It's just sometimes it's hard for me to say things."

Her eyes were huge and silvery with uncertainty. "What things?"

"Like how I wish you'd let me kiss you again."

Beth Ann swallowed, and her tongue flicked nervously over her lips. "You shouldn't talk like that. Ministers are supposed to set examples—"

"I'm not a saint yet," he said in an aggravated tone.

"But—"

Out of patience, he bent and kissed away her protests, feeling the tremulous quiver of her lips beneath his, inhaling the gentle sigh of her sweet breath. He tasted her skin, sipping the salty residue of her weeping, laving her cheekbones and the corner of her mouth with electrifying flicks of his tongue. When he lifted his head again, Beth Ann was heavy-lidded and dazed, her lower lip full and swollen and unconsciously inviting.

"Forget who I'm supposed to be," Zach said deeply. "I'm only a man with feelings and needs just like other men. From the minute I woke up and saw those angel eyes of yours, we've been spitting and sparring and circling like cats at howling time for one reason. *This.*"

Lifting his hand, he stroked her throat, then boldly caressed the swells of her breasts revealed by the ruined shirtwaist.

"Zach . . ." She shivered and moaned, clutching at the strong bones of his wrist, yet too powerless in her frailty to push him away. "You're confusing me!"

He pulled the ribbon from the end of her braid, combed his fingers through the springy strands, and reverently spread them over her shoulders like a cloak. "What we do to each other isn't unnatural, Beth. It's the way the Lord meant for men and women to find out how they feel about each other. You wouldn't respond to your 'friend' Pat this way."

She shuddered. "No!"

"Then tell me you like me, just a little."

"Yes." Helplessly, she couldn't deny what her traitorous body so readily proclaimed.

"And I like you, angel. A hell of a lot." He stroked her skin, caressing the fullness of her breasts through the tattered cloth, and whispered passionately into her ear. "Let Solomon say it for me. 'Behold, thou art fair, my beloved ... Thy navel is like a round goblet which wanteth not liquor: thy belly is like an heap of wheat set about with lilies. Thy two breasts are like two young roes ...'"

Consumed by the sensuality of Zach's words, Beth Ann was barely conscious of being pressed backward against Buck's thin mattress. Zach nuzzled her neck, his lips avid on her flesh, and she shivered and melted, liquid flooding her core in a sweet rush of desire the like of which she's never experienced.

Oh, my, yes! She did like this man! Despite his vocation and the maddening things he'd done, he touched her in ways no man ever had. She liked the way Zach laughed, with that devilish glint in his beautiful blue-green eyes, and the way his hair curled so beguilingly beneath her eager fingers. He was surprisingly worldly and skillful with his kisses, his tongue exploring hers, tickling the roof of her mouth, stealing all her breath. And when he touched her beneath her skirt, squeezing the tender flesh of her thighs, she thought she'd go wild, surging against his hard length and kissing him back with no thought for today, no care for the consequences of tomorrow.

Kissing Zach, clinging to his broad shoulders,

Beth Ann found him marvelous, tender, and vastly exciting, taking her past abandonment to joyous participation. He half covered her, his knee wedged between hers, precariously propped on the edge of the narrow cot, his attention undivided. There was no question of where this was leading, and she knew the marriage act would be no hardship with this man.

Beth Ann stiffened and her eyes flew open, the words of her unguarded thoughts echoing in her brain with the force of a miraculous revelation. It was clear from the way Zach Temple was presently kissing her senseless that he liked— *desired*— her as much as she did him. What if . . .?

No, it was too absurd!

Yet the idea, once germinated, blossomed full-blown: *What if she married the preacher?*

Gasping, she pulled her mouth away from Zach's, trying to marshall her muddled, outrageous thoughts. Zach merely transferred his attentions to her earlobe, breathing gustily against her neck while his hand tugged the folds of her skirt up past her knees.

Beth Ann had always heard that when the Lord closed a door, He opened a window. Maybe this was the solution she'd been searching for. If Zach was willing to rescue her from the likes of Pat Tucker, perhaps he could rescue her from life at Traveler's Rest as well! Marriage to someone as respectable as a minister would certainly restore her reputation, and she knew she could be a good wife, faithful and hardworking—if only Zach would wed her and take her away from Destiny so that she could prove it!

Hadn't it been Saint Paul who'd said it was "better to marry than to burn"? Well, the preacher had just gone up in flames, if Beth Ann was any judge, but to quench his fires by giving herself totally to him now would only prove that she wasn't worthy to be a wife. No, she'd had experience with that before and learned the hard way— consummation was reserved for the man who'd grace her hand with a gold band!

It was desperate. It was foolhardy. It was a definite long shot. But with no options left, it was the only plan Beth Ann had. She possessed something Zach definitely wanted, and if only she could defend what was left of her virtue long enough to make the preacher come up with a marriage license, it just might work. As unlikely as it seemed, the Reverend Zach Temple could turn out to be her salvation.

"Zach." She pushed at his shoulders.

"God, you're luscious." His voice was thick. "Come on, darlin'—"

Beth Ann's desperate, mighty shove threw Zach off balance, and he pitched over the side of the cot. He landed with a thud and a grunt on the hard-packed dirt floor. "What the hell!"

She sat up in a flash, hastily brushing her bunched skirts back down and pulling the ragged edges of her bodice together in a semblance of modesty. "Zach, please! We've got to stop."

Coming to a seated position on the floor, he looked up at her in mystification, his eyes slightly unfocused, as if she'd suddenly sprouted a pigtail and begun speaking Chinese. Then he shook his shaggy head as if to clear it. "Now, wait a minute, honey."

"It's just not right, not without the . . . sanctions of matrimony, and you know it, Zachariah Temple," she said hastily, unnerved by the heated light still lingering in his turquoise eyes. "Think of your calling. You won't thank me if . . . if we go on."

"Jee-sus." Zach buried his face in his hands, then shoved his fingers through his whiskey brown curls.

"Yes, we really ought to pray." She swallowed at the pained, accusing look he gave her. "For strength. Ah, in the face of temptation."

"Sweetheart, listen . . ." Zach managed a strained smile, and began pushing himself to his feet.

Beth Ann jumped up as well, setting a bit of distance between them. "You have to understand, Zach. I've—I've repented of my indiscretion. The Lord knows how sorry I am it ever happened! I can't afford to repeat my sins again, even . . ." She broke off, biting her lip.

"Even what?" There was a dangerous edge to his gravelly tone.

Hot color rose up her neck and washed her cheeks, but her words were even. "Even if I want you desperately."

Zach felt as though he been punched in the gut—again. He took a step toward her, his hands outstretched. "Angel."

"No, Zach." She edged backward, keeping the space between them constant, and gave him a smoky glance through her lashes. "I can't. I want you to like me, but more, I want you to respect me, too."

Zach groaned inaudibly. *Respect her?* She wasn't going all prim and proper on him at this late date, was she? That was the last thing on earth he wanted—but he couldn't tell her that! Trying to ignore the aching bulge between his legs, Zach strove to bring himself under a tenuous control.

He had to remember that his late night searches through Wolf's papers had failed to turn up any clue to the location of Wolf's mine. Even though he was ready to explode with frustration, his instincts said not to force the issue with Beth Ann now, not if he hoped for her help with his search, and especially not if he hoped to win her affections on another day. And he had no doubt there would come another day of reckoning—Beth Ann was too passionate a woman to deny herself indefinitely.

He took a deep breath. "You're absolutely right, darlin'. I do heartily beg your pardon if I've offended you."

Her cheeks burned even brighter. "Not that, exactly. I think you know how much I like it when you ... touch me. But it really shouldn't go any further, not without ... well, not without benefit of clergy. You of all people must understand that."

What was the minx up to now? Zach wondered. Fishing for a marriage proposal? Not danged likely! However, having an inkling of what she was plotting put everything back into perspective. He wasn't obliged to be noble if the little hellion wanted to play the game for higher stakes. She'd dealt this hand, but he was more than ready to call her bluff.

"I appreciate your reminding me of my duty, honey. I think in the—er, heat of the moment, things got out of hand."

"Yes, I was upset about losing Nellie, you see." Beth Ann brushed her fingers through her long hair and bit her lip. "Paw will be furious at the scene I made."

"Let me take care of it."

She gave him an apprehensive look. "You won't tell him about Pat?"

"Not if you don't want me to."

She shuddered. "No. I'd rather forget it."

"Then don't worry about a thing. Come, we'll

go back now. You can tidy up while I talk to Wolf.
I'm sure he'll understand."

Beth Ann looked up at Zach in gratitude and
shyly allowed him to take her arm. "No one has
ever been this kind to me, Zach. I only wish there
was some way I could show you how much I appreciate it."

Swallowing back the urge to offer an explicit
suggestion or two, Zach hid a twinge of grim humor behind a mild tone. "I'm sure you'll think of
something."

"Female trouble!"

"I'm afraid so," Zach said, watching embarrassed color suffuse Wolf's ruddy countenance.
"You know how, er—delicate these things can be
with women. Beth Ann was in an overly emo-
tional state, sir, but I know your heart contains
sufficient Christian love and charity to forgive her
outburst. She's most upset over the grief she
caused you."

Wolf leaned back in his straight chair, studying
Zach as he perched on the veranda railing. "Think
I should call the doc? Who'll do the cooking if that
gal comes down ailing?"

"A good night's sleep and some forbearance on
your part should be all that's needed," Zach said
hastily. He knew Beth Ann would be mortified
when she heard this excuse, and he certainly
didn't want that cricket of a doctor poking her and
asking embarrassing questions when there was
nothing at all wrong with her that a night in
Zach's bed and a trip out of the territory of Arizona wouldn't cure!

"If you say so, Reverend. I won't say anything
more about it." Wolf snorted. "Can't have things
going to pieces around here because the girl's

taken a liking to the vapors or such nonsense, though. Too much work to do. Where is she, anyway?"

"Ah, resting in her room. She was upset about selling the mare, I believe."

"Such a lot of fuss over a swag-backed nag! Never was worth a plugged nickel," Wolf said defensively. "Couldn't turn down a fair offer for her, now could I?"

Zach shrugged. "That's your affair, I'm sure."

"Yeah. Well, Robert's been kinda on edge lately. This trip ... ah, to Tucson, and business pressures down at the bank. Lot on his mind, including that boy of his. Wouldn't have been Christian to ignore a friend when I could help out, now would it?"

"Indeed not."

Wolf curled his paws around the brass handle of his cane and gave Zach a sly look from behind the bush of his black and silver beard. "You could help Robert out, too, if you would."

"Me? How's that?"

"By agreeing to preach to our congregation come Sunday."

Alarm bells went off in Zach's head. "Oh, well, now, that's very flattering, but—"

"Why, Robert was just saying this morning how blessed we'd all feel if we had a real clergyman to lead our worship services for a change."

And let the cat out of the bag when I make some gaffe like mixing up Peter and Paul and the rest of those jokers? Zach thought. *Uh-uh!*

"Much as I'd like to oblige, Mr. Linder, I've been delayed long enough."

"Those hooligans down in Tucson can wait, Reverend. You ain't scared of decent folk, are you?"

"I simply wouldn't want to presume on you or your congregation's hospitality," Zach demurred.

"Robert and me speak for the deacon's board. And don't worry, we guarantee to make it worth your while." Wolf winked. "Why, you ain't never seen a man squeeze a tightfisted congregation better than Robert. Besides, I've got something in the works maybe fixin' to pan out big, and I appreciate your special prayers. So do us the honor of carrying the Word of God to us."

Talk of money always made Zach more agreeable. What the hell. He'd had enough experience fast-talking his way out of tough spots to give it a shot. Maybe Wolf would be so grateful afterwards, Zach could flat out *ask* him about the damn mines. And there was that unfinished business with Wolf's daughter. Beth Ann had anticipated a wedding night in the past, and before he left Destiny, Zach was going to do his damnedest to get her to repeat the experience—with him.

"All right, Mr. Linder, I accept."

"Splendid, Reverend, splendid!" Wolf levered himself heavily to a standing position and waved for Zach to follow him. "Come inside. I've got quite a few texts and treatises that might be useful. I've always favored a sermon on the Lord chasing the money changers from the temple, but there's the Sermon on the Mount for the more faint-hearted, or maybe . . ."

Reluctantly Zach followed the older man as he disappeared inside, and for the first time in a great while, he actually sent a prayer of his own heavenward—a prayer that he would survive this without ending up wearing a tar-and-feather overcoat and straddling a rail on his way out of Destiny!

* * *

For the first time in a long while, Beth Ann actually found herself looking forward to Sunday. Since Paw's surprising announcement that the Reverend Temple would be staying on at Traveler's Rest in response to the Gospel Assembly Chapel's invitation to preach, she'd been hardpressed to keep her mind on anything but Zach and her growing certainty that he was going to ask her to marry him—soon.

Now, seating herself beside her paw on Wolf's favored first pew, Beth Ann adjusted her black gabardine skirts and folded her gloved hands around her Bible. Surreptitiously she watched Zach move quietly around the stifling little room, shaking hands, introducing himself to Sheriff Nichols and his wife, renewing his acquaintance with the Hardys, Mrs. Cunningham and Mayor Ike, Miss Kellogg, and the Barlings men. Bobby Barlings leaned past his father's shoulder to wave and grin at Beth Ann, then subsided at his father's quiet admonishment, but not before Beth Ann returned his smile from beneath the brim of her prim black bonnet.

Then, like iron filings drawn to a magnet, her gaze found Zach again. He looked dignified and handsome in a dark coat and clerical collar, his burnished curls shining, his smile easy and welcoming. Beth Ann's heart tripped over.

It was remarkable how often that was happening these days, and it was all Zach's doing. Since becoming her champion and comforting her in the barn, he'd been as attentive as the most besotted suitor. Gallant and sweet and funny, making her laugh, helping her with the heavy kitchen chores, walking with her beside the river in the evening twilight, wooing and charming her just like any young lover would his beloved. They hadn't ar-

gued about the slightest thing, persuading Beth
Ann that they would indeed make a compatible
pair. Her prejudice against preachers had been the
source of their initial friction, after all, and now
that it was gone, she could see what a fine, upstanding individual he was, kind and generous
and deserving of all regard.

And those sweet, stolen kisses! How they made
her heart race, even though they had been few and
necessarily chaste. Thanks to Beth Ann's explicit
instructions, Ama was never far away, playing du-
enna with her giggling presence, just in case Beth
Ann's own willpower failed her. And well it might
have, for there was nothing more enticing than being in Zach's arms and feeling his lips upon hers.

Beth Ann sighed longingly. She felt Zach's powerful needs and desires fully as much as her own,
and the tension between them had grown to almost unendurable levels. The merest touch of his
hand would send her heart into palpitations and
melt her center. There had even been times when
they'd exchanged a fleeting embrace and she'd felt
the hard length of Zach's turgid manhood pressed
against her.

She would marry him in a moment, not only to
escape her life here, but also so they could indulge
the urges of their flesh without guilt, as the Cre-
ator meant, with pleasure and intimacy and a
commitment to the future. If only he would ask!
Surely there was some way that she could give
him the necessary push in the right direction.

Her musings were interrupted when Robert
Barlings stepped to the pulpit to start the services.
He led the opening hymn, "Lord of All Being,
Throned Afar," in his deep baritone, made a wel-
come speech introducing Zach, then asked for
prayer requests.

Wolf was the first to stand, as always, but Beth Ann stiffened when he took her elbow and dragged her to her feet. Somehow she'd forgotten for a moment, or perhaps hoped for a change from her habitual Sunday penance, but no, her father would never forget his duty to his daughter.

"I ask the community to pray for the soul of this woman," Wolf intoned, his voice as loud and wrathful as Jehovah's. "She is a sinner, a foul fornicator, and as weak as her woman's flesh."

Head bowed, cheeks fiery with humiliation, Beth Ann held herself still beneath the murmurs of supplication that poured from the members of the congregation. Behind her, she could hear Mamie Cunningham's strident voice over the subdued hum of the others.

"God, grant redemption to this sinful creature." Wolf lowered himself back into his seat, bowed his head in preparation of a good half hour of exhortations, and began to pray loudly. "Tear the flesh from her bones, send your plagues upon her with foul sores and suffering, but teach her repentance, for she is guilty of the most loathsome of sins—"

"Yea, a sinner!" Zach's voice rang out over the hubbub.

Beth Ann's head jerked up, and her pulse throbbed with trepidation. Was he condemning her or joining his prayers to the congregation's? Zach stood and raised his voice even louder.

"Are we not all sinners?" He lifted his arms in entreaty. "Do we not all carry guilty secrets in our hearts?"

The men and women seated on the pews exchanged confused glances.

"Yes, I mean you!" Zach said, pointing at random into the crowd. "And you. And you!" His finger aimed right at Wolf himself.

"I am!" Bobby Barlings jumped to his feet, grinning, delighted at this game. "I'm a sinner!"

Zach smiled back at the young man. "That's right. Stand up, brother. Stand up, sister! And a little child shall lead them. Everyone stand up!"

Reluctantly several members of the congregation rose, followed by another and another. A few smiled hesitantly, but others looked uncomfortable and would not meet their neighbors' eyes. With a great shuffling of feet, soon everyone in the small adobe building was standing. Everyone—except Wolf Linder. Seated in the pew, Wolf scowled in confusion, his thick neck growing red as heads turned his way, and stares and glares poured down on him.

" 'He that is without sin among you, let him first cast a stone . . .' " Zach quoted, his voice earnest. "Is it right to condemn others when our own faults and failures lie in the Lord's plain sight?"

Beth Ann met Zach's bright blue-green glance, and she gave a soft gasp as she took his purpose. He was shielding her, restoring a portion of her pride by making her one of many, rather than the single sinner. She felt a warmth grow inside her heart that filled her with gratitude and hope.

Zach continued. "Confess your sins before the Lord in the silence of your own soul and find His forgiveness and mercy. Isn't that what we all want? And yes, brothers and sisters, grace and mercy is what the Lord wants us to have—*all* of us."

Mamie Cunningham leaned forward in the pew behind Wolf, poked a chubby forefinger in his broad back, and hissed at him. "On your feet, you heathen!"

His ears crimson, Wolf scowled from beneath his bushy eyebrows, but he could not resist the pressure of an entire roomful of expectant, rebuking stares. His jaw working with chagrin and reluctance, he pushed at his cane and finally levered himself to a stand.

"Well done, brothers and sisters! Now, forever after this day, we pledge to rise together at this time and repeat this community confession together in humility and repentance. Let us pause for a moment of silent reflection on this promise."

With her head bowed, Beth Ann's thoughts tumbled and flitted with the realization of what Zach had done for her. He'd risked the censure of the entire congregation to end her solitary Sunday penances. With a start, she knew that she was very close to falling in love with Zach Temple, and the knowledge made her feel breathless and sweaty-palmed and wonderful. Was this how it happened? With Tom, love had been all intensity and desperation and forbidden excitement. It was all that and so much more with Zach, a terrible sweetness that intoxicated her and made her dream again.

After what he'd done, he must really care for her, too. Why, it was practically a declaration! Happiness bubbled up inside her, and she couldn't wait for the service to end.

"Amen," Zach concluded the silent prayer. "The Lord will reward you all. Please be seated now, and we'll begin today's lesson."

The chapel's occupants settled somewhat noisily into the pews again. They were more attentive now, livelier somehow, as they waited to see what other surprises the visiting preacher had up his sleeve. What they got was a friendly, humorous listing of the ills of the world and some down-to-earth suggestions for dealing with them.

Beth Ann was too delirious with joy to attend

closely, her head full of daydreams. They would have a cottage, she was certain of that, and she would make it into a perfect home, with starched curtains at the shining windows and her woven rugs on the spotless floors. Perhaps Zach could find a church in a town where there were green and growing things and friendly faces all year long. She would plant marigolds at the front door and roses in the garden so that she could take bouquets to the sick when she went out to visit Zach's parishioners. And she would teach Sunday school to the children of the congregation, and someday their own babies as well, telling them the Bible stories her mother had taught her as a girl, especially the tale of Noah and his ark and how God gave the world a second chance.

Later, outside in the sunshine, everyone agreed that the Reverend Temple's sermon was quite a success, the offering plate heavier than it had been in years as positive proof. Church members crowded around him to offer their congratulations. Impatient, but knowing it would be some time before Zach would be released from the duties of cordiality and her father would finish bending Mr. Barlings's ear, Beth Ann walked to where their buggy was parked by itself in the meager shade of a gnarled piñon tree. Maybe, in time, she might even be allowed to join the knots of chatting women catching up on the week's news. For now, she was happy enough with the knowledge of Zach's devotion not to mind.

She found a seat on the buggy's step facing away from the churchyard so she'd be shielded from curious eyes, and let her daydreams reclaim her. After a time, she heard the crunch of footsteps and looked up to find Zach coming around the rear of the buggy. Damp curls hugged his forehead, and his turquoise gaze was bright with victory.

"So," he asked with a cocky smile, "how'd I do?"

Smiling and eager, Beth Ann was on her feet in an instant, her hands outstretched. As he folded them within his own, she gazed up at him, adoration mingling with admiration. "Wonderful!"

His light laugh was self-deprecating. "Well, not quite that good, honey."

"No, I mean it! They loved it. They loved *you*."

His thumbs made circles over the backs of her hands. "At least no one fell asleep."

"You were ... great." Behind the brim of her staid bonnet, her eyes were luminous. "And, Zach, what you said, what you *did*—" Her voice choked, became tremulous. "I can't tell you what it means to me ..."

He grinned, a roguish, wicked twinkle that made her toes curl inside her high-buttoned shoes. "Maybe you can show me later tonight, sweetheart."

Blushing, her heart pounding, she nodded shyly, then, giving in to impulse, she raised up on her toes and kissed him, throwing her arms around his neck. "Oh, Zach!" she whispered. "I'll make you such a good wife, I swear! When can we tell Paw?"

His body stiffened, and he began to disentangle her neck lock. "Whoa, hold your horses, angel. Who said anything about marriage?"

Something cold and icy wrapped around Beth Ann's heart, and the blood drained from her face. "But I thought ... you said ..."

"I've never made you any promises."

Bewildered, she couldn't take it in. "Then why court me the way you have?"

His lids drooped. "Why do you think?"

She felt as though he'd punched her in the chest, and her breath wafted out on a single, devastated "Oh." She swallowed. "Is that still what . . . ?"

"It's *all* I've been able to think about. You and I both know that if we don't lie down together soon, we're liable to explode."

Surprisingly, his matter-of-fact attitude and the fact that, fresh from the pulpit, he could make her such an indecent proposition still had the power to shock her.

"You've got to get me out of your system?" she asked faintly.

"Something like that." He ran a finger down her cheek. "Might be kinda hard to do. But after the way we've been smoldering, we owe it to ourselves to give it a try, don't you think?"

The sun beat down on her bonnet, the heavy knot of her pinned-up hair underneath it pulling painfully at her scalp with the beginnings of a migraine. How could she have believed, even hoped, that he might actually *marry* her? Her stupidity mocked her. She squinted against the brilliance, looking out across the arid plains to the cool blue mountaintops on the horizon, and wishing that she had the wings of Noah's dove so that she could fly away forever.

"What I think, preacher," she said woodenly, "is that you've had enough fun at my expense."

His laugh was a husky, masculine rumble of pure intent. "We haven't even begun to have fun, angel."

His cavalier attitude transformed her hurt into pure fury, and her gaze became venomous. She hissed at him, feeling the poison of hate and betrayal foul her system. "You despicable sidewinder! No need to worry about soiling someone who's already been ruined, is that it?"

His eyes narrowed against the dusty glare, and he gave a shrug. "At least you know the stakes."

"Whereas some simpering virgin wouldn't?" she sneered. "How *honorable*."

"I have my standards."

"Well, believe it or not," she said, furious, "so do I! And I'll sell myself in the worst flea-bitten bawdy house in the territory before I let you touch me again, you varmint!"

"Now, don't go getting your dander in an up-roar, darlin'. We can get this all straightened out tonight."

"I may be slower than most women to recognize a two-legged, four-flushing badger, but I do learn from my mistakes." Climbing into the buggy, she settled her skirts and unhooked the reins. "Your days at Traveler's Rest are over, preacher!"

"Huh?" His sandy brows knit together in puzzlement.

"What I'm saying is good-bye and good riddance! You're fit to travel, and I'm sure that after that brilliant pulpit performance, you can wangle any number of invitations to Sunday dinner." She gave a sharp laugh. "Better try to smoke it up a bit for them, though. There's nothing the good people of Destiny love with their roast beef better then the smell of brimstone."

"Hold it, angel, are you kicking me out?"

"Now you're getting the picture! Buck will bring you the rest of your things."

Jaw tight, Zach grabbed her wrist. "And what's your paw liable to say when he finds out?"

"That any fellow who can make Wolf Linder as uncomfortable as you did today is healthy enough to be on his way!"

Wolf stood at the church door waiting to be picked up. Shaking off Zach's hold, Beth Ann reached for the reins, her gray eyes as cold as Arctic ice.

"Don't you ever come back to Traveler's Rest, Zach Temple," she warned. "The biggest mistake I ever made was letting you live to torment me. The next time I shoot someone, I'll be damned sure I do the job right!"

Slapping the reins, she clucked to the team and drove away. Mamie Cunningham's shrill, unctuous voice carried over the sound of the horses' hooves.

"What did that hussy mean by that, Reverend? Well, never mind her! You simply must come to Sunday dinner. Isn't it wonderful? The deacons want to offer you the pastorship—permanently!"

Chapter 9

"Thank you, Reverend," Mamie Cunningham said, batting her stubby lashes and simpering like a debutante. "I find our little talks so . . . edifying."

"That's why I'm here, Mrs. Cunningham." Zach walked her to the door of the room in the rear of the Gospel Assembly Church that had been both his office and sleeping quarters for nearly a month. "And thank you for the cake."

"I just love to see a man eat well. You are coming to supper tomorrow night?"

If her dinner was anything like the cake—leaden and tasteless—there wasn't much to look forward to. "I wouldn't miss it."

She beamed at him, her long, horsey face quivering with gratification. "We'll see you then. Good evening."

Zach closed the door behind her with a sigh of relief, then threw himself down in the chair at the desk that took up half the small room. Behind him, a canvas curtain strung on a rope hid his bed and washstand from prying eyes. The atmosphere outside was heavy with late day heat and humidity, and not even a breath of air whispered through the room's open windows. Zach dragged a finger around his neck to loosen his sticky skin from the choking clerical collar. The townspeople assured him the June rainy season would deliver welcome relief from the oppressiveness, but so far

Mother Nature had perversely withheld her seasonal blessings of moisture.

That was bound to be why he was so fidgety these days.

Yeah, and jackrabbits fly with little pink wings.

Zach grimaced and rubbed his jaw, his palm making a raspy sound against his afternoon stubble. Almost against his will, he found himself reaching into the desk drawer for the thin leather wallet stored there. His mouth twisting in self-mockery, he lifted out the tintype he'd stolen from Tom Chapman and stared at Beth Ann Linder's tiny portrait. Damn, but this woman was eating at him!

As a rambling man, he had a knack for knowing when to fold a hand, cut his losses, and move on, but this little filly was a challenge he just couldn't back away from. He'd been so close to claiming her, but then his code of honor wouldn't let him take her into his bed under a misguided assumption that he was going to marry her. Lord, that would have made him as bad as Tom! She ought to have at least given him credit for that, but she'd literally kicked him out of Traveler's Rest, and he'd never seen a woman so coldly furious ... or so hurt.

Zach grimaced. Oddly, no one had found anything unusual about his somewhat precipitate departure from the way station, but hell, he'd only accepted the deacons' offer to become the Gospel Assembly Chapel's pastor—temporarily, of course—for the sole purpose of finding time and a method to make the contrary woman understand the compliment he'd paid her! He figured when she calmed down, he might be able to recover the ground he'd lost, but now the hardheaded filly wouldn't give him so much as the time of day!

When he'd ridden out to pick up his few possessions, she'd refused to come out of her room. The few times he'd seen her in town, she'd turned on her heel at the sight of him. For the past three Sundays in church, she'd been stone-faced and steadfastly refused to meet his eyes. When he'd been lucky enough to address a private word to her, she'd pretended he wasn't there. It was a chilly sensation, and he understood the power of the Indian tribes that punished by ostracism, declaring the guilty party "dead" to all so that it was worse than being a ghost. It was downright unnerving to have those silvery eyes look right through him.

Not that he hadn't had his successes over the past few weeks. Zach Madison always landed on his feet, and after all, there was still Wolf Linder's gold mines to consider. He'd invested too much time and effort on the old scoundrel to give up now, and Wolf's resentment at being forced to stand up with the sinners hadn't lasted long. His regular visits to the new "parson" gave Zach plenty of opportunity to lecture the man about financing God's work.

To his surprise, Zach had found that a man could live comfortably, if modestly, on what the collection plates were bringing in, and he had more supper invitations than he could shake a stick at. More interesting than that, however, was the number of individuals who had come to the preacher's door to lay their problems before him and seek advice. Since Zach was smart enough to do more listening than talking, these folks generally worked their way around to their own solutions, then gave Zach credit for it.

Actually, it was kind of satisfying, Zach admitted. He'd listened to a grieving father, counseled a hot-tempered teenaged boy, and arbitrated a family quarrel between two middle-aged sisters. Even pretty Kitty Hardy had come to see him, hesitant at first, then unable to stop the flood of unhappiness over her marriage to her dour, domineering shopkeeper husband, a choice that had given her security but no true affection. Suitably sympathetic, Zach allowed Kitty to talk out her feelings, but he was totally unprepared for the question she finally asked.

"So I was wondering . . ." Kitty bit her lips and squeezed her reticule flat. "That is, if you know . . ."

Zach smiled encouragingly. "Yes, Mrs. Hardy? If I know what?"

She looked everywhere around the little office but at him. "Oh, you are going to think me incredibly bold, but I have no one else I can ask, and . . . and . . ."

"And what?"

"I don't think Douglas and I are . . . are ready for children yet!" she blurted. "So I must know if there is some *way* . . ."

Zach swallowed and felt his ears grow hot. He gulped again and cleared his throat. "To prevent . . . um, conception, you mean?"

Face flaming, Kitty stared at her hands in her lap and nodded.

Zach had never thought ministering to a flock would push him into this kind of corner! He deliberated for a long moment.

"Ah—in my experience, there's only one sure-fire method. I prescribe an apple."

She looked up eagerly. "That's it? But that's so simple! Wait—is it to be taken before or after?"

Zach smiled wryly. *"Instead."*

Kitty blinked. "Oh, I see." Something like resignation flickered behind her eyes, and she rose to her feet. "Well, thank you, Reverend Temple. You've been most helpful."

"I'm at your disposal, ma'am." He walked her to the door. "Ah, one thing I've been meaning to ask you—you were once a friend of Miss Linder's, weren't you?"

"Yes. School chums, you know. I didn't like to turn my back on Beth Ann," Kitty said, looking a bit shamefaced. "But Douglas wouldn't hear of my continuing to see her, and so I couldn't ... you know." She shrugged.

"Seems to me Miss Linder has lived an exemplary life since her unfortunate experience with this Chapman fellow," Zach remarked. "Shouldn't she have a second chance? Following one's heart is more an error in judgment than true wickedness."

Kitty sighed. "That's what I tried to tell Douglas. It's so sad, really. Beth Ann was always so lively and happy before all that happened. Now she seems more like that old bear of a father of hers. I miss her."

"Perhaps you could reach out to her in some small way?"

"I'd like to, but how?"

"I want to thank Miss Linder for her hospitality—"

Kitty looked startled. "But, Reverend Temple, it was the least she could do after shooting you!"

"The accident was as much my own fault as Miss Linder's, and she went out of her way many times to see to my—er, comfort," Zach explained smoothly. "Could you deliver a gift for me? It might make it easier to reestablish your relationship in some small way. I know she'd welcome it."

"Well, Douglas wouldn't like it . . ." Kitty bit her lip, then her childish features took on a new maturity that was partly defiance. "But I knew Beth Ann before I married him, and . . . and I owe it to her, don't I? What would you like delivered?"

Zach had smiled then. "There's a certain bonnet in your shop . . ."

Now Zach's gaze returned to the tintype in his hand.

Beth Ann had gotten Buck to return that bonnet faster than you could say "go to hell." She and Kitty might have come to an understanding, but Beth Ann was still having nothing to do with one Reverend Zach Temple. Not that Zach had been trying to bribe himself back into her good graces as Buck reported she'd thought. It was just that he'd wanted to give her something pretty . . . and hell, he missed her, too!

Zach growled under his breath and shoved the picture into his coat pocket. What he really needed was a drink.

Since waltzing into the saloon for a whiskey hardly fit his current disguise, it looked as though he would have to settle for a walk before his scheduled chess game with Wolf Linder. Shoving back his chair, Zach headed for the door. He met the older man stumping down the sidewalk moments later.

"Howdy, Reverend," Wolf bellowed. "Just the man I was aimin' to see."

Zach glanced toward the horizon, but the sun was fast disappearing behind a glowering line of gray and purple clouds. The same clouds had blown up every day this week without dropping a sprinkle of rain. "Am I running late, sir?"

"Better late than never," Wolf quipped, guffawing at his own wit. He seemed strangely frenetic, almost electrified, as if he were building up a storm like the clouds above them. "No, it's me that's early, but I'm going to have to cancel out. Got some business to tend to with Robert. Great things happening, son. Great things, and it's about time. Meeting may last all night. Hope you don't mind."

"Not at all."

But that was a lie. Frustration suddenly overcame Zach. He'd been working to gain the old man's confidence for weeks now, with no result. Zach couldn't afford to hang around this dumpy town forever, even if the "pickin's" as minister were pretty good. The old restlessness was back, the prickles on the back of his neck that said it was time to move on. Maybe subtlety was wasted on Wolf.

Zach gave the older man a considering look. "You know, Mr. Linder, you've been telling me all the old stories about the mines around here. I sure would like to see a few for myself. Give it a try, so to speak."

"Dirty your hands with that kind of backbreaking work?" Wolf laughed and clapped Zach's shoulder in a friendly fashion. "No, sir, wouldn't dream of it! Don't worry, Reverend. Things are finally turning around for old Wolf Linder. And about time, too. No more scraping and toiling for me. It's going to be Easy Street from now on. And don't you fret, I'm going to see that the Lord gets His share. Yes, sir, I don't ever short the Almighty, nor His servant, neither!"

"That's very reassuring." Zach's tone was dry.

Wolf gave Zach's shoulder another hearty cuff. "Listen, we'll have that game tomorrow evening, all right? See you then."

Fists bunched in his pockets in frustration, Zach

watched the older man hobble off, then head across the street toward the Destiny Savings Bank. The establishment was closed for the day, the shades drawn at the windows, but Wolf pounded on the door. Zach caught a flash of Robert Bar- lings's annoyed face when he let Wolf in and the surreptitious glance he sent up and down the nearly deserted street. Then they both went inside. Wolf's "business" intrigued Zach mightily, for his instincts told him he smelled a swindle, but he couldn't expect to cash in on it if the old man kept Zach on the outside looking in.

Chewing on that thought, Zach strolled down the boardwalk. He wished again for a shot of whiskey—mescal, rotgut, a beer—hell, he didn't care! Between Wolf Linder and his daughter, this whole business was beginning to stink. But drop- ping this preacher's charade would mean burning a bridge Zach might find he couldn't afford to lose, and innate caution turned his steps away from the saloon. Maybe he'd better settle for a cup of coffee at the two-bit restaurant where he took his meals.

The food at the Destiny Café didn't hold a can- dle to Beth Ann's, of course, and Zach could un- derstand Wolf's desire to keep her cooking at Traveler's Rest. Zach wondered if in twenty years Beth Ann would still be at work over her father's stove, growing more sour and resentful by the day, turning, as Kitty had predicted, into a hard, feminine version of her father. It was a grim picture.

Zach approached the café entrance just as Sheriff Tristan Nichols stepped outside, wiping his damp forehead with a blue bandanna, then slapping his hat onto his lank brown hair. He was a tall man with a hawkish nose who always rode a palomino and took his lawman's duties seriously.

"Evening, Sheriff." Zach nodded.

"Reverend. Ain't you and Wolf due at a checker game?"

"Chess." Zach's cheek twitched. Jeez! A man couldn't scratch his ass in a town this small without everyone knowing about it! "It's been postponed. Think it'll rain?"

The sheriff peered at the sky from under his bushy eyebrows and sniffed. "Yup. Be a real gully washer when she blows. Hope it gets it over with soon. This kind of weather makes folks loco. Had a killing down in the Mexican quarters earlier, and little Kitty Hardy's done packed up and left Douglas."

"What!"

Nichols nodded. "Took the afternoon stage to Yuma, she did. Douglas is fit to bust a gut, saying she got the notion from Beth Ann Linder."

"That's not true." Zach's jaw grew taut. "You can quell that rumor immediately, Sheriff. Mrs. Hardy was troubled about her marriage and came to me for guidance."

The sheriff lifted an eyebrow. "So you're the one who told her to skedaddle?"

"Absolutely not. Everything we discussed was in confidence, of course, but I can tell you she never gave a hint of such a plan to me." *But I'd have given her my blessing.* "And she certainly didn't mention Miss Linder."

"Well, Douglas is pretty upset."

"I can imagine," Zach replied in a wry tone. "And you don't look like a happy man either, Sheriff."

"That ain't the worst of it, Reverend."

"There's more?" Zach smiled. "Don't tell me Ike Cunningham refused to wash the dinner dishes?"

Sheriff Nichols grinned, then rubbed the smile away with the back of his hand. "Mamie wouldn't countenance such a rebellion. Naw, I just got in a whole stack of bulletins and wanted posters."

Zach stiffened. "Anything important?"

"Usual rustling, horse thievin', and such; a couple of towns around Prescott got a lookout for a sharp player name of Madison, but that ain't nuthin'. Big news is the jailbreak at the Territorial Prison."

Hearing his own name on the sheriff's lips hadn't rattled Zach as much as that last bit of news. "Yuma?" he croaked.

"Yup. Bad'un name of Chapman and a bunch of his gang killed a couple of guards and got clean away. He used to hang out around these parts. Hope he don't come back."

"Why would he?" Zach asked uneasily, but he was afraid he already knew the answer.

"Beth Ann Linder."

Zach's collar suddenly seemed two sizes too small. He cleared his throat. "I understood this Chapman fellow left her high and dry before."

"Yeah, but once the bee gets a taste for nectar, he always comes buzzin' around his favorite flower."

Zach frowned. "Surely Chapman wouldn't risk coming here? A man on the run would be better off getting himself lost in the mountains for a spell, wouldn't you guess?"

"Love is a peculiar thing, Reverend. Makes perfectly normal folks act like idiots sometimes." Sheriff Nichols shrugged and pulled the brim of his hat down against a frisky little zephyr whirling a dust devil across the main street. "Reckon we'll find out soon enough. Enjoy your supper, Reverend."

Minutes later, Zach sat at a tiny table in the grimy little café, staring down into a cup of very black, very bad coffee. He took another sip of the scalding brew and winced at its bitterness. The bad taste in his mouth wasn't just due to the coffee, but to a rising certainty that he wasn't long for Destiny. As old Boone, the saloonkeeper in Calliope, had liked to say, it was time to "lift the bull's tail and look him square in the eye."

What Zach saw wasn't promising. The law had the word out on him, Tom Chapman would slit his gullet if they crossed paths in Destiny, and Zach was no closer to Wolf's mines than the day he'd arrived. Zach gave a philosophical shrug. Sometimes schemes panned out; sometimes they didn't. It was time to cut his losses and vamoose.

The only bonus in this swindle was Beth Ann herself, and Zach's gut tightened every time he thought about her and Tom together. What if she were so desperate to leave this town that she ran off with that bastard again?

A surge of something primal and possessively male made Zach bare his teeth in a silent snarl. Beth Ann deserved better. She deserved ... well, a man who'd look after her. Someone who'd take her out of this narrow-minded, one-horse town for good and show her the time of her life in the process. Someone like ... him.

Zach leaned back in his chair, eyes narrowed, thinking hard. Why else had he hung around these past weeks but for the chance to finally woo that feisty, fascinating woman into his bed? She was like a burr under his saddle blanket, the memory of her sweet flesh an ache that wouldn't go away. He'd never wanted a woman the way he wanted

Beth Ann Linder, and while he might give up on a cache of gold nuggets, he wasn't as willing to give up on her. At least not yet.

Wolf's meeting with Barlings gave Zach the perfect opportunity to ride out to Traveler's Rest and make Beth Ann listen to him. When all else failed, there was always the truth. Maybe she'd think of him a bit more kindly when she discovered he wasn't any kind of a preacher at all.

Zach smiled to himself, picturing her face. Yes, that was the ticket! He'd make his confession and play the white knight by taking her away from Destiny and rescuing her from a life of drudgery under Wolf's fat thumb. They could go to Mexico, California maybe, where there were always opportunities for a quick thinker like him. Lord, what a team they'd make! The way they set each other on fire, they'd have a high old time before the flames burned out.

If she'd listen to him.

If she didn't shoot him on sight first.

Zach's grin widened. As a gambling man, he understood the odds might be a little risky, but once he had Beth Ann back in his arms, he knew a few tricks that would help turn the tables in his favor. A burning flared low in Zach's belly, and he pushed back from the table, his thoughts already halfway to the livery stable.

Hell, what did he have to lose?

It didn't look good.

Sweating under the heavy slicker, Beth Ann tipped her head back to peer from under the dripping brim of Paw's old sombrero at the rapidly rising Gila River. Fat raindrops pounded the parched earth, whipped by the wind into a near-horizontal curtain, and thunder echoed across the desert floor. Though Beth Ann knew it was a good hour until sundown, the sky was the color of a bruise, the oily twilight fast diminishing as the storm front drew ominously closer.

"Sweet sassafras."

Chewing her lip, Beth Ann stood poised on the rise above the river, straining to see through the murk at the rush of muddy water that had already made the ford leading to town nearly impassable. Limbs and brush and floating debris she didn't care to examine too closely bobbed past, evidence that the long-awaited storm had already unleashed its fury farther north. The dry earth couldn't accept such a volume of moisture quickly enough, and now the runoff from a thousand small arroyos careened together in a violent rush that could spell disaster for anything or anyone caught in its plummet to the sea. Traveler's Rest, standing on its high ground, would be safe enough, but despite Buck's earlier—now unfounded—assurances to the contrary, at the rate the water was rising, the low-lying corrals holding the Linders' prize string of horses was going to be the first thing to go—and fast.

At least she'd had the presence of mind to have Buck take Ama back to her village when the sky began to take on that menacing purple color, Beth Ann told herself grimly. Now she wouldn't have to worry about the woman's safety, only the fact that with Paw stranded in town and Buck unable to get back across the river from the Pima village, she was the only one left to move the string up to the relative safety of the barn or else watch them drown.

And she had to hurry.

Rain beating into her eyes, Beth Ann rushed down the rise, her boots sliding in the mud as she raced through the cottonwood thicket. Her hems were already soaked where they showed beneath the edge of the voluminous slicker, and her footing was so precarious, she skidded with each new buffet of the wind. A cottonwood branch caught her across the cheek, making her cry out with the stinging surprise of the blow, but a distant flash of lightning and another peal of thunder urged her to greater speed.

Beth Ann was briefly and somewhat ironically thankful that Nellie and the foal were safe in town. Of course, if Paw hadn't interfered, they'd be on a ranch near Yuma and she would have reached California by now. Instead, Bobby Barlings had her filly, and out of desperation, she'd let a fool's dream of happiness with Zach Temple lead her to new humiliation. A region around her heart still hurt whenever she thought about him, about how foolish she'd been to trust, to hope. And yet the dream had been so sweet . . .

But the pain of seeing him in town every Sunday, and knowing how he'd used her, was intolerable. She couldn't remain here, growing more and more bitter, the ruins of her dreams lying shattered at her feet, still wanting him. For shamefully, as much as she tried to harden her heart, her blood still beat faster in her veins at the mere sight of him, and she lay in her solitary bed at night, tormented by the memory of his scent, the way he stroked her skin, the taste of his mouth . . .

With a little desperate groan, Beth Ann shook off the recollection, leaning against the wind and stomping through the ankle-deep puddles toward the corrals. At least she'd had sense enough not to resort to any more half-baked plans to run away.

Thank God for Whiskey Jean. As soon as the rainy season came and the roads became impassable for the bull teams, Jean had promised to help Beth Ann leave Destiny. All Beth Ann had to do was hold on until then. Despite the water lashing her face, Beth Ann grimaced wryly. It looked as though her wait for the rainy season was over with a vengeance.

A dozen nervous horses huddled miserably in the corral, but it was a high, frightened whinny from a different direction that froze Beth Ann in her tracks. Turning, she scanned the curve of the undulating river, then gasped.

"The damn fool!"

A lone rider struggled with his buckskin horse in the middle of the turbulence. The strength of the current had forced him out of the normally shallow ford into the deeper channel, now swollen and dangerous with rushing water and debris. Pushed by the stream, the horse and rider swam at a diagonal, attempting to reach the opposite bank where Beth Ann stood, but the force of the water was so powerful, they made little headway. The horse was tiring, and if the weary beast didn't find purchase on the river bottom soon, both horse and rider would be pulled under or swept away around the curve of the river for good.

Beth Ann took a step forward, her fingers curling into helpless fists. There was nothing she could do but watch the struggle. The horse foundered, dunking both himself and his rider, and Beth Ann held her breath in horror. But then they broke the choppy surface again. The man had lost his hat, but she thought they were a little closer . . .

In a blinding flash of lightning, she recognized

the glint of whiskey in the curls plastered against the rider's head. "Zach!"

Beth Ann plunged down the incline toward the riverbank, her heart in her throat, terrorized at the drama unfolding before her eyes. Screaming his name again and again, she waved and hopped like a Bedlamite, urging him on while the rain fell in torrents. She couldn't tell if he even saw her, but in the last moment when she feared he was lost, the buckskin found solid ground beneath its hooves. Lurching forward, horse and rider struggled out of the water and up the muddy bank, both soaked to the skin.

With a sob of relief, Beth Ann hurtled toward Zach and the winded horse. "Zach!"

He wiped the water from his eyes and found her. "Angel?"

"Are you *crazy?*" She skidded to a sloppy halt beside his stirrup, then, infuriated, struck his drenched thigh with both fists. "You could have been *killed!*"

The tired horse jerked backward, forcing Zach to concentrate on his reins for a moment. "Dammit, woman! Will you hold off your bitching for just a minute!"

Relief and fury mingled, but any tears she might have shed were lost in the instantaneous ignition of her flayed temper. "How *dare* you frighten me like that! Didn't I tell you to stay away from here?" Her howl of rage nearly matched the wind's. "Where's my rifle? I'll teach you, you mangy, low-down skunk!"

Zach slid from the saddle in one lithe movement and grabbed her arm. "Hold your tongue, you foulmouthed termagant!"

"Get your hands off me!"

The driving rain pasted Zach's hair to his brow,

and his turquoise eyes glinted with temper. "Beth Ann, I swear to God I'll throttle you if you don't shut the hell up!"

"I'd like to see you try!" she spat, then jerked so hard, he lost his grip. She overbalanced and landed butt-first in a puddle the size of New Hampshire. "Now see what you made me do!" she railed.

"What the devil are you doing out here anyway?"

She matched his bellow with a yell. "Trying to save my stock!"

Zach cast a weather eye toward the rising river and the clot of nervous animals in the lower corral. He offered her a hand. "I'll help you."

"I don't need your help!" She dragged herself free of the mudhole's suction, then pitched a fistful of sticky dirt at him. It struck his chin and once white clerical collar with a satisfying splat. "Oh, go soak your head!"

Turning her back, she stormed back up the incline and threw open the corral gate.

"Come back here, woman, I want to talk to you!"

"Now?" Despite the comical way her wide-brimmed hat spilled channels of rain in all directions like a fountain, her look was withering. "Forget it, preacher. I've got work to do."

Clucking smoothly, she approached the group of fractious animals and managed to grab a mare's halter just as an ear-shattering boom of thunder rent the sodden air. "Whoa, Buttercup, easy!"

Buttercup was as eager to leave this terrible place as Beth Ann was, and half dragged her mistress straight through the gap. Holding on for dear life, trying not to stumble and end up trampled,

Beth Ann whistled for the others. Another clap of thunder was all the urging they needed, and the entire group bolted. Beth Ann gave a little shriek of dismay. She heard Zach's shout.

"Lead them toward the barn. I'll herd the rest from behind!"

She would rather have been beholden to a diamondback rattler, but there didn't seem much point in arguing. Hanging on to Buttercup's halter, she slogged toward the barn. She nearly lost her grip on the horse while trying to open the barn door, but finally it swung open and she shooed the animal inside. Buttercup seemed delighted at the dry and relatively quiet haven, trotting happily into a stall and picking up a mouthful of hay.

The rest of the herd wasn't so sure it was a good idea.

"Come on, you stupid toad-brains," Beth Ann crooned in her sweetest voice, gritting her teeth in an encouraging smile. A duo made the decision and bolted inside, but despite Zach's urging from atop his mount, the next one balked at the strange-looking creature in the wide hat and black slicker directing traffic.

"That's right, you sorry little boneyard," Beth Ann urged. "Come on, you reject from a glue factory—"

The air crackled, and the hairs on the back of Beth Ann's neck stood on end. In the next instant, a searing flash blinded her, and the world exploded above her head. The balky horse panicked, reared, then charged past Beth Ann, nearly knocking her down.

"Beth Ann, look out!"

She looked up at Zach's warning, then froze. Lightning had struck the ridgepole extending from the barn loft, and the roof was ablaze in places that quickly smoldered out under the onslaught of the downpour. As she watched in frozen horror, the ridgepole cracked—and fell right at her.

Something caught her hard in the back, knocking her breath from her lungs and lifting her off her feet. It took her a moment to realize it was Zach, who'd grabbed her at a dead run and flung them both out of the way just as the heavy beam slammed into the muddy ground behind them.

Zach rolled to his knees, his hands busy on Beth Ann's person, looking for signs of injury. Beth Ann's lungs were empty, and for that frightening moment before she could inhale again, she wondered if she was dead. Then life returned with a gush of air, and she began to wheeze and struggle, pressing herself up from the sloppy earth.

"Are you all right?" Zach's voice was strained. "Where are you hurt?"

"I'm fine," she said, gasping. "The horses . . ."

"The hell with the damn horses!" he snarled, jerking her to her feet. "They scattered with that last bolt. Let them take care of themselves!"

"But—"

"I've had it, Beth Ann!" he bellowed. "We're getting out of this *now*. The horses will find their own shelter—which proves they're smarter than *we* are!"

Without waiting for her inevitable argument, he half led, half carried her toward the main building. Beth Ann was disgracefully grateful for his support, for her knees felt like noodles and she was shaking all over with shock.

They all but fell through the rear door of the

kitchen. The reprieve from the rain's pounding was a great relief—until she looked down.

"Oh, no!" An inch of water covered the kitchen floor.

"Upstairs."

"But—"

"There's not much we can do about it now." Zach grabbed a stack of kitchen towels from a shelf, and then his features softened. "Come on, honey. You're soaked through."

Helplessly she allowed him to guide her up the stairs into the main parlor. Their sodden garments made puddles on the floor, which Beth Ann ignored for the first time in her life. Outside, the rain barreled down unceasingly.

With shaking hands, Beth Ann pulled off the oversized hat. Her soaked hair spilled from its braid, curling down her back in wet ringlets. She couldn't manage the fasteners on the slicker.

"Let me." Zach had peeled off his drenched coat and shirt and applied a hand towel to his face and bare chest. Now he undid her slicker and deftly stripped it off. Then his breath caught, and he lifted a gentle finger to the welt on her cheek.

"What happened?"

Mystified, she raised her hand to examine the place. "Oh. It's nothing. A twig caught me, that's all."

"You were lucky."

Trembling, she tasted the rain lingering on her upper lip. "What—what are you doing here, Zach?"

He was unbuttoning her cuffs, for her shirtwaist was sodden, too. "I wanted to talk." He looked up with a humorous gleam in his eye. "I just didn't know the bottom could drop out so quickly."

She gave a little cry of desperation. "You could have drowned!"

He went instantly solemn. "And that beam would have killed you. Good thing I showed up, huh?"

Beth Ann looked at him with wonder and terror, and shuddered uncontrollably. They could have both died, and what a waste, what a tragedy! It was stupid, *stupid* not to admit what she'd secretly known for a very long time.

"You're cold," he murmured, chafing her hands. "You need to get those wet things off."

For answer, her trembling fingers found the buttons on her blouse and slowly undid them from neck to waist. She caught his startled gaze with her own, her silvery eyes never wavering as she pulled the blouse free of her waistband then let it slide down her arms.

Zach's Adam's apple bobbed. "Honey?"

She undid the button of her muddy skirt and let it and her petticoats drop to the floor. In her chemise and drawers, she reached for him, placing her palms flat against his hair-dusted chest. "Warm me, Zach."

He shuddered, and his arms circled her like vises. "Sweetheart, this isn't ... I don't think I could stop if ... Are you *sure?*"

Heart beating like a drum within her chest, she nodded. Whatever he was, however they'd come to this, no matter what came after, she couldn't bear to think that she'd let this moment pass without choosing to *live* it fully. She might never have another chance.

"Please, Zach," she whispered, already conscious of the heat radiating against her skin from his thighs, his belly, his chest. She pressed her lips to his breastbone and felt him quiver. "I love you."

He cupped the back of her head in a fierce movement that tilted her face up to his. His eyes blazed.

"You damn well better," he muttered.

When his lips took possession of her mouth, she knew her soul was lost, and she rejoiced.

Chapter 10

She was sweeter than paradise.

Zach tightened his arms around Beth Ann, groaning deep in his throat with the heated, dizzying need spilling through his blood. Her mouth was lush and exotic, potent with the taste of desire, entirely enticing.

Temptress. Eve. Angel and demon in one. She stirred against him, her hands clasping his neck, her skin like silk and roses, and he was utterly lost.

The damp translucency of her thin chemise was no impediment to his questing hand, and he cupped the swollen heaviness of her breast while his tongue took unlicensed liberties within her mouth. The movement brought her to her tiptoes, straining upward to meet him, elongating the soft swell in a mystifying manner that forced the peaked nub into greater prominence against his palm. Control slipped within Zach, while beyond the dim parlor's steamy windows the roaring heavens crashed and fell.

Breathing heavily, he touched the corners of her mouth with his tongue, then grazed along her jawbone, feeding on the shivers that coursed across her flesh. The contrast between their cool, damp garments and the heat generated by the contact of their skin was shocking, as if somehow the lightning had transmitted itself through the air into their bodies, crackling and sizzling with a life of its own. Zach pressed his forehead into the curve of her neck, sliding the strap of her chemise off her shoulder and letting his thumb do wicked things against her nipple. She arched with a gasp of surprise, but then he sensed her almost immediate languor, a subtle acceptance of the pleasure, a feminine melting that stoked his masculine fires.

"Jee-sus, you're sweet," he said, his voice husky with need.

How could Tom have given this up he wondered? He knew that he wouldn't tell Beth Ann the news about her former love. He didn't want her sparing so much as a thought for that bastard, not when, by her own admission, it was Zach she cared for now. He reveled in the selfishness of that powerful knowledge, overcome by a primitive need for possession that surged like flame through his aching loins.

Beth Ann caressed his nape, her fingers twining into his damp curls, and her expression was dazed. "Zach . . ."

He dropped to one knee, sliding his hands around to cup her buttocks intimately, leaning in to lick her puckered pink nipples through the thin fabric. Her hands convulsed against his shoulders, and she moaned softly.

Pressing his face into the curve of her belly, Zach inhaled the heated womanly scents, musk and honey, and Beth Ann swayed against him, shuddering, her fingers tightening unthinkingly in his hair. Running his hands down her lithe flanks to the garters at her knees, he pushed down her stockings, caressing her slender calves, then fumbled clumsily with the wet laces and removed her shoes.

Reversing his direction, he explored the tops of her thighs, then plucked loose the button at the waist of her drawers, soothing her instant tension with murmured nothings, then slowly peeling the damp garment down her slender legs. He sucked in a sharp breath at the sight of the triangle of tight black curls at the apex of her thighs. Unbearably moved, he bent and pressed a kiss there, holding her still against his mouth when she jerked and gave a tiny squeal of surprise.

Sensing her resistance, he reluctantly retreated, moving up to circle the indentation of her navel with the tip of his tongue, smiling to himself as her knees buckled and she slid down his chest and back into his arms. He supported them both, kissing her ardently as they kneeled on the hard wooden floor together.

Beth Ann's responsiveness staggered him. Her tongue was nimble and as rapacious as his own. Her hands explored his shoulders, his biceps, the sensitive turn of his elbow, then her fingers raked through the mat of hair on his chest and her nails traced the round coins of his nipples. He growled low in his throat in pleasure, and she grew bolder, her hands sliding down his flat belly to his belt buckle.

"Yes," he encouraged, his teeth tugging gently at her lower lip. "Touch me."

But she hesitated, drew back. Zach caught her hand and pressed it to himself through his soaked trousers, letting her feel his hardness. She gasped and shivered, but did not resist, and her touch, even through the layers of fabric, drove Zach toward the brink of madness.

Circling her waist with both arms, he buried his mouth in the valley between her breasts, shaking in every fiber, struggling for breath, for control. He wanted to make it good, and so he strove to slow the pace, but his body screamed in denial, everything in him urging him to take her now, here on the hard floor with the rain beating down outside.

Her lips were beside his ear, her breath warm and beguiling. "I . . . can't breathe."

"That makes two of us, honey," he said against the lacy edge of her chemise.

Suddenly impatient with even that frail barrier, he leaned back, lifted the garment over her head, and tossed it aside, catching her about the waist again when she murmured in soft protest and blushed hotly. Fascinated, he watched the rosy tide climb up her chest and neck, then followed its path with the backs of his knuckles.

"Beautiful. You are so damned lovely."

"Zach—"

"Let me," he said against her lips. She sighed and leaned back against his arm, quivering and acquiescent, and he ran his hand from her collarbone to the turgid dusky tip of one breast, across the downy plane of her belly, and lower, lower into the nest of crinkly hair.

Zach plunged his tongue into her mouth as the tip of his finger parted her soft feminine petals. Exploring deeper, he inhaled her quick, excited gasps, taking her soft moans within himself, feeling her eagerness and need from both within and without, and making it an extension of his own. His fingers found moisture, the feminine dew of arousal, and he thought he'd explode with wanting.

With a rumbled growl of pure male intent, he caught her in his arms and rose to his feet in one swift movement. Leaving behind the trail of discarded clothing, he carried her into her own shadowy bedroom. He swept back the bedcovers with one hand, then deposited her gently on the snowy sheets. A flare of lightning, farther away now, illuminated her for a scant second—her dark hair spread in undulating waves over her shoulders, her body pale and almost luminescent, her eyes the color of twilight, watchful and shy and shining with a silver intensity that shattered his composure.

He couldn't shed the rest of his clothes fast enough, but finally he was beside her in the gently swaying rope bed. As he covered her with kisses, his large hands molded her slender form from shoulder to hip, torturing himself with the sweet agony of his overwhelming need. She touched his waist, his hipbones, and murmured his name, and he couldn't wait any longer.

Kissing Beth Ann deeply, Zach moved over her, letting her feel his weight, parting her legs and probing the dark mysteries between her thighs with his arousal. She arched against him a little, a sudden tension possessing her, and he soothed her with little nuzzles against her neck, then took a nipple between his teeth and suckled strongly.

Crying out, she writhed and squirmed against him, and he almost cursed, it was so good. She was hot, so hot, and his tip parted her wetness, slid into silkiness a little distance. He stopped, teasing them both, catching her wrists and pressing them down against the mattress beside her ears. His eyes met hers.

"God, I want you. You're tearing me apart." He moved slightly, evoking a strangled gasp from her.

"I love you. I do." Her whispered words held a strange tremor, as though they were meant to reassure her more than him.

"I know, angel. Hold on." He pressed more forcefully. She was tight, and though he didn't want to hurt her by going too fast, not giving her the time to accommodate him, the exquisite pleasure of her flesh gloving him urged him inexorably forward.

She stiffened, her eyes opening wide, and Zach backed off with a silent curse. Sliding his hands down her rib cage, he palmed her hips and lifted her slightly to ease the penetration, and tried again, slowly, slowly, gritting his teeth with the effort.

And came up against resistance.

"Relax, honey." Zach panted, his breath hissing between his teeth. "You're so tense, I can't—"

"I'm trying." Her voice was raw, strangely vulnerable.

"Maybe too hard," he muttered, covering her mouth again. With his hands, he urged her to lift her knees. Her thighs flexed beneath his hands, and she clung to his neck, opening to him fully, defenseless and giving, yet womanly and powerful at the same time. He was humbled, exalted by her trust.

"We're so good together, sweetheart," Zach said, his voice raspy with strain. "Can you feel it? Let it happen."

Passion clouded his eyesight. Need drove him. She was so tight, he'd thought he'd die of pleasure. The pressure. Ah, the heat . . .

Face buried against her neck, he pressed, every atom in his being urging him to bury himself deep, deep in her sweet body. But her resistance was still there, and the cords of Zach's patience and his control were fraying fast. He pushed harder, and she arched against him with a tiny cry, her features in the shadowy light pinched with pain.

He could have wept with frustration. "Beth, please. I don't want to hurt you. It'll be so much better if you relax."

"It's all right." Her hands smoothed his shoulders in unspoken forgiveness. "I want you."

Zach caught her face between his hands and kissed her deeply, his tongue carnally mimicking the joining of their bodies. But she remained stiff with apprehension, and when the demands of his body insisted he thrust against her entrance and she gasped again, he groaned aloud.

"I don't understand. What are you scared of, angel?"

"So many damn questions!" She flexed and pressed her heels into the small of his back.

It was too much for Zach's system. With a groan that was both defeat and triumph, he surged strongly against her. From some distant plane he felt the moment her resistance ended. And he plunged deep inside her, the way he'd always wanted, sheathed so closely, he could feel her heartbeat.

She quivered like a bowstring, and he knew he'd hurt her, but regret was beyond him in that moment when heaven and hell commingled in a flash of ecstatic sensation. Enfolded, enveloped, enraptured, he cradled her to him, kissing the straining cords in her neck, licking at her nipples, then taking her mouth again. He tasted salt and tears, but she clung to him, kissing him back, and his mind melted and his body moved of its own accord.

Thrusting deeply, he captured her little shudders within his mouth as the tempo increased, and suddenly there was no way to wait for her completion, no way to deny the explosion that caught him and hurled him straight into the heart of a fiery sun.

After a long time, his spinning senses slowed. Vaguely he realized he was still a part of her body

and that his full weight rested on her. Overcome
with the lassitude of exquisite release, his nose
pressed into the fragrant hollow of her shoulder,
he lifted himself slightly, and she drew a shaky
breath that was close to a sob.

"My God, you're wonderful," he murmured,
nuzzling her skin. He felt her shift uncomfortably,
and reluctantly lifted himself from her, sliding
onto his side and cradling her in the curve of his
body. He swept her tumbled hair back from her
face and kissed her tenderly. It disturbed him to
find her weeping.

"Don't, angel," he begged softly. "It'll be all
right next time, you'll see. I'm a clumsy oaf, and
you're so sweet, I went off like a green boy, but I
promise it'll be better . . ."

He stroked her breast, her stomach, felt the
sticky evidence of their passion on her inner thigh.
It gave him a strange, possessive feeling to know
how they had marked each other. He lifted his fingers, then frowned.

The storm still beat its fury against the windows, but the room inside was suddenly an oasis
of silence. Only Beth Ann's quiet shudders broke
the stillness. Zach looked down at the dark smears
on her thighs, the sheets, himself. For a dizzying
instant the world turned upside down. Nothing
made sense.

And then everything did.

"Merciful God." His whisper was harsh; he was
stricken with the enormity of his discovery. Tom
Chapman was a goddammed liar, all right. "Son of
a bitch!"

Beth Ann tried to roll away, but Zach caught
her, pinned her shoulders down, his eyes glittering
with fury and shame and a disgraceful pride.

"Why? For God's sake, Beth Ann, all this time

you let me think, you let everyone think ... You
never lay with Tom Chapman!"

"I—I did ..."

"Don't give me that! Not with your virgin's
blood covering us both!"

She looked disconcerted, then closed her eyes in
utter mortification. "Is that what ... ? I didn't
know."

Zach's voice was harsh, not to be denied, and
his hands tightened on her shoulders. "What happened with Tom? Tell me!"

"H-He tried, but I was afraid, and it hurt. He
couldn't stay ... you know, *up*, and blamed me."
Tears seeped from under her spiky lashes. "Said I
wasn't a real woman, and then Paw came, and it
was so awful. Anyway, it was too late, because
Tom had taken my virtue."

"No, I just did that," Zach grated, appalled.
He'd been so blinded by his own need, he'd failed
to see the most basic truth. Though she was tech-
nically innocent, he'd taken Beth Ann as if she
were an experienced woman, and his arrogance
and the hurt he'd done her choked him with remorse. "Jesus Christ! Why didn't you tell me?"

Looking as stricken as he felt, she began to weep
in earnest, and he had to strain to understand her
whispered admission.

"Because you might have stopped."

Wretched and wicked, and aching in places
she'd never dreamed, Beth Ann cried against the
curve of Zach's shoulder. He held her until her
storm passed. She could hardly bear his tenderness, and was glad when he finally rose from the
bed and left her.

Huddled on her side, she listened miserably to
the rain that continued to fall, then water splash-

ing from her pitcher and the sounds of discreet washing. Beth Ann closed her eyes, confused and mortified.

She was bound to burn for sure now. Seducing a preacher was certainly high on the list of mortal sins. At least, she thought glumly, she finally really deserved to be called a fornicator.

Still, how curious and deliriously delightful to become part of a man you loved. Imagine having him place himself *there, inside.* How unsettled and muddled it made you afterward. How utterly wanton to wonder what it would be like again.

She felt the edge of the bed sink with Zach's weight, and closed her eyes, praying he'd think she slept.

"Turn over, Beth." Zach pressed her shoulder back into the rumpled bedclothes when she didn't respond. "Come on, honey, I know you're not asleep."

She peered at him cautiously through the fan of her lashes, feeling the heat of a blush rising from her nipples. He was still as naked as she was, and she didn't know how to act in such a situation. Zach gave her a crooked smile.

"I thought this might help."

Lifting a cool, damp cloth, he bathed her hot face, looking very dark and masculine and totally out of place performing such a common service. She couldn't prevent a sigh of pleasure at the cooling whisk of cloth that moved from her face down her neck to her collarbone. But when he touched her legs, she sat up suddenly, reaching for the top sheet, thoroughly embarrassed.

"I can do that," she managed.

A long way off, the rush of the Gila overflowing its banks hissed and murmured like a thing alive, a living entity that surrounded and protected and isolated Traveler's Rest even while it threatened. They might be the only ones left on earth. Beth Ann certainly felt as though she'd dropped off the edge of the world.

"Let me." His voice was deep, his eyes blue-green fire in the near-darkness. Inexorably he pushed the sheet away. "I want to see how I hurt you."

"It wasn't so bad." She realized it was true. The pain had been fierce but fleeting, the soreness passing away already. This was much more mortifying. "Zach, please."

Ignoring her breathy plea, he carefully wiped the dark smears from the inside of her thighs. "These stains are the fruits of the gift you gave me tonight. You think I would not honor them?"

She didn't know what to say. He cleaned gently between her legs, marking the transitory fidgets and winces. Her breathing hastened subtly, and she chewed her lip, silly tears prickling behind her eyes again.

"Angel, don't." Zach tossed the stained cloth aside and pulled her into his arms. "It's going to be all right."

"H-How?" Her breath was catchy with the weight of tears in her chest. He kissed her gently, with such tenderness, her heart nearly burst.

"We'll worry about that in the morning. Rest now. You've been through a lot."

Zach settled them back into the pillows and covered them with the sheet. Beth Ann's cheek lay against his chest, and Zach's arms surrounded her protectively. Exhausted, she allowed herself to savor the embrace as her mind grew hazy.

It was sweet to be held like this, against his heart, and so she fought sleep, drifting in and out, conscious of his hard length next to hers, startled by the brush of hair-dusted limbs when next she surfaced. She wanted to hold on to each sensation as something precious but ephemeral and fleeting, a treasure to be stored in her memory against a grayer day.

The room was black, but the rain had ceased when she became aware of the shadowy weight of him again. Her lips rested against his throat and her legs tangled with Zach's. Drowsy, at ease, she inhaled the musky maleness of his skin like the finest perfume of Arabia. If she turned, thusly, she could kiss the stubble where it began to sprout under his jaw, feeling its rasp against the tip of her tongue.

A warm hand fondled her breast, slowly, softly, without the pressure of time or passion. Blindly she moved closer, seeking warmth, purring as the stroke of a lazy fingertip pebbled her nipple into a hardened nub. She touched his chest, learning his muscular contours by feel in the blackness—the crisp layer of hair, the corrugated outline of ribs and belly, the raised flesh of the scar she'd put on his shoulder.

His hand drifted down her spine, coming to rest at the top of her buttocks, making little soothing circles in the small of her back. She sighed softly. A deeper shadow rose over her, and then his lips traced her features, featherlight kisses on her lashes, the tip of her nose, finally settling upon her mouth like a butterfly alighting on its chosen blossom. And like the blossom, she opened for him.

Beth Ann reached for Zach's face, molding his strong cheekbones between her fingertips, tracing the line of his jaw so that she would know him forever. She threaded her exploring hands into his hair, loving the way it clung and curled over her fingers, mapping the texture of it, learning the nuances that made him unique.

As they lay cocooned in darkness, there was no time, no place, only the two together, brightly burning for each other with a light no ordinary mortal could perceive. Hearts beat in time; sighs sang a sweet duet. Bone became liquid, and flesh as weightless as air. Touching him, she knew herself. When he touched her body, she discovered him.

When, after a long, patient wait, he rolled onto his back and pulled her atop him, she sighed and took him within herself, free of pain and doubt. Awash with pleasure, shivering with desire, she felt dreams and reality merge. Man and woman became one.

Zach held her hips, guiding her to power but letting her choose the path. She rose and fell in a rhythm as ageless as the tides surging upon the shore, enthralled by the rapture building between them, lost in a sea of tender passion. He cupped her breasts, rubbing their crests with increasing urgency, his hips pumping to meet hers, and something wild flared within her.

Loosed from guilt and fear by the darkness and the man, she found her freedom, crashing upon the sands in an incandescent wave of ecstasy that took her by surprise. Arching to the heavens, she cried out, the light of revelation and love flooding her every cell.

And Zach caught her as she fell back down to earth, then poured his strength into her and sent them both flying again.

Reborn, washed clean, the sky sparkled and the earth rested.

Head on her crooked arm, Beth Ann watched

the pearly predawn light illuminate Zach's features, carving them out of the shadows into wonderful prominence. He slept deeply, affording her the undiluted pleasure of looking her fill at him.

She loved his eyelashes, she decided. Never had there been eyelashes as beautifully colored, as fascinatingly thick. And the rusty freckles on his handsome chest—had there ever been freckles so adorable? So absolutely masculine. She meant to count and catalog each one, and give thanks and blessings for them all.

Lying beside the man she loved, Beth Ann basked in a golden euphoria. She knew there were things she should think about—the whereabouts of the horses, whether Traveler's Rest had sustained any major damage, when Buck or Paw were likely to return—but for this one fragile bubble in time, she allowed herself to ignore both responsibilities and consequences. It was enough to just *feel*. It was miraculous to be this happy.

How many times had she and Zach reached for each other during this night of discovery? She hardly knew. But she did know they'd explored the boundaries of delight together. She'd had no idea that the pleasures of the flesh could be so all-consuming, that being held with tenderness and concern and passion could expand the horizons of a woman's very existence, that loving a man with one's body could make of you *more*, not less.

What she and Zach had done with and for each other felt so very right that she could not bring herself to doubt or fear the future. Zach would never hurt her. How could he, when he'd been so tender and remorseful over the little injury that she knew now, proudly, had made her a whole woman? And the delight he'd shown when she'd come to completion, dissolving in his arms in resplendent pleasure. Surely such a man would never fail her. Somehow she was certain things would work out.

The room had grown brighter, but Beth Ann was still loath to disturb Zach. She wanted to extend this first time together as far as possible, keep it inviolate just for the two of them before the world intruded. Smiling, she slipped quietly from the bed and reached for her white cotton wrapper, thinking about sharing a cup of coffee, watching him shave—perhaps helping him again! The image made her shiver with a sensual rush. The things they had left to discover about each other filled her with happy expectation.

Padding on bare feet through the deserted house, she paused in the parlor, bemused by the scene of seduction. Clothes lay everywhere, piled in such a manner that there was no question of what had occurred. It was damning evidence which she'd just as soon no one, especially her paw, discovered.

A quick glance out the front windows proved that the Gila had returned to much its original course. Despite the litter of debris, the ford would be passable again, the privacy she and Zach had shared nearly over. Anxious about his way station, if not his daughter's safety, Wolf would no doubt make his appearance too soon for her peace of mind.

Beth Ann's bubble of unconcern popped. Before the reality returned, it would be wise for her and Zach to talk. Taking a deep breath, she hurried down the inside stairs to inspect her kitchen.

A thin layer of mud covered the stone flags, but luckily, there was no other damage, With the expertise of long practice, she quickly built a fire in the stove and started the coffee. She and Ama would have to spend some time getting the place back into her usual spick-and-span order. Depending on the roads, there might even be a stage through today, and passengers to feed.

That thought led her to the back door. The yard was muddy, and scattered with windblown litter, but down past the barn in the cottonwood thicket, several horses grazed peacefully. It was likely that the rest of the herd was nearby as well. Even Buck would have an easy time retrieving them.

The smell of fresh-brewed coffee filled the kitchen as Beth Ann stepped back inside, her mind clicking over with things to do. No matter that her life had changed substantially, the world still rolled on. She crossed to the pantry and opened the locked storeroom, breathing a sigh of relief to find that her sacks of flour and sugar, the boxes of canned goods, and the other staples stored in the windowless, shelf-lined room were also undamaged.

The lid rattled on the bubbling coffee pot. Without bothering to lock the storeroom again, Beth Ann rushed to rescue the pot before it boiled over. Pouring a cup, she hurried up the stairs again, this time pausing to pick up the clothing scattered around the parlor, her muddy skirts and underthings, Zach's stained shirt and sodden coat. She carried her load back to her room, satisfied with the removal of the most blatant evidence of her fall from grace.

Zach was still asleep as she quietly set the coffee cup on the bedside table. Beth Ann smiled to herself as his nose twitched at the warm aroma and he threw his forearm across his brow as if to ward off the invasion of wakefulness. The stubble on his jaw gleamed with reddish lights, and his mouth, relaxed and unsmiling, seemed rather more determined, even ruthless, than when he was awake and animated with his usual charm. Though his whiskey-tinted curls were boyishly endearing to her, there was nothing childlike about Zach Temple in repose. A tiny shiver ran down Beth Ann's spine, but whether it was a response to the sexual longing that filled her or a premonition of disaster, she wasn't sure.

Shaking off the phantasm, Beth Ann threw the curling, tangled mass of her hair over her shoulders and stealthily moved around the room, quickly sorting out their clothing. She had fresh things to wear, but Zach's would have to be laundered. Laying his damp, crumpled trousers across the back of a chair, she examined his shirt, then threw it into the pile with her own muddy things. She held up his dark coat, inspecting the damage his dunk into the Gila had done with a critical eye. Perhaps if she brushed it down well, it wouldn't be a total loss.

Taking her hairbrush, she moved to the window to see better, then briskly whisked the bristles over the damp wool, loosening bits of mud and grass. It was a homey, wifely task that made her smile to herself. So this was what it felt like. The intimacies of the night bled over into the daylight, giving a woman a proprietary right to care for her man, to perform the little domestic services that linked and bound a couple in bonds of familiarity and affection to last a lifetime.

Bemused, Beth Ann stroked the lapels of Zach's coat lovingly. One of the buttons hung by a thread, and when she touched it, it popped off in her hand. When the coat was dry again, she'd stitch it back on for Zach. A minister of the gospel couldn't appear looking tattered and tawdry. She slipped the button into the coat's side pocket for safekeeping, and her fingers touched a sodden slip of paper. Frowning, hoping it wasn't something important, she eased the nearly disintegrating square from the pocket—and stared into her own eyes.

For a long moment her brain refused to work. Then, creaking over like old machinery, the inevitable questions formed. It was an old picture, over two years old, and she'd only had the one . . .

With a little start of dismay and growing dread, she turned the tintype over, but she didn't need to strain her eyes to decipher the washed-out shadow of an inscription: "For Tom, with love from Beth Ann."

The coat dropped from her hands. The black ice of cold suspicion and dire foreboding congealed her blood and froze her heart. Compelled, she turned slowly, and met the turquoise gaze of a man she didn't know.

Raised on one elbow, Zach looked at her face, then the picture slowly dissolving between her fingers. His mouth twisted.

"Beth—"

Disillusion and fear made her eyes stark. "Who *are* you?"

Chapter 11

It's not what you think."

"Since I've no idea what I think, that could well be true," Beth Ann said in a voice that shook only slightly.

Zach sat up on the edge of the bed, his bare feet dangling to the floor, the sheet twisted about his hips. Beth Ann was silhouetted against the muslin-covered window, her dark mass of hair backlit with a nimbus like an angel's halo. The crumpled, shapeless garment she wore fell open at her slender neck, revealing the pulse jumping in the hollow of her throat.

Zach was amazed by his involuntary leap of arousal. He wanted her again, but her silver eyes were accusing, more avenging angel than sweet devil lover now, and guilt rose up in Zach's throat like gall. His reckoning was at hand, but he was at a loss where to begin.

"I can explain," he said, knowing how lame that sounded.

"Just tell me where you got this." Her fingers trembled on the small portrait. "Tom?"

Zach nodded uncomfortably, the easy charm that had served him well in so many tight places unaccountably missing.

Beth Ann sucked in a breath, as if she'd been punched in the stomach, as if she'd braced for the blow but was still surprised by the force of it. "He gave it to you?"

"Not exactly." Zach tried to tread carefully. "It . . . came into my possession in Yuma."

"In prison." Her eyes widened imperceptibly when he made no denial. "You weren't there ministering to the prisoners, were you?"

The muscle in Zach's jaw twitched. "No."

"You aren't a preacher. Never have been."

He shook his head.

"You son of a bitch!" She pitched the tintype print into his face, and the picture fluttered down and landed on the floor between his feet. She was furious, gloriously enraged, her eyes burning with silver fire and her breasts heaving beneath the wrapper in agitation. "All this time, I thought—but you're nothing but a rotten, lying, stinking *convict!*"

"I did my time," he said tightly.

"For what? Have I been harboring a bank robber, a murderer? If you knew Tom, there's nothing could surprise me!"

Zach shrugged. "Fraud."

"How utterly perfect! How delightfully absurd." Haughty as a queen, she looked down her nose at him. "Why? Why did you come here?"

"Something Tom said." Zach saw the dangerous glint in her eye and added hastily, "About your paw. It . . . it was a bad idea."

She blinked in comprehension, then gave a derisive, caustic laugh meant for them both. "Of course. You're just another jackass after Paw's gold. Paw's *nonexistent* gold. He's been played out for years. Only, fools like you and Tom never believe it!"

Abruptly she turned her back, staring out the window, and her voice was low and bitter. "And God knows I never learn."

Zach came off the bed then, clasping her bent

shoulders, his mouth twisting with remorse. "Beth, honey—"

She rounded on him with a she-cat's enraged hiss, throwing off his hands. "Don't touch me! I can't bear it."

That hurt.

"You didn't mind it so much last night," he muttered.

"How dare you remind me!" She was livid, her color high from both fury and an unobstructed view of his magnificent, unabashed nudity. "I must have been mad! Why don't you just go?"

"I will. Things . . . Well, it's time for me to leave Destiny. That's what I rode out last night to tell you."

Beth Ann caught a strangled breath, a twisted, sharply painful sound, and she swayed on her feet. Zach caught her waist between his hands to hold her steady, and this time she lacked the strength to protest.

"Couldn't get what you wanted, so you took what you could get, is that it, preacher?" Her question ended with a choked laugh, and then she couldn't seem to catch her breath. "I'll bet you never had such a send-off before, have you, Zach? It is Zach, isn't it? Or is that another lie?"

"It's Zach. Zach Madison."

She nodded. "But perhaps spectacular good-byes are your specialty, Zach Madison. Along with fraud and deception."

Zach winced. "Give me some credit, Beth Ann. Last night took me as much by surprise as it did you. And as much as I enjoyed it, it didn't mean good-bye."

"What did it mean?" Her words were barely a whisper.

"How about . . . a beginning? For us. I want you to come with me."

She frowned, her gaze going slightly unfocused in confusion. "Come with you? Where?"

"Does it really matter? Anywhere would be better for you than this hellhole."

Gentling her with the pressure of his hands, he tugged her closer, burying his lips in the curls at her temple. His sex brushed the soft folds of her wrapper, pressing against the womanly curves beneath the fabric, and he nearly groaned with a fresh surge of lust.

"We'll go anywhere you want," he said thickly. "I've got . . . skills, of a sort. Why, you've never seen a better man at three-card monte or the old soap game! God, we'll have a time together."

"Are you asking me to marry you?"

He was startled, then his mouth curved into a persuasive grin. "Come on, honey. We're both too savvy to fall for that old trap."

"I suppose. So we'll move about like two will-o'-the-wisps plying your 'trade,' and I'll be your mistress. And then what, Zach?"

"Hmm?" He nuzzled the hollow of her neck, drinking in the heated, feminine essences, his fists dragging at her wrapper.

She stood still and patient under his attentions, her voice strangely dispassionate. "After you've made me your doxy and used me like a whore, then what?"

He drew back a little, scowling. "Don't talk like that, angel. I'll take care of you."

"Liar!" She shoved him away viciously, her eyes glimmering with furious tears. "You low-down varmint! When I think of what you put me through—give me one reason why I should believe a word you say!"

Zach shoved his fingers through his hair in exasperation. "Jesus Christ, woman! I'm being as honest as I know how."

"Honest?" she sneered. "Now, there's an interesting word coming from you. The whole damned town swallowed your tales. *Reverend* Temple this and *Reverend* Temple that! So good, so understanding, such a worker for the Lord. Everyone thinks you're some kind of saint!"

Zach couldn't repress a grin. "Everyone but you. So what do you say, angel? Shall we be sinners together? I guarantee it'll be a whole lot more satisfying."

She gasped in outrage. "You abominable swine! You lied to me. You made me believe and hope, and I—I trusted you. I gave ..." Her breathing grew choppy, painful. "I gave you ... *everything*, and you made me ... Oh, God, now I really am a fallen woman!"

"Don't go hysterical on me!" Zach snapped, reaching for her.

She darted under his arm, her panicked movements throwing her into the side of her loom frame and sending it crashing to the floor. "Stay away from me!"

His brows lowered into an angry glower, Zach stalked her through the tangle of yarns and spindles like a mountain lion tracking its prey. With a little squeak, Beth Ann backed away, only to find herself trapped between the bedside table and corner window. "Don't come any closer!"

"You're being overemotional, Beth Ann," he said firmly. "You can make a few virtuous protests for appearances' sake, if you must, but don't expect me to drag out the sackcloth and ashes over this. You wanted what happened as much as I did—more, even."

"Liar! Lying pig!"

He gave a long-suffering sigh. "I wasn't alone in that bed, Beth. I came out here to tell you everything, to ask you to go away with me, and that's the God's truth, I swear. Things just happened a little faster than I'd counted on, that's all, but the end is still the same. Just because you're feeling a little postcoital remorse doesn't mean you should throw it all away."

"There's nothing worth keeping!" She spit like a cornered kitten, her fingers curling into claws as if she'd like to tear him to pieces.

Zach gave her a disgusted look. "Hell, I thought you had better sense that to swallow the guilt Wolf's been spoon-feeding you."

"At least Paw tries to make me do what's right," she said defiantly.

"By torturing you mentally with a pile of self-righteous garbage? By never forgiving you for the one mistake you made? By keeping you a virtual prisoner, like a slave in your own home?" She looked so stricken that he modulated his tone and reached to gently touch her cheek. "You've been trying to escape for a long time, honey. Why not with me?"

He saw her little guilty start and knew he'd guessed right. From her flight with Tom to that foolish runaway attempt that Pat Tucker's attack had spoiled, to those days when she'd allowed Zach to court her while she looked for respectability—oh, yes, she'd dreamed of escape in lots of ways, and the truth of that flickered in her fine gray eyes.

But, stubbornly, she held on to her defiance. "I don't need you to escape. I—I'll do it on my own! I'm going to San Francisco and train with a great chef. I'll have a career. You'll see . . ."

She caught a ragged breath as he stroked her

throat, and her lashes fanned down, shadowing her cheekbones. "Don't, Zach."

Crowding her closer, he cupped her breast through the wrapper, gently pinching the crest into prominence. "We've got this, and it's good. You can't deny that."

"Bastard," she moaned, leaning in to him. "You're trying to use my weakness against me."

He caught her close, letting his arousal press against her feminine mound, laughing softly in her ear. "I'm counting on it."

Zach kissed her then, a soft, deep mingling of mouths that lit fires neither could deny. She murmured incoherently, and her arms stole around his neck, the sweet silkiness of her ebony hair surrounding them like a dark, fragrant cloud. Zach gathered fistfuls of her wrapper, tugging it upward until he could cup her rounded buttocks with his bare palms, lifting her against his tumescence and grinding circles that left them both breathless.

He could sense the heat building in her, the subtle softening underlaid with fine tension, and was staggered anew by her responsiveness. His tongue delved deeper, twining with hers, tasting the heady wine of her mouth and feeling her deep, interior shiver, the melting pliancy of surrender. She was his for the taking, every sweet, luscious inch, every succulent curve, and he wanted to lift her against the wall and pound into her until they were both convinced of that essential truth.

His chest heaving, his skin burning, his loins aching, Zach began to back her into the corner, smiling against her mouth in triumph. "Tom said you were hot in bed. Pity the poor bastard never knew how right he was."

A shriek pierced Zach's eardrum the same mo-

ment a cup struck his temple and a shower of still
hot coffee rained down his back. Zach jumped and
yowled. "Ow!"

Beth Ann jerked free of his hands, murder in her
eye. "Goddammed lying, stinking bastards—
you're all alike! God, I hate you! I hate you all.
Where's my rifle? I'm going to shoot you so full of
holes—"

She darted toward the door, but Zach caught
her wrist in a punishing grip and swung her
around against the tan adobe wall with an angry
growl. Brown streams of coffee dripped down his
back and trickled through the hair on his legs.

"Damnation, woman, have you lost your
mind?"

"Yes!" she howled, wild-eyed with fury and humiliation. "Yes! To ever think, to ever believe I
could care for you! Get out of my house. Get out
of my life!"

She struck out at him, and her palm clapped
painfully against his ear. Zach pinned her wrists
against the wall and pressed his body into hers to
control her struggles.

"That's enough, you hellcat!"

"Let me go!" Panting hard, she glared up at
him. "I hate you!"

"No, you don't." Smiling a little at her puny resistance, he bent closer, relishing the fact that he
didn't have to play the saint any longer. "And I'll
show you why."

His kissed her hard, wielding his superior
strength ruthlessly, then drew back sharply with a
grunt of pain. Amazed as much as angry, he tasted
the metallic, salty-sweet flavor of blood on his lip.
She'd bitten him!

"Damnation, what's got into you?" he snarled,

squeezing her wrists. "Will you settle down and be sensible?"

"Sensible!" The word was a scream of rage. Straining furiously within his grip, she tried to knee him, to stomp his toes—anything! "You misbegotten half-wit! You have no idea—"

Her voice cracked suddenly. Her eyes filled, and her whisper came from a low, husky register, full of desperation and despair. "I'll never forgive you. Never."

"So what the hell difference dose it make!" Zach's anger was born of confusion. He'd offered her a way out, hadn't he? What did she want from him? "You're loco, lady, plum loco!"

"And you're a thief and a liar!" she shrieked. "Your mother should have drowned you at birth!"

Crimson fury blinded Zach. "You bitch, that's—"

"Enough!"

The infuriated bellow lashed them like the whip of an Arctic wind, freezing them in place. In the doorway, Wolf Linder raised the ugly black muzzle of a Colt revolver and cocked the hammer with an ominous click that echoed bizarrely in the now silent room.

"That," he repeated with a quietness that was worse than a shout, "is quite enough." Leaning on his cane, his fat face suffused with choleric color under his bushy beard, he waved the barrel at Zach. "Step away from my daughter."

Oh, God, I'm going to faint! Silver spangles floated in blackness on the edge of Beth Ann's vision. Paw! It was like with Tom, only a thousand times worse. Her heart wouldn't beat and she couldn't breathe and she wished the floor would open and the earth would swallow her alive. Hell itself would be better than this!

Zach slowly unclenched his hands from around Beth Ann's wrists, frowning at the red rings his fingers had made. Unperturbed by his own nudity, he faced Wolf instead of moving away, shielding Beth Ann with his body.

"Take it easy, Wolf," he warned softly. "This isn't as bad as you think. I wasn't going to harm her—"

"Shut up and get your pants on, preacher!" Wolf growled. "Before I do something I shouldn't."

Zach's eyes narrowed on the gun, and he nodded. Jaw working, he grabbed his trousers from the back of the chair and pulled them on.

Her ears ringing and her mouth dry, Beth Ann sagged against the rough plastered wall, praying her knees wouldn't give way. Wolf's black eyes took in everything—her well-kissed lips and the rumpled sheets—and condemned her utterly. In a swift move that belied his size and disability, the older man stepped forward and struck Beth Ann a stinging blow with the back of his hand. She fell sideways into the window indention.

"*Jezebel!*" he hissed. "Wicked abomination! You reek of the foulest sin."

Knuckles pressed against the trickle of blood in the corner of her mouth, Beth Ann cowered and quivered at each word as though from another blow. Numb, humiliated, she wished she were dead.

"Leave her be, Wolf," Zach ordered angrily, a muscle ticking in his clenched jaw. "I'm the one at fault."

"Your flesh is no weaker than any man's, Reverend. It's this strumpet here who's tempted you to sin." Wolf's ebony eyes burned with a zealot's righteous fire.

"You've got it wrong," Zach protested, both

sickened and amazed. "Don't you understand it was me who took advantage?"

Wolf shook his head sorrowfully. "God knows you're an honorable man to try to defend this heathenish slut, but she's cast in the mold of Eve. Wickedness and vile degradation flow in her veins which no amount of penitence and prayer can cleanse!"

His florid face the picture of grim determination, Wolf waved the gun in the direction of the door. "But I can sure try. You best go now, Reverend."

"The hell I will!" In one swift movement, Zach shrugged his coat on over his coffee-stained back and reached for Beth Ann. "Come on, honey, find some clothes. We're getting out of here. Now."

"I can't allow that, Reverend." Wolf pointed the pistol at Zach's midsection. "I won't let this harlot spawn of mine spoil a promising career. You do proper repentance before the Lord and we'll say nothing more about this ... unfortunate mistake."

"Goddammit, Wolf!" Exasperation fueled Zach's anger and revulsion, but Wolf's state of mind was explosive, and Zach didn't dare move, only tightened his hand on Beth Ann's upper arm in silent warning.

"Don't add blasphemy to your transgressions," Wolf ordered coldly, raising the gun. "Now, git."

"Don't you threaten a servant of the Lord, you bullheaded buffalo!" Zach retorted, feigning high indignation. "Your daughter and I ..." He paused and swallowed hard. "We're getting *married.*"

Beth Ann gaped, then the weight of a thousand disappointments landed on her chest, and she gasped for air. Married? Oh, sure, *now* Zach offered a respectable solution—when he stood at gunpoint with no other alternative! It was too utterly lowering, too completely mortifying! She might be secondhand goods, she might be in hot water up to her eyeballs, but even a fallen woman didn't have to stoop to accepting a man who didn't really want her! That future was too horrific to contemplate!

"Married?" Wolf echoed uncertainly.

"No, we're not!" Beth Ann denied, provoked beyond all rationality.

"Shut up," Zach ordered, jerking her arm. "It's what you wanted, isn't it?"

"In a pig's eye!" Wiping her lip, she lifted her chin, all traces of craven timidity vanishing in a rush of defiance. "I wouldn't have you if God Almighty served you to me on a golden collection plate, *preacher!*"

"There, I knew it!" Wolf grunted with entirely too much satisfaction. "You little hellion. You tricked the reverend, didn't you?"

"Lured him in, bold as brass," she said wildly, twisting free of Zach with a triumphant smile. "Just like I did Tom, Pat Tucker, and all the rest!"

"The rest . . . ?" Wolf sounded strangled.

"Don't pay any attention," Zach said furiously. "She's lying."

Beth Ann kept gaily on. "What a challenge to see if the preacher could keep his pants buttoned longer than most. But he was so easy to seduce with my countless wiles, he was no challenge at all. It was most disappointing—especially for me when we got down to that all-too-brief business!"

Laughing, she pulled a pout and smoothed Zach's water-spotted lapel with one dainty finger. "Too bad, but won't the preacher's clumsiness in bed make an interesting topic around the sewing circles tomorrow?"

"*Silence!*" Wolf roared, his eyes bulging, his face

an apoplectic color. "By God, you'll not ruin this man if I can stop it!"

"Wolf, listen to me," Zach said tiredly. "I've got to tell you something."

"Out!" Livid, Wolf grabbed a hank of Beth Ann's hair and pointed the pistol at Zach again. "Get out, Reverend, and don't come back! I can take care of my own house; you see to yours!"

Zach took a step closer, his eyes fastened on Beth Ann. Her features tightened in pain at the punishing grip Wolf had on her hair. "Let her go."

The sharp report of the pistol split the air, and Zach grabbed his upper arm. Amazed, he looked down at the shredded coat sleeve under his fingers, at the blood dripping from the hot graze on his biceps. "You son of a—"

Wolf fired again, smashing the window to Zach's right. The glass tinkled a little melody as it fell to the stone floor.

"Do what he says!" Beth Ann gasped. "You're making it worse!"

She was right. Everything Zach said and did only increased Wolf's ire, fired the crazed, irate light behind those black marble eyes of his. This had to stop, before someone—before *she* got hurt. And rushing in like some kind of storybook hero with Wolf in this dangerous mood didn't appear the way to go about it.

Zach held up his hands placatingly and began to back toward the bedroom door. "Keep your hair on, Wolf. I'm going."

Wolf's massive belly heaved with exertion and passion, but some of the frenzy in his expression eased. "It's for your own good, son."

"Sure, Wolf. Just—" Zach's eyes met Beth Ann's frightened silver gaze. "Just don't hurt her."

"We all have much to pray on." Wolf gestured

with the pistol, and with one last agonized look toward Beth Ann, Zach grabbed up his boots and left the room.

Biting back whimpers of pain from hair nearly pulled from her tender scalp, Beth Ann endured her father's painful grasp in silence for several endless minutes. Finally they heard Zach gallop past the front of Traveler's Rest, heading back to town. Only then did Wolf release her, giving her a vicious push away from him.

"Dress yourself. You shame me."

Weak with the aftermath of the scene, glad that Zach Madison was out of her life, yet strangely hurt by his desertion, she buried her face in her trembling hands. Beneath the crumpled wrapper, her body felt cold and strange, bereft and ancient, as if she'd aged a hundred years since dawn. Her tired reply was automatic. "I'm sorry, Paw."

"Why the reverend should have any care for you after what you've done, I can't imagine."

She raised her face, and her smile was bleak. "He has a guilty conscience?"

"Don't make light of this vile offense!" Savage again, Wolf jammed his pistol into his belt and struck the floor with his cane with such menacing force that it nearly shattered the slender shaft.

"I wasn't being funny!" Beth Ann grabbed clean clothing from a drawer, suddenly maddened and choked at the intolerable injustice of Wolf's condemnation, unable to endure it silently any longer. "He was right. I was lying before. I'd never truly been with a man before Zach, but you wouldn't listen. Why must you always believe the worst about me?"

"Harlot! I know you for what you are."

She whirled on her heel, infuriated past endurance. "No, you have no idea! Zach loved me with his body, and it was a beautiful thing! Not sordid or squalid, but lovely and tender."

"I will not listen to this filth!"

"Because you can't conceive of the possibility that you might be wrong about me, can you?" she demanded. "And if you've been wrong all this time, that makes the virtuous, long-suffering Mr. Linder a mean-spirited, vindictive fool, doesn't it?"

Wolf cheeks flushed crimson with rage. "Get downstairs!"

She shook her head. "No. I'm through trying to please you. Cook your own breakfast. I'm leaving Traveler's Rest. Today."

"You're not going anywhere."

Wolf stamped through the debris of the fallen loom, purposely crushing the fragile spindles and narrow frame with his one good foot. Grabbing her arm in a painful, powerful grip, he twisted it behind her and pushed Beth Ann out of the room. They clattered down the narrow kitchen stairs to the cadence of his cane and peg and his furious words puffing into her ear.

"Me and Robert's got too much going for me to play nursemaid to a willful hellion any longer! I'm going to fix you like I should have done months ago!"

The pace he kept and his awkward, painful grip made Beth Ann breathless and light-headed, and she hugged her armload of clothing to her bosom in an automatic, self-protective gesture. Something about the timbre of Wolf's voice filled her with dire foreboding.

"Wh-what are you talking about?" She gasped as they stumbled down the last steps into the muddy kitchen.

Wolf pushed her toward the storeroom. "Ike Cunningham is justice of the peace. He can do it."

Her voice went higher. "Do what?"

Wolf smiled, a terrible, satisfied curling of his heavy lips. "Marry you off to Bobby Barlings, that's what. Today, by all that's holy, I'll get shut of your wickedness once and for all!"

"Paw! No!" She twisted, trying frantically to free herself from his viselike grip, appalled at the ludicrous idea. "I won't! That's impossible. You can't make me!"

Wolf gave her a cold look. "There are ways."

She knew he meant it, and the monster who looked at her from behind her father's black eyes terrified her more than taking vows with a poor dim-witted boy ever could.

"Why do you hate me?" she whispered. "Is it because Mother ran away?"

"She didn't get far," Wolf snarled, and caught Beth Ann around her throat. His thick fingers tightened, and Beth Ann choked and dug at his hands in frantic fear.

"Pray for forgiveness, Eleanor," Wolf rumbled, lost in another time. "I want to hear you pray before you die."

"Paw." Her words and her breath strangled under his constricting grip. "I'm not Eleanor. I'm Beth Ann! I'm . . . Beth . . ."

The kitchen door burst open.

"I heard shots—" Old Buck skidded to a halt on the muddy kitchen floor, his grizzled visage incredulous. "Holy Jehosephat, boss! What are you *doing?*"

Wolf released Beth Ann and shoved her, bundled clothes and all, into the storeroom and shot the bolt home. Wheezing desperately for air, she fell into a pile of flour sacks and lay there, winded and dazed, listening to Buck's indignant squawks through the wooden door.

"You cain't do that to Miss Beth Ann!"

"Don't tell me how to discipline my own child," Wolf replied icily. "She's an affront against God and nature, fornicating with strange men under my own roof, and she'll be punished as I see fit! Where have you been?"

Buck gobbled incoherently on the other side of the stout door. Thin light seeped through the cracks in the wood and around the thick leather hinges, spilling pale bars of illumination into Bath Ann's prison. Blinking, she strained to hear the old cowpoke over the rasps of her own tortured breathing.

"Ama's village ... river up ... mare's stuck in the mud ..."

"Very well, Buck," Wolf said, his voice calm and terrible. "We'll get the mare out first, then I want you to go to town with a couple of messages ..."

Beth Ann scrambled up, pounding her fists on the door. Her throat felt sore and swollen, and she cried out in a frightened croak. "Buck! Buck, please! Let me out. Paw's lost his mind! You've got to be careful. Oh, Buck, please—!"

But Wolf was pushing the old cowboy out of the kitchen with a thousand easy explanations to muddle the man's slow deductions, and then there was nothing left to do but fall down in a heap and cry her heart out in pain, fear, and despair.

With an instinctive certainty, Beth Ann understood that her mother had never found her happiness with the traveling dentist. A vision of Eleanor's beautiful face rose in the darkness, her satiny black hair, the full mouth and striking eyes that were so like Beth Ann's. And then the vision changed. Shifting desert sands covered those lovely, dead features, hiding everything forever, including the evidence of Wolf's foulest crime.

Beth Ann shuddered uncontrollably, and drew the neck of her wrapper closer in a futile attempt to ward off the chill of death and deception. All those years of Wolf's playing the injured husband, calling on the Lord for vindication, making Eleanor's daughter pay and pay . . .

And now Beth Ann knew. Oh, God, she knew.

Beth Ann ran her fingers along the bruises circling her neck, and a tiny whimper of terror escaped her. Her father was mad.

More than what she'd done with Zach, Beth Ann felt it was her final defiance—that bald announcement that she was leaving—that had pushed Wolf to the edge of a violent act against his own daughter. Had Eleanor made a similar pronouncement that had ultimately cost her life? The little girl inside Beth Ann who had always carried the secret hurt of her mother's desertion finally understood . . . and forgave.

"Oh, Mama," Beth Ann whispered, "what am I going to do?"

She'd never consent to Wolf's insane plan for her to wed Bobby Barlings, but what new violence might that defiance evoke? Would Robert Barlings listen to her pleas for help, or was he too determined to provide his boy with everything his heart desired, even to the point of sacrificing Beth Ann? She shuddered and pounded an impotent fist on the bolted door, yelling for help. Surely *someone* would come?

Turning, she rested her shoulder blades against the door and tried to control her panicky breathing. Buck wouldn't have the strength of mind to oppose Wolf, and she didn't know how long it might take them to rescue the trapped mare. They could return at any moment! And as for Zach Madison ... Beth Ann's chest constricted at the memory of the blood on his arm. Wolf might have killed him! She tried to resurrect her fury at his deception, but she was too frightened to feel anything but the deepest hurt. No, the stranger she'd known as Zach had gotten what he wanted, and a clean getaway besides, and the man she'd loved was no more than a myth. She couldn't count on Zach any more than she could count on a stage full of territorial marshals arriving to rescue her from this impromptu dungeon.

She had to count on herself. It was nothing new.

Inhaling deeply, Beth Ann fought for calm and forced herself to evaluate her surroundings. Canned goods, staples, her clean clothes in a puddle at her feet—she was not without resources, and self-reliance was her new watchword.

Hurrying, she felt her way to the back of the storeroom to the casks of stored water, drank deeply, made cursory ablutions, and dressed, twisting her hair into a loose braid. If—*when*—she made her escape, she'd at least make a decent appearance. Knowing the door bolt was heavy and secure, she broke a jar of preserved peaches, then grimly set to work, sawing at the leather door hinge with a shard of glass.

Minutes, hours, an eternity later, with the sweat rolling off her forehead and damp patches staining the armpits of her shirtwaist, she nearly wept with the meager progress she'd made on the lower hinge. The shard slipped, cutting the tip of her finger, and she cried out in frustration, then stuck the abused member in her mouth. In the stillness, she heard a distant commotion of shouts and horses, and froze in dismay. Paw!

Beth Ann cringed back into the darkness, curled

in a ball of fear, her spine pressing against the wall. The cloying scent of cloves and spiced peaches suffocated her, and her stomach lurched with nausea. Overhead! Looking up into darkness, she blindly followed the muffled vibration of footsteps on the porch, raised voices she couldn't identify—and then gunshots!

Terrified, Beth Ann didn't move, didn't breathe. What had Paw done? She thought of Buck and was sorry for every time she'd been impatient and thoughtless with the old man. Surely Paw hadn't . . . ? She swallowed hard. Was she next? What if Robert Barlings wouldn't fall in with Wolf's marriage plans? Would he fall afoul of Paw's escalating violence, too?

Beth Ann forced herself to pick up the shard and began sawing again, even more forcefully. She would not be found sitting in this dark hole like a scared mouse, doing nothing! Pushing her fear aside, she concentrated on scraping the sharp edge of the glass against the tough leather.

Aeons later, the hinge yielded to a final swipe of her rough knife. Nearly sobbing with relief, she broke nails prying the bottom corner of the heavy door away from the casing. The top hinge and the bolt were still in place, but if she could lift the bottom of the door out just a little, she might be able to squeeze through . . .

There! She forced her head and shoulder through the opening, then wiggled and pushed, thankful for the slippery greasing of mud on the floor as lubrication. With a final awful strain, she slipped out in a rush of scraped skin and bruises, but nothing mattered except she was free!

Panting harshly, she crawled to her feet and looked around the empty kitchen, her ears pricked for the tiniest sound. Nothing. That was more un-nerving than Paw's bellows of rage.

Nervously Beth Ann gathered her courage. She dared stop for nothing. No packing, no mementos this time. Only flight from a madman. No horse, either, she remembered, for they were all scattered. She'd have to make it on foot. Whiskey Jean would know what to do, and Beth Ann would find her somehow.

Staggering slightly, she hastened to the kitchen's front door, the one protected by the veranda's overhang, and peered out cautiously, only to be dazzled after the darkness of the storeroom by the bright daylight spilling across the flood-littered front yard. Blinking rapidly, every sense quivering, she raised a hand to shield her eyes and stepped out, leaving the safety of the overhang behind. She picked up her skirts and ran up the slight incline toward the shallow flight of steps off the main ve-randa. She could follow the road as far as the first bend in the river—

Rounding the edge of the steps, she came up short with a startled cry of horror.

Wolf Linder lay sprawled on his back in a bro-ken puppet's tumble of useless limbs, his sightless black eyes staring up into a heaven he'd never see. Two crimson pools blotched his chest, and his Colt lay in the mud at his side.

"Paw?" It surprised Beth Ann that her voice was as plaintive as a child's.

On wooden feet, she shuffled forward, but there was no need to be cautious any longer. In a daze, she bent and picked up her father's pistol. It was heavier than she'd expected, and it hung in her hand within the folds of her muddy skirt. She felt nothing—not relief, not pleasure, not even sorrow—only a faint curiosity that quickly faded as the blood pounded painfully in her temples. Without thinking, she pressed her father's eyelids, closing the blind orbs in a final duty.

And then she began to shake.

Stumbling backwards, she sank down on the bottom step, her eyes dry, the Colt clutched to her stomach like a comforting blanket. She was still there when the horsemen arrived.

From a great distance, she watched Sheriff Nichols examine her father's body, then cover it with a blanket from the house. She noticed vaguely that it was one she'd made herself. Somehow Buck was there, tears seeping down the creases in his weather-beaten face, and Robert Barlings and Kitty's husband, and some other grim-faced men she couldn't remember, but it was Zach who gently pried the Colt from her clenched fingers.

"Oh, God, angel," he said in a voice that seemed to have passed through layers of cotton wadding to get to her ears. "I shouldn't have left you. I'm sorry. I shouldn't . . ."

Passive, cocooned, she smiled.

"You'll have to come with me, Miss Linder." Sheriff Nichols stood next to her, his mouth compressed but determined. "You're under arrest for murder."

Chapter 12

"Murderous whore!"

"I knew it was just a matter of time." Mamie Cunningham's voice sounded high and shrill above the angry murmuring drifting through the high barred window over Beth Ann's head. "As God is my witness, she said the next time she pulled a trigger, she'd make sure the job was done right! Heard her with my own ears."

"She filled my Kitty's head with wicked notions," Douglas Hardy shouted. "If it wasn't for her—"

A rash of other voices chimed in.

"A damned crime against nature!"

"God-fearing man like Wolf Linder—"

"What else did you expect from a slut like her?"

"Patricide cannot be tolerated by a civilized society!"

Beth Ann recognized Robert Barlings's deep voice and cringed, burying her face against the jail cot's scratchy wool blanket and covering her ears with her hands. There was no escape from this waking nightmare, and it just kept getting worse.

How can they think I killed Paw?

The question rattled against the inside of her head, growing more and more painful as the anesthetic of shock wore off. She knew she hadn't made a very good defense at first sight, not with her neck and wrists marked with signs of brutality and a pistol still smelling of cordite clutched to her bosom. She vaguely recalled someone—it might have been Zach, she wasn't sure—saying something about "self-defense." But mostly, after finding her father dead, everything had rolled off her like water off a duck's back, reality barely impinging on her battered consciousness. It hadn't occurred to her that a failure to plead her innocence in those first moments would brand her more guilty than if she'd made a complete confession.

Rolling over on her back, Beth Ann counted the flyspecks on the twig and mud-daub ceiling, trying to ignore the ugly muttering coming from the street outside the Destiny City Jail.

Located through a heavy wooden door in a room behind the sheriff's office, the jail's two iron-barred cells had an unfortunate stench of urine, probably the work of the drunk Sheriff Nichols had evicted to provide complete isolation for his newest prisoner. A single barred window high on the wall over the thin cot on which Beth Ann lay provided only meager ventilation, and the afternoon heat and rare post-storm humidity made the cell an oven.

All in all, it wasn't so bad. She could have been outside facing that increasingly wrathful mob.

Beth Ann swallowed. She knew her reputation—hadn't she embellished it at every opportunity with defiance and outrageousness? But the virulence in the crowd's communal voice startled her. When had she ever really hurt any of those people? Even Mr. Barlings, whom she counted as something of a friend, had deserted her. Despite the heat, she shivered.

"I say we get a rope!"

Beth Ann bolted upright on the cot, a cold prickle of perspiration jumping out under the armpits of her soiled shirtwaist. Her ebony hair fell wild and loose, long since freed from its untidy braid by the ride into town.

"You cain't hang a woman!" someone else objected.

"Tar and feathers then! We don't need her kind in Destiny!"

"You shut your yap, Douglas Hardy," Sheriff Nichols boomed over the cacophony.

A sudden silence fell over the crowd, so complete Beth Ann could have sworn she heard the sheriff cocking his rifle. She could almost see him, feet spread wide, facing down the irate, bloodthirsty group with a glare from under his shaggy eyebrows. She felt giddy with gratitude. When another voice spoke up, her mental picture of the outside events shattered abruptly.

"Friends, consider." Zach Madison's tone was so kind, so saintly, he could have been one of the original apostles. "I know we're all shocked and distraught at today's events, but to act in this rash manner is only to invite further tragedy."

"But, Reverend, you know what she's capable of better'n anybody!"

Beth Ann shriveled inside at the unknowing irony of those words. To have Zach Temple—no, Madison—defending her! She'd rather hang! She gritted her teeth, hating him, yet straining to hear more.

"Yeah, she's guilty as sin, and you know it!" someone else piped in.

"That's for the judge to determine," the sheriff said firmly. "No one's taking the law into their own hands as long as I'm sheriff of this town."

Zach raised his voice in agreement. "We cannot let our emotions run wild here, my friends. I suggest you all return to your homes now and reflect on your own mortality. Like our dear companion

Wolf, we will all meet our Maker sooner than we expect. It is wise to be prepared."

"You heard the preacher," Sheriff Nichols said. 'Get on, all of you! I won't have lawlessness in my town."

There was a rippling undercurrent of resentful muttering, but the crowd reluctantly dispersed under the sheriff's proddings. Beth Ann realized she'd been holding her breath and released it with a shaky sigh. She was reprieved. But for how long?

Pressing the heels of her hands against her burning eyes, she fought tears. The heavy door rattled, and her head jerked up in wary watchfulness.

"Er, Miss Linder?" Sheriff Nichols poked his hawkish nose around the edge of the door.

"Are they gone, Sheriff?"

He flushed, a bit shamefaced, and she wondered if it was because of the uncharitable—to say the least!—actions of the townsfolk, or the fact that he stood on one side of the cage and she on the other.

"Ah, er, yes," he stammered. "You heard . . . ?"

"Just about everything," she admitted with a wry grimace, settling her shoulder blades against the wall and crossing her ankles demurely. "Thank you."

"Just doing my job."

He looked so uncomfortable, she had to smile, although it was somewhat wan. "Yes, I know. I understand."

"Look, you—er, have a visitor."

She straightened suspiciously. "Who?"

"The reverend wants to counsel with you, offer some consolation—"

"No!" Jumping to her feet, she hugged herself,

her fingers digging into her upper arms in a vain attempt to control their tremors.

The sheriff was nonplussed and disapproving all at once. "But, Miss Linder, I really think—"

"No, I said! Not him."

"Now, look here, young lady, you're going to need all the friends you can get. Why, it was him who fetched me out to Traveler's Rest in the first place. If only we'd hurried—" The sheriff shook his head sorrowfully. "But never mind that. The Reverend Temple just wants to help."

"Sweet sassafras! Can't you hear?" The tin slop bucket she threw at the sheriff was, fortunately, empty, but it clanged against the iron bars with such a sharp report, the older man jumped back as if a snake had struck at him. "I never want to see that low-down swine again as long as I live!"

Beth Ann threw herself facedown on the cot and burst into tears.

"Sure. That's all right. I didn't mean . . . You don't have to see anyone you don't want to." Sheriff Nichols hastily backed away and quietly pulled the door shut behind him.

Chest aching and eyes burning, Beth Ann sobbed out her heartache in a stormy release of accumulated fear, tension, disappointment, and grief. Now that Wolf was gone, she couldn't hate him as much as she'd thought, but the few good memories she had would be forever tainted by the horrible certainty that he'd been responsible for her mother's disappearance. Had it been his crime that had shadowed his existence, or had he always been so bitter and vengeful? What a waste of a life. Pity clogged her throat at that unhappy epitaph.

But her tears weren't all for Wolf. How could they be when the man she thought she'd loved had betrayed her so utterly? When she thought of the sweetness she and Zach had shared, and then realized it had been an illusion laced with deceit, her tears were bitter indeed. What greater fool was there than a woman who trusted her heart to a man, only to find her hopes dashed not once, but twice?

Her despair was so enervating, she barely had the energy to care what happened to her now. She could protest that she was innocent of her father's murder, but who among her God-fearing neighbors would believe her? With the townsfolk shrieking for her blood and every shred of circumstantial evidence pointed at her guilt, there didn't seem to be much reason to hope. Wolf's death had freed her from one kind of bondage, only to imprison her in another trap.

Sapped by her weeping but too exhausted to find the escape of sleep, Beth Ann lay on the cot and prayed for a solution. She came out of a half stupor sometime near dusk, roused by a strident spate of words from the outer office.

"Well, o'course she'll see me!"

The stout wooden door flew open, and a robust figure in a mud-spattered duster filled the doorway. Beth Ann swung her feet to the floor and sat up with a tremendous smile as Whiskey Jean swept in like a charging bull.

"Open that there door," Jean ordered. She carried a split-willow basket covered with a red checkered napkin hooked over her arm. "You can't expect a lady to eat that swill you serve, Tristan Nichols!"

"I'm coming. Hold your horses," the sheriff grumbled, jangling a ring of keys.

Behind him, old Buck teetered forward on his

bowed legs, his snaggled grin a mite uncertain. "How do, Miss Beth Ann?"

Sheriff Nichols cast a cautious glance Beth Ann's way. "Don't object to these visitors, do you, miss?"

She shook her head, afraid her voice would betray her if she spoke.

"Well, what are you waiting for?" Whiskey Jean demanded. "Open that there door. You already checked for files and firearms, and the fried chicken's getting cold."

Sheriff Nichols meekly complied. The door swung open, and the minute her visitors entered and the door was securely locked behind them again, Beth Ann launched herself against Jean's buxom chest.

"There, there," Jean said, patting Beth Ann's back awkwardly as Sheriff Nichols withdrew, leaving them alone. "There, there, honey. It's going to be all right."

Beth Ann drew a shaky, watery breath. "Oh, Jean, I'm so glad you're here!" She looked at the faithful old cowpoke mashing his battered hat between his gnarled fingers and reached out her hand. "You, too, Buck. Thank you both."

"As if we'd let you rot in this cell without a never-you-mind," Jean scoffed, her voice gruffer than usual. She pulled Beth Ann down beside her on the narrow cot and plopped the basket in her lap. "Now, you just check inside there. Biscuits and chicken and pickles, and even a jug of cool buttermilk."

Beth Ann smiled helplessly. "I—I'm not very hungry."

"Horse manure!" Jean deftly plucked a chicken breast from the folds of the napkin and handed it to Beth Ann. "You got to keep your strength up."

Beth Ann's stomach growled just then, loud

enough to be heard, and she realized with a start that it had been over a day since she'd eaten. Her body realized it, even if her head didn't. She managed a weak smile. "Maybe you're right."

"O'course!" Jean handed a wing to Buck, who nodded polite thanks, then took a leg for herself.

The three nibbled for a moment in companionable silence, the illusion of a normal family picnic so strong, Beth Ann managed several bites of chicken before her throat began to tighten again. Chewing energetically, Jean passed the buttermilk.

"Try a little of that, child. Nothing like buttermilk to settle a stomach, right, Buck?"

"My mama swore by it, Miss Jean."

Jean beamed at the grizzled cowpoke's courteous address. "See there, Beth Ann? A full stomach makes the thinkin' easier, too, and Lord knows we got us a powerful lot of ponderin' to do about all this!"

Beth Ann took a swallow of the buttermilk and then set both the jug and her unfinished piece of chicken back in the basket. "Jean . . ."

"Not that it surprises me, really. I always said if ever there was a man needed killing for sheer orneriness—beg your pardon, Beth Ann—it was Wolf, but what I can't understand is why you—"

"I didn't do it."

Whiskey Jean nearly choked on a bite of chicken. "What did you say?"

"I didn't shoot Paw."

"I knew it!" Buck hopped from side to side, swinging the chicken wing in wide circles for emphasis. "It just weren't possible. I tried to tell 'em!"

"Great balls of fire, girl!" Whiskey Jean's expression was quite put out. "If you didn't kill Wolf, why haven't you said so before now?"

Beth Ann shrugged. "Who'd believe me?"

"Why, me and Buck, for two!" Jean tossed her well-blasted leg bone back in the basket. "So if you didn't do it, who did?"

"I don't know." Beth Ann shook her head, her gray eyes bleak. "Paw locked me in the storeroom. I didn't see anything."

She related the morning's events sketchily, leaving out about Zach because it was just too humiliating and she couldn't bear to have her last two friends in the world desert her when they learned the truth of her degradation.

"I heard voices, shots—but I couldn't tell what happened. It could have been someone we knew or total strangers, some drifter after cash, anything!" Beth Ann smoothed her wrinkled, mud-streaked skirts in frustration, then glanced at the cowhand leaning against the bars. "I was really afraid Paw had done something awful to you, Buck. I'm real glad you're all right."

"The temper he was in, I was afeared of that, too," the old man admitted with an abashed shake of his head. "I skedaddled toward town like he said, but when I met up with the sheriff headed to Traveler's Rest, I felt beholden to ride back. It's sorry I am I ever left you in the first place, Miss Beth Ann, after seeing him treat you so rough. Things might've worked out different . . ."

"Well, regrets like that don't help none," Jean said, scratching her mousy thatch worriedly. "From what the sheriff says, Beth Ann sittin' there with the gun in her hand made a pretty damning picture folks won't soon forget."

"I realize that." Beth Ann shuddered, thinking about the earlier viciousness of the mob. "It's funny Paw turned out to be such a leading citizen that his death provokes everyday folks to riot."

"The talk's ugly yet." Buck looked upset to have

to add that. "When I passed by the saloon, Douglas Hardy was still spouting off. Drunk as a rooster with a crop freighted with scamper juice, and gettin' just about as mean."

"And folks are listening to that damn fool?" Jean demanded, indignant.

"More than you'd want to believe, Miss Jean."

Beth Ann chewed her lower lip. "Damn."

"Now, don't you worry none, honey," Jean said staunchly, "the sheriff ain't going to let you come to no harm. We'll get all of this straightened out in no time."

Beth Ann thrust the strands of hair out of her face with a weary gesture. "How?"

"You'll see. Just as soon as the judge comes from Wickenburg and you can tell your side of the story. Buck can speak for you, too."

"That's right, Miss Beth Ann." Buck bobbed his grizzled head like a turkey gobbler in agreement. "And how about one of them lawyer fellers? We'll get you one of them, too."

"Good idea," Jean said, impressed. "And in the meantime, we'll do some poking around on our own. Maybe somebody saw something."

A lump thickened in Beth Ann's throat. "Thank you. I don't know what I'd do ..."

"Bear up, child," Jean advised. "I know this ain't the most comfortable set of circumstances in the world, but it won't be for long."

"I—I have one other thing to ask of you," Beth Ann said. She pleated her skirt between her fingers. "It's Paw. The arrangements ... ?"

"They took him to the mortuary, Miss Beth Ann," Buck said solemnly.

"Could you ..." Beth Ann had to stop a moment to catch her breath. "Could you see that the funeral's done proper? Since I can't. Paw didn't love me much, but he was my father, and it's only fitting ..."

"Don't you worry none." Whiskey Jean's lips twitched as if she were holding in a vast emotion, and her answer was a husky rasp. "We'll see to it."

"Buck, see they lay him out in his good black suit?"

"Sure, miss." The old cowboy blinked furiously.

A trickle of tears slid from the corners of Beth Ann's eyes. "Oh, and his new shirt I just finished. It's in his top drawer. He—he never got a chance to wear it."

"Just like you want, honey." Whiskey Jean gathered Beth Ann into a big bear hug, and they clung for a few moments. The older woman's eyes glittered with moisture, and she gave a healthy snort as she released Beth Ann. "We'd best be goin', Buck. Got lots to do."

Rising, Jean hollered for the sheriff, surreptitiously wiping her eyes on her dusty cuffs. Buck reached into his back pocket and silently offered a clean bandanna. "Miss Jean?"

"*Gracias*." The burly bullwhacker wiped her streaming face and smiled. "You're a real gentleman, Buck."

Buck's weather-beaten features turned red under the bronze. "It's a pleasure to help a lady like you, ma'am."

Beth Ann marveled silently at the sudden undercurrent between such an unlikely pair. Jean practically preened, and Buck seemed to stand taller. When the sheriff entered and released them from the cell, skinny Buck gallantly offered his arm to the larger woman. Blushing, she accepted it graciously, nearly simpering at the masculine attention. Beth Ann smiled to herself. If her trouble might be the impetus that helped two lonely people find each other, then she couldn't be totally sorry.

"We'll see you in the morning, child," Whiskey Jean said in farewell. "I'll bring you some clean things and such."

Beth Ann glanced down at herself with a rueful grimace. "I'd appreciate it."

"Fine. You try to get some sleep now."

"Yes, I will." Beth Ann tried to smile. "And thank you again."

Whiskey Jean left on Buck's arm, and as the door closed behind them, Beth Ann heard her speaking to the sheriff.

"Grab a chair, Tristan. You got some wrong-headed ideas about my little gal, and we need to powwow."

When sometime later the sheriff looked in again, it was almost completely dark. He lit a small lantern hanging from a wall bracket and inspected Beth Ann's pale face in the weak yellow glow.

"You should have spoken up earlier, Miss Linder," he said in a troubled voice. "This story of yours—"

"I guess you find it hard to believe," Beth Ann said quietly, rising from the cot. "It's the truth, nonetheless."

"It's what the judge thinks that counts. I'll see about taking you to Wickenburg myself tomorrow."

She looked at him sharply. "Instead of waiting for him to make his circuit here?"

"Feeling is running high right now. I wouldn't want to push our luck. I thought about moving you tonight even, but . . ." He shrugged. "Matthew Gelder'll be relieving me in a while so I can get some shut-eye. We'll leave at dawn if that's all right with you."

Beth Ann looked at the man for a long moment, weighing the unspoken import behind his decision. His concern frightened her more than the earlier heated shouts had. Could public outrage for her assumed crime turn her former friends and neighbors into vigilantes? She wouldn't have believed it possible before, but then lately nothing had turned out as she'd expected. The air was rapidly cooling now that the sun was down, but when she shivered, it wasn't from the chill. "Could I have another blanket?"

"Sure." When the sheriff returned with her request, he passed it through the bars, his craggy face etched with discomfort. "Ain't never had a woman in here before. Is there anything . . . ? That is, ah . . ."

"I'm sure I can manage until dawn, Sheriff." She swept the blanket over her shoulders and reseated herself on the cot. "Good night."

He reached to doff a hat he didn't wear. "Ah, good night, miss."

But as the night wore on and the raucous noise from the direction of the saloon grew louder and more boisterous, Beth Ann found she wasn't managing very well at all.

Every horse that clopped past the jail, every shout of greeting, every half-heard murmur on the street, became something sinister and menacing. Unable to find the solace of sleep, she lay in tense wakefulness, her mind replaying the day's tumultuous events—the moment of revelation about her mother, finding Wolf's body, the instant her cocoon of disinterest dissolved into fear for her life. Most merciless of all were the memories of Zach's hands on her body, and she groaned and bit her lip and prayed the night would end soon.

The tumult from the direction of the saloon

changed its pitch sometime in the early wee hours. Beth Ann sat up in alarm, her ears attuned to the nuances of the sounds by hours of intense listening. She felt the alteration on an instinctive level, sensed the threat in distant words she could not yet decipher.

From the sheriff's office came Deputy Gelder's loud snoring. The fool wasn't even awake! The indecipherable exhortations of drunken brawlers grew louder, and the flicker of torchlight made shadows dance menacingly on the pale adobe walls. Silent panic built within Beth Ann's chest, choking her breath, squeezing her pulse into a thin thread that could not carry the blood to her head.

A scratch sounded above her head, and she jumped, her skin crawling.

"Beth Ann? Angel, wake up."

Zach. His voice came from the high barred window.

For the briefest of instants, gladness filled her with a giddy rush of relief, but then she squashed it down with all her will.

"Go away!" she ordered.

"Beth!" His voice was a cautioning hiss. She could see his hand on the window's bar, the lantern's golden light gilding the fine hair on his wrist. Beth Ann's stomach plummeted, leaving her dazed that such a simple thing could render her weak with desire still. It was intolerable!

She stepped on top of the wobbly cot, peering at the shadowy outline of Zach's face through the bars. Vaguely she wondered how he stood so high, but the immediate rush of hurt and fury that swamped her crowded out everything but the need to be rid of him.

"What are you doing here? Leave me alone or I'll call the deputy!"

"Woman, don't you hear what's going on?" His voice was a low, harsh whisper. "Back away from the window as far as you can."

"Why?"

"Don't ask stupid questions. There's no time!"

She was highly affronted. "I do not ask *stupid—*"

But he had already vanished. Nonplussed, she scowled at the empty window, then suddenly gaped at the length of chain he threaded through the openings between the bars. Before her startled eyes, the slack in the chain tightened and the old adobe in which the bars were seated began to crumble and shatter under the pressure.

With a squeak of pure dismay, Beth Ann leaped off the cot at the same moment that the entire window practically exploded outward, taking a goodly hunk of the wall with it. She sprawled on her knees beside the iron-barred cell door, so taken aback by the abrupt demolition, she could only stare, openmouthed, at the destruction.

Then Zach was clambering through the opening, his clerical collar and dark jacket hardly the costume she would have envisioned for a jailbreak. He grabbed her arm and jerked her to her feet. "Come *on!*"

She gasped. "Are you *crazy?*"

He didn't answer, hefting her up bodily, then pushing her headfirst through the now chest-high opening and diving after her just as Deputy Gelder gave a surprised shout.

Beth Ann hit the ground in a flurry of tumbled skirts and scraped palms. Rubble littered the hard ground. She hardly registered the pair of nervous horses, a blue-gray grulla mare and Zach's buckskin, standing by the abandoned chain. Then Zach had her on her feet and halfway to the mare.

"What do you think you're doing?" she panted, swinging around and pushing at him frantically. "This is insane! I'm not going with *you*!"

"For once in your life, don't argue with me!" Zach snapped.

"But—"

"Unless you'd rather face that lynching party headed this way!"

"Lynch—who, *me?*" Her throat constricted involuntarily.

"Jackasses want you to climb the golden stair on a rope, by God." A bullet whined past Zach's ear. "Oh, hell!"

Vaulting into his own saddle, Zach grabbed Beth Ann's arm and swung her up behind him on the buckskin. He snatched the grulla's bridle, then spurred his mount into an all-out gallop. The two horses burst out of the back of the alley just as a torchlit group of irate men led by a confused Deputy Gelder tumbled into the opening at the other end.

"There they go!"

"Who's that with her?"

"Get the sheriff!"

"After them!"

Zach aimed the sprinting horses straight into the desert toward the mountains. The frantic shouts behind them diminished and were lost as they raced away from Destiny under the starlit sky.

Beth Ann had never experienced such a mad ride. Straddling the horse, her knees and heels flopping uncontrollably, she knew that at any moment she would be thrown to her death. Teeth chattering with terror, she held on to Zach's waist with all her might, her cheek pressed against his back, alternately praying and cursing for all she was worth. Bent low over his horse's neck, Zach covered her knotted-together hands with one of his own, but otherwise ignored her.

They hadn't gone over two miles at this breakneck pace before Zach turned the horses in to a thicket and they plunged down a steep embankment into a narrow arroyo. He was forced to slow down in order to pick out a path through the center of the shallow creek still running briskly with the remnants of the previous day's storm. How he saw at all in the nearly complete darkness was beyond Beth Ann's understanding, but now that her brain wasn't bouncing around inside her skull quite so furiously, she had a chance to focus her scattered wits.

"Stop a minute," she gasped. "I can't—I'm slipping off!"

Zach grunted assent and helped her slide down the horse's rump. "You're right. Unless I miss my bet, they'll be after us quicker than a duck on a June bug. We'll follow this creek to cover our tracks, and as much as I enjoy you pressing against my backside, we'll make better time riding separately."

Beth Ann found herself standing calf-deep in chilly water, and somehow that, coupled with Zach's comment, was the last straw. "Give me those reins!"

She snatched the leather straps from him, then splashed around and stuck her soaked shoe into the stirrup. Ignoring her streaming hems, she hauled herself into the saddle and sawed at the reins to swing the gray around.

"Hold it, angel, wrong way." Zach caught her bridle.

"Get your hands off, you damn fool! I'm going back."

"What! Are you loco?"

"I'm not crazy enough to trust you!" Her tone was scathing.

"Jee-sus H. Christ! I'm trying to help."

"You jackass, you've just made things worse! The sheriff believed me. But after this—now I *do* look guilty!"

"Well, aren't you?"

Beth Ann screeched and gave Zach such a furious shove, his horse spooked and he toppled out of the saddle. He landed in the creek with a splash and a curse. "What the hell's got into you, woman!"

"If you think I'm capable of shooting my own father, then you never knew me at all!" she shouted furiously. "You've fouled things up for me for the last time!"

Zach surged to his feet and hauled her down from the saddle so quickly, she had no time to defend herself. "Now, you listen to me, you hellcat," he growled, shaking her until her teeth chattered. "I saved your hide tonight. The least you could do is show a little gratitude!"

"I was all right until you showed up!"

"Well, you might not have stayed that way if Douglas Hardy had gotten his hands on you! And I suspect the scum he had with him would have taken a great deal of pleasure exploring your virtue—or lack thereof—before they left you looking up a tree."

She choked. "You're despicable!"

"I'm also right. Thank God most of them were too drunk to find their asses, much less a horse this time of night, but you can bet your last dollar that Sheriff Nichols will make it a point of honor to track us down."

"Good! I hope they put you under the jail this

time!" she shrilled, struggling furiously. "And I don't want your help!"

"Well, I certainly wasn't going to let a bunch of stupid cow patties hang my woman."

Incensed, she swung at him, screeching. "I'm not your woman!"

"The hell you aren't."

Eyes narrowed dangerously, Zach sank painful fingers into her hair and dragged her into his embrace, ravishing her mouth with his own in a kiss that staked claims and laid boundaries. It was punishing and consoling, furious and tender all at once, and it left her gasping for breath.

Before she could recover, Zach lifted her into her saddle, grabbed her reins, then remounted. When they were side by side, he reached for her again and kissed her forcefully, his tongue almost brutal. When he finished, he looked down into her dazed face in hard satisfaction.

"Now that we've got that settled, shut up and *ride*."

Chapter 13

Nothing was settled, but Beth Ann was too weary to care.

After riding all night and the better part of the sweltering day, they'd finally left the desert floor and begun to climb into the foothills of the Superstitions. Zach had led them on a convoluted path through the worst possible country, backtracking and circling through the prairie scrub and cactus thickets to confuse their trail, stopping only briefly to rest the horses, then pushing ever onward toward the relative sanctuary of the mountains.

But the punishing pace and the hardships Beth Ann had already endured were taking a toll. Fatigue, hunger, and the soul-deadening certainty that she was in a mess from which she could never escape made her feel like a sleepwalker caught in the throes of a terrible nightmare. When Zach had called for another stop, she'd slid off her tired mount and collapsed in the meager shade of a giant saguaro, so fatigued and demoralized, she could scarcely hold her head up, much less care what the barren, dusty earth would do to her clothes. Gritty, disheveled, she squinted at the blistering sun and pursed her parched lips. Hell couldn't be any worse than this.

"Here, honey." Zach squatted down beside Beth Ann and pushed the canteen into her hands. Sweat dripped from his temples, and his face was caked with red alkali dust. "Drink up."

She looked at him dully, wondering why she'd never seen this steely-eyed stranger before. Zach Madison was definitely a master dissembler. He frowned at her lack of response, then folded her hands around the canvas-covered canteen and helped her lift it to her lips. The impact of his touch brought Beth Ann to life.

"I can do it!" She shrugged him off resentfully and sipped, letting the tepid water ease down her dry throat at first, then taking greedy gulps.

Zach lifted the canteen away before she'd had her fill. "Take it easy. That's all we've got."

"That figures." Beth Ann licked the last of the moisture from her lips, then tiredly pushed her hair back out of her face. She was paying for the lack of a bonnet, her nose already tender with sunburn.

"Try some of this." Zach held out a blackened chunk of sun-dried jerky.

She looked at the unappetizing morsel and shook her head. There were some things she refused to do, whether she was starving or not. "No."

"Don't pull that prima donna crap on me!" Zach snapped, forcing her to take the jerky. "There wasn't time to pack you a champagne luncheon, you know. So eat. You're going to need the strength."

It didn't seem worth the effort to argue, so she stuck the strip in her mouth, wincing at the salty-sour tang. It would take hours to work up enough spit to soften it to chew, much less swallow. Zach's mood was foul enough to convince her, however, so she gnawed dutifully, feeling like a cow with its cud.

Satisfied with her efforts, Zach lifted the canteen and drank sparingly, his Adam's apple bobbing.

Finished, he recapped the container and wiped his sweaty brow on his shirt sleeve. Beth Ann noticed his slight wince, then remembered the bullet graze Wolf had given him. No doubt his arm was sore as all get-out by now. She certainly hoped so.

Zach rose to his feet. "Ready? Let's go."

"No."

"Aw, hell! Don't start that again!"

Beth Ann spit the still solid piece of jerky into her hand and threw it at him. "Go to the devil! I'm not taking another step with you!"

Zach dodged the jerky with a muffled curse. "Look here, angel, be reasonable or I'll hobble you like a half-broke mustang and drag you."

"Drag me where?" she demanded haughtily. "There's nothing within a hundred miles of this godforsaken place!"

"Except Sheriff Nichols and his posse."

Beth Ann's shoulders slumped. She folded her arms around her upraised knees and rested her forehead on her kneecaps. "I don't care."

"Hell!" He kicked a dirt clod. "Are you addled? They'll hang you and me both!"

"So go, then. I'm not asking you to stay." She shook her head against her knees. "What does it matter what happens to me now? I'll never be able to redeem my reputation or clear my name in Destiny after this."

"Why should you want to? What did those holier-than-thou hypocrites ever do to make you care what they think? Shake the dust off your sandals and forget them."

Her head snapped up, and her eyes flashed silver. "Don't you dare quote the Bible at me, you charlatan! And it may seem funny to you, but I'm innocent! I don't want to be known as the woman who shot her own father!"

He held up his hands. "All right, I believe you. But who the hell did?"

"Sweet sassafras, I don't know. It could have been anyone. I've been having the craziest ideas." She shook her head, her expression bleak and frightened. "It could have been a stranger, or someone close. Even someone like Buck. Like ... you."

Zach registered that, then came down on one knee beside her. He touched the bruises on her throat with a fingertip, and his expression was lethally grim. "I wish to God I had."

"I wish to God *I* had!" The gentleness of Zach's touch unnerved her, and her mouth quivered. "He killed my mother, Zach. I'm sure of it. She didn't desert me after all—at least not of her own accord."

"Jesus, Beth, I'm sorry." Zach reached to comfort her, but that moment of vulnerability vanished, and she pushed him away.

"I don't want your pity, Zach Madison! And I'll be damned if I'm going to spend the rest of my life on the run with an outlaw!"

"God Almighty!" Zach ran his hands through his dusty curls. "I don't even have a gun! I may have run into a bit of trouble along the way, but I'm not an outlaw by a long shot!"

"Maybe you weren't, but jailbreaking made you one."

"For you! I did it for you."

"I didn't ask you, did I?" she returned stubbornly.

He grabbed her shoulders. "But you could have, don't you understand? Don't you know I'd do anything for you?"

Her lip curled. "Except give me your name."

"Damn! Is respectability all you can think

about?" Zach ground his teeth and fixed her with an imploring look. "I've been a rambler and lived by my wits all my life, and let me tell you, it's grand! We'll go over the mountains toward Prescott, then head for California. We'll build us a stake, maybe buy into one of those fancy gambling halls in San Francisco. It'll be great. No ties, angel, just you and me against the world."

"No roots. No security. No promises, either." Beth Ann's gray eyes shone with angry hurt. "No, thank you!"

Zach jerked her closer, glowering at her, nose to nose. "You love me. You said it."

She caught a sharp, pained breath. "Not you. Some dream, some illusion. It wasn't real."

"Goddammit! You didn't make love to this collar!" He ripped the celluloid strip free from his shirt and pitched it into the brush, then pressed her hand under the shirt's placket to rest against his heart. "It was me all the time. *Me*, Beth Ann. I'm the one who made you whimper with pleasure, who gave you everything a woman should have when she takes a man she cares about into her bed."

"Stop it." She could hardly breathe. Betrayingly, her fingers curled into the whorls of crisp hair on his muscular chest.

"You remember what it felt like to have me inside you, don't you, angel? How hot, how full. Your skin like velvet, my tongue everywhere . . ." His smile became feral at her involuntary moan. "It was paradise on earth, wasn't it?"

"Damn you," she panted.

Zach bent her over his arm, his hand holding her jaw, his mouth hovering a whisper away from hers. "I could take you right now in the dirt, and you couldn't deny me. Admit it."

His brutal words shattered the breath-stealing carnality of the moment. The most humiliating thing was that he was probably right. In those few short seconds, her feminine center had already begun to melt in both recognition and welcome, and surrender could only follow as her traitorous body overruled the rejection her good sense dictated. Should he discover her response, he'd know in full the power he had over her, and Beth Ann could not abide that ultimate humiliation.

Her eyes burned with defiance. "If you want that kind of empty victory, then do your worst and be damned! You've used and betrayed me, and I hate you!"

"Too bad, because you belong to me now." Releasing his hold, Zach surged to his feet and pulled her up after him. A muscle in his jaw worked, and his mouth clamped down in a furious line. "If we had the leisure to explore the question at length, I'd be glad to prove it to you, but that proof will have to wait until we've lost the posse. Now, get on that damned horse, and if you give me any more sass, I swear I'll turn you over my knee and whale the tar out of you."

Though her knees quaked and her heart thumped within her breast so loudly she was sure the arrogant son of a bitch could hear it, she forced a sneer into her voice. "I'd expect no less from a brute of an outlaw!"

"Then you'd better learn to appreciate my style, and make the best of it, my dear," he retorted grimly. "Because, like it or not, you're stuck with me."

Not for long, Beth Ann vowed furiously. She mounted her horse without further demur, but as they rode, her head was full of plans for escape, not only from the posse, but from Zach and her

own weakness for a man she knew she couldn't
trust—or resist.

"It'll do."

Zach turned his gaze from the hovel of a settlement nestled in the barren crease of valley before
them, then spared a look for the drooping woman
at his side. He was killing her, and it showed.

Dark mauve rings lay under Beth Ann's eyes,
and her lovely mouth hung downward with fatigue. Her gaze was distant and glazed with weariness, and Zach knew that if he didn't let her rest
soon, it wouldn't matter if Sheriff Nichols caught
up with them or not.

"Come on, honey."

"Huh?" She swayed in the saddle, blinking into
the tangerine glare of the sunset whose shadows
mercifully cloaked the more slovenly aspects of
the bedraggled clutch of adobe buildings and rick-
ety corrals.

"The cantina probably has a room with a bed.
And maybe I can rustle us up some grub and
enough water for a wash. Would you like that?"

"Oh, yes." Beth Ann looked at Zach as if he
were her deliverer. It was a pleasant change from
hostility, but he regretted that he'd had to drive
her into a stupor to reach this stage.

"Let's see what we can do, then." Clucking to
the tired horses, Zach led them toward the village.

The settlement was all that was left of a mining
camp that had gone bust. Now only a few Mexican peasants, a broken-down prospector or two,
and the owner of the flea-bitten Joyride Cantina
made up a permanent population that was in-
flated only periodically by a few thirsty miners or
lost travelers. This far off the beaten path, Zach
hoped a disreputable-looking pair like them

wouldn't attract too much attention. He figured they could stock up on a few supplies and find a night's lodging, then head out again at first light. With any amount of luck, Sheriff Nichols wouldn't unravel their trail for days yet, and by then they'd be long gone.

A skinny Mexican boy was glad to tend to their horses for a coin from Zach's pouch. With his saddlebags thrown over one shoulder, Zach lent a supporting arm to Beth Ann, and they entered the cantina. Inside, a dark-eyed señorita in a white off-the-shoulder dress sat at a table smoking a cigarette and watching two crusty miners play five-card stud. A tubercular vaquero plucked a Spanish melody on a battered guitar, while the balding bartender futilely wiped greasy smudges from thick tumblers. A roach scuttled for cover across the dirty floor, and flyspecked bottles of bad whiskey sat in splendor on a raw wood shelf behind the bar. All conversation came to an abrupt halt at Zach and Beth Ann's entrance.

Ignoring the curious, suspicious eyes, Zach approached the bartender and explained what he wanted. The bartender spat tobacco juice onto the floor, shaking his head, then changed his mind at the sight of the gold piece Zach laid on the bar. At the chink of money, the dusky-skinned señorita gravitated toward them, her dark eyes sultry and inviting.

" 'Spect you can have any room in the place at that price, mister," the bartender said, showing his brown teeth. He reached for the coin, but Zach caught his wrist.

"And some food and wash water, as soon as possible. My . . . wife is quite fatigued, as you can see."

Zach felt Beth Ann stiffen, and gave her a hard look in warning.

"Musta been traveling hard," the balding man remarked, pocketing the coin when Zach released him.

"Hard enough, friend," Zach answered, his smile easy and unrevealing. "The room?"

"Show them, Juanita," the bartender ordered with a jerk of his chin.

"Come, *chico*," Juanita said. Dismissing Beth Ann with a glance, she focused her energy exclusively on Zach. With a seductive smile and a provocative swaying of her hips, she escorted them down a grimy hall to the rear of the building, then threw open the door of a stark cell furnished with only a roughhewn bedstead and a slop jar.

Beth Ann stumbled into the little room, then wrinkled her nose in fastidious displeasure at the crumpled bedclothes. Zach lifted his hand, displaying another coin between two fingers, and immediately Juanita's eyes lit up. "See if you can hurry up that food and a jar of water for my wife, señorita."

Juanita snatched the coin and tucked it into her cleavage. "*Sí*, and if you require anything else, señor, anything at all . . ."

Zach smiled. "I'll remember." He shut the door to the sound of Beth Ann's disparaging snort. "What's with you?"

"Nothing, señor," she sneered, jerking off the bed sheets and shaking them vigorously to remove vermin. "Nothing that being a thousand miles away from you wouldn't cure."

He heaved an aggravated sigh. "Don't get your nose in a snit over Juanita. She's just trying to be friendly."

"Friendly!" Beth Ann adroitly flipped the sheets

back into place and made the bed, her corners perfectly square from long practice. "That heifer would climb into your trousers for no more than a wink and a pinch."

"Not jealous, are you, angel?"

Sitting down on the edge of the bed, Beth Ann shot him a fulminating glance and began to pull off her shoes. "Don't be disgusting!"

"Well, a man could get a case of something from a blanket companion like Juanita, so don't be worrying that I'm gonna stray, darlin'."

"Don't flatter yourself, Zach Madison. I've got more to worry about than *you!*"

"You always so crabby when you're tired?" he asked with a half grin. "We're likely to be running in the same yoke awhile, but it's going to take some getting used to."

She spluttered indignantly, but a knock interrupted her before she could launch into a full-fledged blessing-out. Zach opened the door for Juanita, who sailed in bearing a tin plate of beans and a pail of water. He relieved her of her burdens, and she gave him a simpering smile.

"Give me that," Beth Ann said irritably, snatching the plate and pail and glaring at Zach. "Excuse me. I want to clean up. Alone."

"By all means. I've got to check on a few things, anyway." With an appreciative glance for the way Juanita twitched her skirts, Zach followed the señorita toward the door. He gave Beth Ann a mischievous look. "Don't bother to wait up."

The door slammed behind him with such force, Zach grinned. Damn, if he didn't love riling Beth Ann! It made the thought of making up with her all that more appealing.

"Your wife is a she-cat, eh?" Juanita asked, slanting Zach a suggestive look from under her stubby lashes. "A man like you deserves better, softer . . . I am soft as butter, señor."

"Thanks anyway, Juanita, but she'd skin me alive," Zach said, laughing to take the sting out of his rejection, "and I value my hide." He pulled another coin from his pocket, and the woman immediately brightened. "But there is something you can do . . ."

When Zach returned to the room some time later, he'd made use of the outdoor wash trough, gobbled a plate of tasteless beans and salt pork, and done a little horse trading. He knocked, then entered the now dark room quietly, not surprised to find Beth Ann sound asleep on the swaybacked cot, her hand pressed under her cheek like a child. He knew how she felt, for a full stomach made him drowsy and the bed looked mighty inviting, not just because of the feminine hills and valleys hidden beneath the sheet.

Zach placed the bundle of clothes he'd managed to locate—split riding skirt, clean boy's-size shirt, boots, and a soft felt hat—on the bedpost. The rest of his trading hadn't been so innocuous. In fact, he'd had serious reservations about the rifle and gun belt he now placed safely in the far corner, but a man didn't go into Indian raiding territory or light out across a mountain range unarmed. He just might come across a rattlesnake that needed killing—or worse.

Sighing, Zach rotated his head, trying to work out the kinks of fatigue, then stripped and climbed in beside Beth Ann. She murmured but didn't wake, and Zach gingerly cuddled her into the curve of his body, not even minding that they were both too exhausted to make love. Her skin was warm through her thin shimmy and her fragrance enveloped him, clean and fresh and womanly. Just holding her was enough for now, and Zach sighed in contentment, warmed by a sense of homecoming, of belonging. As he drifted off to sleep, he marveled at how good it felt.

"Scoundrel! How dare you! Get out!"

"Oof!" The punch landed in Zach's ribs, jarring him into full, gasping wakefulness with a vengeance. From the bar up front, the strum of a Mexican serenade mixed with drunken laughter, but in the little room, it was the angry rasp of Beth Ann's furious screech that filled his ears.

"You scum! Craven, despicable varmint!" Sitting bolt upright in the darkness, she kicked at him and the twisted sheets and took another swing at his head. "You have no right—"

Zach wasn't too groggy from sleep to duck this time, and he caught her hand. "What the *hell's* the matter with you, woman?"

"Get out of this bed!" she seethed, wrestling with him. The old bedstead creaked and groaned in protest. "Damn you, you didn't even have the decency to keep on your drawers!"

"Blast it to Hades, what for?" Zach demanded, grappling with the slippery hellion.

"What for?" Her voice was incensed and incredulous. "You take a lot for granted, you overgrown coyote! Just because I—we—you've got a hell of a lot of nerve assuming I'd ever let you—" She strangled on her ire, unable to express her outrage. "Just get the hell out of my bed!"

"Since I paid for it, that makes it my bed, angel."

"Then I'll go!" She lunged up, but he hauled her back, pushing her into the bedclothes.

"You'll stay right where you belong," he ground out, furious now himself. "And you'll shut up that caterwauling, too. Do you want to bring the whole town down on us as well as a posse?"

"Almost anything would be better than being mauled by the likes of you," she hissed, her pale eyes glittering in the dimness.

Zach loomed over her, controlling her struggles now with his superior weight. "And you obviously haven't spent enough time in a jail cell to be objective about that. You may not value your freedom, but I sure as hell do."

"Then why don't you just go?" she demanded. "No one got a good look at you when you were pulling down the jailhouse. You can just take off."

"That's what we're both doing, wouldn't you say? But since the law's still after me for some trouble I got myself into up around Prescott, I'd just as soon not call any extra attention my way, either. And the sheriff's sharp. It won't take him long to make a connection between Reverend Temple and those wanted posters he got with my name on them."

"Wanted? For what? Seducing helpless virgins?" she sneered.

He laughed shortly. "As a profession, it's too hazardous for my liking."

"And you're too cowardly to rob banks, so they must want you for something really serious, like eating the pigs' slop or stealing cow pies."

Zach chuckled. "Lord, you've got an imagination. No, all I did was run a pokeno parlor and pretend I was a lawman for a while, but judges just love to throw the book at you for fleecing suckers who should have known better, and I've had my fill of prison." His voice went grim then. "I'm not going back. Ever."

"If there's any justice, there's a cell with your

name on it," she returned, too sweetly, "and I hope they lock you up and throw away the key!"

"Just how long do you intend to keep this up?" he demanded. "I'm getting pretty damned sick of all this abuse."

"It'll take at least a millennium for me to tell you how disgusting and despicable and absolutely revolting you are!"

"You liked every minute of what we did together, and you know it," Zach snapped. "Okay, so I didn't tell you everything. Goddammit, I thought you'd be *glad* to find out I wasn't really a preacher!"

"Glad to know that you'd made a fool of me? You are demented."

"Look, I'm sorry about that, all right? I was going to tell you everything—"

Beth Ann snorted her disbelief. "And the moon's made of green cheese! You were found out, and I thank my lucky stars I finally saw your true colors, you yellow-bellied snake!"

"Will you shut up and listen?" he growled, giving her shoulders a shake. "I asked you to go away with me, didn't I? If you'd had a grain of sense then instead of letting your pride pucker you up like a pickle, none of this would have happened. And it didn't make any difference in the long run, anyway, because here we are together, and that's the way it's going to stay."

"I'm not your property, Zach Madison." She pressed her palms against his bare chest in denial. "I still have something to say about my own life."

"Hell, you still don't get it, do you? We're good together, you and I. Just as soon as we get shut of this mess, you'll see things clearer, but I'll be damned if I'm going to put up with any more of your viciousness and offended pride! You might as well go ahead and forgive me now so we can get on with what's really important."

He insinuated his knee between her thighs, making her gasp, but still she spit her venom at him.

"Forgive you? You've ruined everything! You cheated me out of my virtue with a pack of lies, and now you've fixed it so that I can't go back and clear my name. And my home—I've had to abandon everything I worked so hard to build. Who'll take care of Traveler's Rest now?"

"You little hypocrite!" Zach's words dripped with scorn. "Like most women, you've got a convenient memory—or don't you recall that all you wanted to do was get out of Destiny?"

"Not like this!"

"Well, circumstances being what they were, you didn't have much choice, did you?"

"But I don't have to like them or *you*," she returned in a low, furious whisper. "And you have no right to assume I'm so grateful for that so-called rescue that I'll sleep with you again."

That made him laugh. He nuzzled her neck. "Angel, gratitude has nothing to do with it."

She batted at his head with her hands, but his grip on her shoulders made the assault ineffectual. "Stop that. I don't give myself to lying swindlers."

"Don't speak too soon, angel," he muttered against her throat, smiling as he felt the goose bumps pebbling her skin.

"Damn you," she moaned. "You're just like Tom, only worse! And a thief, too, only not a very good one."

"At least I'm no killer."

"Neither is he!"

"Not according to Sheriff Nichols. Chapman and

his gang killed some guards busting out of the Territorial Prison."

"Tom's free?" She sounded dazed.

Scowling, Zach drew back to look down into her shadowed face, and his hands tightened on her arms. "The son of a bitch is a murderer, Beth Ann. Don't go getting any crazy ideas."

"Why not?" she asked wildly. "He couldn't be any worse than you!"

"You think you're in trouble now, but it's nothing like what you'd find if you hitched up with Tom Chapman." Zach grinned wickedly. "Besides, you said yourself he couldn't service a hot little filly like you. You'd better stick with a man who can satisfy you."

She sucked in an outraged breath, but before she could blast him again, Zach swooped and captured her lips. Lord, even her fury tasted delicious, and her wiggling inflamed him. He breached the seam of her lips easily, stroking the interior of her mouth with his tongue, swallowing her protests, melting her resistance with the ardency and power of his kisses.

Zach curled his arm under the small of her back, arching her body into his, reveling at the soft thrust of her breasts and the narrowness of her waist. Her hips were slender, but rounded in just the right feminine places, and she felt small and fragile and perfect. The need to protect her filled him; the need to possess her again overwhelmed his senses.

Beth Ann moaned softly, her fingers curling into the smooth flesh of his shoulders. When Zach released her lips, she gasped, then her breath feathered out again as he found the peaked crest of a nipple with his mouth and sucked and bit at the tender, distended nub through the thin lawn of her chemise.

"Oh, God. Zach, stop . . ." There was a note of desperation in her voice.

Fire burned in Zach's loins, desire for this woman a cataract of molten need. "Angel. We were meant for this. Can't you feel it?"

Her words were an anguished whisper. "You don't love me."

That's not true.

The unbidden thought startled Zach, and a tremor of something that in another setting would have been fear knifed through him, killing the impulse to voice the words out loud.

"It's close enough," he mumbled.

"Not for me!"

"Will you quit trying to analyze every blame thing?" He cupped her breast and rubbed his throbbing body against her in silent persuasion. "I'll give you what I can. Don't expect more. Just—"

"Just shut up and spread my legs like any other whore?" In the darkness, her voice was husky, and a faint glimmer of moisture glistened on her cheeks. "All right, Zach. If that's what you really want, I can't fight you."

He pulled away, cursing under his breath. "Damnation. That's not what I meant!"

"It doesn't matter, does it? It's what it is."

Passion fled in a rush. Mouthing obscenities, Zach rolled off the creaky bed. "Damned if you aren't the most ungrateful, aggravating female I've ever known! Well, the hell with you!"

He snatched up his clothes and pulled them on, gnashing his teeth.

"Where are you going?" she asked in a small voice.

"To find some convivial company!" He stomped his feet into his boots and buttoned his shirt, knowing it was cockeyed but not caring. "Someone who knows how to treat a man right."

Beth Ann sat up abruptly, rubbing at her wet cheeks. "Good! Go on, then. I hope you and Juanita have fun—and that whatever you catch makes your privates rot off!"

"At least I won't have to put up with a foulmouthed shrew who wouldn't know when she was well off if it came up and bit her on the butt!" he roared.

"Oh—oh, go to the devil!" Bursting into fresh tears, she threw herself into the flat pillow and sobbed.

"And don't try and use those damned female tricks on me, either!"

Furious and frustrated and ashamed all at the same time, Zach jerked open the door. The pale gleam of light from the lantern in the hallway illuminated Beth Ann's tumbled hair and quaking shoulders. Feeling lower than a snake's belly, and helpless to do anything, say anything, *give* anything that would alleviate her distress, he made the usual male choice . . . and fled.

Juanita's dusky face brightened when Zach stalked into the barroom. One look at his glowering expression, and her dark eyes sparkled with knowing sympathy. "Ah, *chico*, you find the bed too hard, eh?"

"You got that damn straight." Zach pulled a chair up to the poker table, grabbed Juanita's arm and pulled her onto his knee, then called for whiskey. With the first shot of rotgut safely down his throat, he gave Juanita a pinch and the other card players a reckless grin. "Deal me in."

The only rooster left in the squalid little community was announcing the arrival of the sun from the hitching post when the game finally broke up. Rising none too steadily to his feet, Zach scraped his collection of gold pieces into his neckerchief and nodded to the other players. He'd shucked them of their stray cash fair and square, and with such good humor that they couldn't even be mad at him. Besides, they were all four sheets to the wind from all the whiskey they'd imbibed.

"Thankee, gents," Zach said, slurring his words. "Maybe next time Lady Luck'll be running t'other way."

"You're a good fellow, Zach," an old miner said with a maudlin sniffle. His weather-beaten companions nodded. "Best I ever seen."

Zach ducked his head modestly and swayed a bit. "Whooee. Better get me some shut-eye."

Juanita sprawled on a bench, snoring softly. She'd have made a pretty corpse, Zach thought kindly, and tucked a couple of gold pieces into her cleavage without waking her. Taking a deep breath, he turned toward the back room, intent on getting things straight with Beth Ann.

After all, a man who'd doubled their stake in one sitting deserved some praise. And dad-blame it! He was still just as hungry for a woman—one particular woman—as he'd ever been. She was just going to have to get all of those fool notions out of her head. Hell, he respected her, didn't he? He was taking care of her, wasn't he? His neck was on the line just the same as hers, wasn't it? Seemed to him, a man willing to do all that, and put up with her female shenanigans, deserved *some* consideration!

Zach paused at the door to steady himself, then wiped his lips on his sleeve and ran his fingers through his hair. He thought longingly for a moment of another bracing shot of "hair of the dog," then regretfully decided against it. A man had to know when to call a halt. After all, liquor had been known to impair a man's performance, and Zach surely didn't want to pull a Tom Chapman on Beth Ann at this critical moment!

He smiled faintly to himself. Yes, sir, he felt fine. They'd have them a little early morning romp, and when they hit the road again, they'd both be wearing smiles. He pushed open the door.

"Honey, you awake? I did so well, we'll be feasting on steak and champagne when we get to—"

Zach broke off with a puzzled frown. The bed was empty. The clothes he'd brought had disappeared from the bedpost, and the rifle was nowhere to be seen. Zach's thoughts swirled in his whiskey-clouded brain for a terrible, endless moment, then the truth hit.

Beth Ann was gone!

And damn if she hadn't made the bed before she left!

Chapter 14

The most aggravating thing about being lost, Beth Ann decided, was that sooner or later you had to admit it.

She reined in her mare, absently stroking the grulla's blue-gray neck for reassurance, and squinted up at the sun from beneath the brim of the hat Zach had so thoughtfully provided. Judging by the length of the shadows from the saguaro, sagebrush, and boulders scattered along the base of the ridge she'd been following, it wasn't even noon, but the heat rising from the sandy soil was enervating and she felt as if she'd been going around in circles for decades.

It had seemed such a simple matter to head west toward Wickenburg and turn herself in to the judge there. How could she have known that nature had planted ridges, cliffs, and outcroppings smack in her way so that she had to turn first one direction and then the other to find a meandering path through this desolate country? Heading out on her own might have been an impetuous, light-minded thing to do, but she didn't really have a choice, not the way things were going between Zach and herself.

Beth Ann shuddered a little. She didn't even know the hard-eyed bandit whose touch threatened to rob her of what little pride she had left. It was better this way, she thought stonily. She had to deal with her problems, and Zach Madison and his grandiose plans were no solution, even if his kisses melted her spine into butter and she ached with desire for him. He wanted a life with no commitments, and in the bitter hours since she'd become homeless and hunted, Beth Ann had realized how precious a home and roots were to her.

Giving the desolate desert landscape another grimace, she dismounted, her stiff joints protesting. Tethering the reins on a spindly bush, she climbed the hill toward a prominent boulder. She might be alone in the middle of nowhere, but to answer Mother Nature's call, she still demanded a modicum of privacy.

She was buttoning the waistband of the split skirt again, wondering sourly if it had belonged to sultry-eyed Juanita, when she caught a whiff of smoke. She jerked her head up, sniffing avidly, the thought of civilization of any kind vastly appealing. Perhaps a local rancher or prospector could point her in the right direction. Following her nose, she scaled the hill to the crest of a rocky ridge.

The sight of the wickiups tucked into the secluded valley froze Beth Ann in her tracks. She knew instantly that this wasn't a motley encampment of peaceful Pimas, and her heart stopped. Apaches!

She gulped as the memory of the Camp Grant Massacre and the Indian retaliation flashed through her head, then she turned back with a flurry of skirts. A squaw gathering grasses on the edge of the valley lifted her head at that moment and gave a shrill cry of alarm. Beth Ann plunged headlong back down the slope, slipping and sliding in a shower of dirt and pebbles. In a near panic, she tore the reins free and flung herself on her horse, then kicked the startled beast into a wild gallop. After about a mile of blind flight, she chanced a quick glance back—and sucked in a ragged gasp of terror. Behind her, three braves on horseback tumbled over the crest of the hill in pursuit!

Sobbing for breath, Beth Ann urged the tired horse to greater effort, praying that the animal wouldn't step in a prairie dog hole. She had little hope that she could outride the trio of braves, especially in unfamiliar country. Gasping, she wondered if she'd have the courage to use the rifle she'd taken from Zach on herself if the worst happened. She'd heard tales of white women held captive by the hostiles, and death was a preferable alternative.

She was galloping through a shallow valley between two rocky ridges now. The slopes were growing steeper, their faces more rugged, and the valley began a gradual curve around the base of a fat hillock crowned by a pediment of red rock cliffs. Another quick glance to the rear told her the braves were fast closing the distance between them.

Panic nearly overtook her then. Panting through her open mouth, she gripped the reins tighter and forced herself to think. When she rounded the curved base of the earthen upthrust, there would be a moment—brief, but real—when she would be out of the sight of her pursuers. It was her only hope.

The thunder of hooves filled her ears, and terror poured like icy needles through her veins, making her feel numb and clumsy. Holding on to her control with the greatest of mental efforts, she desperately scanned the upper reaches of the hillock ... There! In just a few moments, the curve of the mountain would shield her from sight ... now!

Jerking the reins hard, she drew the winded horse to a sliding stop, whipped rifle and canteen from the saddle, and vaulted off. She smacked the horse's rump, and the jittery animal leapt into a gallop again, following the natural lay of the land down the other side of the slope. With a silent prayer, she scrambled up the hillock, pushing through scrappy sagebrush and prickly pear with no more notice than if they were a field of daisies. Her heart pounded in her throat, so loudly she almost didn't hear the thunder of unshod hooves until it was too late. With a whimper, she threw herself down on her belly in the lee of a large boulder, pressing herself into the gritty earth and praying for invisibility.

To her immense relief, the riders passed her by, and the drum of their galloping steeds faded rapidly. Then she was up like a jackrabbit, scrambling and climbing, trying to put as much distance between herself and the Apaches as possible, heading ever upward though the earth became nothing but rocky shards that bruised her feet through her boots and scraped her hands raw when she was forced to climb on all fours.

Sweating, swearing, she came to a point where she could climb no farther, so she worked her way around the circumference of the hill's rocky crown, always away from the direction the braves had taken. When she came at last to a shallow crevice under an overhanging shelf of rock that formed a natural cavelike shelter, she knew it was where she'd have to make her stand.

A thousand years earlier, some other adventurer had carved native glyphs into the ocher-colored rocks, but Beth Ann gave the faded symbols only a brief glance. Of more immediate concern was the litter of broken rocks scattered about the area. She poked around with the rifle's muzzle to make sure no scorpions or other critters shared her hideout, then gingerly took a strategic seat behind a low rock wall, now crumbling with age, that must have been built by that same ancient artist. With her back pressed against the rock face, she could see anyone who approached, and defend herself as long as her ammunition and water held out.

With a sigh, she removed her hat and blotted her sweaty face with her sleeve. Though she was shaded by the rock overhang, already the heat inside her little fort was stifling. She took a cautious sip from the canteen and placed the rifle within easy reach, grimly promising to save the last cartridge for herself.

The vigil was endless, excruciating. As silent and still as the stones surrounding her, she waited, sweat dripping from every pore, occasionally picking a cactus spine from her skin. She tensed at each sound—the rustle of a prairie rat through the sage, the rattle of rock cracking after a millennium of aging, the harsh cry of a Harris hawk gliding in the cloudless blue sky above her rock roof. She quivered with apprehension like a tightly strung bowstring, each noise causing her heart to flutter madly. Hardly able to breathe, she crouched, taut and frightened, wondering how she'd ever come to this, wondering if Zach would ever know what had become of her and if he'd even care, wondering if God would listen if she tried to pray.

Hours passed in nerve-stretching terror. When the shadows at last grew deeper, Beth Ann dared to draw a breath of hope. Had she succeeded in losing her pursuit? Every minute that passed now encouraged her, yet still her mind played terrible games. What if the Apaches were just waiting until dark to come for her? Even if she had escaped detection, how would she walk out of this wilderness with no horse, and no inkling of the direction she should take? "Out of the frying pan, into the fire" took on a whole new meaning in the desert. And who was to say she wouldn't stumble right back into another Indian encampment?

Moaning a little at such images, she rested her forehead on her knees, trembling from fatigue and fear. A sudden rattle of stones jerked her into watchfulness yet again, her hands tightening on the rifle. Ears straining, eyes darting, she pressed her back into the rock wall. Another shower of gravel, nearer this time, made her jump and quiver.

Slowly, her lips pressed together, she lifted the rifle to her shoulder, peering over the sight at the low rock wall facing her. Swallowing, she cocked the hammer, but her finger trembled on the trigger. To brace herself, she bit her lower lip until she tasted blood. A steady, stealthy crunching of footsteps drew closer, closer . . .

He appeared over the wall, drew up short at the sight of the cocked rifle, and looked at her with murder in his blue-green eyes.

"Well, angel, if you aim to shoot, you'd best get on with it. And this time do us both a favor and make it count."

Beth Ann gaped at Zach, his taut jaw glittering with a day's growth of reddish brown beard, his expression belligerent and smoldering under a layer of sweat and dust. She had been prepared for anything except this. With a cry, she dropped the rifle and covered her face with her shaking hands.

Then he was beside her, jerking her up by the shoulders, his face as savage as she'd ever seen. "By God, I could kill you!"

Her knees were so weak, she could hardly stand, but she had to warn him. "Zach . . . Apaches . . . I . . ."

"I know about the goddammed Apaches!" he snarled. "I followed your trail right to the spot where they butchered your horse and had a picnic!"

Her heart sank at the fate of the stalwart beast. "Oh, no."

Zach shook her hard, his words coming from between clenched teeth. "Do you have any idea what I went through until I figured out none of the blood was yours? God, I died a thousand times! Thank goodness that party was more interested in hauling the carcass back to feed their own camp than in tracking you down!"

Beth Ann's teeth chattered with reaction. "How—how did you find me?"

"I backtracked every inch of your trail, that's how! You're just lucky I was more determined to find you than any Apache. What possessed you to play hide-and-seek with a war party?"

"Pretty clever, huh?" Suddenly giddy with relief, she gave him an insouciant grin. "Sorry you had to make the climb, but I'm glad you did. Do you have a horse?"

Bemused by that devastating flash of dimple, Zach blinked. "Uh, yeah. It got too steep, so I left him down the hill a piece."

"Good. Which way is Wickenburg?"

He swore obscenely. "Is that what you were doing? I ought to beat the holy hell out of you! Do you know what Apaches do with white female captives?" He shook her again, roaring. "Do you?"

Shuddering, she clung to his forearms, shaking her head in answer.

"And you never want to find out! God, I thought . . ."

Zach broke off, glaring at her with his bleary, red-rimmed eyes, and Beth Ann realized that he was shaking as much as she was. He was furious, she thought in amazement, but frightened, too. Zach threaded his fingers through her hair and roughly pulled her face up to his. In the diminishing light, his features were harsh and unyielding, terrifying and exciting.

"Don't you ever do that to me again, damn you!"

"No." She gasped softly at his vehemence, and placed her hands on either side of his waist to steady herself before her knees buckled. At her touch, his eyes turned to pure emerald.

"And don't you ever . . . don't ever—" Zach gave a growl of frustration and primal need. Muttering another oath, he crushed her against himself and took her mouth in a punishing kiss.

His lips were hot, insatiable, and he smelled muskily of sweat and horses and fear. His stubble scraped Beth Ann's tender skin, and his hands were hard and possessive.

It was overwhelming. It was wonderful.

With a murmur, Beth Ann laced her arms around his neck, pressing closer than a thought. His tongue demanded, and she opened willingly, gasping into his mouth at the dizzying, rapacious things he did to her.

His hands moved over her as if he couldn't trust his own senses that she was unharmed. She clung to him, knowing only that she was safe at last.

Zach's mouth consumed her, stealing her thoughts and will, creating waves of sensation and melting need. Her insides went liquid, her belly ignited with the peculiar tightening of desire, and she moaned.

The sound inflamed Zach. His capricious tongue explored the tender ridges inside her mouth, feasting on sweetness, and he fumbled at the buttons of her shirt, then lost patience entirely and ripped it open. Buttons flew unheeded and fabric tore, but Beth Ann made no protest, only shuddered and gasped uncontrollably as his large, warm hands freed her breasts from the confines of her shimmy, stroking and caressing and tormenting the velvety flesh until she could barely stand.

He released her mouth and buried his lips in the curve of her shoulder, his thumbs making wicked circles on her sensitive, distended nipples. Goose bumps shivered across her skin, and lightning zigzagged from her breasts to her feminine core, tension building like a summer storm.

"Zach," she said unevenly, not even knowing what she intended to say, only that his name was precious to her.

"Don't say a word, damn you," he muttered harshly. "You put me through hell!"

"I—I'm sorry." Her whisper was strangled by the thud of her pulse beating in her throat.

"You damn well better be!" Bending his head, he took the rosy tip of one breast between his lips and suckled strongly.

Beth Ann cried out, shaking and writhing, her body screaming as pleasure and need and passion built to unbearable dimensions. He smiled against her skin, then transferred his attentions to her other breast, licking and tugging at the tender pebbled nub until she was trembling and incoherent. When he kissed her again, she tasted her own salt on his lips, and the sense of joining, blending, melting into one being was so erotic, she quivered uncontrollably.

Suspended in a burning rapture, Beth Ann hardly noticed when Zach freed the button on her skirt and lifted her free of the garment. She only knew she felt weightless, as if she were falling free of the earth itself, spinning into some other universe where eternity was encompassed by the strength of Zach's arms around her. She rubbed her hands over his broad shoulders, hating the barrier of his shirt, and when he released her mouth, she barely bothered to breathe, nuzzling at the raspy place where his stubble began on his neck, kissing and tasting and inhaling his scent, a prisoner of pure sensation that was all Zach.

He murmured, tasting her skin greedily, bending her back over one arm to lave the swollen mounds of her breasts as if he could never get enough. He touched her intimately through the thin fabric of her drawers; then, impatient with that impediment, he shoved his hand under the waistband, trailing his fingers through the tight black curls at the juncture of her thighs, probing with one finger the tender petals of her womanhood, slick with dew—for him.

There was no control in him then. With a primitive mating sound rumbling deep in his throat, he kicked her discarded skirt into a pile, then pressed her down on it, covering her with his body. Strong fingers snapped the drawstring of her drawers, then he stripped them off her slender thighs, revealing her fully to his heated gaze.

Dazed, she looked up into Zach's eyes, and she felt as though she were drowning in turquoise fire. When he pressed open her thighs, her eyes widened, and then his mouth was on her—*there*—and she squealed in shock and a thunderous, utterly wicked pleasure.

"Zach, no!"

"Yes." His hands held her firmly, allowing no escape as he teased and sucked and tormented her with his skillful lips, his avid tongue.

"Oh, God, stop!"

He breathed against her damp curls, his voice implacable. "I need this. Oh, sweet Jesus . . ."

He kissed her tenderly, his tongue stroking a knob of feminine flesh where every fiery sensation centered like a burning star. Beth Ann's hips bucked uncontrollably, and her fingers dug into the rocky earth. She couldn't inhale, could only make sharp little hiccups of breath while her body arched and yearned and her mind refused to accept the enormity of this outrageous intimacy.

Her sight dimmed and reality became one pinpoint of light, of building, reaching necessity. She was nearly sobbing, so intense was the pressure, and then Zach touched her. The world exploded in a burst of white, blinding sensation, and she screamed. Behind her eyelids, she saw suns expire and comets streak across the heavens, and she was riding that comet, washed with starlight, flaming into one glorious moment of incandescence that lasted forever.

When the sparks faded away, she opened her dazed eyes to find Zach watching her with an expression of extreme satisfaction. Then the tense urgency returned to his face, his burning need reflected in the blue-green flames of his eyes. He opened his trousers, positioned himself, then entered her in one smooth, powerful thrust. Her eyes opened wide with incredulous surprise as the embers of her release were fanned into new flames by the fullness of his possession.

Teeth bared in a grimace of exquisite pleasure, Zach arched his back, holding himself on his hands, looking at the place where they became one.

"You . . . belong . . . to me," he said between his teeth, making circles with his body that stole Beth Ann's breath all over again. "We were made for this."

"Yes." The truth of it overcame her, and her lids fanned shut in wonder as again sensation built to a crescendo.

She slid her hands beneath Zach's waistband and cupped his muscular buttocks, reveling in the flex and roll of his thrusts, pulling him closer, closer. He jerked, then came down on his forearms, rubbing his hair-dusted chest against her tender nipples and taking her mouth again. She tasted herself on his tongue, a sweet-sour tang that was the essence of sex, and she licked at him greedily, engulfing herself in the totality of their experience together.

The rhythm of his thrusts quickened, and she tightened her thighs, needing him even closer, wishing she could dissolve into his skin. Lifting her legs, she locked her heels in the small of his back, and he went wild, pounding into her with a potency and strength that she relished and rejoiced in.

And then the familiar contractions were upon her again and she threw back her head, crying out with the tumultuous power of a new completion. Zach shuddered, his body tensed, and then he added his shout of triumph to hers, a sound that echoed back from the rocky walls as he surged against her one final time and found his own bliss.

All was quiet, only the sibilant sounds of breathing slowly returning to a normal rhythm disturbing the stillness. Zach lay in a boneless collapse on top of her, their bodies still joined. Distant tingles of aftershocks rippled along Beth Ann's nerves, drifting away and faint, but never to be forgotten or denied again.

Rocks poked into her back, and grit sanded her bare skin. She couldn't be bothered to care, and especially not to think, because that would be even more painful than any physical discomfort. But eventually she had to breathe, and she touched Zach's side, wordlessly urging him to lift his weight from her compressed lungs.

He stirred reluctantly, then raised himself on his elbows, frowning as she sucked in a grateful draft of the rapidly cooling air of the desert night falling around them.

"Are you all right?" His voice was gruff. "Did I . . . hurt you?"

"I don't know," she replied, still dazed. Wondering, she ran her fingers over his waistband. "You didn't even take off your pants."

"Not enough time." Chuckling, he lightly touched his lips to hers. "That's how crazy you make me, angel."

"Don't blame me," she protested. "You were already that way."

"Yeah." Zach lazily licked the skin along the underside of her jaw, evoking shivers that, in her overly sensitized state, seemed to wash from her scalp to her toenails. She twisted slightly, but she was still pinned under his weight.

"You're uncivilized," she accused shakily.

"Umm." He nibbled at her earlobe.

"Uncouth!"

"Uh-huh."

"Wicked!" she snapped, pushing at his shoulders.

"If this is wicked, honey, the whole world's going to hell." Zach slanted her a narrowed, knowing look from beneath his sandy lashes and pressed against her intimately. "I'm just a man. *Your* man. And you'd best get used to it."

Beth Ann gasped with the knowledge that his manhood was no longer flaccid, but growing hard again while still within her own body. The realization leaped like ball lightning through her system, the heat and electricity of her own instant response frightening her. Bewildered, she wailed, "I don't understand . . ."

Zach's slow smile was full of promise and passion. "You will."

Then he began to move again, and for a very long time nothing else mattered.

Zach woke from a deep sleep just before dawn to find the woman in his arms weeping silently. They lay on their sides, spoon-fashion, the single blanket from his bedroll wrapped around them both, the tiny fire that was all he'd dared build within their cave shelter long since extinguished. He placed a hand on her quaking shoulder.

"Beth Ann? What is it, honey? Are you cold?"

She shook her head, the wild mass of her dark curls quivering.

"Scared?"

"No."

Zach tugged her onto her back so that he could see into her face. Moisture streamed down her cheeks, and her mouth was tremulous, her lower lip quivering and as vulnerable as a child's. His brow pleated with concern, he traced the path of her tears with a fingertip. "Darlin', tell me. What's the matter?"

Her spiky lashes drooped wearily, and her

breathing was erratic, but she shook her head again. "Nothing."

Irritation compressed his mouth. "All this water isn't for nothing! Spit it out."

She heaved a dejected sigh. "You wouldn't understand."

"Now, isn't that like a dad-blamed fool woman?" His tone was disgusted. "Can't answer a simple question, so you make the man the dummy!"

Her eyes snapped open, and the silver-gray pools were anguished and miserable. "I just don't know who I am anymore."

"Jee-sus!" Zach levered himself to a sitting position and glared his exasperation. "We've got one horse between us, miles of desert to cross, hostiles camped in the next valley, a posse probably right behind us, and *you're worried about who you are?* Lord protect me!"

Beth Ann rolled to her elbow, her tear-glazed eyes resigned. "I knew you wouldn't understand."

"All right." He held up his hands in surrender. "I'm listening. If it'll end this crying jag, make me understand."

She sat up completely, pulling the tattered remnants of her shirt together, wiping futilely at her wet cheeks. "I knew it would be like this between us."

He grinned, the self-satisfied sign of the sated male. "So did I."

"But I didn't want"—she gestured at the blanket, at them—"this."

That pricked his ego and made him huffy. "You didn't have anything to complain about before, not the way you went off like a rocket every time I touched you!"

Lord, females were maddening! Some women

never experienced a sexual release in a lifetime, and yet Beth Ann had come to her climax again and again. How could she cry about that? In fact, his chest puffed out with pride that he'd been the one to unleash the passion within her, to help her discover the joy of truly being a woman in all ways. And she was hot and responsive and insatiable in bed, a gem among women. Was it any wonder he'd lost control of himself time and again? The ability to abandon oneself to such a pleasure was a blessing, but she acted as though it were a curse!

"To my everlasting shame, I lacked the will to resist you . . . and my own desires," Beth Ann admitted, her expression bleak. "I am weak. I'm a failure all the way around. I couldn't even leave you without getting into terrible trouble. If you hadn't come . . ."

"It's not a crime to need somebody," he grumbled.

She shook her head. "Paw knew me better than I did myself. I guess I'm just as frail and wanton as he always said."

"Dammit, that's not true!" Zach exploded, angered by her self-condemnation.

Beth Ann eyed him sadly, the first pale rays of dawn catching the tears slipping down her cheeks and making them shimmer like crystal dewdrops. "Isn't it? I only know that now that this has happened again, I'll never have the strength to deny you anything you want to take from me."

Zach brightened. "Now, that's the first sensible thing you've said!"

"Yes, that pleases you, doesn't it? Think of the aggravation you'll be spared dealing with a woman with no will of her own, who's lost every shred of independence she ever had." Her lovely mouth twisted. "But I should have had more pride than to give myself to a man who doesn't love me."

He felt as though she'd slapped him. Standing, he perched his fists on his hips and scowled at her. "Hell, woman, what do you want from me?"

She gave a tiny, hopeless shrug, fidgeting with the raveled hem on her shirt. "Something you can't give, I guess. Never mind. It's my problem."

He threw up his hands. "All right! I'll say it, if that's what it takes! I love you. I've always loved you. I loved you from the minute you plugged me in the shoulder and began to siphon sage tea down my throat! There. Does that satisfy you?"

Her look was pitying. "You can lie better than that, Zach. I've seen you do it. Try it again, and this time make me believe it."

"What makes you think I'm lying?" he muttered uncomfortably.

"There, that's a good start." Dashing the tears from her cheeks, she rose to her feet and gave him a brittle smile. "Tell me more, Zach. Whisper in my ear and make me believe that you'll never grow tired of me and move on as you have all your restless life, searching for something new and exciting. Convince me that the passion will never fail, and that I won't care what people think when we're together."

"That again!" Disgusted, he caught her shoulders. "When are you going to learn that none of that matters! It's how you feel about yourself inside that counts."

"I feel witless and weak and confused inside—" she faltered momentarily, and then met his gaze courageously "—loving you despite everything."

"Angel." He swallowed on a sudden lump of feeling, and tried to cover his discomfiture with a laugh. "Give yourself some credit for having a little taste!"

She shook her head slowly, her voice low and hurting. "It's not so smart, caring for a man who's afraid of anything permanent, who has so much talent and potential but fritters it all away on schemes and games and wanderlust and wild dreams! Even when things were at their worst at Traveler's Rest, my dreams were always small—work that had meaning, and if I was lucky, someday a peaceful home, babies of my own to love, a man who'd rub my back. What do I know about the gay life or the dangerous games you play?"

Zach's hands convulsed on her shoulders as her words touched painful chords, the secret fears about himself that dwelt in his deepest heart. Was he a roamer because he didn't like what he saw in the empty center of himself whenever he stopped too long? Her ability to see him so clearly, to know him down to the bone, made Zach unsettled and anxious. "Beth . . ."

"Tell me everything will work out, Zach," she pleaded softly. "Make me believe we have forever, even if it's a lie. I need my small dreams, but God help me, as bad as it hurts, I need you more."

Guilt constricted Zach's throat and made his words husky. "I won't hurt you."

"Now you're lying to yourself, Zach. You already have."

Stunned by her words, Zach let her step out of his nerveless grip. She folded the blanket, then performed a few basic ablutions. With her back to him, she used his comb on her tangled curls, idly examining the native glyphs carved into the rock wall face while Zach's mind foundered in a morass of remorse.

Had he been so blinded by his desire for Beth

Ann that he'd failed to truly understand what a selfish bastard he was to pursue her and win her surrender, knowing that he could never offer her the kind of life she needed? Zach scrubbed his palm across his bearded chin and cursed silently in frustration.

He knew firsthand she was courageous and caring, a real fighter with a heart so giving she could even love a despicable, deceitful, lying varmint like him. Hadn't those qualities in her attracted him from the very beginning? And she'd suffered so much already. Would keeping her with him only convince her that she was all the awful things her father had accused her of? Zach's thoughts shied away from that answer, though he knew it already. She was too willing to believe the worst about herself, so vulnerable her only defense was a wall of defiance to hide her hurt from the world.

Beth Ann's only sin was that she'd been looking for a little love and kindness, but with Tom Chapman and Zach Madison, she'd drawn twice to an inside straight and lost both times. A woman like her needed respectability. She needed neighbors to care about and children to love and raise into upstanding citizens. She needed to be the heart and center of her own home, the one person to whom those she loved could always turn for renewal and loving acceptance.

Zach watched Beth Ann dragging the comb through her glorious ebony locks and swallowed hard. Could he deprive her of all that? She was right. He'd already hurt her, and there would only be more to come as long as she was hooked up with him. She didn't deserve the kind of misery a future with a scoundrel would bring. She needed someone solid, stable, and dependable to take care of her, and Zach Madison wasn't it.

But Jesus, how could he bear to give her up? Zach groaned silently. Even now he wanted her again, longed to hold her close and give himself up to the ecstasy of making her his own. It was the only time in his life he'd ever felt whole. But if there was an ounce of anything honorable left within him, Zach knew that he had to let Beth Ann go, to free her from the chains of passion that bound them so that she could find her own destiny.

Zach came up behind her. With a fingertip, she traced the outline of a brighter set of glyphs scratched into the rock face, chewing her lip in concentration. When he placed his hands on her shoulders, she ignored Zach's touch, and a pain like a burning blade sliced his heart. Silently cursing his own weakness, he clenched his jaw in determination.

"You still want to go to California?"

"Huh?"

"I won't allow you to put yourself in jeopardy by turning yourself in," he said sternly. "I'll take you to California and find you a place, that chef's job or something that suits you . . . before I leave you in peace."

"What? All right." Her words were distracted.

"Dammit, Beth Ann!" he growled, spinning her around. "Would you stop that playing a minute and listen to me? I've had no practice at being noble, and I'm trying to figure out where we go from here!"

"I think . . ." She licked her lips and began again. "I think maybe we could go to Paw's mine."

"What?" He scowled incredulously. "What the hell do you mean?"

She pointed at the glyphs with a shaking finger.

"It's Paw's secret code, the one he used for book-keeping. 'North, two miles to the mushroom,' it says. It's got to be directions!"

A tic of excitement jumped in Zach's jaw. "Are you sure?"

"I'd recognize it anywhere." Suddenly Beth Ann began to laugh, a wild sound that bordered on hysteria.

Alarmed, Zach pulled her into his arms. "Angel, what is it? What's wrong?"

"Oh, Zach." She gasped with laughter, but her eyes were bright with tears. "Even from the grave, Paw's still telling me where to go!"

Chapter 15

"**W**olf Linder was one damned suspicious bastard."

Beneath a many-armed saguaro, Beth Ann scowled and pressed her palm protectively against another set of glyphs carved into a petrified log poking from a drift of sand. "It isn't proper to speak ill of the dead," she replied.

Zach snorted and dumped silt out of his boot. "I swear, you'd defend Satan himself to spite me. And the devil doesn't hold a candle to a devious old galoot like your paw."

"Because his directions have made us crisscross our own path ten times today?"

Zach's mouth twisted beneath his scraggly growth of stubble, and he gave the deep cut of desolate, rock-lined canyon surrounding them a bad-tempered glance. "No. Because he couldn't even trust his own flesh and blood with the location of her inheritance."

A day of following Wolf's trail of clues through the canyons and mesas of the unrelenting Superstitions had drained Beth Ann's reserves of forbearance and energy. Emotionally as well as physically spent, she vacillated between the urge to give vent to either blazing anger or uncontrollable weeping, in the end opting for neither because in the late afternoon heat, both would take too much effort.

"What does it matter?" she asked wearily, pushing her hair back from her damp temples. "I told you. We're not going to find anything there anyway."

"Then why did Wolf guard his secret so closely?" Zach demanded, pulling on his boot again. "Why all these games?"

"Maybe he didn't trust his memory. It's only a map of sorts, after all."

"Or maybe he just wanted to see how many suckers would fall for a wild-goose chase. It's just the kind of sick joke he'd play."

Beth Ann shook her head. "I'm the only one who could read the markings besides Paw."

"How can you be sure of that? Maybe your paw had a partner you didn't know about. Hell, he could even be Wolf's killer. That's possible, isn't it?"

"I suppose, maybe ... Oh, I don't know!" Beth Ann sat down on the petrified log and massaged her tired neck muscles. "I don't know *what* to think anymore!"

Zach unhooked the canteen from his saddle horn and squinted into the rugged, sun-drenched vista. Here and there the late spring rains produced a flash of brief color amid the gray-green sage. Golden blossoms tipped the treelike stems of cholla, lavender saucers topped fat, knobby peyote, and dainty pink petals sprang from the vicious heart of a thorny fishhook cactus.

"It's a damned muddle, all right," he muttered.

Beth Ann gave him a morose look. "We make a fine pair, snared by greed and curiosity, risking our lives for—what? The mythical pot of gold?"

Squatting on his haunches beside her, Zach passed Beth Ann the canteen and gave her an oblique look. "You never know when you might get lucky, angel."

"I'd hate to think I had to depend on my luck." She took a drink, then returned the canteen. "I hope yours is better."

"Lady Fortune has been kind in the past."

"Do you think she would smile long enough for you to snare a jackrabbit? I'm starving." Zach opened his mouth to make a suggestion, but Beth Ann forestalled him with a glower. "And no, I don't want any more of your damned jerky!"

He grinned and gave her an encouraging pat on the knee. "I'm sick of it myself, honey, but you know what they say about beggars."

"Yeah." She stared at the arid landscape, and her mouth drooped. "This wasn't a very good idea, was it?"

"I've had better," he admitted.

"Maybe we should give it up."

Zach slanted her a look from under his sandy lashes. "Is that what you want?"

"It's the sensible thing. There's not much water left."

"No. And I'm afraid the horse is going lame."

"I'd noticed." Beth Ann's brow furrowed in worry. "Between the Apaches and the posse, we've got enough trouble, haven't we?"

"Uh-huh." Zach drew patterns in the rocky earth with his fingertip.

Questions hung in the silence, and the moment stretched out endlessly. Finally Beth Ann sighed.

"We're going on, aren't we?"

Zach lifted his head. "Looks that way."

"We're both loco." She gave a reluctant laugh. "Sunstroke. That's the only explanation."

"No, that's what Wolf owes us—an explanation. He kept things from both of us. That mine of his seems to be at least a place to start discovering some answers."

Despite the heat, Beth Ann shivered. "It was the only thing Paw really cared about. I—I'm afraid of what I might find."

"Look, if you're thinking I'm going to jump Wolf's claim or something—" Zach began indignantly.

She waved away his protest. "I don't care about that, just that you're going to be disappointed."

"Let's worry about that when we find it, all right? Have a little faith."

"That's funny coming from you, *preacher.*"

"Hey, I didn't do so badly, did I?" Zach demanded defensively.

She lifted an eyebrow. "For a hypocrite, you mean?"

"Damn! I never said I didn't believe . . . exactly. I may be an unprincipled scoundrel by some folks' reckoning, but I have some standards!" Anger glittered in Zach's turquoise eyes. "Didn't I put a stop to that verbal Sunday stoning your paw put you through? And no sermon of mine ever advised passing judgment or condemning your neighbor, either."

Beth Ann flushed. "You're right. I'm sorry. But I still think Paw's mine played out long ago. If I'm wrong, you're welcome to it all. I couldn't abide living off of something that's caused me nothing but misery all these years, and after your fine performance as Reverend Temple, I'd say it's the least you deserve." She attempted a wry smile. "We wouldn't want your time in Destiny to be a total waste."

Zach scowled. "Hell, you know I wouldn't do that to you! You're going to need everything you can get to start a new life after . . ."

"After you move on?" Her mouth quivered briefly, but she clamped her lips together and lifted her chin. "I heard you earlier, so you needn't tread on eggshells regarding the subject."

His face darkened. "It's best, isn't it?"

"For whom, Zach?" she asked softly.

He jumped to his feet, jerkily returning the canteen to the saddle and then making a production of checking the horse's tender front hoof. Her eyes followed him in silent reproach, and when he turned back to her, a truculent expression marred his handsome features.

"I won't abandon you, you know. When we get to California, I'll see to it that you're set up someplace nice. If there's anything workable in your paw's mine, the money will just make things easier for you, that's all. Hell, maybe you can open your own fancy restaurant!"

Beth Ann spread her hands and opened her eyes wide. "Why would I welcome anything that makes it easier for you to leave me?"

His brow lowered thunderously. "Look, there's nothing to be gained from this."

"Maybe you're right." She looked down at her hands. "And maybe I'd do anything I could to stay with you—even play on your avarice to keep you tromping through these mountains with me until doomsday."

Zach's sandy brows pulled together in puzzled consternation. "What?"

"Did you never stop to think that you've been awfully trusting? How can you be sure that I've been reading Paw's shorthand to you correctly?"

A dull flush rolled up Zach's neck. "You mean . . . ? Good God, Beth Ann, you didn't!"

She held his gaze for a long moment, then allowed a tiny smile of satisfaction to curve her lips. "No."

"God! You hellion! I ought to—"

"I know. Beat me."

"Not on your life." Striding to her side, he bent and kissed her hard, his bristly cheeks rasping deliciously against her skin, his hand tangling in her hair possessively. "There are better ways to keep you in line, woman."

"You've been taking a lot for granted," she murmured against his lips. "Just because you've got everything all planned out doesn't mean that's the way it's going to be."

Nudging her chin up with his knuckle, he smiled at her challenge. "Is that a threat?"

"Call it fair warning, because things are about to change."

"How?"

Looking down at the rock log on which she sat, Beth Ann rubbed her palm across the crude carvings again. "We're close. To what, I don't know. But this says we'll find what we seek at the top of that ridge."

Zach straightened, using his hand to shade his eyes as he examined the rocky slope. Eagerness tightened his jaw. "You up to it, angel?"

Beth Ann rose to her feet and tugged on her hat. "Let's just get it over with."

It took another hour of excruciating labor to ascend the slope, leading the limping horse, picking a path through the gorse and brush and over the clumps of reddish rock that slid and shifted with each step. A scorching wind buffeted them, draining Beth Ann of her strength, and when they finally reached the windy, barren spine of the ridge, she was gasping and light-headed.

Staggering, she let Zach give her a hand up the last few feet, then clung to his arm, blinking at the undulating spill of land falling down the other side of this small, rock-strewn plateau. In the clear desert air everything looked closer than it should, but Beth Ann realized the glint of silver peeking out of a fold in the landscape below was a creek, the precious water it carried only a few miles distant.

The ridge overlooked a small cliff, a litter of rocks and boulders spreading out only four to five feet below where they stood. Beth Ann looked at the jumble of stone and piles of rocky, barren earth in dismay. "There's nothing here!"

"Look again." Zach pointed at the fool-the-eye maze of rocks amid the lengthening shadows. "That pile is a cairn of some kind, probably a claim marker, and there's a rock corral and a piece of a hut. And look, that has to be the *arrastre*, the ore-grinding mill . . . Come on!"

Tying the tired horse to a tenacious sagebush, Zach jumped down the low cliff, then turned to help Beth Ann. She could pick out the features he'd mentioned now, her eyes adjusting to the ubiquitous redness of the rocks lying everywhere. Sure enough, there was a crude hut, little more than stacked stones for walls with a rough fireplace visible through the door opening and the remnants of a sagebrush roof rotting to pieces above. Wolf's handiwork? Was this desolate place her father's mine site? The achievement he'd thought of with more affection than he'd ever given either his wife or daughter?

Beth Ann pivoted, drinking in the stark place in both wonder and horror, then gasped. "Zach."

He turned, following her gaze. A funnel-shaped hole the height of a man opened its black maw against the jumble of fallen rock at the base of the cliff. The angle of the incline made it all but invisible from above.

"That's it," Zach said.

"It *is?*" Beth Ann hadn't really known what to expect, but for all their trouble, surely Paw's mine must be more than a mere hole in the ground! Zach laughed, an exultant rumble that mocked her disappointment.

"You'll see." He led her to the hole, then gingerly inspected the shadowy entrance. "There should be . . . ah! Here it is."

A match scratched, and then light bloomed inside the lantern Zach held aloft, illuminating the tunnel painstakingly chopped out of the mountainside. Ancient-looking timbers shored up the roof, and a litter of rusty tools, buckets, and mysterious equipment cluttered the downward-sloping floor.

"Stay here," he cautioned, stepping farther into the hole. A sifting of sand drifted down on his head, and Beth Ann's heart leapt into her throat.

"Zach, be careful!"

Zach flashed her a smile over his shoulder. "Easy, angel. Someone might think you really care about me. I'm just going to take a look around."

She compressed her lips in annoyance. "Well . . . make sure you don't get yourself killed! I've got enough to explain."

"I'll do my best."

Hovering at the opening to the mine, Beth Ann chewed her lip as Zach disappeared down the corridor, then nearly jumped out of her skin when he gave a shout just moments later. She plunged down the tunnel after him, only to meet him coming out with a wooden cask perched on his shoulder.

"Didn't I tell you to stay put?" he demanded, swinging her around by the elbow and hustling her back the way she'd come.

"I thought you were in trouble." She hadn't realized how jittery she'd become until she heard herself blurting questions. "Why did you cry out? Did you find gold already?"

"Something almost better." Back at the opening, he set the cask down on the ground, then used his knife to pry open the wax-sealed lid. "God forgive Wolf's black heart, the old bastard did us a favor."

Liquid sloshed as Zach removed the cover.

"Water," Beth Ann breathed, dipping her fingers into the barrel.

"Stockpiled in casks. It may taste like horse piss, but it makes things a bit easier."

"Yes." She lifted her cupped hand to sip. The water was brackish with a faintly oily aftertaste, but potable enough. "I'll water the horse. Poor thing, he needs this worse than we do."

"Can you manage?" Zach was already reaching again for the lantern. "I'd like to—"

"Go ahead. I'd rather stay busy doing something than stand here worrying."

Zach smiled and touched her cheek. "That's my girl."

If only you believed it, Beth Ann thought, her throat constricting as he disappeared again.

Zach's very eagerness spelled the death knell for her hopes. After all, hadn't he admitted the reason he'd come to Traveler's Rest in the first place was to get his hands on Wolf Linder's gold mine? And now, whether there was anything worth mining left or not, he'd reached his goal. It wouldn't be long before he heard the siren's song calling him to a new game, another chase—away from her.

Since Zach had made her so thoroughly his, nothing—not the charges pending against her, not their survival in this desert, not even the identity of Wolf's murderer—concerned Beth Ann more than the future of their relationship. If she were a sensible woman, she'd make a clean break when they came down off this mesa, and they would go their separate ways as she'd intended when she'd first left the cantina. But where loving Zach Madison was concerned, she was neither sensible nor strong.

Though she lectured herself sternly, her foolish heart could not be persuaded to give up hope. Staying with Zach as long as she could might make him see that their being together wasn't so impossible. Perhaps they could go to California. Her trials to this point had proven her both flexible and resilient. Maybe there was a place for her in the kind of life he led.

And maybe I'll find out what true heartbreak really is.

Apprehension squeezed Beth Ann's throat even tighter. She only knew that for all his faults and weaknesses, there was a goodness and a genuine liking for and understanding of humanity within Zach Madison that she loved with all her heart. Knowing that she stood above a dangerous precipice, she couldn't let her fears—of society's scorn, of Zach himself—make her give up on them just yet. He might be a gambler, but with their happiness at stake, she had no choice but to take the risk herself. Resolutely she lifted the little cask and went to tend to their mount.

By the time she found a narrow path, led the weary buckskin down from the ridge into the old rock corral, and watered the grateful animal, she was again in control of herself. But the longer she waited at the mine's entrance for Zach, the more tenuous her grasp on her anxieties became. Mysterious thumps and bumps reverberated from the depths of the mine shaft while the evening shadows grew deeper and the air cooled. Finally, unable to stand the waiting any longer, she ventured into the mouth of the tunnel.

"Zach?"

A muffled response echoed from the darkness ahead. Biting her lip, she trailed her fingers against the sandy wall, stepping carefully in the dimness, straining ears and eyes. She gave a sigh of relief when the golden illumination of the lantern appeared ahead of Zach's returning figure.

"You took so long," she said. "Are you all right?"

"Yeah, fine. The tunnel is a bit shaky in places." Under the haze of his beard, Zach's scowl was abstracted. He carried a corroded pickax and chunks of quartz and gray-black rock. Passing the lantern to Beth Ann, he led her toward the mouth of the mine. "Let's get out into the light."

Puzzled by his reticence, she turned the wick down to kill the lamp, then trailed after him. "Did you find anything? Did you see any gold?"

Zach deposited his booty on the top of a table-high boulder outside the cave's mouth. "There was plenty of color."

"Was?"

"Must have been a chimney of quartz from the looks of it. Probably with a gold vein as rich as Midas running through it. It played out about eighty feet down."

Beth Ann's shoulders slumped. She was disappointed despite her predictions. There wasn't even the lure of the mine to hold Zach any longer. "So there's nothing left?"

"The gold is finished, as far as I can see. From what you said, Wolf must have gotten all of it early on. There's some other minerals, though—galena, quite a bit of copper—and in the lower shaft there's evidence of recent diggings. That's where I found this."

Zach stirred a collection of translucent gray stones with a fingertip, and his expression held a strange tension that confused Beth Ann. "What is it?" she asked.

For answer, Zach took the lantern from her, then picked up one of the stones and scratched a pattern into the glass chimney. His jaw flexing, he laid the stone in the center of his palm and held it out to Beth Ann.

"Diamonds."

Stunned, Beth Ann couldn't breathe. "What?" she wheezed. "D-Diamonds? Are you sure?"

"Positive."

Her head spun with the implications of such a find. "No wonder Paw was so secretive. I can't believe it!"

Zach's eyes glittered with a cynical light. "Good thing, darlin', because it's a fake."

Her whirling thoughts crashed to a halt that was painfully abrupt. Dazed, she shook her head. "I don't understand."

Zach closed his fist over the uncut gemstone and chuckled without humor. "They say it takes one to know one, and I guess they're right. I thought I smelled a swindle."

"Quit talking in riddles!" Her confusion mingled with irritation, taking her temper to the flash point. "What do you mean? Are these diamonds real or aren't they?"

"Oh, they're real enough. But I'd be surprised if they turn out to be anything better than second-rate stones. But then, that's all you need for bait."

Her lips parted in incredulity. "You're saying they were purposely planted?"

Zach nodded. "Your God-fearing paw was salting his own mine, angel."

"But why?" She pressed fingertips to her throbbing temples. "This doesn't make sense."

"Sure it does, if you're figuring to sell the claim to some unsuspecting investor. Even the greenest prospector knows diamonds are sometimes found in gold veins, and the mineral deposits in this territory are still largely unexplored. It's just the kind of odds a gambler likes, and what else is an investor but a man willing to risk his money on the chance of a big return? By God, with the right kind of front man, it should work like a charm."

"It's just so . . . so unbelievable," Beth Ann said faintly.

Zach's voice held a note of grudging admiration. "I have to hand it to old Wolf. This is one masterful hoax. Too bad it got him killed."

"You think the two are related? But who? How?"

Zach retrieved a small, crumpled band of gilded paper from his shirt pocket and held it out. "Does this answer your question?"

Puzzled, she smoothed out the slender strip, then stiffened in dismay as she recognized the exclusive cigar brand logo. "Oh, my God—Mr. Barlings!"

Zach's mouth was grim. "That's right, angel. The banker and your paw never went to Tucson. They came here to plant these stones. This is the 'something big' Wolf kept hinting about, only it looks like the partners had a serious falling out."

"So Mr. Barlings killed Paw and then blamed me," Beth Ann concluded bitterly. Another illusion fell apart, leaving only betrayal. "And I made it all so easy for him."

"Not only that, but I'll wager good money

there's some sort of written document in the vault of the Destiny Savings Bank deeding Barlings Wolf's half of any partnership, should you not be around to inherit. It's perfect—whether you hang or go to prison for Wolf's death, or escape, never to be seen again—Barlings gets Traveler's Rest, the mine, everything."

Beth Ann stared at the pile of uncut stones and minerals littering the top of the boulder, soaking in the implications of Zach's words like the last red-gold rays of the setting sun. The pieces of the puzzle fit perfectly. Everything she'd ever hoped and dreamed, worked for and believed in, lay in ruins, and the devastation was like ashes in her mouth. Then her lips twitched, and soft laughter burbled from her throat.

Zach's warm fingers closed around her upper arm. "Honey?"

"Oh, it's rich, isn't it, Zach?" Her silver eyes glittered with tears that burned too hot to shed. "I wanted to fit into your life, and now I know I can—as one of the greatest dupes you'll every hope to know!"

Zach rinsed the last of the lather off his cheeks, dumped his cup of shaving water, and shivered at the touch of the chill desert air on his bare, damp chest. Wolf's cache of water had made a wash possible, and the Lord knew he needed it after the dirt he'd collected gathering up all the salted diamonds from within the mine. Zach stuck his shaving paraphernalia back into his saddlebag and paused, looking up to admire the stars peppering the night sky, brilliant pinpoints of light brighter than any diamonds.

He shook his head. It was still nearly incomprehensible that Wolf Linder could have come up with such a scheme. Surely Robert Barlings had been the mastermind behind it all along. Only in the end he'd found he couldn't control his partner and resorted to a violent act, letting an innocent woman shoulder the blame like the coward he was. Zach bared his teeth in a silent snarl, and his palms itched with the need to do a little violence of his own—preferably on Robert Barlings's dignified countenance.

Suppressing a growl, Zach gathered up his belongings and stalked toward the rock-walled hut where they'd made their camp. Ducking under the lintel of the low door opening, he came up short. Though the roof was still mostly open to the sky, the interior of the hut had been tidied, the bedroll laid out neatly, and the lantern hung on a hook. Zach sucked in a silent breath at the sight of Beth Ann in the warm yellow circle of lamplight.

She'd taken advantage of the surplus water to wash up, too, even rinsing the dust from her curling ebony tresses. Wearing only her lace-edged shimmy and skirt, she sat before the fire glowing in the rough hearth, knees drawn up in a pensive pose as her hair dried. Occasionally she stirred a pan of something bubbling aromatically on the coals, and as she moved, the curve of her breasts pressed against the thin fabric. Her golden skin was flushed with becoming heat, and the scent of her—fresh, womanly, warm—was an exotic and enticing perfume.

Zach wanted her instantly, but the unhappy curve of her lush mouth kept him from reaching for her. Despite the lust that consumed him, there was a more urgent need to comfort, a tight knot within his chest that throbbed with empathy. She'd been through a lot, emotionally as well as physically. There was no doubt that her emotions were raw and confused. Wolf Linder surely deserved what he'd gotten if he'd murdered Beth Ann's mother, but how could his own daughter rejoice in his death? And as for Barlings's manipulation of both Wolf and the present situation, could she contend with all that implied?

No, she needed time to think things through and heal, and as much as he hated it, Zach hardened his resolve not to make things worse for her by giving in to his desire. She deserved better than a will-o'-the-wisp hustler taking advantage of her when she was at such a low ebb. Besides, as soon as they arrived in California and he got her settled, he was going to have to become accustomed to being without her. It was best if they both began the process of disconnecting here and now.

A very noble ideal, Madison, an inner voice sneered. *Now explain why it hurts so damn much!* Grimacing, Zach stepped inside the hut and dropped his gear in a corner.

"That smells good," he said.

Beth Ann jumped and glanced over her shoulder at Zach. Her eyes widened at his bare chest and clean-shaven cheeks, and she blushed.

"Ah, it's just beans and jerky," she said, hastily turning back to her stirring. "Paw left a little stash of supplies, so there's baking powder biscuits, too, but they're liable to be heavy ..."

"Sounds fit for a king." Self-conscious with a semiclad female for the first time since he'd been a kid in a hayloft groping at his first girl, Zach pulled on his dirty shirt, but stopped short of buttoning the sweat-stained garment. "Er, you sure do take to rough camping like a real pro, Beth Ann."

"At last I'm good for something. Here, it's ready. Why don't you eat?" She dipped up a tin plate and added a biscuit from the pan she'd improvised out of a piece of broken shovel.

Zach sat down in Indian fashion across from her and accepted the dish, acutely aware of the brush of her fingers against his. "Uh, thanks." It was surprisingly good, and he ate with the concentrated enjoyment of a hungry man for several minutes before he realized she was only nibbling the edge of a biscuit. "Aren't you going to eat more than that?"

Startled from her thoughts, she looked down in surprise at the bread she was absently crumbling between her fingers. "I guess I'm not very hungry."

"Maybe this will improve your appetite." He pulled a small drawstring pouch from his pants pocket and tossed it to her. "Your jewels, my lady."

Her lip curled with distaste. "The diamonds?"

"All I could find. Wolf did a good job of making it look like a natural occurrence. There may be others planted so that with a little more poking around, the gullible could find them and *really* be convinced."

Beth Ann opened the pouch and poured a few of the clear, nondescript-looking stones into her palm. "They hardly appear worth a man's life, do they?"

He set his empty plate aside. "They may not be a king's ransom, but at least they'll give you a little grub stake."

She shuddered and returned the gems to the pouch. "I don't want it. It's like ... like blood money."

"You can't afford to be too squeamish, honey."

"You mean I should be more like you?" she snapped, scrambling to her feet. "Deny any standards that interfere with what I want? Lie and cheat and steal without compunction as long as it suits my purpose?" Her features tight with disdain, she dropped the pouch into his lap. "I won't."

Scowling, Zach rose also. "Be practical, Beth Ann."

"Practical?" She laughed. "Is that what you call it? How convenient for you that the rules can always be bent for Zach Madison."

"It's called survival, honey," he drawled, annoyed at the way her sharp words pricked a part of him he'd thought long discarded—his conscience. "And it may be all that stands between you and ruination."

"Perhaps, but how can a life without dignity or values have any meaning?"

"When have any of your fine ideals done you any good?" he retorted. "Come down out of that ivory tower, and see what the real world is like. You're going to need the damn diamonds."

"I'd rather starve!" she raved. "I'd rather sell my body on the streets! I'm certainly accustomed to people thinking I'm that kind of woman. What's the slight inconvenience of actually performing the act after enduring the slurs and barbs for so long?"

Zach's mouth tightened. "Cut it out, angel. You don't mean that."

Her anger abruptly deflated, and she buried her face in her hands. "No." She took a deep, shuddering breath and lifted her face. Her eyes were wide with remorse. "No, I don't. I'm sorry, Zach. You've been so kind. I shouldn't take out my foul temper on you."

Kind? The word made him wince with guilt. He rested a comforting hand on her shoulder. "Never mind. It's been a difficult day. You're overwrought, fatigued. You should go to bed."

She bit her lip and nodded. "Yes."

Zach's palm burned where he touched her velvet skin. He released her abruptly and turned toward the doorway. "Uh, you take the blanket. I'll sleep outside."

The small sound she made was a cross between a gasp and a whimper of pain. Zach chanced a glance back, and his resolve dribbled from his veins at the stricken look on her face.

With her dark hair curling about her shoulders, and her gray eyes wide in her pale face, she looked like a lost little girl. Then a single tear slid from under her sooty lashes, and that's how Zach felt—utterly lost.

"Don't, honey," he murmured, pulled to her side as though by a magnet.

She looked up into his face, her lower lip tremulous with hurt. "Have I lost you already? What I said ... I didn't mean ..."

"Shh." His insides twisting, Zach thumbed a tear from her cheekbone, only to have it instantly replaced by another crystal droplet. "It's not that."

"Don't ... don't you want me anymore?"

Zach groaned, and his body leapt to throbbing life. He ground his teeth and prayed for control. "You're not making this any easier, angel. For once in my godforsaken life, I'm trying to do right by you."

She licked a teardrop from her upper lip in an unconsciously provocative gesture that made Zach's blood heat. "I don't understand."

"I've wronged you, making us lovers, knowing that it couldn't be forever."

Her color heightened, and her whisper was husky. "I wanted it, too."

He shook his head regretfully. "You lacked the experience to resist an all-out assault from an unprincipled bastard with lust in his heart. But I'm trying to make it up to you now. What we share in bed is perfect, but a woman like you needs more than I can give."

"You're so wrong, Zach," she said, her voice husky. "I'm not asking for anything but to be with you."

"No, you'll only come to regret it. Believe me, it's best this way, even if leaving you crying is the hardest thing I've ever tried to do."

She touched his chest, curling her fingers into the crisp hair. "Then don't."

Her light caress jolted him, and his crooked smile held an element of strain. "You're undermining my good intentions."

She pushed at his shirt, her look intent. "Good."

"No." Zach caught her wrists, holding her hands between them. "Listen to me. You were right. I haven't had a very clear view of right and wrong in the past. But after knowing you, I feel ashamed of all the rotten things I've done. You make me want to act in an upright fashion, to be a better man than I am. And God help me, that's what I'm trying to do."

Her lips parted in surprise. "Why, Zach?"

He grimaced. "So . . . so you'll think better of me, maybe even be a little proud of my effort, I guess."

"Why?"

He shook her in growing exasperation. "Because I care about you! That's why I'm trying to walk away now. I don't want you hurt anymore. *I* don't want to hurt you."

She pushed against his grip, her voice insistent and compelling. "Why, Zach? Tell me why."

"Because I love you, dammit!" he roared, astonished by the first real truth from his liar's lips in years.

And it was true. His heart ached with it, desire and affection centering on this slender, valiant woman who'd given him so much—her laughter, her passion, her generous heart. But it made no difference, only made it more imperative that for once in his life, he make the unselfish choice and give her up, to spare her the unhappiness she'd inevitably find with a no-account drifter like him.

With a sound of frustration and fury, Zach pulled Beth Ann into his arms and kissed her fiercely. When he raised his head, she lay in a boneless collapse against his chest, caught somewhere between laughter and tears.

"Do you believe me this time?" he growled in her ear.

"Does it matter?" she murmured, pulling his head down again.

It did.

It mattered incredibly to Zach that she should know what she meant to him. In an instant of blinding realization, he saw how loving this woman changed everything for him and within him. His universe tilted, then spun in a new and infinitely more promising direction, centering in the soft silver eyes of a woman who loved him—*him*, with all his imperfections and failings. It was a heady, humbling sensation. But did he have the skill and courage to win them a future in his newly created world? How could he prove his devotion to the one who mattered most to him?

Chapter 16

❦❦

"Return to Destiny?" Beth Ann stared up into Zach's blue-green eyes, baffled and alarmed. "Why?"

"You'll see." Tenderly Zach cupped her face between his palms. "It's the only way."

Blinking away the remnants of tears, she shook her head in confusion, unbalanced by Zach's lightning-quick shift from a declaration of love to talk of new travel plans when all she really wanted was for him to kiss her again. "The way to do what?"

"Clear your name and bring Barlings to justice."

"That's impossible." Beth Ann frowned, her fingers curling around Zach's strong wrists, the crisp sandy hairs on the backs of his hands glittering in the lamplight. The masculine odors of soap and musk tantalized her senses, interfering with her efforts to focus her attention on Zach's incredible statement. "Who'd believe me over an upright businessman like Mr. Barlings, anyway?"

"Sheriff Nichols for starters," Zach said, "especially now that we've got the diamonds. Wolf and Barlings had to purchase these uncut stones somewhere. I'm sure with a little persistence they can be traced to the banker. Then the sheriff will have his motive—"

"No!" She backed out of Zach's hands, her eyes frightened.

Zach heaved a deep breath. "Look, honey, I see

now that you can't live under a murder charge. We've got to get this straight if you're ever to have the kind of future you deserve."

"But, Zach, even if the sheriff listens to us about Paw's killing, you'll face jailbreaking charges." She wrung her hands, the pulse leaping in her throat in alarm. "And you said Nichols had already connected you to the wanted notices—you could be arrested. You could go back to prison!"

"I'm willing to take that chance."

"Well, I'm not!" Shivering violently, she turned toward the little fireplace, running her hands up and down her bare arms in agitation. "I don't want you in jail! It would be like caging an eagle. I won't have it. I—"

"I'd do anything for you." Zach came up behind her, covering her nervous hands with his own and nuzzling the satiny crook of her neck with his mouth. Her head fell back, and as always when he touched her, her knees melted to butter.

"Zach . . ." His name was a breathless murmur.

"Anything," he repeated in a strange throaty rasp. "Including serve my time and go straight—if I know you'll be waiting for me when I get out, ready to wear my wedding ring and keep me to the narrow path for the rest of my life."

Beth Ann caught a stunned breath, and her heart raced so furiously that when she finally spoke, her voice was a mere whisper. "Are—are you asking me to marry you?"

Zach threaded his fingers through the thick, dark hair at her temples and pressed a soft kiss to her hairline. "I reckon I am."

Almost timidly, as if afraid of what she'd find, she turned to face him, searching his features. "You'd do all that for me?"

"Yes."

His simple sincerity illuminated her heart with radiance and dispelled all doubts. Her lips parted in dazed wonder. "You do love me."

Zach gave her a crooked, roguish grin and ran his knuckles down her cheek. "Isn't that what I said?"

"I've been afraid to believe."

"What? That a sinner can turn over a new leaf if the right woman is there to bring out the best in him? I can do it with your help, Beth Ann. And if you'll honor me with your trust, I'll take my vows with you before God and man so that you'll never doubt what I feel for you again."

Her lower lip trembled. "Truly?"

Zach nodded solemnly. "Yes, angel, truly."

"Oh, Zach." She threw herself at his neck, holding him tight, pressing against him fervently. It was impossible to get close enough, for the feel of him, so solid and strong, was an incandescent delight amid the ardent flood of her emotions. "I love you so much!"

"Then say yes," he said with a husky laugh.

"No, I can't bear to see you shackled against your will, either by a marriage license or a prison cell. I won't let you sacrifice your freedom for me!"

"Freedom?" Zach shook his head, and his fingers slipped beneath the shoulder strap of her shimmy, soothing the overtense muscles beneath it. "Drifting around, I was never really free. I've been searching for you all my life, I think. When I look into your angel eyes, I know you're the reason I was put on this earth. If it means my paying my debt to society in order to help clear you of Wolf's murder, then I'm willing. We can both make a fresh start, and that most definitely includes making you my bride." His expression became different, almost bashful. "If you'll have me."

"But I'm yours already, no matter what," she cried, caught in the throes of happiness and terror. Was she destined to win her heart's desire only to have him throw it all away on some grandiose gesture?

"We don't have to go back to Destiny to redeem my worthless reputation! It doesn't matter anymore." She tugged on his shirt for emphasis, trying to make him *see*. "You were right. What you believe about yourself counts more than what anyone else thinks. I think God sent you to Destiny to free me from that burden. I'm not going to hang my head in shame ever again for making the choices that are right for me. And I chose you, Zach Madison."

Zach held her, his arms cupped about her waist possessively. "Honey—"

She touched his face. "Don't you understand? I'll follow you anywhere—to California or Mexico, it doesn't matter. Nothing does as long as you love me and we're together. That's what I've learned from loving you."

"Well, I sure as hell love you," he rumbled, "and we're together now, but we're going to do it my way, angel."

Her fingers dug into his shirt in anguish. "Zach, please."

"All my life I've had no more moral fiber than a boiled noodle." His chin firmed, and his tone was adamant. "For once, I'm going to do the right thing. I want us to begin as we mean to go on. Will you do it? Will you wait for me?"

Beth Ann read the earnestness in his handsome face and understood his sacrifice and his pride and his determination. How could she stand in the way of a man like that?

"Yes, I'll wait," she said, choking. "Forever."

"Don't cry," he murmured, pressing kisses on her lashes, her nose, the curve of her cheek. "I can't bear to see you cry."

"A woman can cry the day she becomes engaged to marry the man she loves, can't she?" Beth Ann demanded. She caressed his cheeks, the rusty curls at his nape, then pushed his shirt off his shoulders. "I'm just happy."

"You've got the dangedest way of showing it," Zach muttered, his tongue licking at the moisture seeping from under her lids.

"And frightened," she admitted softly.

"You understand why it has to be this way? It's not just for you. It's for me, too. A kind of redemption, to balance the scales of my life."

"Yes, I understand." She raised up on her tiptoes and pressed her lips against his, tasting the salty residue of her own bittersweet tears. "I'll do whatever you want. But that's for tomorrow, and I need tonight just for us."

Zach's hand covered her breast, and a shudder of desire shook his body. "God! So do I."

She gave him a vixenish smile. "Then show me how much."

He needed no further invitation, and bent his head to kiss her. With an arm clamped around her back, he pulled her against the thickening part of himself, letting her know how she excited him, how much he desired her.

She felt response leap like wildfire through her veins, and a heaviness grew between her legs where his hardness pressed insistently. She loved his taste, the hot tang of his mouth, and opened eagerly for the sweet invasion of his lips, twining her arms around his neck, meeting the voluptuous thrust of his tongue with a boldness that made him groan.

The audible proof of his susceptibility to her inflamed Beth Ann with the heady knowledge of her feminine power. She drank of him, taking and giving, her tongue nimble and beguiling against the rasp of his. Smoothing her hands down his neck, she traced the corded tendons, followed the strength of his collarbone, then raked the sandy brown bramble covering his chest. She explored the little puffy scar on his shoulder with regret, and when her nails discovered the bronze coins of his flat male nipples, Zach jerked uncontrollably and used his weight to push her against the uneven stone wall. With his hands pressed flat beside her ears, he savored her mouth and ground his hips against her sensitive delta, greedily inhaling the little spurts of her breath the movement produced.

"Let me see you," he said, reaching for the hem of her shimmy. He drew it over her head, his eyes igniting at the golden ivory and pink of her breasts. "Oh, God, your skin . . . It's wonderful."

His mouth was open against her neck, and his thumbs found the peaked crests of her nipples, his touch shooting pure sensation through her down to the throbbing secret place between her legs. He left a damp trail of kisses down her breastbone, then took one rosy crown between his teeth, making her cry out and sink her fingers into his burnished curls.

"Zach . . ." She was enthralled by the sight of his avid mouth against her flesh and the supple flex of his muscular back as he moved to capture the other nipple. Her knees buckled, and it was his arms behind her hips that supported her as pleasure liquified her core and need built.

He licked at the sheen of perspiration coating her skin, laving the velvety underside of her breasts, his fingers suddenly busy with the fastening of her skirt. Then he was pushing her garments down to puddle at her bare feet and pressing his cheek against her belly, his lashes quivering as he tasted the delicate indentation of her navel, then lower, his tongue dampening the arch of crinkly hair.

"Oh, that's not fair," Beth Ann wailed, panting, leaning back against the stone wall with her hair tumbled over her shoulders. She felt wanton and wanted and womanly.

"I wanted to go slow," Zach said, breathing her scent, holding the round womanly curves of her hips in his large palms. "But I can't . . . seem to."

He nuzzled the mysterious folds, tasting her there, too, a subtle, breath-stealing exploration that made Beth Ann cry out with delight. He held her there, tormenting her to near insanity until she clutched at his hair, wiggling and insistent.

"Not so fast," she complained softly, pulling him back up her body.

He tangled a fist in the silky skein of her long hair and gently bit her shoulder. "Don't you like it?" he rumbled.

"You make me feel so beautiful." Her hands moved over his trouser buttons, unfastening them one by one. "But I want to be a part of you."

Zach gasped as she freed his surging manhood from the confines of his pants, and his words were suddenly strangled. "I think that can be arranged."

"Mmm." She concentrated on the wonder of him, stroking the hard, pulsing velvet with her fingertips, feeling the involuntary quiver that he could not control, smiling when he growled. Kicking completely out of his trousers, Zach took her mouth again, hot and demanding, his tongue rapacious and electrifying.

Pressed totally unclothed to his hard masculine length, Beth Ann reveled in their differences, in how his angles complemented her curves, how his taut, sun-bronzed flesh contrasted to her soft white skin, how his strength played to her weakness. She explored the rippling muscles of his back and lean buttocks, then the hair-dusted perfection of his strong thighs. Bending, she dropped kisses down his collarbone to his navel, emulating his earlier path across her own body. Then, with a boldness she had not known she possessed, she touched her lips to his heated sex and was rewarded by a deep, visceral groan.

He caught her across the back, lifting her one-armed and pressing her against the wall. "Talk about too fast!" he gritted, his features quivering as he sought for control. "Do that again, angel, and I won't be responsible for the results."

"I trust you," she said, her chest heaving with her ragged breathing, her silver eyes bright with love and desire. She wiggled against him in invitation. "Let's see what happens."

"Hoyden!" He kissed her again, his mouth open, his tongue doing a wicked dance inside the sweet cavern. "God, I love you!"

Holding her against him, he cupped her mound, grinding the heel of his hand against the sensitive flesh until her hips lifted involuntarily. Then he slipped his fingers inside her tightness, sliding into the slick, dewy warmth, making her arch and cry out with the sudden exquisite pressure.

"Zach!" Head thrown back, throat exposed, the

ivory globes of her breasts flattened against the wall of his chest, she clung to him, then lifted her foot and stroked the back of his knee.

He went wild, surging forward and thrusting into her, lifting her nearly off her feet as he held her pressed against the wall, one arm supporting her hips, the other protecting her shoulders. She gasped at the sudden entry, the heat and power of his penetration filling her. He held her poised, the position pushing him deep, deeper, until she was certain that he touched her very soul.

Perched on the brink of something momentous, she buried her face in Zach's shoulder, hanging on to the only firmament that existed for her. She felt his hot breath on her neck, the flick of his tongue on her skin, and shivered with the delicious sensual stimulation. When he moved, he took her very breath, sliding into her, taking possession, stretching and filling her. Yearning, she held on, taking him within her, reaching, then lifting one leg over his flexing hips and pulling him even closer.

Zach stiffened and jerked, then groaned deep in his throat as the pulsations overtook him. With a raw male sound of pleasure, he buried himself to the hilt within her softness. After an endless moment, his sweat-dampened muscles relaxed, and he blew out a gusty breath, still holding her against the wall.

Breathing hard, itching for a fulfillment that hadn't come, she squirmed. He roused then.

"You didn't? Angel, I'm sorry. I warned you—no, stay where you are."

Cupping her hips, their bodies still joined, he lay down on the unrolled blanket, letting her straddle him.

She gasped. "Zach, what . . . ?"

"Your turn. Use me." He caught her neck in the curve of his elbow and drew her mouth down to his, kissing her deeply, urging her to move with his other hand on her hip. "Let me pleasure you, my love."

The unquenched flames within her leapt to new life as she tried a tentative move. His erection was still full within her, his hardness only beginning to fail after his completion, but what made her gasp was the control she wielded over her own pleasure. If she moved, just so . . . ah!

"That's it, honey," Zach encouraged, caressing her breasts, her stomach, then reaching between their bodies to press the kernel of sensation between her thighs.

Whether it was Zach's experienced touch or her own movements that hurled her over the precipice didn't matter, for in that instant, sensation exploded in a cascade of iridescent pleasure. Arching, Beth Ann shuddered and cried out. Zach's firm hands pulled her even harder against himself, and she trembled again, catapulted into a voluptuous rapture of the senses that went on and on until she collapsed, totally spent, into a boneless, breathless heap against his chest.

Zach's arms cradled her, rocking gently from side to side, his chuckle whispering into her ear. "God, you're good. We are so damn good together!"

"When you love someone, it's always new, isn't it?" she murmured, her voice wondering and drowsy.

He was silent a moment, and then his arms tightened around her and his voice was suspiciously thick. "You know, angel, that just may be one of the great secrets of life."

Beth Ann understood. Together, they could forever rediscover the intimacy they shared, reinvent their love in an endless variety of ways. No longer would the siren's call tempt Zach to move on to someone new. Oh, perhaps he'd always need new challenges in other areas, new schemes to tempt a man of action and imagination, but Beth Ann knew she'd never again fear the Juanitas of the world.

Raising her head, she pressed a gentle kiss to Zach's lips. "No, my darling, it's the secret of love."

"Are you sure?"

"Sure as God made tasty little chuckwallas."

Beth Ann chewed her lip, her trepidation too overwhelming to be diminished by Zach's levity. "We can still turn north, or go west to—"

"Though I still can't believe I'm saying this—*south*," Zach said firmly. "To meet our destiny."

She scowled. "You're not funny."

"And I can't resist you when you pout." Zach swept Beth Ann into his arms, kissed her soundly, then lifted her onto the buckskin's back.

After a night of surrender and loving exploration, they'd taken the morning to work their way down to the little silvery creek visible from Wolf's mine, then spent the heat of the day frolicking like children in the shallow water before ending up, as they'd both known they would, in a lusty encounter and a lazy siesta afterwards. But with miles of desert ahead, and only one half-lame horse, they had to make the most of the cooler hours for traveling. And now that the moment of truth had arrived, now that they had reached a literal crossroads and they had to make the actual choice of which direction to take, Beth Ann was not at all certain that the decisions they'd reached the night before were reasonable—or even sane.

"I do not pout," she pouted. "But all the same . . ."

"Hey." Zach looked up from adjusting her stirrup, then laced her trembling fingers into his reassuring grip. "We're in this together, remember? It may not be as bad as you think."

"No, it may be worse! Oh, Zach, I don't think I can bear to be parted from you, not now, not after . . ." She blushed prettily.

"I know, angel." His smile deserted him, and he brushed a kiss over her knuckles. "I don't like to think about that either. But you know what's got to be done, and why."

She took a shaky breath and tried to smile. "The preacher won't succumb to temptation, eh?"

"Though you're enough to tempt Saint Peter himself—not this time. So our future will be free of old shadows."

"Yes." Bending down out of the saddle, she kissed him tenderly, then straightened, a determined glint in her gray eyes. "Well, then, to Destiny, if you please, sir. I'm ready to have this over."

It was slow going, walking and taking turns on the horse, but Beth Ann didn't really mind putting off the inevitable, for this time with Zach had a particular sweetness about it, poignantly enhanced by both their newfound understanding and the uncertainty before them. They followed the stream for a while, then took a well-marked trail through rugged foothills. Keeping a vigilant lookout for hostiles, they followed this sign of civilization, wending their way ever southward, back toward the Gila River and Destiny. Beth Ann knew it was only a matter of time before they encountered other travelers along this thoroughfare, and her trepidation grew with each step.

"How long do you think it will take us?" she asked at one point. She'd abandoned the limping buckskin, and now walked beside Zach with the horse following along behind them.

Zach shrugged and kicked a stone. Clumps of prickly pear and a few hardy sagebushes were all that marred the sandy slopes around them. "Couple of days, at this rate. We'll look for a campsite soon. Can't afford to push the horse or we may be completely afoot."

With a sigh, Beth Ann twisted her hair back into a rough knot and stuffed it under her hat. She'd managed to secure the placket of her much-the-worse-for-wear shirt with a couple of thorns used as straight pins, and she thought longingly of fresh underthings and crisp calico.

"It would probably help the situation if you dumped all those samples you loaded into the saddlebags," she pointed out. "What did you want them for, anyway?"

Zach lifted a sandy eyebrow. "Curiosity. Thought you might want an assayer to analyze the other minerals I found. You own that mine now, you know. Maybe you could sell the claim to the lesser minerals to tide you over. It would make things easier, and you wouldn't have to work so hard at Traveler's Rest while I'm ... er, gone."

"How can you be so calm about going back to jail?" she cried. "And we've assumed I'll be cleared of Paw's murder. What if I'm not? At the very best, I'll wind up in prison, too. Zach, this is crazy! Let's turn back. I'd rather take my chances with the Apaches. We don't have to do this—"

"I'm afraid it's too late for second thoughts, angel."

"No, it's not! Why, we can—"

"Look." Zach tipped his head, indicating with his hat brim a cloud of dust roiling toward them across the valley floor.

Horsemen!

Beth Ann grabbed Zach's arm, sudden alarm making her pulse race. "Oh, dear God, Zach! Is it the posse? What are we going to do?"

"Find a shady place to sit until they get here. My feet ache like the devil, don't yours?"

His equanimity infuriated her. "Never mind your feet! What's going to happen?"

"Why, we'll turn ourselves in, of course." His blue-green eyes narrowed as he watched the outlines of half a dozen riders materialize. He unbuckled his gun belt. "Hang this over the saddle horn, will you, angel? We don't want to provoke any trigger-happy deputies, but keep it near, just in case . . ."

"In case what?" she demanded, slinging the belt over the horn.

"That's the raggediest looking posse I ever saw," Zach murmured. He stiffened. "They've seen us."

Her fingers convulsed on his shirt sleeve. "I love you, Zach."

"Courage, angel." Giving her hand a supportive squeeze, he set her a little behind him, his attitude protective. "Whatever happens, follow my lead."

Beth Ann didn't really have time to question his curious order, for within minutes the first of the riders galloped up in a swirl of dust. Squinting against the dirty haze, Beth Ann blinked and sneezed, trying to see. But it was no one she recognized from Destiny. The rider was heavily armed, dressed in soiled denims and sweat-stained shirt, his bearded visage and sour, snaggletoothed smile nothing less than sinister. The man drew his dun mount to a halt a few feet away.

"Howdy."

Zach took a step forward, smiling and amiable and nonthreatening in the extreme. "How do, partner. Mighty nice to see a friendly face in these parts, ain't it?"

The rider spat a mouthful of brown tobacco juice into the dirt as the rest of his party approached. "Where you headed?"

Zach pointed. "South. How 'bout you?"

"North."

"Uh, you fellows from around here?"

"Mebbe. Gotcha a peck of trouble, don't ya?"

Zach perched one hand on his hip and lifted his hat with the other to scratch his head ruefully. "You could say that. Lost my wife's mare to a group of hungry Apaches a few days back, and now this one's come up lame."

Beth Ann started slightly at the use of the word "wife," then began to relax. Sheriff Nichols's large frame and trademark palomino gelding were nowhere to be seen in the pack of riders. Thank God, they'd been reprieved! If she could just convince Zach to change his mind now, everything would be all right.

Zach continued to speak easily. "You folks could sure do me a service if I could buy another horse off of you. Any chance of that?"

"Could be." The first rider's dark eyes narrowed. "Say, stranger, don't I know you?"

Zach hesitated. "Can't say that we've ever met, friend."

"Why ... why, hell! It's Zach!" The rider whipped off his sombrero and beamed like a maniac. "Don't you know me, Zach? It's old Dogger!"

Beth Ann perked up. This was a friend of

Zach's? Unsavory as he appeared, he could be their salvation.

"Dogger." Zach's voice was noncommittal, as if he were searching his memory for something.

"Sure, you remember!" Dogger cuffed his thigh in delight and leaned forward the better to make them out through the silty haze stirred up by the rest of the riders. "And gotcha a wife, ya say? Howdy, ma'am."

Beth Ann smiled uncertainly, nervously pulling off her hat to adjust her sliding hair, trying to put herself to rights with a fussiness that was typically feminine.

Dogger broke off his garrulous welcome and starred at her, as pie-eyed and openmouthed as if he'd been poleaxed. "Well, I'll be a long-eared, blue-lipped son of a mule!"

"What the devil's goin' on, Dogger?" A thickset man sporting a drooping, ink black mustache above several days' growth of dark stubble spurred his large bay stallion through the pack.

Beth Ann froze, her breath dying in her throat. The burly form, the hirsute complexion, the ice blue eyes. Recognition zigzagged through her like a lightning bolt. From a great distance, she heard Zach utter one low, succinct obscenity.

Beth Ann felt like swearing, too. Light-headed with shock, she reached a hand out toward the buckskin to steady herself before she fell on her face.

Images rocked her. False-hearted lover. Bank robber. Outlaw. Killer. *Tom.*

"Lookee here what I done found, Tom," Dogger hooted. "It's Zach, sure as spit, and he's done hitched up with your woman!"

"What the hell!" Tom Chapman swung down

from his bay in a fluid movement that belied his size.

Clad in a cattleman's checkered shirt and bandanna with the ubiquitous gun belt of the Southwest strapped to his hips, he appeared on the surface no different from a thousand other cowpokes—until you looked into his emotionless blue eyes. Then you knew this was a man who could lead by sheer animal magnetism, ruthless and deadly as a predator, who'd take what he wanted without regard for morality or consequence.

Beth Ann watched him approach with something like her old awe, but now the features she'd once found so boyishly appealing only seemed weak, the animal attraction of his masculinity repellant and coarsely vulgar.

"Well, Tom!" Zach stepped forward with his hand outstretched. "If you ain't a sight for sore eyes! I figured you'd be laying low up in these parts."

"Shaddup, Madison." Pushing past Zach, Tom stopped in front of Beth Ann and looked her up and down. "Hello, Beth Ann."

Feeling as though Tom were stripping her naked with his eyes, she flushed in hot humiliation. Then all the old, unresolved hurt became a blazing anger. Straightening her shoulders, she gave him a chilly glare. "Tom."

"God, she's a looker, Tom, just like you said!" Dogger declared. "Cain't you say hello better'n that?"

"Yeah, Tom!" Another rider egged him on. "Whatcha waitin' for?"

"Ain't you got guts to make it a real reunion?" a third prodded. The others joined in with ribald shouts of encouragement, some still on horseback, others edging in for a closer look at the infamous Miss Beth Ann Linder.

God, what lies had he told them? Beth Ann remembered the picture Zach had taken from Tom. What did all of these men know about her and Tom Chapman? What had they guessed? She wished the earth would open up and swallow her and end her mortification.

"Now, that's a right fine idee." Grinning like a lascivious jackal, Tom wiped his mouth with his forearm and curled his grimy forefinger at Beth Ann. "Come on, sugar. Ain't you going to show me how much you missed me?"

"No, thank you, Tom," she snapped coldly. "Seeing you again is about as refreshing as being burned at the stake."

Her hostility surprised him, and to her shock, she saw the minute hesitation, the fear. For a moment, she was mystified by it; then she understood. Only she knew of Tom's ultimate failure. When the pressure was on, big, brave Tom, the scourge of the outlaw bands, hadn't even been able to bed a woman! Her lips tilted in a knowing smile that was almost a sneer.

Tom's dark cheeks reddened. "You was always part bitch, Beth Ann. That's what made takin' you so damn sweet."

Without warning, he reached out, jerked her against his broad chest, and ground his mouth against hers.

Beth Ann gagged at the repulsive stench of him. Had she ever really welcomed this man's caresses? Impossible. It seemed a thousand years ago. She must have been mad with desperation to have ever believed she loved him. With a furious squeal of rage, she bit at him, slamming her open palm against his ear. Howling, Tom jerked back, then

Zach was on him, pulling him away with such force, Tom sprawled in the dirt.

"Keep your damn hands off her!" Zach snarled.

"Said she's his wife," Dogger interjected, then continued slyly, "but I don't see no wedding ring."

"You son of a bitch!" Tom rolled to his feet and landed a backhanded blow against Zach's jaw that bloodied his nose and knocked him flat onto the seat of his pants. Chest heaving, Tom loomed over Zach.

"I normally kill any man who horns in on my territory!"

"You left her to two yeas of misery at Wolf Linder's hands!" Zach wiped his nose on his cuff and spit. "You got no claim to this *territory* anymore, so leave her be, you cockless wonder!"

That pricked the bully's fragile ego, a whisper of weakness that he could not let go unchallenged before his men. With an infuriated snarl, Tom drew his pistol.

"No!" Beth Ann screamed, and started forward, only to be caught up short by Dogger's horny fist.

Ignoring her outburst, Tom cocked the gun. With an ugly laugh, he waved it menacingly at Zach's crotch. "I'll take what I want, when I want it, old friend. What's to keep me from putting a slug in you and reclaiming my rights here and now?"

Leaning back on his hands, Zach gave Tom a look of utter contempt and let loose a string of curses that made the dry desert air smoke. "You sorry bastard! I always thought you were a smart man, but turns out you're as dumb as dirt. Hell, I ain't got time to waste on the likes of you when there's big money to be made!"

"Money?" Tom's beady blue eyes narrowed suspiciously. "What money?"

"Women come and go, Tom, but a scheme like

this comes along only once—maybe twice—in a lifetime." Zach shook his head. "I thought you were a man with vision, but you don't know dung from wild honey. Makes me feel like a fool for ever coming after you."

Beth Ann gasped, shaking her head in confusion. What did Zach mean? Tom seemed to share her befuddlement.

"What the hell are you talking about?" Tom demanded.

Zach touched the streak of blood on his upper lip, grimaced, then gave Tom a cunning grin. "Riches beyond your wildest dreams, Tom. You were after Wolf Linder's treasure, weren't you?"

"That sumabitch was all talk," Tom grumbled. "He never had nothing worth a barrel of shucks."

"Wrong again, Tom. Wolf's dead, and I got his winnings right here." Zach removed a pouch from his pocket and pitched it to Tom.

The burly outlaw caught the pouch one-handed and glared at Zach in distrust. "What the devil's this?"

"Diamonds." Zach grinned at Tom's slack-jawed amazement. "And, friend, I know where there's a whole damn bank full of them!"

Chapter 17

❦

Sacrilege.

Her mouth set, Beth Ann grimly turned her back on the group of rowdies and sat down on what had once been the kneeler of an altar rail. Behind her, Tom Chapman and his men drank and cursed and boasted around a campfire built directly on the blackened stones of their temporary hideout, a mission chapel constructed a century or more before by an outpost of Spanish priests, but long since abandoned to the hostile environment and even more hostile Apaches. In the church portal, the outlaw band's horses stomped and munched feed and defecated in a makeshift stable. Even though the apse of the small structure was open to the night sky and the plaster walls were ancient and crumbling, Beth Ann found the blatant disregard for the sacredness of this holy place vastly disturbing.

Even more distressing was Zach Madison's chameleonlike behavior. She picked out the sound of his robust laughter from the cacophony of conversation, and shivered. Since the moment Zach had handed over the diamonds, and hinted of more to be found, he and Tom had fallen into instant camaraderie like a couple of long-lost pals, all trace of acrimony forgotten.

As if it had never been. The golden web of firelight flickered into the corners of the forsaken chapel, throwing the sinister shadows into a macabre dance, and Beth Ann's skin crawled with a nameless apprehension.

She'd been hoisted up to ride behind the redolent Dogger with no more regard for her sensibilities than if she were indeed some sort of camp follower, and basically ignored since then. Tom had ordered one man to hand over his horse to Zach, taking their lame buckskin to follow at a slower pace, and they'd rattled across the countryside to this out-of-the-way cloister and the promise of a little "talk" with Tom.

"Tequila, missy?"

A stubble-faced outlaw sidled out of the shadows, bottle in hand. Beth Ann threw her loose curls over her shoulder, fixed him with her silver gaze, and squelched the hopeful bandit with a look so frigid, the very air crackled with frost. "Thank you. No."

The man opened his mouth to argue, took another measure of her icy countenance, thought better of it, and shuffled away. Beth Ann turned back to her examination of the altar rail with a silent sigh of relief. So far, she'd been able to deter every proposition, decent and otherwise, that she'd received, but she cursed Tom Chapman yet again for bragging about their relationship in such livid detail that every man jack of his gang felt beholden to test his manhood on the loose woman who'd so suddenly and providentially appeared within their midst.

Had that been Zach's intent when he arrived at Traveler's Rest? Unbidden, the hateful, insidious doubts jumped into her brain. Had Zach and Tom planned this all along? Had it all been a conspiracy to capture Wolf Linder's wealth, with her as the expendable pawn? Beth Ann moaned, then stifled the painful sound with a knuckle to her mouth. Leaning against the oak rail, she breathed deeply and fought the feelings of panic and betrayal, her eyes darting everywhere in search of answers.

But the statues had long since vanished from their niches, the candles burned out, the devout worshipers disappeared from before the heavy wooden altar, now stripped of its gilt and fine linens. Nothing was left but the ghostly echoes of prayers, and even that was masked by the noise of the roisterous gang desecrating this sacred hall. Beth Ann's long penance at her father's falsely pious hands and her resulting resentment of all things religious should have made her feel satisfaction at such a scene, but instead, she was uneasy and disturbed. Then her gaze fastened on a shadow on the wall behind the rustic altar, a lighter patch where a cross had once hung as a symbol of reverence for the faithful.

Faith.

Did she believe or not? That's what it all boiled down to. Was her faith no more than a wavering shadow on a crumbling wall, worn down by her trials to nothing? For the first time, she searched her inner self for what *she* believed—not what had been drummed into her by Wolf Linder's perverted exhortations, not even what she'd heard in church over the years—but what was inside her own soul. And a feeling of peace stole into her heart and calmed her fears.

Of course she believed. She believed in a merciful God who loved His creations and was always willing to give a poor sinner a second chance. And she found that she didn't blame God anymore. How could she, when everything she'd ever been or endured had led her to Zach, to her other self? She drew a deep breath.

Have a little faith. Isn't that what Zach had said?

If she loved him, then she had to trust that her doubts were groundless and that she would know in good time his reasons for his actions. Comforted by what she recognized as a gift of grace, she felt her mouth soften and tears prickle behind her lids. Silently she offered up her gratitude.

"Don't worry, Tom, I'll sweeten her up."

She jerked at the sound of Zach's voice, then watched him swagger toward her, carrying a bundle of clothes. The lazy, insinuating smile on his face made her flush hotly. She hardly recognized him, so easily and completely had he adopted the rough language and manner of these outlaws.

Gulping, she turned her head away again, shielding her expression from the avid stares of the gang, breathing shallowly to control her wildly thumping heart. *Courage,* she thought. Wasn't Zach a master at both prevarication and landing on his feet? This had to be part of his game, a display of the talents that had served him so well during his roving life.

Follow my lead. It was the only thing she could do. She felt Zach standing over her. Lifting her chin, she concentrated on the faint outline of the cross and refused to look at him.

"Aw, don't be so hard to live with, honey," he crooned, flicking her hair back from her neck with a fingertip.

She snatched herself away. "Don't!"

"Ornery woman," Zach announced loudly enough for the rest to hear. He shook his tousled head, good-humored but rueful. "Can't live with 'em; sure as hell can't live without 'em."

There were several nods and chuckles of agreement, and a snort from Tom, who tipped back his bottle and took a deep pull. Zach grinned at the gang and winked, as if sharing a profound masculine secret, then squatted down on the kneeler and tossed the bundle into Beth Ann's lap.

"Think you can wear this?"

Startled, she looked aghast at a gown of the most amazing shade of crimson she'd ever seen and a wide-brimmed lady's hat, complete with overblown cabbage roses and veil.

She tossed the bundle back at him. "Why would I want to wear this trash, you scoundrel?"

" 'Cause I know how pretty you'll look in it," he purred, his turquoise eyes intense in the golden glow of the fire. Spreading the silky dress out across her lap again, Zach leaned closer and spoke out of the side of his mouth in a voice meant for her alone. "Don't lay it on too thick, angel. We're supposed to be in this together, you know."

"No, I can't imagine what you're up to!" she hissed between her teeth. "And as for this . . ." She rubbed the fabric between two fingers in distaste. "It looks like, like . . ."

Zach settled more comfortably beside her, keeping his voice low and his general attitude smiling and persuasive for all to see. "Yep, hiding out or not, Tom's kept busy robbing folks headed up to Prescott. Last stage carried a load of whores— excuse me, soiled doves—but they took away more gold than they brought, if you know what I mean."

"Unfortunately, I can guess. But what has this"—she shook the dress at him—"to do with us?"

"Well," Zach drawled, "my prediction is you're going to make quite an impression when we rob the Destiny Savings Bank."

"What!"

He grabbed her wrist and squeezed a warning at her involuntary squeak of dismay. "Easy! Don't look too upset. Remember, you're out to get your fair share of Wolf's ill-gotten gains."

Beth Ann fought for breath. "But rob the *bank?* Are you mad?"

"I had to say something to get Tom's attention."

"Oh, my Lord." She pressed a trembling hand to her face. "This is horrible! You mean for us to fall in with these thieves and murderers? If we go back to Destiny surrounded by killers, we'll be judged guilty by association before we do a thing! And if we actually follow through with the robbery—" She broke off with a shudder. "What happened to all your talk about 'moral fiber' and a 'new leaf,' Zach?"

"Dammit, woman! I'm doing the best I can," he muttered, his frustration showing in the white-knuckled grip he kept on her wrist. "I had to do some fast talking just to keep us alive—or hadn't you noticed that old Tom was pretty near ready to bore a hole in my hide with his Colt?"

"Yes, of course I did. I was so frightened!"

"Well, if Tom kills me, what do you expect his gang will do to you?"

She blanched. "Oh."

"Yeah, *oh.* I've got Tom convinced that you're the only way we'll ever get close enough to Barlings to get our hands on more diamonds, but since you're still a mite het up against him for walking out on you before, that he needs me to sweet-talk you to keep you in line."

Despite herself, Beth Ann's lips twitched. "And he bought that?"

Loosening his grip, Zach rubbed his thumb against the inside of her wrist. "Let's just say that right now Tom's greed outweighs his lust."

Beth Ann was beginning to feel a trifle warm, and when she looked up at Zach, her eyes were soft. "Tom's a pig, and, as you know, not man enough to make good that kind of threat."

"Don't remind him of that, honey," Zach warned. "He's on a hair trigger as it is. One wrong step from either of us, one hint of a double cross, and he'll kill us both."

"Is that what this is, Zach? A double cross?"

He frowned. "You didn't really expect me to hitch up with that hairy bastard, did you?"

"There for a minute . . ." She took another breath. "You were so *convincing!* I'm sorry I doubted you."

"That's quite a compliment, coming from the only person who really knows me." Zach's lips twisted wryly. "Damn, I'm better at this than I thought."

"You've got a knack for handling all sorts, that's for sure," she said with a soft, admiring laugh. "Maybe you should consider a career in politics or something."

He snorted his disdain for that idea. "Let's just worry about getting through the next day or two, all right?"

She was instantly sober again. "What if Mr. Barlings doesn't have more diamonds?"

"He owns a damn bank, doesn't he? Surely a haul of cash will satisfy Tom."

"If Tom gets what he wants, he's liable to kill us anyway. But if we go through with the robbery, no lawman will believe us and we'll never be able to turn ourselves in!" She drew a shaky breath. "Then what, Zach?"

He flashed a quick look over her shoulder at the raucous gang, and grimaced. "Hell, I don't know. I'm making this up as I go along."

"Sweet sassafras," she breathed, her fingers

clenching in the crimson silk. Zach covered her hands with his own.

"Don't give up on me now, angel," he said. "I'll think of something."

Loving him, all she could do was have faith that Zach hadn't completely run out of ideas.

The idea was to stay calm, but as Beth Ann and Dogger drove a stolen buggy into Destiny two days later, her heart was pounding and her palms were sweating inside her gloves, and any semblance of that wished-for state of mind was beyond her. The fact that she was drenched in a cheap floral scent and wore a harlot's crimson dress so low-cut it barely hid her nipples didn't help. Thankfully, the swath of pale veiling spilling from her equally outrageous hat concealed her features to her chin, filming her face with both mystery and anonymity—she devoutly hoped. After all, the success of this scheme and her future with Zach depended upon her playacting.

They certainly caught the attention of the few people populating Destiny's dusty main street this hot morning. Heads turned and conversations came to a dead halt as the buggy wheeled past, then rolled to a stop in front of the impressive redbrick facade of the Destiny Savings Bank. Dogger, polished up a bit in his role as driver, tied the reins, then leaped down and proffered his horny hand to help her alight. With a daring flash of black stockings, Beth Ann stepped down, striving to look as regal and haughty as possible.

Dogger hustled to open the bank's tall, glass-fronted door. Swallowing hard and praying for courage, Beth Ann swept inside in cloud of sweetness, pausing on the highly varnished floor to assess the premises.

The two regular tellers sat behind their window cages, and beyond the oak and brass rail, the paneled door to Mr. Barlings's private office stood half-open. She could see the shiny steel door of the walk-in vault through the grilled gate. The air held a hint of lemon oil, musty currency, and ink. A pair of customers stood at the tall work desk in the public area, busily applying pen to paper, and Beth Ann stiffened in recognition.

Mamie Cunningham, of all people! Beth Ann barely stifled an audible groan of dismay. And Harold, the milksop husband of the woman she'd insulted that day in Hardy's mercantile! Had fate ever chosen two more unlikely witnesses? But there was nothing to do but go on.

"You may wait with the buggy, Mr. Dogger," Beth Ann announced, keeping her voice low and husky as Zach had instructed. *Play the part,* Zach had said. *Seduce with illusion.*

"Yes'm." Dogger tipped his hat, his eyes darting avidly around the quiet office, then he backed out the way he'd come. His presence beside the buggy would be the signal to Tom Chapman to proceed.

Their exchange had caught the attention of the customers. Mamie Cunningham looked up curiously, then her jaw dropped at the sight of the gaudily dressed strumpet poised on the threshold of this respectable financial institution. For a giddy instant, hilarity threatened to overcome Beth Ann. Dressed as she was, she looked the part of the scarlet woman she'd always been branded—and thus she had finally rendered the opinionated Mrs. Cunningham speechless! It was almost worth it.

Knowing her mirth was a product of nerves, and therefore dangerous, Beth Ann forcibly squelched it. Sailing up to the nearest teller, she heaved her reticule onto the counter and lifted out

Zach's ruse—a neatly wrapped package of ore samples.

"The manager, if you please, and be quick about it, young man," she commanded in an imperative tone. "I've come a great distance with specimens to be assayed immediately."

The dewy-faced young man gaped at her exposed bosom, then blushed to his roots. "Mr. Barlings? Y-Yes, ma'am."

He darted away, only to return in seconds. "Mr. Barlings is—er, engaged, ma'am. But he says if you leave your samples, he'll have them analyzed by this afternoon."

"What!" Her outrage was only partially feigned. What if Barlings wouldn't cooperate with their plan? Impossible! He *had* to! Too much depended on everything happening on schedule. She cast around for some way to coerce his participation.

"These samples are entirely too valuable to leave my person, young man!" she snapped, her breath making the veiling puff slightly at the level of her mouth. "I shall wait upon Mr. Barlings right here."

Grabbing her parcel, Beth Ann took a straight-backed chair positioned beside the rail in full view of every entering customer. She thrust out her chest, and for good measure crossed her legs, displaying a ruffled petticoat and entirely too much slender calf.

Harold's eyes nearly bugged out of his head. Noticing him, Mamie Cunningham screwed up her sour face in disapproval and rapped him soundly on the back with her reticule. The harried teller took one look, then disappeared again. When he returned, Mr. Barlings followed in his wake. His deeply lined face stiffened when he saw the creature in the rose-festooned hat lounging on his furniture, then he adjusted his spectacles and put on a manner of resolute politeness.

"Thank you for waiting, madam," Barlings said smoothly. "I find I've completed my business. Would you care to step into my private office now?"

Faced with her father's murderer for the first time, Beth Ann nearly quailed. Robert Barlings appeared so *normal*, just a man somewhat past his prime, with the usual worries about his family, his business, and what he'd have for supper. It still seemed incomprehensible that such a sedate, pompous businessman could be capable of cold-blooded violence. But even the devil could smile.

Forcing herself to concentrate on her task, Beth Ann jumped to her feet. "Indeed I would, sir! That's more like it."

Clearly relieved that he could rid his outer office of this unwelcome and embarrassing occupant so easily, Barlings escorted her past the railing and into his walnut-paneled office. His longish nose twitched, and he kept his distance from the cloying haze of perfume that surrounded her, which was exactly Beth Ann's intention. When he waved her inside, he was equally careful not to close the door completely.

Behind her veil, Beth Ann's mouth twisted with contempt. A killer who prized his reputation—how droll! It would be a pleasure to see him brought to justice.

"Now, madam, how may the Destiny Savings Bank be of service?" Robert Barlings asked, sitting down behind his desk and folding his hands over his paunch.

"I understand this is the only place in the vicinity where ore may be properly assayed, sir," she said in a throaty voice, taking the seat opposite.

She placed the ore samples on his shiny mahogany desk beside an expensive humidor. "Please do so immediately. Price is no object, but time is."

Barlings fingered the parcel speculatively. "May one inquire why this is so?"

"I have received an offer on a worthless mining claim of . . . of my late husband's." Beth Ann's lips tightened at the knowing look that flickered behind Robert Barlings's eyeglasses. He assumed the "husband" was the fabrication of a woman of easy virtue. He didn't know how right he was.

As she continued, her words were flat. "The amount of the offer is overly generous and raises some suspicion. If I know exactly the worth of my property, I may be able to obtain more elsewhere, but I do not wish to lose the present offer, which, unfortunately, I am compelled to either reject or accept no later than six o'clock this evening. You understand my urgency to have this problem resolved?"

"Perfectly, madam. It will be a matter of short work." He picked up the samples. "Would you care to wait here?"

"Thank you."

Barlings left the office, and Beth Ann could hear him speaking to one of his employees. Trembling with reaction, she peeked out the door in time to see him twist the heavy handle on the vault door, then step inside, where she knew he kept his assayer's instruments. Mission accomplished! Groping backward, she sank down again in the chair, fighting a sudden wave of nausea, so great was her relief. She lifted a gloved hand under her veil to blot away the sheen of perspiration on her brow and neck. Now, if only Zach would come!

"Papa? Wait'll you hear what the filly did! I—" Bobby Barlings skidded to a stop inside the door of his father's office, his light brown hair boyishly tousled, his cotton shirt crumpled under his striped suspenders, shirttail half hanging out from some boyish escapade. When he saw the strange woman sitting there, his smile faded, and he scowled. "Where's my papa?"

Beth Ann hastily removed her hand from her face, tugging down the veil again. *Oh, no!* she thought, dismayed. *Bobby, what are you doing here? You could be hurt!* She pointed in Barlings's direction wordlessly.

"Oh." Bobby's hazel gaze was frankly curious. "Who're you?"

"Nobody," Beth Ann answered, too quickly, forgetting to keep her voice low. Realizing her mistake, she gave a sharp, guttural order. "Go home, young man. You're interfering with your papa's business! Now, go!"

"I am not either interfering!" Bobby said, highly indignant. "I'm a big help! He says so. I take good care of my papa!"

"I—I'm sure you do," Beth Ann murmured, terrorized. She had to get Bobby out of here before . . .

On inspiration, she dug in the bottom of the reticule, nearly whooping when she found a couple of forgotten pennies. She shoved them at Bobby. "Here, a helpful youngster like you deserves a reward. Why don't you go buy yourself some red licorice? It's one of your favorites, isn't it?"

"Gosh, thanks!" Beaming, Bobby took the pennies, then frowned and tried to peer through the hazy veil. Beth Ann hastily averted her face.

"Go on, now," she said gently. "Go get your candy."

Recalled to the pleasure ahead, Bobby nodded vigorously. "I sure will!"

Bobby dashed out of the office as quickly as he'd appeared, and within a minute Beth Ann heard his cheerful farewell and the rattle of the glass front door as he slammed it behind him. She slumped in the chair, shaking in every fiber.

She'd never make it! This bank robbery business was altogether too harrowing! Despite her quaking knees, she forced herself to her feet again, hesitating in the office doorway. Mamie Cunningham was busy giving one of the tellers a piece of her mind, and Harold had taken up what looked to be permanent residence at the work desk, evidently waiting for one last look at the harlot before going about his business.

Beth Ann chewed her lip. Oh, why wouldn't they just go? And where were Zach and Tom? This was the tricky part, the timing, for if Mr. Barlings closed the vault before they were ready, they were lost.

Zach's plan was simplicity itself. Tom assumed that his two cohorts shared his intention of robbing the bank and making a quick getaway. Zach and Beth Ann would cooperate with that plan, but only until the opportunity arose for them to duck into the vault together and close it behind them. Tom was welcome to take what he could and escape, and since the sheriff would undoubtedly arrest them as soon as they were released from the vault, they'd have the opportunity to make all suitable explanations and confront Barlings with Wolf's murder. Zach calculated a few minutes in that dark and airless space would be a lot healthier in the long run than riding the outlaw trail with Tom Chapman and his band of cutthroats.

As Beth Ann watched, Barlings stepped out of the vault, his balding pate inclined in preoccupation over the paper report from his hand. Instantly her heart tripped over in panic. Where was Zach? The vault had to remain open until he arrived! She darted out of the office and past the open metal gate, infusing eagerness into her voice.

"Mr. Barlings, sir! Never say that you are finished already?"

He looked up in surprise. "Ah, it is a simple procedure, madam."

"This is certainly wonderful service, indeed." Ignoring his instinctive reaction away from such a questionable personage as herself, Beth Ann ingeniously tucked her arm into his, effectively forestalling him from securing the vault door. She tried not to shiver in repulsion at a murderer's touch. "Quick, do tell me. What are your results?"

"Madam, four of the five samples are valueless."

"Ah. No more than I suspected."

"But the fifth . . ." Mr. Barlings's expression showed an unusual excitement as he thrust the report at her. "Here, see for yourself."

Forced to release his arm to accept the paper, she gave a high, coquettish laugh that drew Mamie Cunningham's scornful glare. "Land's sake, you can't expect a woman to know about such things, sir! Just tell me. You didn't find any gold, did you?"

"No, madam, but if the vein from which the fifth sample came proves true, you may well own one of the purest copper deposits in all of the Arizona Territory."

Beth Ann stared at him through the gauzy veil. "You must be joking."

"Indeed not, I assure you!" Barlings said eagerly. "And if you are still in the market to sell, a lady of your, er—sensibilities having no wish to dirty her hands with the brutal work of mining—

then I am prepared on behalf of my usual investors to offer you a fair price which I'm sure will be much more acceptable than your current proposition."

"Oh, my God." She lifted a hand to her temple, overcome by the enormous irony. Wolf's mine wasn't worthless after all! All those years, he'd merely been looking for the wrong thing. He'd schemed and died—for nothing. Rage and futility and hate made her light-headed, and she swayed drunkenly, catching herself against the iron gate.

"Madam!" Barlings's voice seemed to come from a great distance. "Madam, are you ill?"

"Just . . . faint," she said, breathing through her teeth. "At such good news."

Barlings supported her elbow. "Here, let me find you a seat. There must be smelling salts around here someplace. Perhaps a glass of water?"

"Just let me stand here . . . a moment and catch my breath."

Mr. Barlings bent nearer in solicitous concern, loath to have a swooning female disgrace herself on his premises. Beth Ann felt the moment he stiffened, and she knew her charade was over.

"Yes, of—of course," Barlings stuttered, dropping her elbow as if she were a live coal and stepping back. She could see the quick calculation behind his eyes. "A drink. That's the ticket. I—I'll just get it—"

And sound the alarm? Not on your life!

Desperation gave Beth Ann the strength to act. Like a striking snake, she reached out, latching her fingers around his forearm and letting her weight sag toward the floor. Barlings had no choice but to support her or be dragged into a heap as well.

"Don't leave me," she begged. "I am . . . indisposed."

"Then let me send for the doctor," Barlings suggested, trying to shake her off, obviously uncertain, his gaze flickering hopefully toward the front of the office.

"No, don't go. I fear I shall be sick!" Beth Ann lurched, her top-heavy hat sliding to one side as she sent the older man staggering.

"Enough of this!" His hands closed painfully around her shoulders, his patience at an end, and he spoke in a low growl. "Cease this deception. I know who you are. Have you run mad? Why have you come back here?"

With a hiss of outrage, Beth Ann whipped the concealing veil free and sent it and the detested hat tumbling to the floor. "To see justice done, you assassin!"

Barlings cringed, then his jowly face hardened. "A foolish error, Miss Beth Ann—"

Mamie Cunningham stood at the dividing rail, her gossipy nose intrigued by the quiet ruckus occurring between the prominent banker and his not-so-respectable customer. "Anything the matter, Mr. Barlings?" she called, then gaped. "Good God, it's Beth Ann Linder! Murderess! Oh, Lord help me! It's her! Hold on to her, sir!"

"Now see what you've done!" Barlings grated. "I—yeow! Damn, you hellion, stop that!"

Beth Ann's big toe throbbed where she'd kicked Mr. Barlings's shin. Struggling against his grip, she made another swipe at him, and his yelp and Mamie's howling produced a commotion that brought the rest of the staff at a run. Only Harold noticed the two men who burst through the front doors with drawn pistols. Prudently, Harold immediately raised his hands toward heaven.

"Everybody shut the hell up!" Tom Chapman roared, waving his Colt.

Dead silence reigned. All eyes swiveled toward the interlopers, and a collective gasp rose to the ceiling. Beth Ann slipped out of Barlings's suddenly lax grasp, and she met Zach's turquoise gaze across the room. To her utter chagrin, she was trembling so much, she could barely stand.

"That's better," Tom said in satisfaction.

"Reverend Temple." Mamie Cunningham's normally strident tones were weak as a newborn kitten's mewing, her eyes as big as two cart wheels. "What . . . how?"

"The name's Madison, ma'am." Zach tipped his hat. "Zach Madison, and the closest I ever got to a seminary was cleaning out the privies at Sister Sadie's Burlesque."

Mrs. Cunningham's plump hand fluttered at her throat. "Oh, dear Lord."

"Praying's a good idee, Mamie." Tom chuckled, then lowered his heavy black brows into a ferocious scowl. "Now, haul your fat ass down on that floor and git started! The rest of you, too."

Harold, Mrs. Cunningham, and the two tellers hit the floor fast enough to make Tom smile again. He drew a bead on the banker, stopping his slower descent. "Not you, Barlings. We got business."

"What kind of business?" Robert Barlings demanded angrily.

"As if you don't know!" Zach sauntered casually past the cowering hostages, pushing through the swinging gate in the dividing rail and moving toward Beth Ann, the pistol he wielded looking curiously out of place within his hand.

Darting a look toward the open vault, Zach encouraged her with his eyes. Carefully, so as not to tip off Tom that anything was afoot, Beth Ann began to back toward the steel door, her blood roaring in her ears.

"We know everything, Barlings," Zach continued in a conversational tone. "About Wolf Linder's mine, about your defrauding buyers with salted diamonds, everything."

"That's right, banker, so hand over the rest of them diamonds!" Tom ordered.

"This—this is utterly ridiculous!" Barlings spluttered. "I don't know anything about diamonds."

"Don't give me that!" Tom drew the hammer back on his pistol, and at his feet Mamie Cunningham gave a small, fearful shriek and covered her head with her arms. "I ain't got time for none of your funny business."

"Better listen to him, Barlings," Zach advised. Reaching Beth Ann's side, he gave her a surreptitious push, subtly herding her toward the vault door. "You're too cautious to have salted all those stones into the mine. You had to have some in reserve to show the suckers, didn't you? So where do you keep them, banker? In the vault with the rest of the valuables? Or did you resort to a loose floorboard somewhere?"

Robert Barlings's face flushed with ruddy choler. "This is preposterous! I deal in coin, not gems!"

"Damn, he's stubborn," Zach commented easily. "But it won't work, Barlings. We found your particular brand of smokes *inside* Wolf's mine."

Barlings's high color bled from his features, leaving him white and guilty-looking.

"We're wasting time!" Tom growled, chancing a glance out the front. "The boys can't keep watch forever."

"I'll check the vault," Zach offered, holstering his pistol. "Might as well take the money while we're at it, huh, Tom? Come on, Beth Ann. You can help."

Swallowing, she moved stiffly, nearly overcome with giddiness. The maw of the vault opened before her, not a menace, but a sanctuary. They were going to make it!

"Get it all, Madison," Tom ordered, his pale eyes lighting up with avarice.

"You—you'll ruin me!" Barlings protested.

Tom grinned maliciously. "Seeing as how I always figured a banker is about as useless as a wart on a pretty girl's bottom, all the bett—"

The bank door exploded inward, and Bobby Barlings's gangly form spilled over the doorstep. Eyes wild, clutching a fistful of red licorice whips, Bobby bellowed for his father, in such a state he registered neither the gunmen nor the bodies sprawled on the floor.

"Paw! It's her! Miss Beth Ann's come back! I saw her!"

"Bobby, no!" Beth Ann's involuntary warning came too late.

Tom jumped the younger man, grabbing him around the neck and kicking the door shut in one lightning-swift movement.

"Well, if it ain't the half-wit," Tom sneered, squeezing Bobby's neck between his beefy fingers. Bobby gagged and dropped the red candy strands, digging futilely at Tom's powerful grip, his hazel eyes wide and startled. The elder Barlings charged forward, fists clenched, an inarticulate protest on his lips.

"Inside, angel, now," Zach ordered, shoving Beth Ann toward the vault door.

"No." Steadying herself on the grilled gate, she shook her head, terrified, but certain they couldn't abandon an innocent like Bobby to Tom Chapman's violence. She met Zach's frustration with a look of transparent appeal that begged, *do something*. "No one's supposed to get hurt!"

"Hold it, banker!" Tom barked, jamming the barrel of his pistol into Bobby's jawbone.

Barlings froze in his tracks just beyond the railing, his breath wheezing from his chest in apoplectic gusts. "Just don't hurt him . . ."

"Well, now, I'd sure like to oblige, but . . ." Smirking his malevolent satisfaction, Tom shrugged and cocked the trigger of the Colt. "Does this refresh your memory about them diamonds?"

Chapter 18

Robert Barlings gulped and held his hands up in surrender. "All right. I'll get what you want. Just don't . . ."

"That's more like it," Tom said with an oily smile. "Get moving!"

Zach's jaw unclenched a notch, and he let his breath slide between his teeth.

At least the banker had sense enough not to play stubborn with Bobby's life on the line. Now if only Beth Ann would show as much intelligence about their own predicament! She was white-faced with dread at Tom's threats to the boy, but Zach gave her a hard look, jerking his head toward the vault a fraction, urging her inside again. She ignored him, and Zach swore silently.

"I—I'll just go get the stones," Barlings said, taking a step. "They're in my desk—"

"Don't trust banks, do you?" Tom mocked. His eyes hardened, and he took a choking grip on the back of Bobby's shirt collar, practically lifting the younger man off his feet. "Beth Ann, you fetch it. Bound to be a Peacemaker in that desk. Wouldn't want the banker to make a mistake he'd regret."

Barlings dug a key out of his vest pocket and passed it to Beth Ann over the dividing rail.

"Top left-hand," he muttered, furious but impotent in the face of Tom's determination. "The bag's stamped 'Solomon Brothers, New York.' "

Nodding wordlessly, she hurried into the office,

the crimson silk of her costume whispering across the varnished floor.

Barlings turned back to Tom. "Let him go now."

"Not worried, are you, banker?" With an ugly glint in his blue eyes, Tom lightly tapped Bobby's temple with the gun barrel. "You better be playing square with me."

"Don't mess with my papa!" Gasping, Bobby struggled, swinging wildly, but his efforts were useless against Tom's massive grip. "Bad things happen to people who mess with my papa!"

"Quiet, Bobby!" his father ordered sharply.

"Out of the mouths of babes, eh, Barlings?" Zach demanded, suddenly intense. As long as Barlings had a reason to be cooperative, there was the small matter of clearing Beth Ann's name. "You and Wolf had it all planned, didn't you? Salt Wolf's worthless mine, then defraud some unsuspecting investors. But something happened, didn't it? Wolf got greedy."

"He was . . . mad." Barlings's dark gaze darted around the room. He licked his lips nervously, the words tumbling out as if Bobby's danger had loosened all his self-control. "Full of wild ideas. Unmanageable."

"Why, Barlings? Why throw your lot in with a loose cannon like Wolf?"

"It was just business. I'd had a run of bad luck, nothing an infusion of cash wouldn't cure, you see, and . . . and the scheme was perfect. No one would really get hurt. But Wolf was never satisfied. He—he threatened to expose me." The banker's lined face darkened with suppressed fury. "I'd planned it so carefully, and the fool was spoiling everything!"

A small distressed sound made Zach look up. White-faced with strain, Beth Ann stood in the office doorway listening to Barlings's strangled words, wringing a purple velvet sack between her hands. Setting his jaw, Zach pushed harder for the truth.

"He'd have ruined you, right, Robert? Your business, your reputation—everything you worked for, the security for your son, all gone."

"I tried to reason with him!" Barlings's gaze strayed to the pistol barrel leveled at his son's temple. "Wolf wouldn't listen."

"So you killed him." Zach noted Mamie Cunningham's faint gasp with satisfaction. Good, she was listening.

Tom's dark, bushy brows pulled together in puzzlement. "Hell, Zach! I thought you plugged the son of a bitch!"

"That's what you get for trying to think, Tom," Zach snapped, then glared at the banker. "Admit it, Barlings. *You shot Wolf Linder.*"

With a child's plaintive cry, Bobby squirmed in Tom's brutal neck lock. "Papa—"

"Yes," Robert Barlings said, his voice a harsh rasp. "I killed him. Now, let my boy go!"

The four floor-bound hostages rustled and stirred at the banker's shocking confession.

"Keep still!" Tom roared. He noticed Beth Ann hovering in the doorway. "Got 'em?"

She nodded.

"Show 'em to me."

Wordlessly, her silver eyes so pale they were almost transparent, she opened the sack and spilled the collection of nondescript stones into her palm. As she returned the stones to the pouch, Tom flashed a white-toothed smile at the banker.

"Any man who'd kill Wolf Linder deserves a break, I reckon."

Tom thrust Bobby at his father and reached

across the railing to snatch the sack from Beth Ann's hands. With a shuddering gasp that was almost a sob, Barlings clasped his son in his arms.

"You got the rest of that cash, Zach?" Tom demanded.

"Right away, Tom." Zach motioned Beth Ann toward the vault once more. This time she moved, and Zach lifted a paean of silent thanks—which was instantly shattered by a harsh clamor of gunshots from the street outside.

Dogger stuck his head in the door, his look almost comically panicked as Tom's pistol swung at him. "Holy smokes, boss! Hold yer fire! The jig's up."

Tom swore fluently. "I knew there was too damn much talking going on!"

"The boys'll keep the sheriff pinned down at the jail," Dogger said excitedly. "Let's get the hell out of here!"

As Dogger disappeared out the door again, Tom jerked his head at Zach. "C'mon."

"Not this time, Tom." Ignoring Tom's dumbfounded expression, Zach moved to Beth Ann's side.

"What're you, *crazy?*" Tom demanded, jumping as another round of gunfire erupted. Then his face darkened with understanding. "You set me up, you son of a bitch!"

"No, but I guarantee the sheriff's going to be here quicker than hell can scorch a feather thanks to the hole I busted in his jail wall a few days back. You'd better get going."

"And leave you here to lead the law straight back to me? Not on your life!" Tom leveled his pistol at them with an ominous click of the hammer. "Drop your gun right there and *move* before I blast the both of you to kingdom come!"

"*Think* for once, you jackass!" Zach gritted his teeth but nevertheless carefully drew his pistol and laid it down on the floor beside the railing. Dammit! He hadn't counted on Tom's cantankerous nature! "We're willing to take our medicine, and that'll take the heat off of you!"

"Shut up!" Tom snarled, stuffing the velvet pouch into his waistband. "You're extra insurance. Get over here, woman! Hurry!"

Biting her lip, Beth Ann took a step toward the outlaw.

"No!" Bobby Barlings clenched his fists, and his lower lip had the sullen, petulant jut of a thwarted child. "You can't take Miss Beth away again! I'm going to marry her! Papa promised!"

"Bobby! Hush up," the older man hissed, jerking his protesting son back by his suspenders.

"But, Papa!" Bobby wailed.

Zach's insides heaved with frustration. This wasn't the way it was supposed to work! And, damn it all, it was his own arrogant belief in his flimflam ability that was responsible! Even if they managed to dodge a hail of bullets, outrace another posse, and convince Tom they hadn't meant him any real harm, all Zach and Beth Ann's plans would be for naught. They were caught up in a web of lies and lawbreaking they'd never be able to unravel, much less explain.

That was no kind of life for Beth Ann. Barlings's confession had given her a chance. Zach couldn't do less than make her take it—even if it meant giving up his opportunity for a new life, even— God help him—if it meant giving *her* up. Beth Ann's happiness was worth any sacrifice.

Catching her arm, Zach pushed her back behind him. "All right, Tom. Don't get excited. I'm coming. But leave Beth Ann here."

Tom's low growl was a warning that his patience was at an end. "Dammit, Madison!"

"She'll just slow us down, and she's no use to you anyway. Admit it, Tom. She just ain't no fun."

Tom's dark countenance puckered, then he spit on the floor. "You're damned right about that, Zach. She kept her legs crossed tighter than a spinster schoolmarm the whole time I knew her! Reckon a cold fish like her will do for a half-wit, at that."

"Zach, don't," Beth Ann said in a soft, urgent rush, her voice trembling. "I want to be with you! 'Whither thou goest . . .'"

Zach caught her shoulders. "Listen to me! It's the only way. At least you'll be safe, now that these people know the truth! You heard it all, didn't you, Miss Mamie?"

"Yes. Yes, I heard," came the muffled reply from the floor. "I was so wrong . . ."

"But I might never see you again!" Beth Ann's silver eyes were smoky with anguish. "Oh, Zach . . ."

There wasn't time to say the things he needed to say, to make a proper farewell, to explain that loving her had redeemed his worthless soul, so he touched her cheek in a fleeting caress that had to say it all. "Angel."

Another flurry of gunfire sounded in the street. Zach turned toward the door. "We'd better get, Tom."

"You've gone soft, Madison," Tom accused. "You wouldn't be fit to shoot if all I wanted was to unload my gun! You're liable to get us all kilt! Aw, the hell with you both!" He patted the pouch sticking over his waistband and grinned. "I got what I came for, anyway. *Adiós.*"

With a dip of his head, Tom Chapman ducked

out the bank door, leaving Zach standing dumb-founded. "Well, I'll be . . ."

"Zach!" Overjoyed, Beth Ann flung herself into his embrace. His arms closed around her, and it was heaven.

Outside, riders thundered down the dusty street. For a breathless moment, the town held still, then the silence was broken by excited shouts. Zach knew it wouldn't be long before the sheriff appeared. Meanwhile, Harold helped Mamie Cunningham to a chair and fanned her with her reticule while the two tellers talked among themselves, slanting horrified glances to-ward Barlings and his son. Oblivious to the rever-berations his confession had produced, the older man dusted Bobby's shoulders and tucked in his shirttail, checking him for injuries as if he were five years old. Bobby's gaze as he watched Zach holding Beth Ann grew steadily more mutinous with an adult's dark jealousy.

"I'll be . . ." Zach repeated, shaking his head in amazement.

"It's going to be all right, isn't it?" Beth Ann's voice was shaky, her grip around Zach's waist viselike, for she never intended to let him go again.

Zach smiled down at her, then gently tilted her face up and kissed her, a soft brush of lips that was infinitely exciting and full of promise. "Not easy, angel, because we've still got some ex-plaining to do, but—yes, I think we're both going to be all right." Then he threw back his head and laughed.

"Zach?"

He snorted, shaking his head. "Poor Tom. I hope he doesn't regret his generous impulse when he finds out what he got for his trouble."

"What he got?" Beth Ann frowned in confusion. "He got a sack full of diamonds!"

"Practically worthless." Zach turned to face the banker. "Isn't that right, Barlings? Those second-rate stones of yours—how much would you say they're worth?"

"Huh?" Haggard, Barlings leaned heavily on the dividing rail and shrugged in disinterest. "Uh, couple of hundred dollars at most."

Zach cocked a roguish sandy eyebrow at Beth Ann. "See?"

"Oh, dear." She giggled. "And he never got his hands on any of the bank's cash, either, did he?"

"No." Zach's lips twitched. They looked at each other for a long, helpless moment, and then both exploded into mirth. Holding on to each other, they let laughter take them in a release of tension and undiluted joy. Bewildered, Mamie Cunningham and the others looked on in amazement.

"You don't know the best part," Beth Ann managed between whoops. "Paw's mine—it's full of copper!"

"You don't say!" Chuckling, Zach cradled her against his side. "Diamonds to copper—what a comedown!"

"It'll be good, honest work for anyone who wants it," she protested, thumping her fist against his chest. Her smile grew serious. "We'll be able to do whatever you want with it—even buy into that gambling palace you talked about."

It amazed him that she'd remembered such a thing. Zach's blue-green gaze softened, and his voice turned husky as he pulled her closer. "Dreams change, angel. You and I will build one we can both share when the time—"

"Stop touching her!" Bobby Barlings shrilled the order, his hands bunched belligerently at his sides.

Angry red mottled his cheeks, and his eyes were wide and disturbed.

"Bobby—" Robert Barlings's warning went unheeded.

"You leave her alone," Bobby told Zach. "I'm warning you . . ."

"Take it easy, son." Zach smiled. "I'm not hurting her."

"You don't have the right! Miss Beth Ann is mine. Papa said so!" Bobby's agitation made him shake with an uncontrollable fury.

"It's all right, Bobby," Beth Ann soothed, hardly surprised that what had transpired had produced his excitable state. Had he even understood what his father had confessed? She sincerely hoped not. "Zach's my good friend. Just like you are."

"You're *my* lady." Bobby's lower lip trembled. "You're mine! When we get married, you'll see."

Zach shook his head, his mouth going a bit stony. "Sorry, son, but you've got to understand. Miss Beth Ann is going to marry me."

"No! That's not true! I won't let it be true!"

Tears spurting, Bobby looked around wildly, then dove for the railing. Scrambling up, he waved Zach's discarded pistol in a dangerous arc. Mamie Cunningham shrieked, and the rest of the bank's occupants scattered.

"I'm going to shoot you!" Bobby cried, near hysteria. "I'm going to kill you just like I did that bad Wolf!"

"Bobby!" Barlings started forward, absolute horror written on his florid countenance. "Don't say another word! And give me that thing!"

"No, Papa. I've got to." Sobbing, Bobby steadied the pistol in two hands and pointed it at his rival.

Zach shoved Beth Ann behind him, shielding

her with his body, his features slack with pure
amazement. "You? You killed Wolf?"

"Don't answer that, Bobby!" Barlings ordered,
reaching for the gun. His son shook him off.

"I did it! Wolf hollered at Papa. He made Papa
mad. I had to help, don't you see?" The distracted
light in Bobby's eyes focused in sudden vicious intent. He aimed the pistol at Zach. "And it was
easy. All you have to do is pull this—"

"No, Bobby, don't!" In a spurt of pure fear, the
stunned immobility left Beth Ann, and she flung
herself forward to confront the young man. "This
won't make me happy. You want me to be happy,
don't you?"

"But—" His face awash with moisture, Bobby
chewed the inside of his cheek, suddenly unde-
cided.

"You see?" Beth Ann crooned, ignoring Zach's
frantic signals to get back. "You don't really want
to hurt anyone."

"But I hate him!" Bobby cried passionately.

"Hate's no good," she said, stepping closer, her
hand outstretched. Her heart pounded so hard, it
threatened to close her throat, but she pasted a ca-
joling smile on her face and tried to reach the disturbed boy. "Believe me, I know, Bobby. Love is so
much better. And friends love each other in a very
special way. Will you be my friend now, and let
me have the gun?"

She could see him wavering, the hurt and rejection and indecision roiling within his erratic, tumbling thoughts. "Please, Bobby."

His expression miserable, his tears streaming,
Bobby gave her a slow, sorrowful smile. "I can't."

When he swung toward Zach, Beth Ann was already in motion. When he pulled the trigger, she

was committed. And when the searing pain struck, all that mattered was that Zach was safe.

"Angel!"

Crumpling on the shiny wood floor, Beth Ann heard Zach's ragged voice and the high keening that was Bobby's contrition from a vast distance. Over her head, a shadowy surge of bodies overpowered the boy, abruptly ending the painful wail of an animal in torment.

Then Zach was there, holding her with hands stained as red as her silly dress, but the darkness pressed down and she fell into a pool of scarlet, forever lost . . .

She was lost in a rosy cloud bank and found it beautiful, like sunlight filtering through her eyelids. Floating and peaceful, she wandered, serene at last. After a great while she noticed a tiny pinpoint of brightness. Drawn by its warmth, she moved toward the light . . .

No, my angel, not yet.

Beth Ann stopped, her heart catching at the familiar, beloved voice. "Mother?"

It's not your time. You must go back.

Longing pierced Beth Ann with such intensity that tears trembled on her lashes. "But I want to be with you!"

And you will, beloved, but in the proper order of things.

"I love you, Mother. Don't send me away!"

You have so much more to do, so much more love to experience. Take the chance I never had.

The tears fell. "But, Mother . . ."

Someone's waiting, my dearest.

Beth Ann remembered then. "Yes."

And the love flooded through her being, giving

her the courage to turn from the beckoning light. "Good-bye, Mother."

Farewell, my darling. The voice was already a distant whisper, but the words were a loving promise. *When the time is right, I'll be here . . .*

Smiling, Beth Ann sifted through the cloud bank, entranced to find the rosy hue changing, becoming deeper, shifting into violet and magenta, then blue. A peculiar shade of blue-green that surrounded and filled her with wonder, a color like the sky just after daybreak, like the light in her true love's eyes . . .

Climbing free of the cloud bank, Beth Ann opened her eyes to meet Zach's anxious turquoise gaze, and smiled. "Zach . . ."

"Angel." Seated in a straight-backed chair beside her bed, Zach folded Beth Ann's hand tighter into his. His whiskey-tinted curls were tousled and he wore a clean shirt, but his face was haggard with worry, and his voice choked. "Thank God."

She became conscious of a number of things all at once: the unfamiliar room, the crisp linens, the lace-edged nightgown, the bulky constriction of a bandage covering a painful place on her left side. She was physically tired, although not dreadfully so, but conversely, she felt spiritually refreshed and rested, and finding Zach beside her made her joy complete. It was all so very puzzling.

"Where . . .?" she asked.

"Ah, Mrs. Cunningham's. She wouldn't hear of anything else when you were hurt."

Memory slid into place for Beth Ann. "Bobby!"

Zach stilled her weak attempt to sit up, knowing instinctively how to answer her unspoken question. "He's safe."

"Really?"

Zach pursed his lips and glanced away.

She squeezed his hand insistently. "Zach?"

Bowing his head over her hand, he mumbled, "His mind . . . uh, snapped. There's a hospital . . . He'll be well cared for there, they say."

"Oh." It was a shaky sigh.

Zach bent closer, nuzzling her temple. "Don't cry, angel."

"Am I crying?" Mystified, she touched her fingertips to the moisture at the corner of her eye.

"You wept in your sleep."

She frowned, searching through the rosy haze that still lingered in the back of her mind. A slow smile of certitude curled her lips. She cupped Zach's jaw lovingly. "I dreamed about my mother."

"That's nice. You know, when I was in your shoes, I dreamed about angels."

Her look held a sweet contentment. "It's the same thing."

"Well, this is one habit I'd just as soon not see us take up, all right? Jee-sus, you scared me!" Zach admitted on a raw tone, pressing a fervent kiss into her palm. "There for a while, Doc Sayers wasn't sure . . ."

"I'm fine. Don't you know I'd never go anywhere without you?" Her eyelids were growing heavy again. "Oh, Zach, I'm so glad you're here. Don't every leave me . . ."

"Angel." The word was a tortured rasp. He bent to kiss her, but even in his gentleness, she sensed his desperation.

"What is it?"

He smoothed her hair back from her forehead and gave her a crooked smile. "Time to face the music, love. Sheriff Nichols has those warrants on me. Looks like I'll be cooling my heels for a spell in the Territorial Prison at Yuma again."

Suddenly there wasn't enough blood flowing through her brain for her to comprehend his words. Denial leapt instinctively to her lips. "No."

"I explained everything and did some of the fastest talking of my life, but his hands are tied, honey." Zach gave a philosophical shrug. "We expected it all along, didn't we? When we decided, we knew I'd have to pay the piper sooner or later."

"When?" Beth Ann could barely form the word between lips that felt white and bloodless.

Zach grimaced. "Soon. The sheriff was kind enough not to force the issue until you were out of danger."

Now her side ached, and her throat was full. Beth Ann turned her face toward the wall to spare Zach her anguish. "I'll see if I can't manage to languish a bit, then."

"Don't." Carefully he climbed onto the bed beside her and gathered her into his arms, cradling her shaking form with such tenderness that she thought she might die of love. "Be brave for me, angel. I couldn't bear it otherwise. Get well so I know you're safe and . . . and that you're waiting for me."

"As if I had a choice," she scoffed.

And then she wept in earnest.

"Well, it's about time you woke up again and rejoined the living!"

Beth Ann turned her head on her pillow, peering in amazement at the female figure blocking the doorway.

"What's the matter?" Whiskey Jean demanded, striding in with a loaded tray balanced on one massive palm. "Ain't you never seen a lady in skirts afore?"

Beth Ann gaped. Whiskey Jean's lined face was free of its usual layer of road dust, and her hair, still mousy but shining clean, was tumbled into a frowsy topknot that was really quite flattering.

"Jean. You look . . . wonderful."

Depositing the tray on the bedside table, the amazon delicately touched the lilac calico of her dress. "Kinda nice, ain't it? Buck favors me in purple, too."

"Buck?" Beth Ann felt a little light-headed.

"Now, don't you worry, gal!" Jean plumped pillows and eased the younger woman into a half-sitting position with no more effort than if she'd been an infant. "Buck's taking fine care of Traveler's Rest. Why, I daresay things ain't gone as smooth in years. I'm sure Ama's cooking don't hold a candle to yours, but the passengers ain't complaining, far as I can see. I tell you one thing, though, you need to get rid of Wolf's bookkeeping—I can't make out hide nor hair of it!"

"You—you're helping out, too?"

"Sure. I was tired of whacking them bullocks, anyway."

Beth Ann felt emotion swell her throat. Two good friends were treasures indeed. "Thank you, Jean."

"Now, don't go getting all weepy on me!" Jean admonished hastily. "Think you can manage a little broth? We gotta keep you built up, if we don't want that fever to come back."

Listlessly Beth Ann inspected the cup of pale golden liquid, then her friend's encouraging expression. "I'll try."

"There you go." Jean sat down on the edge of the bed and handed Beth Ann the cup, watching her closely as she took a cautious sip. "Had you quite an adventure, didn't you?"

"Umm." The chicken broth was flavorful, salty against Beth Ann's tongue, and astonishingly bracing. Her soul might be in black despair, but her body didn't want to give up just yet. "I suppose."

"You suppose?" Whiskey Jean lifted her craggy eyebrows in mock amazement. "Bank robbing, diamond mines, outlaws! Huh! You coulda stepped right out of one of them dime novels!"

Beth Ann set the cup on the bedside table with a dejected thump. "Everyone's talking? Well, that's nothing new."

"No, what's new is the amount of crow one small town can swallow in just a few days' time!" Jean chuckled heartily. "O'course, everybody's saying how they knew all along you'd been misjudged—sweet, fine, dutiful young woman that you are! That Tom was just a lying blackguard, after all. And nobody is surprised that the preacher didn't turn out to be a preacher either. No, sir! Amazing how many folks always thought he was kinda shifty-eyed."

"Zach is not shifty-eyed! He's got the most beautiful eyes in the whole world." Beth Ann's heat dissolved as fast as it had erupted, and her chin trembled. "Where is he?"

"Down in the jail."

"Oh." Beth Ann drew a deep, ragged breath. Since the moment she'd awakened again without Zach's comforting arms around her, she'd had a secret terror that he'd already been sent away—in manacles. The image chilled her with a soul-deep pain. Didn't anyone understand Zach's crimes were minor compared to the scale of things they'd just experienced? "When will the sheriff take him to Yuma?"

Jean sobered. "Half an hour. That's what I came to tell you."

Beth Ann's cheeks went as pale as snow. "Oh, no."

"They'll come by here first so you can say good-bye."

Fighting back her dismay, Beth Ann held her aching side and flipped off the covers. "Help me up."

"Now, wait a minute, honey, you can't go off half-cocked—"

"I refuse to send the man I love off to prison for God knows how long with me looking like something the cat dragged in!" Beth Ann's voice caught. "He'll need to remember . . . so help me to that chair, and hand me that shawl. Oh, and I need a comb!"

"All right, keep your shirt on." Jean helped Beth Ann reach the straight-backed chair, then whipped a yellow crocheted shawl off a hook on the back of the bedroom door and dropped it around Beth Ann's shoulders. "I guess we gotta give the sheriff credit for some Christian feeling."

"If he truly had any, he'd let Zach go! After all, if it hadn't been for Zach, we'd never have learned who really killed Paw, and Tom Chapman might have gotten away with the whole town's savings!"

"Yeah, instead, all old Tom got was a bunch of nearly worthless diamonds." With a laugh, Jean situated herself behind Beth Ann and began to comb the tangles out of her ebony curls. "I'd sure like to see the look on his face when he tries to peddle them out California way. The sheriff didn't even waste time sending a posse after him. Course, it was kind of ticklish, them diamonds belonging to Mr. Barlings in the first place. Took Tristan a bit of skull scratching to finally figure that one out."

Beth Ann stopped trying to adjust the shawl into a more becoming drapery and frowned in confusion. "Meaning?"

"Well, Barlings said he didn't care about the diamonds. And since only *contemplating* fraud ain't exactly a crime, it turns out the only thing the banker was guilty of was trying to protect Bobby. I'd have knocked Mr. Barlings around for saying nothing when they tried to pin Wolf's murder on you, but there's no accounting for the power of a parent's love, I guess."

Beth Ann sighed, tormented by her own guilt. Had she selfishly encouraged Bobby's devotion too much? Or had he been beyond reach long before anyone realized? "Poor Bobby. He seemed so harmless. Who would have ever guessed?"

"Yeah. Mr. Barlings has already turned over his interest in the bank to the Tucson investors and left town. Heard tell he's going to stay near that hospital, but the doc don't hold out no hope that Bobby will ever get any better."

"What a tragedy," Beth Ann murmured. Voices from beyond the door caught her attention, and she tensed.

"That must be them," Jean said. Despite her finery, she still walked with a man's firm swagger, and she stalked to the door. When she pulled it open, Mamie Cunningham, looking grim, escorted Sheriff Nichols and Zach inside. Her husband, Mayor Ike Cunningham, trailed along behind. Beth Ann was relieved to see that Zach was unfettered.

"Angel, you shouldn't be up!" Catching her hands, Zach kneeled at her side, only the faint line of strain bracketing his mouth marring his usual insouciant expression.

Though her heart was breaking, Beth Ann tried to match his chipper manner. "A lady never greets visitors while lying flat on her back if she can help it. Bad form, you know."

Zach's lips quirked, and he leaned forward, murmuring in her ear. "Flat on your back is my favorite, angel."

"You are a rogue, Zach Madison." The laugh in her voice caught painfully, and her silver eyes blazed with sudden fierceness. "Don't ever change!"

Zach touched her face, her hair, as if memorizing her, then pressed a gentle kiss to her trembling lips. "Never."

Foreheads pressed together, they made their own little cocoon of privacy while the other visitors looked elsewhere.

"I wish I had a photograph to give you," she whispered. "I'll have one made and send it!"

"I don't need anything to help me remember. Every breath I draw, every word I hear, everything I touch or feel or see, is caught up in the way I love you." Zach pressed her palm against his heart. "It won't be forever. Every day that passes brings us that much closer to being together. Try to hold on to that."

She drew a shaky breath, ignoring the tear that trickled from the corner of her eye. "Yes, Zach. I love you, too."

Behind them, Sheriff Nichols cleared his throat. "We need to get movin', son."

"Tarnation, Tristan!" Whiskey Jean exploded. "After all that's happened, taking this boy off to the hoosegow don't hardly seem fair. Ain't there nuthin' you can do?"

"Just my duty," the sheriff answered stiffly.

Zach stood. "I've learned it doesn't pay to step outside the law, and I'm willing to take my medicine. No hard feelings, Sheriff." He extended his hand.

The sheriff shifted his bulky form uncomfortably, then took Zach's hand. "You understand, the way things stand, I ain't got a choice."

With a comforting hand pressed to Beth Ann's shoulder, Zach shrugged. "Sure."

"Well, I sure don't understand!" Mamie Cunningham snapped. "And even though Reverend Temple—er, Mr. Madison—was a real scamp to fool us all, I think the whole town's learned a valuable lesson. 'Judge not, that ye be not judged.' Ain't that right, Ike?"

"Yes, Mamie."

Mamie warmed to her topic. "Amen to that! In fact, all things considered, especially the way he run off Tom Chapman and exposed a murderer, I'd say Mr. Madison could turn out to be one of Destiny's most valuable citizens. So I—we—the town, that is—have a proposition. Tell 'em, Ike."

"You're doing fine, Mamie."

"You're the mayor!" she hissed at her husband. "Tell 'em!"

Ike gave his wife a pained look, then scratched his jowls. "See, Sheriff, it's like this. If Zach and his fiancée—Miss Beth Ann there—are free to develop old Wolf's mine—it's full of copper, you know—we'd likely be in for a spell of prosperity here in Destiny."

"That's right," Mamie agreed, nodding. "Miners coming from everywhere! Men who need livery stables and groceries and equipment, and folks passing through on the stage and staying at Traveler's Rest. Why, Destiny *needs* this young couple!"

Beth Ann looked up at Zach in amazement, but his expression was as puzzled as her own.

"Just what are you getting at, Mamie?" Sheriff Nichols demanded.

Mamie crossed her arms over her bosom and gave him a smug look. "Tell him, Ike."

Ike rolled his eyes, heaved a long-suffering sigh, then continued as ordered. "A parole, Sheriff. Since Mr. Madison ain't no kind of killer or nothing like that, if I—we—the whole damn town!—vouches for him, and makes sure he's gainfully employed right here in Destiny, ain't there some way we can get the authorities to parole him into our custody?"

Zach's fingers dug into Beth Ann's shoulder, and she held her breath.

"Ya know"—slowly, like rock cracking, the sheriff's features formed a half smile—"that just might work."

Whiskey Jean let loose a whoop.

"That is," the sheriff interjected, "if you have no objections to such an arrangement, Mr. Madison."

Stunned, Zach shook his head, and Beth Ann turned her cheek against his leg and bit her lip to keep from crying.

Sheriff Nichols appeared relieved of a great burden. "Well, Mayor, that's settled, then. I'll see to the paperwork, and I guess if Mr. Madison agrees to go no further than . . . say, Traveler's Rest, then we're all set."

Mamie Cunningham clapped her hands in delight. "Wonderful!"

Ike offered his hand to Zach. "Congratulations, son. Looks like you're a free man—more or less."

Zach swallowed hard. "I—I don't know what to say. I'll try to be worthy of the town's confidence."

"Maybe this time around, we'll all try a little

harder," the sheriff added, clapping Zach on the back. "I'm right happy not to have to ride all the way to Yuma, I can tell you that."

Zach grinned. "My sentiments exactly, Sheriff!" Jubilant, he reached for Beth Ann, lifting her to her feet with care and holding on to her as if she were infinitely precious. "Did you hear that, angel?"

"It's like a miracle." Dazed, she smiled through a blur of tears, looping her arms around his neck.

"No, you're the miracle—for loving me! But don't think I'm going to let my own angel fly away. Quick! Tell me when you'll marry me!"

She laughed, joyful, not even minding the painful stitch in her injured side. Nothing could spoil her elation. "As soon as you want. Today!"

"Nonsense!" Mamie Cunningham scoffed. "We'll have to find a minister, and then there's your dress, and, of course, the cake will have to be enormous to feed the whole town!" She looked delighted at the prospect. "Lots of work ahead of us, eh, Jean? Better tuck the patient back into bed so we can get to work."

"That's a fine idea, Mamie," Whiskey Jean stated with a broad grin, and started toward Beth Ann.

Beth Ann's arms tightened around Zach's neck, and he shook his head. "Appears the patient doesn't plan to go anywhere just yet, ladies."

Mamie simpered and made shooing motions with her hands at the rest of the room's occupants. "Then perhaps we'd all better leave you to that agreeable task, Mr. Madison."

"My pleasure, ma'am," Zach murmured, dropping another kiss on Beth Ann's willing mouth. He looked up with a question just as Ike Cunningham reached the door. "Oh, say, Mr. Mayor, what was that about gainful employment?"

Epilogue

"I simply must have another slice of that coconut cake, Mrs. Madison! *And* your recipe."

"I'll be happy to copy it out for you, Mrs. Nichols."

Beth Ann smiled at the sheriff's wife and carefully added a piece of cake to her plate from the bountiful buffet laid out on impromptu tables of boards and sawhorses. Decked out in their Sunday best, Destiny's populace had turned out in force for a brush arbor revival and dinner on the grounds of the Gospel Assembly Chapel, now that September's arrival heralded some much welcomed relief from the summer heat.

"Beth Ann's cakes are much in demand at Traveler's Rest." Zach appeared at his wife's side out of nowhere and gave her a wink. "But her claim to fame is her chuckwalla! You should taste it."

Beth Ann blushed. "You, sir, are an unconscionable tease! Pay him no mind, Mrs. Nichols."

The other woman twinkled merrily. "I'm sure I'd love to sample something so exotic, my dear, though it might shock Tristan to find lizard on his plate."

"It can be an experience worth repeating, I assure you," Zach said so solemnly, Beth Ann had to choke back a laugh.

"You really ought to collect your best recipes in

403

a book, my dear," Mrs. Nichols advised. "I know I'd purchase a copy."

Somewhat startled, Beth Ann considered the idea with growing excitement. "A collation of recipes for indigenous Arizona produce and game? How novel. I'll have to think seriously about it."

"But not today," Zach said, grinning. "Excuse us, please, ma'am. I'd like a word with my wife before the services resume."

"Certainly." Mrs. Nichols took a bite of cake and wandered off to join the crowd.

"Zach Madison, you are incorrigible," Beth Ann mock-scolded. She held out a plate of cake. "Here, have you had dessert?"

Zach swiftly set the plate aside, pulled her arm through his, and growled in her ear. "You're what looks good enough to eat."

"It must be the hat," she said tartly.

He leaned back to inspect her, his turquoise eyes glowing with pleasure as he noted her new bronze faille gown and the matching confection of lace and veiling perched atop her glistening black curls. "Quite fetching."

"Thank you again, Zach, but I'm sure that you really shouldn't have been so extravagant."

"It's a man's prerogative to gift his bride with pretty things for a wedding present."

"But you'd already given me the best present, Zach." She squeezed his arm gratefully. "I can't tell you what having Nellie back again means to me."

"I knew, honey, and I'm glad I could arrange it." His tender look became teasing again. "And if I want to dress you in pretty things—especially those silky bits that only I get to enjoy—then you're simply going to have to humor me. Although I'm not sure that I like all the admiring looks you're getting today in that outfit. Maybe sackcloth would be safer for my peace of mind at that!"

"Jealous?" Smiling, Beth Ann pulled a flirtatious fingertip down the lapel of his navy blue jacket, finding the string tie he wore with his white shirt quite dashing. She gave him a mischievous look from under her lashes. "Good."

Zach grinned and led her through the throng toward the lean-to made of heaped-up brush and the rough benches set up before it for the congregation. "Minx. Just wait until I get you home."

"Oh, how shocking," she mocked in a whisper. "I am a respectable married woman, sir!"

Pausing in the shadow of a large yucca plant, Zach caught her left hand and rubbed the plain gold band gracing her ring finger. "Who, thankfully, knows how to leave that respectability outside our bedroom door."

Beth Ann caught a little breath, her cheeks heating again, her insides melting at the warmth in Zach's look. They'd married as soon as she'd been able, and she was certain she owed the rapidity of her recovery to her desire to become Zach's bride. In the past weeks of their marriage, they'd made Traveler's Rest into a real home for the first time, full of laughter and quiet, tender moments. Zach had taken to the challenge of developing the copper mine as if he'd been born to it, reveling in every aspect of equipment, manpower, and logistics, meeting every new demand with unbridled enthusiasm. Still, Beth Ann would not have been human if she hadn't had occasional doubts.

She watched him toy with her ring now. "You don't regret it, do you, Zach?"

He looked startled. "That I married you? Angel, how could you even think it?"

"Not just that," she said, flustered, "but giving up your freedom, changing your roaming ways, and . . . and . . ."

"Becoming a solid, upright citizen?" His mouth quirked. "It is pretty amazing, isn't it? And no, I don't regret a thing. In fact, I'm still amazed that the Lord has let me be this happy."

"You are, aren't you?" she asked softly, her silvery eyes shining with love.

For answer, Zach bent his head and kissed her, the fire in his salute boding well for the evening to come. "Very happy, my love."

"Me, too." She sighed.

"We'll finish this discussion at home?"

Smiling, she gave her husband a look that made him catch his breath. "I'll look forward to it."

Zach cleared his throat. "Ah, I think I'd better find you a seat before this gets out of hand, Mrs. Madison."

"Certainly," she said demurely. "There's Jean and Buck. I'll sit with them, shall I?"

"Good idea, angel. Maybe they can keep you out of trouble."

Laughing, she wrinkled her nose at him, then went to join Jean, who sported another new lavender dress, and Buck, his thin hair slicked down with oil and his best jacket brushed and pressed to perfection.

"Shore is a good turnout, ain't it?" Jean fanned herself with her handkerchief and shifted her skirts so that Beth Ann could sit beside her on the plank bench. Beyond the brush arbor, the magenta outline of the Superstition Mountains formed a lofty backdrop against the pure blue sky, a natural theater for the worship of God's majesty.

"Downright gratifying," Buck agreed, nodding to Beth Ann and handing her a dog-eared hymnal. Solicitously he opened a second hymnal for him and Jean to share. Hiding a smile of pleasure, Beth Ann contemplated the possibility of another wedding in the future for Traveler's Rest.

The deacon announced the afternoon's opening hymn, and they all rose to join in singing "Crown Him with Many Crowns." Beth Ann found her mind wandering from the uplifting lyrics, her thoughts forming a thanksgiving prayer for the many blessings she'd been given already.

Her lips curled in a tender smile at the thought of the new blanket she'd set to her loom just the day before, a smaller one than usual, but just right for the gift that would come to them in the spring if all went well. It didn't matter if the border to that blanket would be pink or blue, Beth Ann knew a miracle when she experienced it, and tonight she'd share the news with Zach.

She sat up straighter as the deacon introduced the new assistant pastor and he took the podium to speak.

"Friends, not everyone hears the Lord's call. In fact, sometimes the Lord has to bust you up pretty good before He captures your attention." Zach Madison met his wife's loving gaze across the space that separated them and smiled. "You all know I'm living proof of that!"

There was a general nodding and murmur of approving laughter, and Beth Ann knew she'd never been prouder of the man she loved. Zach had been both amazed and humbled when Mayor Ike had told him the town still needed a part-time parson. As Mamie pointed out, a reformed sinner made the best preacher, anyway.

"Sometimes it's the simplest truths that are the

Avon Romantic Treasures

Unforgettable, enthralling love stories,
sparkling with passion and adventure
from Romance's bestselling authors

MY WILD ROSE *by Deborah Camp*
76738-4/$4.50 US/$5.50 Can

MIDNIGHT AND MAGNOLIAS *by Rebecca Paisley*
76566-7/$4.50 US/$5.50 Can

THE MASTER'S BRIDE *by Suzannah Davis*
76821-6/$4.50 US/$5.50 Can

A ROSE AT MIDNIGHT *by Anne Stuart*
76740-6/$4.50 US/$5.50 Can

FORTUNE'S MISTRESS *by Judith E. French*
76864-X/$4.50 US/$5.50 Can

HIS MAGIC TOUCH *by Stella Cameron*
76607-8/$4.50 US/$5.50 Can

COMANCHE WIND *by Genell Dellin*
76717-1/$4.50 US/$5.50 Can

THEN CAME YOU *by Lisa Kleypas*
77013-X/$4.50 US/$5.50 Can

Buy these books at your local bookstore or use this coupon for ordering:

Mail to: Avon Books. Dept BP. Box 767. Rte 2. Dresden. TN 38225   C
Please send me the book(s) I have checked above.
❏ My check or money order— no cash or CODs please— for $_____is enclosed
(please add S1.50 to cover postage and handling for each book ordered— Canadian residents
add 7°o GST).
❏ Charge my VISA MC Acct#_____Exp Date_____
Minimum credit card order is two books or $6.00 (please add postage and handling charge of
S1.50 per book — Canadian residents add 7°o GST). For faster service. call
1-800-762-0779. Residents of Tennessee. please call 1-800-633-1607. Prices and numbers
are subject to change without notice. Please allow six to eight weeks for delivery.

Name_____
Address_____
City_____State/Zip_____
Telephone No._____   RT 0693

Avon Romances—
the best in exceptional authors and unforgettable novels!